Into The Gray

A Benjamin Cole Story

The Ghostline Protocol series
Book 2

Keven Perkins

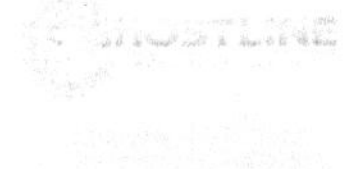

WWW.GHOSTLINEPUBLISHERS.COM

Cover design by Author

Published by: Ghostline Publishing

ISBN: 979-8-218-94626-5

Printed in the United States

FIRST EDITION

To Chris, Robin, Bill, John, Penny, Stephanie, JT, Lisa, Tammy, Joel, Christine, Michael, David, Daniel, Evan, and Mel, Diane, Blake, Stephen, and so many others for your love and support of my hobby. Without you all I probably would have given up on this. Your excitement to what comes next inspires me to keep writing.

KP

Special Shout out to my little brother Patrick for helping me edit this book. Thank you for bearing with my lack of understanding, and for being such a great Ghostline fan.

I love you brother. K

If you or the veteran or service member in your life show signs of crisis, contact the Veterans/Military Crisis Line. In the United States, dial 988, then press 1 or text 838255.

"The moment you are seen, the mission changes."

INTO THE GRAY

BY:
KEVEN PERKINS

Prologue

M*anagua, Nicaragua, December 1984, 2115 Hours*

The checkpoint appeared without warning, a cluster of oil drums and sandbags blocking the Carretera Norte, illuminated by a single flickering streetlight that cast more shadows than it dispelled. Deputy Director Marcus Lawson watched through tinted windows as his driver slowed the battered Toyota sedan, one hand dropping casually to his lap where Lawson knew a Browning Hi-Power rested beneath a folded newspaper.

"Sandinistas," the driver said quietly. His name was Ortega, or at least that's what the local station chief had called him. Lawson hadn't asked for clarification. In his experience, the less you knew about local assets, the easier it was to burn them if things went sideways.

Three soldiers emerged from the shadows, AK-47s slung across their chests. Young. Nineteen, maybe twenty. The kind of kids who'd grown up in the revolution and knew nothing else. One of them carried a flashlight, sweeping it across the windshield with the casual arrogance of someone who'd never been shot at.

Lawson's hand moved to the diplomatic passport in his jacket pocket, but he didn't pull it out yet. Better to let Ortega handle it.

The driver rolled down his window, letting in a wave of humid December heat that smelled like diesel exhaust, rotting vegetation, and the particular stink of a city at war with itself.

The soldier with the flashlight leaned in, said something in rapid Spanish.

Ortega responded, his tone bored, annoyed, perfect. The soldier's eyes flicked to Lawson in the back seat, lingered for a moment, then moved on. Lawson kept his face neutral, his posture relaxed. Just another businessman, another gringo trying to make money off someone else's misery.

The soldier waved them through.

As they pulled away, Lawson checked his watch: 2118 hours. The meeting was scheduled for 2200. He'd built in extra time for exactly this kind of delay. Checkpoints, traffic, the general chaos of a capital city that had been bombed, rebuilt, and was slowly tearing itself apart again. Managua at night was a study in controlled anarchy. Half the streetlights didn't work. Soviet-made trucks rumbled past, carrying troops or supplies or bodies. It was hard to tell in the dark. Sandinista propaganda posters peeled from walls, competing with Contra graffiti that appeared overnight and was painted over by morning.

Lawson had been in Managua twice before, both times under official cover, both times staying in the secure compound near the embassy. This was different. This was off the books. The kind of meeting that, if it went wrong, would end with his body in a ditch and a terse statement from Langley about a tragic accident.

He'd spent the last hour running countersurveillance. The flight from Panama City had been clean. A private charter, no manifest, paid for with cash that couldn't be traced back to the Agency.

Ortega had picked him up at a private airstrip north of the city, and they'd spent forty minutes driving in circles, doubling back, watching for tails.

Lawson had spotted two possible surveillance vehicles, a white Lada that stayed three cars back for too long, and a motorcycle that appeared twice in different locations. But both had peeled off eventually, and for the last twenty minutes, they'd been clean.

Probably.

In this business, you were never really sure.

They turned onto Avenida Bolívar, heading into the Bolonia district. The neighborhood changed immediately. The streets here were wider, cleaner. The streetlights actually worked. Colonial-era mansions sat behind high walls topped with broken glass and razor wire, their courtyards hidden from view. This was where the old money lived. The families who'd survived Somoza, survived the revolution, and would probably survive whatever came next. The kind of people who understood that ideology was temporary, but wealth was forever.

Lawson noted landmarks as they drove. A church on the corner, its bell tower dark. A pharmacy with steel shutters pulled down. A gas station, closed, two-armed guards sitting outside in plastic chairs. Escape routes. If things went bad, he could go north toward the lake, or south toward the embassy district. East would take him into the barrios, where a gringo would stand out like a searchlight.

West led to the old city center, still rubble from the '72 earthquake.

The estate appeared on the left.

A two-story Spanish colonial behind twelve-foot walls, the kind of place that had probably belonged to a coffee baron before the revolution. Lawson could see the tops of palm trees swaying in the night breeze, and the soft glow of lights from the upper windows.

Two guards stood at the gate. Not Sandinista regulars, Lawson could tell from the way they held themselves. These were professionals. Private security. Expensive.

They wore civilian clothes, but their posture was military, and the way they tracked the approaching car suggested training that went beyond the usual rent-a-cop bullshit. One of them had his hand near his waistband, where Lawson assumed he carried a sidearm. The other held a radio.

Contra rebels wouldn't be caught dead in Managua, not in the Sandinista-controlled capital. These were mercenaries. The kind of men who worked for whoever paid best and knew when to look away.

Ortega slowed at the gate. The guard with the radio said something, listened to his earpiece, then nodded and stepped back. The gate swung open—electric, Lawson noted, which meant backup power, which meant someone had money and planning.

They pulled through into a circular driveway. Manicured lawn. Flower beds. A fountain in the center, currently dry. The house itself was immaculate, fresh paint, intact roof tiles, windows that weren't covered with plywood or steel shutters. In a city where half the buildings still showed bullet holes from the revolution, this place looked like it belonged in a different country.

Lawson checked his watch again: 2147 hours. Thirteen minutes early. Perfect.

"Wait here," he said to Ortega. "Engine running."

The driver nodded, understanding the implication. If Lawson didn't come out in ninety minutes, Ortega would leave.

If anyone tried to stop him, he'd shoot his way out. And if he made it back to the airstrip, he'd burn everything, the car, the safe house, the contact numbers. Standard protocol for a meeting that officially didn't exist.

Lawson stepped out into the humid night. The temperature had to be pushing eighty-five, even at this hour.

His shirt stuck to his back immediately. He could hear insects buzzing in the garden, and somewhere in the distance, the faint pop-pop-pop of gunfire. Could be Contras. Could be Sandinistas shooting at shadows. Could be someone settling a personal score. In Managua, gunfire was like traffic noise, constant, meaningless, easy to ignore.

The front door opened before he reached it. A young officer stood in the doorway, mid-twenties, wearing an immaculate uniform with no insignia. His boots were polished to a mirror shine, and his posture was parade-ground perfect. He didn't smile, didn't speak, just stepped aside and gestured for Lawson to enter.

Inside, the temperature dropped twenty degrees. Air conditioning, a luxury in a city where electricity was rationed and brownouts were daily occurrences. The floor was polished hardwood, probably mahogany, covered with Persian rugs that looked genuine. The walls were decorated with colonial-era paintings, religious scenes, pastoral landscapes, the kind of art that wealthy families had been collecting for generations.

The young officer led him through the house without

speaking. They passed a library, floor-to-ceiling bookshelves, leather-bound volumes, a reading chair positioned near a window.

Then a sitting room, antique furniture, a grandfather clock ticking softly in the corner, fresh flowers in a crystal vase. Everything was understated, elegant, expensive. The kind of wealth that came from knowing which colonial antiques to loot before the revolution, and which officials to bribe afterward.

They arrived at a study overlooking a courtyard garden. Subtle ground lights illuminated tropical plants and a small reflecting pool. Through the window, Lawson could see more guards patrolling the perimeter, at least four, maybe more in the shadows.

Senior Commander Tomás Reyes stood at the window, hands clasped behind his back, silhouetted against the garden lights. He didn't turn as Lawson entered. The young officer withdrew, closing the door with a soft click that somehow felt final.

For a long moment, neither man spoke. Lawson used the time to assess. Reyes was younger than he'd expected, mid-forties, maybe, with the lean build of someone who still trained with his troops. His uniform was tailored, expensive, but worn enough to suggest he actually wore it in the field. His hair was cut military-short, graying at the temples. His hands, clasped behind his back, showed calluses, not the soft hands of a desk officer, but the rough hands of someone who still handled weapons.

"Deputy Director." Reyes turned, and Lawson got his first good look at the man's face.

Strong features. Intelligent eyes. A slight smile that didn't reach those eyes. He extended his hand. "Thank you for coming."

His grip was firm, controlled. His English was unaccented, American university, Lawson knew from the file.

Stanford, Class of '71. International relations. The kind of education that produced either diplomats or revolutionaries, depending on which way the wind was blowing.

"Your message suggested urgency," Lawson said.

"Please, sit." Reyes gestured to two leather chairs arranged near a sidebar. A bottle of Flor de Caña rum stood beside two glasses, already poured. The bottle was seven-year, Lawson noted, not the cheap stuff. "I thought we might speak frankly, away from the usual channels."

Lawson remained standing. "I requested this meeting, Commander. I have information you need to hear."

Reyes's eyebrows rose slightly. "Indeed?" He picked up one of the glasses, swirled the rum gently. "I'm listening."

"First, I need to know what you've heard. What rumors have reached you."

Reyes studied him for a long moment, then gestured again to the chairs. This time, Lawson sat. The leather was soft, expensive, probably imported.

"Rumors," Reyes said, settling into his own chair. "Whispers, really. My intelligence networks have picked up... anomalies.

American operators who appear and disappear like ghosts. Unexplained casualties among our officers, clean executions, professional work, but no claims of responsibility from the Contras. They lack that kind of precision."

He paused, watching Lawson's face. "And a name. Ghostline. Though no one seems to know what it means."

Lawson felt something cold settle in his chest. The leak was worse than he'd thought. But that made this easier. Reyes already suspected. All Lawson had to do was confirm it.

And use it.

"Ghostline is real," Lawson said quietly. "It's a covert operations unit. Highly trained. Operating outside normal command structures."

Reyes leaned forward slightly, his casual demeanor sharpening into focused attention. "Go on."

"They're teenagers," Lawson said. "Recruited young. Trained at Fort Bragg by Delta Force operators. They answer directly to the President through a single handler, no congressional oversight, no paper trail, no legal authorization. It's completely off the books."

The silence that followed was profound. Reyes set down his glass carefully, his eyes never leaving Lawson's face.

"Teenagers," he repeated.

"Seventeen, eighteen years old. Some younger when they were recruited." Lawson picked up the second glass, took a sip.

The rum burned going down. "The President created the program through a classified finding. Direct presidential authority. No one else has access, not Congress, not the intelligence committees, not even most of the Agency. It's compartmented beyond anything I've ever seen."

"And you're telling me this because...?"

"Because it's unconstitutional," Lawson said, and he heard the conviction in his own voice.

"It's everything the Founding Fathers feared, unchecked executive power, secret operations with no accountability." He paused, then made his decision. "And because I've already tried to stop them. Directly."

Reyes's eyes sharpened. "Explain."

"Two months ago, I leaked their operational location to the Soviets. Through a proxy, a cutout that couldn't be traced back to me." Lawson's voice remained steady, clinical. "The GRU sent a Spetsnaz team. Six operators. Elite. The best they had in the region."

"And?"

"Ghostline neutralized all of them and blew a hind helicopter out of the air." Lawson met Reyes's eyes. "Every single one. The Soviets lost an entire team, a helicopter with crew, and those kids walked away without a scratch. That's when I realized indirect approaches wouldn't work. These aren't normal teenagers. They're weapons.

Highly trained, highly lethal weapons operating with presidential authority and zero oversight."

Reyes sat back slowly, reassessing. "You've already committed treason."

"I've already tried to protect the Constitution from a dangerous precedent," Lawson corrected. "And I failed. That's why I'm here. That's why I need your help." He leaned forward. "Today it's Nicaragua. Tomorrow? Domestic operations? Political opponents? This is how democracies die, Commander.

Not with tanks in the streets, but with programs like this operating in the shadows."

Reyes studied him with new intensity.

"You're asking me to help you expose this program."

"I'm asking you to help me protect American democracy from a dangerous precedent." Lawson's voice hardened. "The President has created a private army accountable to no one. If Ghostline is exposed, if the world sees what he's done. It will force him out of office. Congressional hearings. Media scrutiny. Criminal investigations. The kind of scandal that ends presidencies."

"And you want me to provide that exposure."

"Yes." Lawson set down his glass. "Ghostline will

deploy to Nicaragua. Probably within the next sixty days. When they do, you'll have two options. Option one: capture them alive. Parade them in front of international press. American teenagers conducting illegal operations on foreign soil. The scandal would be immediate and devastating."

"And option two?"

"Eliminate them. Display the bodies.

Prove that the United States is sending children to fight covert wars."

Lawson's voice remained steady, clinical. "Either way, the President is finished. The program is exposed. And the constitutional crisis is resolved."

Reyes sat back in his chair, and for the first time, something like surprise flickered across his face. "You're volunteering classified information about an active operation. You understand what that makes you."

"A patriot," Lawson said. "Protecting my country from tyranny."

"A traitor," Reyes corrected, but there was no judgment in his voice. Just observation. "By any legal definition."

"The law is whatever serves the Constitution. And this program violates everything the Constitution stands for." Lawson met his eyes. "I'm not doing this for money. I'm not doing this because I've been compromised. I'm doing this because someone has to stop this before it destroys everything we claim to defend."

Reyes picked up his glass again, took a slow sip. "You've thought this through."

"For three weeks. Ever since I learned Ghostline existed." Lawson's jaw tightened. "A colleague mentioned it in passing, complained about resources he couldn't reallocate because of 'presidential authority.' I pushed. He said too much. And once I knew it existed, I started connecting dots. Unusual activity reports. Unexplained casualties. Teenagers who disappeared from the system and reappeared with skills they shouldn't have."

"And you decided to burn it down."

"I decided to protect the system." Lawson leaned forward again. "You want American support for a new government in Nicaragua.

I want to eliminate a threat to constitutional governance. We both get what we need."

"And the teenagers die."

"They signed up for this. They knew the risks." But even as Lawson said it, a small voice in the back of his mind whispered the truth he didn't want to hear. These were kids. Seventeen, eighteen years old.

They'd been recruited, trained, turned into weapons. And now he was sending them into a trap.

He pushed the thought away. This was bigger than a handful of teenagers. This was about the future of American democracy.

Reyes was quiet for a long moment, studying Lawson with those sharp, calculating eyes. "You're offering me intelligence on when they deploy. Where they'll be. What their mission is."

"Yes."

"In exchange for what?"

"Proof," Lawson said. "Proof that the program exists. Proof that the President authorized it. Proof that will force congressional hearings and criminal investigations." He paused. "And six months from now, when Nicaragua has a new government, the United States will have a grateful ally. Someone who understands the value of cooperation."

"A coup," Reyes said.

"A restoration of stability. With American support, weapons, intelligence, diplomatic recognition. It could be accomplished cleanly. Minimal bloodshed. A new government friendly to U.S. interests."

Reyes smiled slightly. "You've thought this through very carefully, Deputy Director."

"I've had three weeks to think about nothing else."

"And you're certain you want to cross this line? Once you give me operational intelligence, there's no going back."

Lawson thought about Ghostline. Teenagers operating with no oversight, answerable only to the President. Secret missions with no accountability. It was exactly the kind of unchecked power that destroyed democracies from within.

He was protecting the system.

He had to believe that.

"I'm certain," Lawson said. "When Ghostline deploys, I'll give you seventy-two hours' notice. Location, mission parameters, team composition. Everything you need to be ready."

Reyes set down his glass and stood, walking to a desk in the corner. He pulled out a folder and spread a map across the surface. "Then we need to establish secure communication protocols. Dead drops in Panama City. Three locations." He pointed to specific streets. "Here, here, and here. A café, a bookstore, and a church. You'll leave packages in the men's room, behind the toilet tank. Standard tradecraft."

Lawson joined him at the desk, studying the map.

"Encryption?"

"One-time pads. I'll provide the key sheets." Reyes pulled out a stack of thin paper, covered in random number sequences. "Burn after use. No copies."

"Radio frequencies?"

"For emergencies only. 7.435 MHz, upper sideband.

Transmission window is 0300 to 0315 local time, Tuesdays and Fridays. Use the call sign 'Compass.' I'll respond as 'True North.'"

Lawson memorized the details. "Timeline for information exchanges?"

"Weekly, if possible. Every two weeks at minimum. I need advance warning when Ghostline deploys. At least seventy-two hours to position my forces."

"And if I'm compromised?"

"Then we never met. This conversation never happened." Reyes's voice was flat, matter-of-fact. "I'll deny everything. You'll be on your own."

"Same from my end."

"Understood." Reyes extended his hand. "We're both taking significant risks, Deputy Director."

Lawson shook his hand. The grip was firm, final. A covenant sealed. "The risks are worth it. This program represents everything the Founding Fathers feared. If we don't stop it now, we never will."

"And when it's over? When this covert team is... exposed and the President is forced out?"

"Then the system is protected.

Democracy survives. And Nicaragua has a government that understands the value of American friendship." Lawson picked up the one-time pads, folded them carefully, and slipped them into his jacket pocket. "Everyone wins."

Except the kids, a small voice whispered. But he pushed that away. They'd signed up for this. They knew the risks.

And if they were good enough to survive, they'd be fine. If not... well, that proved the program was flawed from the start.

Reyes studied him for a moment longer, and something

like respect flickered in his eyes. "I didn't expect you to be so... forthcoming.

Most intelligence officers play games. Dance around the truth. You walked in here and laid everything on the table."

"Because we don't have time for games," Lawson said. "Ghostline could deploy any day. We need to be ready."

"We will be." Reyes walked back to the sidebar, picked up the bottle of rum, and refilled both glasses. "To patriots," he said, raising his glass. "Doing what must be done."

Lawson raised his glass. "To patriots."

They drank.

They spent the next twenty minutes working through additional details. Contingency protocols if one of the dead drops was compromised. Recognition signals for in-person meetings if absolutely necessary. A timetable for the coup, contingent on Ghostline's elimination. Reyes had thought it through carefully, Lawson noted with approval. The man was thorough.

Professional. The kind of officer who planned three moves ahead.

The kind of man who could be useful.

When they finished, Lawson stood. Reyes walked him to the door.

"One more thing," Lawson said. "When you take them, alive or dead. make sure the world sees it. International press. Photographs. Proof that can't be denied or covered up."

"I understand perfectly, Deputy Director."

Reyes extended his hand one final time. "The exposure will be complete. The President won't be able to hide from this."

Lawson shook his hand and walked out into the humid night. His shirt was soaked with sweat within seconds.

The insects were louder now, a constant buzz that filled the darkness. Somewhere in the distance, another burst of gunfire echoed across the city.

Ortega had the car running, as instructed. Lawson climbed into the back seat, and they pulled away from the estate. He looked back once at the lighted windows, at the guards standing in the shadows, at the walls topped with razor wire.

Two predators had made a covenant tonight. Each believed he was using the other. Each believed he was serving a higher purpose. Only one of them would be right.

The car turned onto the main road, heading toward the airport and the unmarked plane that would take Lawson back to Washington.

Behind them, in the study, Reyes poured himself another glass of rum and smiled at the Nicaraguan night.

The pieces were in motion now.

All that remained was to wait for this Task Force to arrive.

Chapter One

FORT BRAGG, North Carolina.
Delta Force Compound, Hangar 97
January 1985

The briefing room at Fort Bragg smelled like stale coffee and the particular brand of institutional disinfectant that the Army used in every secure facility from Bragg to Beirut. Cole sat with his boots propped on the chair in front of him, staring at the acoustic tiles on the ceiling and counting the water stains. Fourteen. Same as yesterday. Same as the day before that.

Three weeks they'd been back. Three weeks of debriefs and waiting and the kind of silence that came from knowing someone had tried to get you erased.

The room itself was buried in the basement of Hangar 97, behind two cipher-locked doors and a security checkpoint manned by Delta operators who didn't ask questions and didn't remember faces. Concrete walls painted institutional beige. Fluorescent lights that hummed with a frequency that made Cole's teeth ache after the first hour. A conference table that had seen better days, scarred with coffee rings and the occasional cigarette burn from before the no-smoking policy that nobody followed anyway.

Maps covered one wall, topographical surveys of Central America, satellite imagery of Soviet installations, target folders marked with classifications that didn't officially exist. The other wall held a whiteboard covered in operational timelines that had been hastily erased.

Leaving ghost images of dates and grid coordinates that told stories to anyone who knew how to read them.

The climate control system cycled on with a mechanical wheeze, pushing cold air through vents that hadn't been cleaned since the Carter administration. It was always too cold in here. Cole figured that was intentional it kept you alert, kept you uncomfortable, kept you from getting too relaxed in a place where relaxation could get you disappeared.

Across from him, Vail was methodically field stripping a Sig Sauer P226 that didn't need cleaning. He'd already cleaned it twice today. Cole had watched him do it, the same precise movements, the same careful attention to components that were already spotless. Slide off. Barrel out. Recoil spring. Guide rod. Each piece laid out on the table in perfect order, like a surgical array.

It was ritual. Control. The kind of thing you did when your brain needed something to focus on besides the fact that someone in the intelligence community had burned your operation before it even started. Vail's hands were steady, his face expressionless, but Cole knew him well enough to read the tension in his shoulders, the way his jaw was set just a little too tight.

Operation Ember Knife had been a success. They'd extracted SPARROW from Camp Mantis, destroyed the

Rebel communications infrastructure, and made it to the exfil point with zero casualties.

Textbook operation. The kind of mission that should have ended with quiet congratulations and a week of downtime.

The Operation Night Arrow With the six man neutralize team that were there to target his team.

That's when they'd walked into a nightmare.

The operator-elimination team had hit them during exfiltration, two klicks from the extraction zone. Not Sandinistas. Not regular forces. Russians no doubt.

The hind helicopter gave that away. Professional operators, trained, equipped, and positioned exactly where the team would be. They'd moved like Delta, fought like Delta, and they'd known things they shouldn't have known. Grid coordinates. Timing. Routes. Spetsnaz

Someone had sent them. Someone who knew about us. Someone who wanted Task Force dead.

Cole had smelled it thirty seconds before contact, wrong movement in the tree line, wrong shadows, wrong everything. They'd fought their way through, left four bodies behind, and made the exfil by the skin of their teeth. But the message was clear: someone on their own side had tried to eliminate them. The operation was compromised. And somewhere in the chain of command, there was a leak.

Riker was doing what Riker always did when forced to sit still bouncing his knee and looking like he might crawl out of his own skin. His right leg jackhammered against the floor in a steady rhythm that had been going for the last forty minutes. Combat adrenaline was a hell of a drug, and Riker's system was still processing three weeks' worth of it.

He'd been on point during the exfiltration when the team of operators materialized from the tree line.

He'd seen them first, wrong silhouettes, wrong movement patterns, professionals where there shouldn't have been anyone.

He'd engaged first, dropping the lead operator before the rest of Ghostline even knew they were compromised. He'd been running hot ever since.

"Think they're gonna tell us we're compromised?

"Riker asked, breaking the silence that had stretched for the better part of an hour.

"We already know we're compromised," Vail said without looking up from the pistol. His voice was flat, matter of fact, the tone of a man stating an objective truth. "Someone sent a team of highly trained men after us. Professional operators. Our own people."

"Mission was clean," Riker said, more to himself than anyone else. "We got SPARROW out. Destroyed the comms facility. Did everything right. And someone still tried to smoke us."

"Which is why we're sitting here instead of drinking somewhere warm." Cole dropped his feet and leaned forward, elbows on his knees. He could feel the weight of the last three weeks in his bones, the hypervigilance, the paranoia, the constant awareness that someone in their own community had tried to bury them. "Relax. If they were gonna burn us, we wouldn't be waiting in a briefing room. We'd be in a basement somewhere having a very different conversation."

It was true, and they all knew it.

The fact that they were still breathing, still armed, still operating out of the Delta compound meant someone upstairs was protecting them. The question was who, and for how long.

Cole's jaw tightened as he thought about it.

Three weeks of sitting on his ass while Harrow chased ghosts through the intelligence community. Three weeks of watching his team get more wound up, more paranoid, more ready to snap. They were operators, not analysts. They were built for action, for movement, for solving problems with violence and precision. Sitting still made them dangerous in all the wrong ways.

He wanted to go downrange. Wanted to find whoever had leaked their operation and put a bullet in their skull.

Wanted to finish the job they'd started in Managua. But Harrow had been clear: stand down, stay quiet, let him handle the investigation. Cole understood the logic. If someone was hunting them, better to be invisible than to be a target. But understanding didn't make it easier.

The door opened with a metallic click that echoed in the concrete space. Colonel Harrow walked in carrying a manila folder, and Cole read him in the first three seconds. Tired. The kind of tired that came from spending three weeks trying to figure out how a black operation got compromised before it even started. His uniform was crisp, his bearing was professional, but there were shadows under his eyes that hadn't been there a month ago. He'd lost weight. His face had the drawn, hollow look of a man who'd been living on coffee and four hours of sleep.

He didn't sit down. That was the tell. When Harrow sat down, it meant a conversation. When he stayed standing, it meant orders.

"Gentlemen," Harrow said. His voice carried the rasp of too many cigarettes and not enough rest. "Good news. You're going back to school. Well, some of you are anyway."

Cole felt his jaw tighten. "The fuck does that mean?"

He wanted action, not training. Training was always needed, they trained constantly, honing tradecraft that could degrade in a matter of weeks without practice. But right now, training felt like a punishment. Like being benched. Like being told to sit in the corner while the adults handled the real work.

Harrow's eyes flicked to him, and there was something in that look, understanding, maybe, or sympathy.

Or maybe just exhaustion.

"It means while I sort out who leaked your operation, you three are going to Marine Corps Base Quantico to attend Scout Sniper School. Starts Monday. You leave tomorrow."

Riker's knee stopped bouncing. "We just got back from eliminating people and now we're going to fucking sniper school. At a Marine Corps base. Fucking jarheads."

"The Marine Scout Sniper School is an elite, demanding eight-week course focused on advanced marksmanship, fieldcraft, and stalking," Harrow said, his tone suggesting he'd given this speech before and didn't particularly care if they liked it.

"And it gets you out of sight while I handle the intel leak. You're not exactly low-profile right now. Someone in the community knows about us, which means someone's asking questions. Better you're not here to answer them."

Cole understood immediately. It wasn't about training. It was about protection. Get them off the base, out of the system, somewhere they couldn't be found by whoever was digging into Task Force Ghostline. Quantico was perfect, a legitimate training pipeline.

Far enough from Bragg to break any surveillance, isolated enough that three Army operators would blend into a class of Marine students.

Vail reassembled the Sig with practiced efficiency, the

slide snapping back into place with a metallic click. "Marine Scout Sniper's eight weeks?"

"Seven if you don't fuck around," Harrow said.

"And you won't, because you're going to keep your heads down, learn what they have to teach, and not tell anyone who you are or what you do. As far as the Marines are concerned, you're three Army kids who got lucky with a training slot."

"They're gonna ask what unit," Cole said.

"And you're going to tell them you're with the 313th Military Intelligence Battalion's LRS platoon, 82nd Airborne Division. I've got paperwork that says so." Harrow dropped the folder on the table with a heavy thud. "Orders, medical records, training jackets. Everything you need to fit in."

Cole picked up the folder and flipped it open.

The paperwork looked legitimate because it was legitimate, real documents, real signatures, real unit designations. The 313th MI Battalion was a real unit with a real Long Range Surveillance platoon that conducted real reconnaissance operations. The cover story was solid because it was built on truth, just attached to operators who didn't actually belong to that unit.

The training jackets showed a progression that made sense: Airborne School, Ranger School, advanced reconnaissance courses. Nothing that would raise flags.

Nothing that would suggest they were anything other than competent soldiers who'd earned a slot at a prestigious school.

"What if they push?" Cole asked.

"They won't.

Marines don't give a shit about Army politics. You show

up, do the work, don't embarrass yourselves, and they'll leave you alone." Harrow moved toward the door, then stopped. His hand was on the handle, but he turned back, and his eyes locked on Cole. "And Cole. Don't do anything stupid."

He said it because he knew. Knew how competitive Cole was. Knew that Cole would see a room full of Marine instructors as a challenge, as a test.

This was an opportunity to prove that Army operators were the apex predators in any environment. Knew that Cole would push, would excel, would dominate, because that was what Cole did.

"Define stupid," Cole said with a vulpine grin.

"You know exactly what the fuck I mean.

These Marine instructors are professionals. They're not the enemy and they're not targets. You're there to learn, not to prove you're the baddest motherfucker in the room. Until the Army sets up its own Sniper course, we will be grateful guests."

Cole met Harrow's eyes and held them. The grin was still there, sharp and predatory. "I will be the baddest motherfucker in the room."

For a moment, Harrow just stared at him.

Then he shook his head, muttered "Goddammit," and left. The door closed behind him with a heavy metallic thud that echoed in the concrete space. His footsteps receded down the hallway, quick and loud, the sound of a man who'd just lost an argument he knew he was going to lose before it started.

Riker waited until the footsteps faded completely. Then he looked at Cole and grinned. "He thinks you're gonna do something stupid. You are going to give that man a stroke one day, brother."

"I'm always doing something stupid," Cole said. He

stood up, stretched, felt his spine pop in three places. "And maybe the Colonel needs to take better care of himself. If he has a stroke, it won't be because of me."

He smiled, but there was no humor in it. Just the cold calculation of a man who'd been sidelined for three weeks and was finally being given something to do, even if it wasn't the mission he wanted.

Vail holstered the Sig and stood. "When do we leave?"

"Tomorrow, 0600," Cole said. "Pack light. We'll be gone seven weeks."

"Eight," Riker corrected.

"Seven," Cole said. "Because we're not going to fuck around."

They filed out of the briefing room, past the security checkpoint, up the stairs and into the cold January air. The Delta compound sprawled around them, low buildings, training ranges, the constant sound of gunfire from the shooting houses. Somewhere in the distance, a helicopter was landing.

Cole looked up at the sky. It was overcast, gray, the kind of day that promised rain but never delivered. In seven weeks, they'd be back. And by then, maybe Harrow would have found the leak. Maybe they'd know who'd tried to neutralize them in Managua.

And maybe, Cole thought, as he lit a cigarette, they'd get a chance to close the loop.

Chapter Two

Quantico in January was cold and wet and exactly as miserable as Cole expected Virginia to be. The kind of cold that wasn't dramatic, no blizzards, no ice storms, just a persistent, bone-deep chill that worked its way through your fatigues and settled in your joints. Gray skies hung low over the base, threatening rain that came in sporadic bursts throughout the day, never enough to wash anything clean, just enough to make everything damp and uncomfortable.

They'd driven up from Bragg in a borrowed Chevy Impala that smelled like stale cigarettes and decades of government neglect. The heater worked intermittently, and the windshield wipers left streaks across the glass. Cole had driven the first half, Vail the second, while Riker slept in the back seat with his head against the window. They'd stopped once for gas and coffee that tasted like it had been brewed during the Carter administration. Nobody complained. Complaining was for people who had better options.

They arrived at the main gate just before 1800 hours. The Marine sentry checked their orders with the kind of methodical precision that suggested he'd done this ten thousand times and would do it ten thousand more. He waved them through without comment, pointing toward the visitor processing building with a gloved hand.

Check-in was efficient and impersonal. A staff sergeant named Billings, according to the name tape on his woodland cammies.

Processed their paperwork with the dead-eyed efficiency of a man who'd seen a thousand students come through and didn't give a shit about a thousand more. He was maybe five-six, compact, with what was left of his blonde hair shaved down to stubble.

He looked at their 82nd Airborne patches, looked at their orders, and pointed them toward the barracks without a word. Formation was at 0600. Don't be late. Dismissed.

The barracks were standard Marine Corps: two-story cinderblock buildings painted in that particular shade of institutional beige that existed nowhere in nature. Inside, the floors were polished to a high gloss that smelled like industrial wax and petroleum. The bunks were arranged in neat rows, footlockers at the end of each rack, everything squared away with the kind of precision that made Army barracks look like college dorm rooms.

Cole claimed a rack near the window on the second floor. The mattress was thin, the springs creaked, and the pillow felt like it was stuffed with sawdust. Perfect. Vail took the bunk across from him. Riker sprawled on his like he was already asleep, arms behind his head, staring at the ceiling. The barracks were quiet. Too quiet. Most of the other students hadn't arrived yet, and the ones who had been keeping to themselves, unpacking gear, checking weapons, doing the pre-course rituals that every shooter developed over time. The building had that particular silence of men who didn't know each other yet, who were sizing each other up, waiting to see who would wash out and who would make it.

"Think the Marines are gonna be pricks about us being Army?" Riker asked the ceiling.

"Probably," Vail said, pulling his cleaning kit from his ruck.

"Definitely," Cole said. "But they'll get over it once they see we're not complete shitbags."

"Speak for yourself," Riker said. "I'm a total shitbag."

"Yes..., yes you are," Vail responded, not looking up from his kit.

Cole pulled his ruck onto his bunk and started unpacking. He'd brought the minimum.

Three sets of fatigues, boots, field gear, cold-weather layers, and his personal weapons cleaning kit. Everything else, rifles, optics, ghillie materials, the Marines would provide. That was the theory, anyway. In practice, Cole had learned a long time ago that you never trusted someone else's gear with your life. But they were here under cover, three Army guys attending a Marine sniper course, and showing up with Delta-level equipment would raise questions they couldn't answer.

"So," Vail said, threading a bore snake through his Sig Sauer. "What are you going to do here that will give Harrow a stroke, Cole?"

Cole looked up from his ruck. "According to the training folder, no one has ever come closer than 200 meters to the instructors during the stalking phase."

Vail stopped cleaning his pistol. Riker sat up on his bunk.

"There it is," Vail said, shaking his head. "The stupid Harrow was talking about. Nate is going to have a heart attack. You are not seriously thinking about doing that, are you?"

"I'm always thinking about it," Cole said. "Doesn't mean I'm gonna do it."

Vail gave him a flat look that said he didn't believe a fucking word of that. He knew Cole's competitive tendencies better than most. This crazy motherfucker is going to sneak up on the instructors, he thought with a grin. "I'll get Price to say a prayer for Harrow."

Cole smiled but said nothing. The idea had been forming since he'd read the course description back at Bragg. Two hundred meters was the standard. It was achievable, respectable, what the Marine Corps expected from its Scout Snipers. But Cole wasn't here to meet expectations. He was here because someone had tried to neutralize his team in Managua.

And until Harrow found the leak, they were stuck in holding patterns and training courses, waiting for permission to do what they did best.

If he was going to be stuck at Quantico for eight weeks, he might as well make it interesting.

Chapter Three

The first week was classroom work.

Ballistics. Range estimation. Weather effects. Spin drift, bullet drop, minutes of angle, and the kind of technical knowledge that separated snipers from guys who were just good shots. The Marine instructors were exactly what Cole expected: competent, professional, and utterly unimpressed by the three Army kids in the back of the room.

Gunnery Sergeant Keller, no relation to their Keller, which Riker thought was hilarious, ran most of the classes. He was compact and weathered, maybe forty-five, with the kind of face that suggested he'd spent more time behind a rifle than in front of a mirror. His hands were scarred, his eyes were sharp, and he didn't waste time with motivational speeches or Marine Corps mythology. He just taught.

"Wind's gonna fuck you more than anything else," Keller said on the second day, pointing at the diagram on the whiteboard. "You can know your dope, you can have perfect form, you can do everything right, and a gust you didn't read will still put your round in the dirt. So, you learn to read it. You learn to feel it. And you learn to wait for the shot instead of forcing it."

Cole started writing. He didn't have a photographic memory, and the information Keller was providing was worth absorbing. Harrow had taught him most of this already, Delta's sniper program was arguably better than the Marines'.

But there were details here, small refinements in technique, that were worth cataloging.

"Observe how different elements in the environment are moving to estimate wind speed," Keller continued, tapping the chart. "One to three miles per hour: smoke and dust drift, but the leaves are still. Four to seven, light breeze, you can feel it on your face, leaves rustle, tall grass moves slightly. Eight to twelve: leaves and small twigs move constantly, light flags extend. Thirteen to eighteen: small branches move, dust and loose paper lift off the ground. Anything above that, you're not taking the shot unless you're desperate or stupid."

He looked directly at the class. "Don't be desperate. Don't be stupid."

Cole wrote it all down. Vail was doing the same, his handwriting neater, more methodical. Riker was half-listening, half-staring out the window at the range beyond. He'd learn it when he needed to. That was how Riker operated, instinct first, technique second.

The Marines had been doing this longer than the Army had. There was no shame in learning from people who knew their shit.

The range work started in week two.

They shot from every position: prone, sitting, kneeling, standing, supported, unsupported. They shot at known distances, 100, 200, 300, 500, 800 yards, and unknown distances where they had to calculate range, wind, and elevation on their own. They shot in rain, in wind, in the cold gray dawn when your fingers were numb and your breath condensed in front of your face.

The rifles were M40A1s: Remington 700 actions, heavy barrels, Unertl 10x scopes.

Reliable, accurate, and cold as hell when you'd been lying in the mud for three hours. Cole's groups were tight and consistent. Vail's were tighter, the man was a perfectionist, and it showed in his shot placement. Riker was good but not great.

He had the instinct, the natural feel for windage and elevation, but he lacked patience, and it showed in his follow-through. "You're jerking the trigger," Keller told Riker after one string of fire on a freezing Thursday morning. The range was slick with mud, and a light rain was falling. "You know the round's going off, so you're flinching before it happens. Anticipation. It's fucking up your follow-through."

"I'm not flinching, goddammit," Riker said, his breath misting in the cold air.

Keller picked up Riker's target and held it up. Five rounds, all of them low and right, clustered in a pattern that told the story of a shooter who was pulling the shot. "This says you are. So, either fix it, or get used to missing." He paused, then added with a slight grin, "We could just send you back to your unit. It's the Army, they're used to failures."

A few of the Marines chuckled. Riker's jaw tightened.

He fixed it. And he fixed it fast. The shit he'd get from the team if he failed a Marine sniper course would be nonstop and vicious. By the end of the day, his groups were clean, centered, consistent. Keller nodded once and moved on to the next shooter.

Cole watched it all, absorbing, evaluating. He wasn't just here to learn; he was here to understand how the Marines trained.

How they thought, what their standards were. And he was planning. From day one, he'd been planning the final stalk, the moment when he'd prove something that didn't need proving but that he needed to do anyway.

Two hundred meters was the standard.

Cole had no intention of stopping at two hundred meters.

Chapter Four

By week four, they'd moved into fieldcraft and stalking.

This was the part of the course that separated Scout Snipers from everyone else. It wasn't about shooting anymore; it was about becoming invisible. Moving through terrain without being seen. Getting close enough to neutralize without ever being detected. Concealment, movement techniques, route selection, final firing positions. The use of ghillie suits that each candidate had to construct themselves from burlap, netting, and whatever natural vegetation they could scavenge from the training area.

Cole was very, very good at it.

The first stalking exercise was basic: move 400 yards through open ground to an observation post without being spotted by instructors with binoculars and spotting scopes. Most students got caught within the first hundred yards, a reflection off a watch, an unnatural shape, movement that was too fast or too straight. A few made it halfway before an instructor called them out.

Cole, Vail, and Riker all made it to the OP without being detected.

"Army's doing something right," one of the instructors muttered.

The exercises got harder. Shorter distances, more observers, less cover, worse weather. Cole adapted.

He moved in inches, using every depression in the ground, every shadow, every moment when the instructors' attention shifted elsewhere.

He didn't think about it consciously, it was the same instinct that had kept him alive in Nicaragua, the same predatory patience that made him good at killing people.

Vail was almost as good, methodical and precise. Riker was good enough, learning to slow down, to think before moving.

But Cole was already thinking about the final test. The moment that mattered.

The final stalking test came in week seven.

The instructors set up an OP on a hillside overlooking a wide, gently sloping field with scattered brush and a few small trees. The students' objective: stalk to within 200 yards, set up a firing position, take a blank shot at a target near the OP, and extract without being detected.

Two hundred yards was the standard. It was achievable. It was what the Marine Corps expected.

Cole had no intention of stopping at 200 yards.

He started his stalk at 0600, moving out with the rest of the students in a loose skirmish line. The instructors were already in position on the hillside, scanning the field with optics, looking for movement, for unnatural shapes, for anything that didn't belong. The morning was cold, the grass wet with dew, the sky just beginning to lighten in the east.

Cole went to ground immediately.

Dropping into a shallow drainage ditch that ran perpendicular to the OP. The grass was soaked, and the ground was cold enough to leach the heat from his body within minutes. He barely noticed. He was already gone, already something other than human, just another piece of the landscape, patient and still.

He moved in increments. Six inches. Wait. Another six inches. Wait. He used his elbows and the edges of his boots, keeping his body flat, his rifle secure in the drag bag he'd fashioned from canvas and netting. Every movement was deliberate, controlled, invisible. The ghillie suit he'd built over the past three weeks picked up mud and grass as he moved, blending him further into the terrain.

It took him two hours to cover the first hundred yards.

At 300 yards, he could see the OP clearly, two instructors behind spotting scopes, one with binoculars, all of them scanning the field with the methodical patience of professionals. He watched them for twenty minutes, learning their patterns, the rhythm of their searches. Left to right, slow sweep, pause, back again. They were good. Professional. But they were looking for students who would stop at 200 yards and take their shot.

Cole kept moving.

At 250 yards, he heard one of the instructors call out a student who'd been spotted. "Grid 4-7. See him?"

"Yeah. Dumbass is wearing his watch. Caught the glint."

"Someone was not paying attention in class."

The student stood up, frustrated, and walked back to the start point. Each candidate had three attempts to pass the course.

Cole didn't move. Didn't react. He was a stone, a

shadow, nothing. His watch was in his pocket. Had been since the stalk started.

At 200 yards, he could have taken his shot. Instead, he angled slightly left, using a line of scrub brush that ran almost to the base of the hill. His ghillie suit was picking up debris as designed, making him indistinguishable from the vegetation.

The instructors weren't watching the brush line closely, it was too close, too obvious. No one would be stupid enough to use it.

Cole used it.

At 100 yards, he was below the OP, hidden in the dead ground at the base of the hill. He could hear the instructors talking, their voices carrying in the still morning air. He began moving up the hill, using the terrain, the rocks, the scattered vegetation. It was steeper here, harder to move quietly, but the instructors were focused on the field below. He'd emptied his canteen on the slope ahead of him to keep dust down from his drag bag. They weren't expecting anyone behind them.

At fifty yards, he stopped and waited. One of the instructors stood up, stretched, and walked a few feet away to piss. The other two kept scanning.

Cole moved again.

The physical toll was significant now.

The cold had seeped into his bones, his muscles were cramping from hours of controlled movement, and his throat was dry from thirst. But he barely registered it. He was in the zone now, that predatory state where time stretched and compressed, where every blade of grass was a landmark, every shift in light a signal. He wasn't Cole anymore. He was an operator, and the instructors were objective.

At twenty yards, he could see them clearly. Gunnery Sergeant Keller and two others whose names he didn't know. They were focused, professional, doing their job. They had no idea he was there.

Cole covered the last twenty yards in forty-five minutes. He moved like water, like smoke, like something that didn't exist. And then he was there, close enough to touch, close enough to neutralize.

He reached out and tapped Keller on the boot.

Keller jerked, spun, and found himself staring at Cole, who was lying prone in the grass three feet away, his rifle aimed at the target downrange.

"Bang," Cole said quietly, and pulled the trigger. The blank round cracked across the field, the sound sharp in the morning air.

The other two instructors whipped around, their faces registering shock, confusion, and something that might have been respect. Keller stared at Cole for a long moment, his expression unreadable. Then he started laughing, a short, disbelieving bark of sound.

"What in the fuck," Keller said. "What in the actual fuck."

Cole low-crawled backward, down the hill, and disappeared into the terrain. All he could think about was the look that was going to be on Harrow's face when they got back to Bragg.

He had a wide grin on his olive drab and loam-colored face.

Chapter Five

The debrief happened that afternoon. All the students who'd completed the stalk were called into the classroom to review their performance. Cole, Vail, and Riker sat in the back while Keller went through each student's approach, pointing out mistakes, offering corrections. When he got to Cole, Keller stopped and looked at him for a long moment.

"You," Keller said. "Stand up."

Cole stood, reluctantly.

"You want to explain what in the fuck you were doing up there?"

"Stalking, Gunny" Cole said.

"The objective was 200 yards. And its Gunnery Sargeant, piss ant."

"I got closer. Not too bad for a piss ant aye Gunny"

Keller grimaced "You got close enough to slit my fucking throat." Keller's voice wasn't angry; it was something else. Curious, maybe. Impressed, definitely. "Where'd you learn to move like that?"

"Here and there," Cole said.

"Here and there." Keller folded his arms. "You're not 82nd Airborne. I've trained 82nd guys.

They're good, but they're not that good. And that attitude is oozing Spec ops So, what are you?"

Cole said nothing.

He could see the curiosity in Keller's eyes, the professional recognition of skill that went beyond what a standard infantry unit would teach.

Keller looked at Vail and Riker. "You two the same?"

"We're just here to learn," Vail said smoothly. "That was some top-notch instruction, Gunny. Thank you for the lessons."

Keller studied them, his expression unreadable. Then he nodded slowly. "Right. Well. You passed. All three of you. Top marks." He looked back at Cole. "But if you ever sneak up on me again, I'm gonna shoot you on principle."

"You have to find me first, Gunny," Cole said, his expression flat, unreadable—the thousand-yard stare that Stanley Kubrick would have appreciated

After the debrief, the three of them walked back to the barracks in silence. The sun was setting, the temperature dropping, the base settling into its evening routine. Riker was grinning like an idiot. Vail looked thoughtful. Cole felt nothing in particular, just the quiet the noise in his head went quiet.

"Harrow's gonna be pissed," Riker said.

"Harrow's always fucking pissed," Cole said.

"Yeah, but now he's gonna be right about you doing something stupid."

Cole shrugged. "Wasn't stupid. I didn't get caught."

"You got caught on purpose, dumbass. You tapped the instructor."

"Had to let him know I was there," Cole said smiling. "Otherwise, what's the point?"

Vail shook his head but didn't argue. There was no point. Cole was going to do what Cole was going to do.

The rest of them would just have to deal with it. That was how this team worked. That was how they stayed alive.

Chapter Six

PART ONE

"By the time you start asking who talked, you already know the answer is going to hurt."-George R.R. Martin

They were Secret covert operators pretending to be Army infantry, attending a Marine sniper course that only increased their lethality, waiting for permission to hunt the man who'd tried to neutralize them. And in the meantime, Cole had just proven something that didn't need proving, that he could get close enough to neutralize anyone, anywhere, anytime.

It wasn't arrogance. It was just fact.

And somewhere back at Fort Bragg, Colonel Harrow was going to hear about it and have that stroke after all.

The barracks at Quantico smelled like floor wax and stale sweat, the kind of institutional odor that permeated every military building Cole had ever slept in. The heating system rattled and clanked through the walls, fighting against the January cold that seeped through the single-pane windows. Outside, wind moved through the pine trees with a sound like rushing water.

Cole lay on his bunk in the darkness, eyes open, staring at the ceiling tiles he'd counted seventeen times since lights out. His mind was running through the stalking exercise again, frame by frame, analyzing every movement, every decision. The approach had been good. The concealment better.

But there was always something. Always a detail that could be improved. A second that could be shaved off. A movement that could be more efficient.

His internal clock told him it was 0245 hours. Two minutes before the knock came.

He heard the footsteps first. Boot heels on linoleum, measured and deliberate, coming down the hallway outside. Not the random pattern of someone heading to the latrine. Not the quick pace of someone late for duty. This was purposeful. Military. Coming directly toward their door.

Cole's hand moved to the knife under his pillow. Old habit. Probably unnecessary at a Marine Corps base in Virginia, but habits kept you alive. The footsteps stopped outside their door. Cole counted heartbeats. One. Two. Three. The knock came at exactly 0247 hours. Three sharp raps, official and impersonal. Riker stirred in the bunk across from him. Vail was already sitting up, silent and alert in the darkness. They'd all heard it. They'd all been awake. The door opened without waiting for a response. Light from the hallway spilled in, silhouetting a Marine captain Cole had never seen before. The man was tall, maybe six-two, with the rigid posture of someone who'd spent his entire career in the Corps. His uniform was immaculate even at this hour. His service Charlies, perfectly pressed, ribbons aligned with geometric precision.

Navy and marine Corp Commendation medal with V device. Navy Cross. Purple Heart with two clusters. This wasn't some admin puke. This was a Marine who'd seen the elephant and lived to talk about it. But it was his face that told Cole everything he needed to know. Carefully neutral. Professionally blank. The expression of a man who'd been given orders he didn't understand and had been specifically instructed not to ask questions about.

"Cole, Vail, Riker," the captain said. His voice was flat, emotionless. "Get your shit. You're leaving."

Riker sat up, blinking against the light. "When?"

"Now. You have ten minutes to be outside."

"Guess we will miss graduation." Vail commented

The captain's eyes swept the room once, cataloging, assessing. Then he turned and walked away without another word. The door remained open. Light from the hallway cut across the floor like a blade.

Cole swung his legs off the bunk, his bare feet hitting the cold linoleum. His mind was already working through the variables. Middle of the night extraction. No advance warning. A captain delivering the message personally instead of sending a sergeant. The careful neutrality in the man's expression.

"The fuck did we do?" Riker asked, pulling on his pants.

"Nothing," Cole said, reaching for his duffel bag. "This isn't disciplinary."

"How do you know?"

"Because they'd have sent MPs, not a captain who looks like he's trying not to ask questions." Cole started packing with the efficiency of someone who'd done this a thousand times. Clothes folded tight and compact. Boots at the bottom for weight distribution. Personal items in the side pocket. "And he would've read us our rights."

Vail was already moving, pulling his gear together in the

darkness. He didn't need light. None of them did. They could pack their bags blindfolded, drunk, under fire. It was muscle memory now, ingrained through repetition until it became instinct.

"Something happened," Vail said, zipping his bag closed.

Cole nodded, though Vail probably couldn't see it in the darkness. Something had happened. Something bad enough to pull them out of a Marine Corps school in the middle of the night with no explanation, no warning, no official paperwork. This had Colonel Harrow written all over it.

The kind of thing that happened when operations went sideways and people needed to disappear quickly.

They were packed in eight minutes.

The captain was waiting outside with a Humvee, engine running, exhaust visible in the cold air. He didn't speak as they threw their bags in the back and climbed in. Just put the vehicle in gear and drove, his face illuminated by the green glow of the dashboard lights.

The base was quiet at this hour. A few lights burning in the headquarters building. A pair of MPs at the main gate, who waved them through without checking IDs.

The captain drove with the practiced ease of someone who knew every road on the base, taking them away from the main facilities, toward Turner airfield on the eastern edge of the complex.

Cole watched the landscape slide past through the window. Pine trees. Chain-link fences. Concrete buildings that all looked the same. He was reading the situation, analyzing it, building a picture in his mind of what was happening and why.

No official paperwork meant this was off the books.

Middle of the night meant urgency. A captain as courier

meant someone high up the chain of command wanted this done quietly. And the destination, the airfield, meant they were going somewhere fast.

The Humvee crested a small rise, and Cole saw it.

A C-130 Hercules sat on the tarmac, engines already running, the four turboprops creating a wall of sound that vibrated through the Humvee's frame. The aircraft was painted matte black, no markings, no identification numbers, no unit insignia. Just flat black paint that seemed to absorb light rather than reflect it. This wasn't a regular Air Force bird.

This was 23rd Air Force, the umbrella command for Air Force Special Operations. The kind of planes that flew missions that didn't officially exist, carrying people who weren't officially there, to places that weren't officially visited. The captain pulled up next to the aircraft and stopped. For a moment, he just sat there, hands on the wheel, staring straight ahead. Then he turned and looked at Cole.

"Good luck," he said.

Cole met his eyes. The captain held his gaze for a moment, then looked away, like he'd seen something he didn't want to see. Or maybe something he recognized. The look of a man who knew he was being sent into something bad and might not come back.

"Yeah," Cole said. Something bad.

They climbed out into the roar of the engines. The prop wash hit them like a physical force, cold and violent, carrying the smell of jet fuel and hydraulic fluid.

The loadmaster was waiting at the ramp, an Air Force sergeant, short but powerfully built, with the kind of compact muscularity that came from years of hauling cargo and equipment.

His name tape read MASUR. He waved them aboard with the impatient gesture of someone who had a schedule to keep.

Cole grabbed his bag and headed up the ramp. The cargo bay was cavernous and empty, just bare metal and tie-down points and their three duffel bags looking small and insignificant in all that space. No other passengers. No cargo pallets. No equipment. Just empty space and the smell of metal and oil.

The ramp started closing before they'd even sat down. The hydraulics whined, and the gap of night sky narrowed and disappeared. The interior lights were red, night vision friendly, casting everything in a crimson glow that made the cargo bay look like the inside of a beating heart.

The aircraft lurched forward, taxiing toward the runway.

Cole grabbed a seat along the bulkhead and strapped in. The nylon webbing was worn smooth from years of use, and the metal frame was cold even through his clothes.

Vail sat across from him, face unreadable in the red light. Riker was already leaning back, eyes closed, but Cole knew he wasn't sleeping. None of them were sleeping.

The C-130 turned onto the runway. The engines spooled up, the sound building from a roar to a scream that made conversation impossible. Cole felt the vibration through the seat, through his bones, through his teeth. Then the brakes released and they were rolling, accelerating, the airframe shaking and rattling like it was going to come apart.

The nose lifted. The main gear left the ground. And they were airborne, climbing steeply into the night sky.

"Fort Bragg," Vail said once they'd leveled off and the engine noise had dropped to a manageable roar.

It wasn't a question.

Cole nodded. "Where else?"

Riker opened his eyes. "Fuuuck."

The flight took three hours. Cole spent it thinking, analyzing, preparing. The C-130 was loud, the kind of bone-deep vibration that made sleep impossible even if you wanted it. The cargo bay was cold despite the heating system, and the red lights made everything look like a crime scene.

Cole watched his teammates. Vail sat perfectly still, eyes closed, but his breathing pattern said he was awake and thinking.

Riker kept shifting position, unable to get comfortable, his leg bouncing with nervous energy. Both of them were running through scenarios, building contingency plans, preparing for whatever was waiting for them at Bragg.

The loadmaster, Masur, sat near the cockpit door, reading a paperback novel by the red light. He'd glanced at them once when they boarded, cataloged them as special operations, and then ignored them completely. Smart man. In this business, the less you knew, the longer you lived.

Cole's mind kept circling back to Nicaragua. The ambush. The timing. The fact that the enemy had known exactly where they'd be and when. That kind of intelligence didn't come from luck or good guessing. That came from someone on the inside. Someone with access to operational details. Someone who'd decided that Task Force Ghostline was a problem that needed to be eliminated.

The question was who.

And the answer, Cole suspected, was going to be bad.

The C-130 began its descent at 0545 hours. Cole felt the change in engine pitch, the subtle shift in the aircraft's attitude.

Through the small porthole window, he could see the

sky beginning to lighten, that pre-dawn gray that came before sunrise.

They landed at Pope Air Force Base just after 0600. The sun was coming up, cold and pale over the North Carolina pine trees. The ramp dropped, and Cole got his first breath of North Carolina air, crisp and clean, carrying the smell of pine sap and red clay.

Chapter Seven

Thursday, March 14th, 1985

A black Suburban waited at the edge of the tarmac, exhaust visible in the cold morning air. Harrow was driving. That told Cole everything he needed to know about how serious this was. Colonel Nathan Harrow didn't do pickups. Harrow delegated pickups to junior officers and NCOs while he did more important things like planning operations and managing the political bullshit that came with running a black operations task force. If Harrow was here personally, driving the vehicle himself, then whatever had happened was bad enough that he didn't trust anyone else with the information.

They threw their bags in the back and climbed in. Harrow pulled away before Riker had even closed his door, accelerating hard, taking them away from the airfield at a speed that suggested urgency.

"The rest of the team?" Vail asked from the back seat.

"Waiting," Harrow said. His voice was tight, controlled, but Cole could hear the anger underneath.

Harrow was always some degree of angry, it was his

default state, the baseline from which he operated. But this was different. This was the kind of anger that came from betrayal.

"What happened?" Cole asked.

Harrow's jaw tightened. The muscles bunched and flexed. "I'll brief everyone at once."

They drove in silence. Not toward the main base. Not toward any of the official buildings where Task Force Ghostline officially didn't exist. Harrow took them north, away from Fort Bragg proper, into the pine forests that surrounded the base. The road got narrower, less maintained. They passed through two checkpoints, both manned by MPs who checked IDs with the kind of thoroughness that suggested they'd been told to be extra careful today.

Finally, Harrow turned onto an unmarked road that led to a facility Cole had only been to once before. A nondescript concrete building, three stories tall, no windows on the first two floors. It sat behind two chain-link fences topped with razor wire, with a guard post at the entrance that looked like it could withstand a small arms attack.

The guard checked their IDs three times before letting them through. Not just a glance at the photo, a real check, comparing faces to pictures, running names checking names on a very short list on the clipboards they carried, calling it in and waiting for confirmation.

Cleared.

They all got the green light.

This was the kind of place that didn't exist on any map. The kind of place where people planned things that never officially happened. Where operations were discussed that would be denied by everyone from the President on down.

If they ever came to light. The kind of place where

careers ended and people disappeared if they talked about what happened inside.

Harrow parked in a lot that held only three other vehicles, all of them black Suburbans identical to the one they'd arrived in. He shut down the engine and sat there for a moment, hands on the wheel, staring straight ahead.

"Whatever you hear in there," Harrow said quietly, "stays in there. You don't talk about it. You don't think about it.

You don't even fucking dream about it unless you're behind a locked door in a bunker. Are we clear?"

"Clear," Cole said.

Harrow nodded and got out.

They followed him inside. The building's interior was exactly what Cole expected, institutional and sterile. Fluorescent lights that hummed with a frequency just at the edge of hearing. Linoleum floors polished to a high shine. Concrete walls painted in that particular shade of government beige that seemed to exist nowhere else in the world.

They went down a hallway. Through a door that required a cipher lock. Harrow punched in a six-digit code without hesitation. Down another hallway. Through another locked door, this one requiring both a code and a key card. The security got tighter with each layer, each door, each checkpoint.

Finally, they reached a briefing room at the end of a corridor.

Harrow opened the door. The room smelled like coffee and mold. A long conference table dominated the center, surrounded by chairs that had seen better days.

The walls were bare except for a large map of Central America and a whiteboard covered in notes written in Harrow's distinctive block letters. A coffee maker sat on a side table, surrounded by empty cups and a box of donuts that nobody had touched.

The rest of the team was already there.

Torres sat at the far end of the table, cleaning his fingernails with a folding knife, the blade catching the fluorescent light with each pass. Bishop was next to him, arms crossed, face set in an expression of cold fury. Price leaned against the wall, coffee cup in hand, watching the door with the kind of alertness that never really turned off.

Ward sat perfectly still, his hands flat on the table, his engineer's mind already working through whatever problem they were about to be presented with.

Holt, Mason, Hawke, Draven. All of them. The entire team. Sitting around the conference table with expressions that ranged from pissed off to coldly furious.

Torres looked up when they walked in. "The fuck did they teach you at Quantico? How to show up late?"

"How to sneak up on assholes," Riker said. "Want a demonstration?"

"I am surrounded by a bunch of Juvenile delinquents," Harrow said, shaking his head. He closed the door and locked it, a deadbolt that slid home with a solid thunk that said this conversation was not going to be interrupted. Then he walked to the head of the table and stood there for a moment, looking at each of them in turn.

"Nicaragua wasn't random," Harrow said.

The room went very still. Even Torres stopped cleaning his fingernails.

"The ambush," Harrow continued. "The timing. The fact that they knew exactly where to hit us and when. The fact that they had a six-man spestnaz team in position thirty minutes before we arrived." He paused, letting that sink in.

"Someone leaked information about this team to hostile Soviet forces."

Nobody spoke. The only sound was the hum of the fluorescent lights and the distant rumble of the building's HVAC system.

"Who?" Bishop asked. His voice was quiet, controlled, but Cole could hear the rage underneath.

Harrow reached into his briefcase and pulled out a folder. He opened it and laid a photograph on the table.

A professional headshot, the kind that appeared in official directories and on office walls. A man in his fifties, gray hair, expensive suit, American flag pin on his lapel. The kind of face that appeared on C-SPAN and in Washington Post articles about intelligence policy.

"Deputy Director of Operations at the CIA," Harrow said. "Man named Marcus Lawson."

For a moment, nobody spoke. Cole watched the information settle over the team like a blanket of ice. He saw the way Torres's hand tightened on his knife. The way Bishop's jaw clenched. The way Price set down his coffee cup with exaggerated care, like he was afraid he might throw it if he wasn't careful.

"Our own fucking people," Mason said quietly.

"Not our people," Harrow said. "Lawson's people.

He's working with a GRU cut-out to inform the Soviets of Operation Night Arrow. Local assets in Nicaraguan tell us that he had met with a Nicaraguan Sandinista commander named Tomás Reyes, Senior officer in the Nicaraguan military. After the operation that Lawson set in motion failed. The goal we think is to expose or eliminate this team when we head into that AOR again. So as to embarrass the President and force him out of office. So, they are now going to be expecting you guys. So, we need to be extra careful. Opsec has to be perfect from here on out"

Harrow laid out more photographs. Reyes in uniform, standing in front of a military compound. Reyes meeting with Soviet advisors. Reyes at a political rally, surrounded by armed guards.

"Why?" Ward asked. His analytical mind was already working through the problem, building a model of motivations and consequences.

"Because Lawson thinks the President is weak," Harrow said. "Thinks we're losing the Cold War.

Thinks a covert team operating outside official channels is dangerous and illegal." He paused. "He's not entirely wrong about that last part."

"How'd he find out about us?" Vail asked.

"Hayes." Harrow said the name like it tasted bad. "CIA Special Activities Division liaison. He provided information to Lawson without knowing what Lawson was planning to do with it. Once Hayes realized what was happening, he came to me. He's helping with the investigation now."

"Helping how?" Torres asked. He'd started cleaning his fingernails again, the knife moving in short, precise strokes.

"Tracking Lawson's communications. Identifying his contacts. Building a case." Harrow leaned forward, his hands flat on the table.

"But we're not waiting for a case. We're not going through channels. We're not filing reports or waiting for someone in Washington to decide what to do."

Cole felt something settle in his chest. Cold and certain. He knew what was coming next. Had known since the moment Harrow had picked them up personally.

"We're going after them," Cole said.

Harrow looked at him. "Yes."

"Both of them," Vail said. "Reyes and Lawson."

"Yes, gentlemen. We are going to hunt them both down."

"When?" Cole asked.

"Soon. We're still gathering intelligence on Reyes's location and security. Lawson's movements are easier to track, but he's in D.C., surrounded by people who think he's a patriot." Harrow straightened. "This is going to be complicated. We'll need to operate completely black. No official support. No backup. If this goes wrong, the President will disavow us, and we'll all end up in Leavenworth or dead."

"So, business as usual," Torres said.

A few of them smiled. Dark humor.

The kind that kept you sane when the world went to shit.

"How do we want to handle it?" Hawke asked.

Everyone looked at Cole. It was automatic now, instinctive. When it came to operational planning, Cole was the one they turned to. Not because of rank, they were all the same rank, officially. But because Cole had a gift for seeing the angles, for finding the vulnerabilities, for building plans that worked.

Cole thought about it. Ran through the variables. Two targets. Two different environments. Two different security situations. Two different approaches required.

"Reyes first," he said. "He's the immediate threat. He's got resources, territory, and a reason to keep coming after us. We eliminate him, we cut off Lawson's foreign support."

"And Lawson?" Bishop asked.

"After Reyes is dead, we make it look like Lawson committed suicide." The room was quiet. Cole's voice had been flat. Emotionless. Like he was discussing the weather or a training exercise. "With the time difference between

Nicaragua and Washington, there's no way Lawson learns of Reyes's death before we neutralize him."

"Jesus, Cole," Riker said.

Cole looked at him. "You got a problem with that?"

"No. Just... fucking ruthless, man."

"He tried to fucking end us," Cole said.

"He leaked our fucking existence to people who want us dead. He's planning to do it again." He looked around the table, meeting each man's eyes in turn. "This isn't operational. It's personal. They're targets. We fucking eliminate targets."

Vail nodded slowly. "God damn right."

"I know he's right," Riker said. "Doesn't make it less fucked up that we're going after the Deputy Director of the CIA."

"We're going after a traitor," Ward said quietly. "There's a difference."

Chapter Eight

Operation Dead Letter

Harrow watched them, his expression unreadable. "I need to know you're all in. This crosses lines we haven't crossed before. We're not just operating in the black anymore. People know about us, this task force. We're out of the black and into the gray. We're exposed. If we do this right, we might be able to slip back into the black. But operating on American soil is in violation of the Posse Comitatus Act. For those of you who don't know what that is, it's a U.S. law that prohibits the use of military forces for domestic law enforcement."

He paused, letting that sink in.

"What we're about to do," Harrow continued, "is technically treason. If anyone finds out, we'll all hang. The President will disavow us. The Agency will disavow us. We'll be erased from every record, every file, every database. Our families will be told we died in training accidents. And we'll spend the rest of our lives in Leavenworth if we're lucky, or in unmarked graves if we're not."

The room was silent.

"I'm in," Torres said immediately.

"In," Bishop said.

And one by one, they all said it. Price. Ward. Holt.

Mason. Hawke. Draven. Vail. Riker. Keller.

Cole didn't say anything. He didn't need to. Everyone knew.

Harrow nodded. "All right. We start planning today. Ward, Bishop, you're on intelligence gathering. I want everything we can get on Reyes's location, security, routines.

I want to know where he sleeps, where he eats, where he fucks his mistress. I want to know his guard rotation, his vehicle routes, his communication protocols. Everything."

Ward pulled out a notebook and started writing.

"Hayes, logistics. We'll need weapons, equipment, transportation. All of it untraceable. Nothing that can be traced back to us or to any U.S. military unit."

"I've got contacts," Hayes said. "Will need some money."

"Use them. I'll get you the cash. Hundred thousand to start. More if you need it." Harrow turned to Price. "Price, Vail, Ward, you're on Lawson. I want to know everywhere he goes, everyone he talks to, every fucking cup of coffee he drinks. I want his schedule, his security detail, his home address, his mistress's address if he has one. I want to know his vulnerabilities."

"On it," Price said.

Harrow looked at Cole. "You're running point on mission planning. Figure out how we get to Reyes and how we get out. I want multiple options. I want contingencies. I want exfiltration routes and backup plans and plans for when the backup plans fail."

Cole nodded.

Harrow looked at Keller. "Let's get comms up to coordinate.

I want encrypted channels, burst transmissions, dead

drops if we need them. Nothing that can be intercepted or traced."

"Questions?" Harrow asked.

Nobody spoke.

"Good. Get to work."

The team started to move, but Harrow held up a hand. "One more thing. This doesn't leave this room. You don't talk about it on base. You don't talk about it in your sleep. You don't even fucking think about it unless you're behind a locked door in a bunker." Repeating what he had said to Cole earlier now to the whole team. He paused. "We're hunting one of our own. That makes us traitors too, if anyone finds out. Remember that."

They filed out in silence. Cole stayed behind, waiting until the room was empty except for him and Harrow.

"You good?" Harrow asked.

"Yeah."

"You sure? Because you just volunteered to execute a Deputy Director of the CIA."

"With his actions." Cole said. "He asked for it. When anyone tries to take out me or my team, we will hunt them to the ends of the earth. I don't give a fuck who they are or what position they hold."

Harrow studied him for a long moment. "You don't feel anything about this, do you?"

"Exactly what the fuck should I be feeling about this, Nate?"

"Maybe you should be feeling that assassinating an American, on American soil, is not what you signed up for," Harrow said quietly, the word *Nate* still hanging between them like a fault line. His voice was flat, almost calm, but there was iron underneath it, the kind that warned he was holding himself back. "It sure as hell is not what this team was put together for, Ben."

Cole met his eyes. "You want someone who feels bad about fucking burying traitors, get someone else. Until you find that individual, I am all you have."

"I don't want someone else," Harrow said. "I want you. Because you'll do what needs to be done without hesitation." He paused. "Just remember you're still human, Benjamin. Even if you don't feel like it."

Cole didn't respond. There was nothing to say.

He left Harrow in the briefing room and walked out into the cold January morning. The sun was higher now, bright and indifferent. The air was crisp and clean, carrying the smell of pine trees and the distant sound of artillery fire from the training ranges.

Cole stood there for a moment, letting the cold air fill his lungs, thinking through the mission parameters. Two targets. Two different operational environments. Two different security situations. Multiple variables. Multiple contingencies. Multiple ways it could go wrong.

He thought about Reyes first. Nicaragua. Hostile territory. Foreign military compound. Armed guards. Soviet advisors.

The man would be paranoid, careful, surrounded by security.

Getting to him would require surveillance, intelligence gathering, pattern analysis. They'd need to find his vulnerabilities, his routines, his habits, the places where his guard was down.

Then Lawson. Washington, D.C. American soil. A senior CIA official with security details and protective surveillance. A man who knew how special operations worked, who understood tradecraft, who would be watching for threats. Making it look like suicide would require precision, planning, and perfect execution.

Cole's mind was already building the framework. Surveillance teams. Communication protocols. Weapon selection. Exfiltration routes. Contingency plans. Backup plans for the backup plans. This was what he was good at. This was what he'd been trained for. Not the killing itself, that was just mechanics, just the final step in a long process. But the planning. The analysis. The ability to see the angles and find the vulnerabilities and build a plan that worked.

He was getting tired of people questioning his lack of feeling about what he did, what he was trained to do, hell what they fucking recruited him to do. Harrow wanted someone who would do what needed to be done without hesitation. Well, that's what he had. That's what Cole was.

Somewhere in Nicaragua, Reyes was planning his next move. Somewhere in Washington, Lawson was doing the same. They thought they were hunting Task Force Ghostline. They thought they had the advantage. They thought they were safe.

They were wrong.

Ghostline was coming. Cole was coming.

And Ghostline didn't leave witnesses.

Cole turned and walked back toward the building. There was work to do. Plans to make. Intelligence to gather. Weapons to acquire. A mission to plan.

One man had tried to bury his team. and another would try again with help. Now those two men were going to die.

It was that simple.

Chapter Nine

Friday March 15th, 1985

The planning room was three levels down, behind two cipher locks and a Marine guard who checked their IDs even though he'd cleared them ten minutes earlier. Cole heard the metallic click of the second lock disengaging, felt the pressure change as the heavy steel door swung open. The walls were bare concrete, painted institutional gray decades ago and never touched since. The air was recycled and cold, pushed through HVAC ducts that hummed with a constant low frequency that got into your bones after a while. A long table dominated the center, already covered with maps, satellite photographs, and folders stamped with classifications that meant federal prison if you talked about what was inside. In the mid-eighties, this was what passed for a SCIF, (Sensitive Compartmented Information Facility).

The fluorescent lights overhead cast everything in harsh white light. No windows. No natural light. Just concrete and steel and the weight of secrets that could start wars or end careers. The room smelled like stale coffee, paper, and the particular odor of men who'd been working too long without sleep.

Ward stood at the head of the table like a professor about to teach a class on murder. He'd been up all night; Cole could tell by the empty coffee cups lined up on the side table like soldiers. Seven of them. Ward's hands had a slight tremor, and his eyes were too bright, pupils dilated from too much caffeine and not enough sleep.

He kept shifting his weight from foot to foot, unable to stand still, his mind running faster than his body could keep up with.

Ward's 160-plus IQ was why he was the intelligence arm of this little group of rebels. He knew he was the smartest person in the room, and he never missed an opportunity to remind everyone. But Cole didn't mind. Smart was useful. Smart kept people alive.

Cole just smiled his trademark smile and listened.

The team filed in and took seats around the table. Torres moved with controlled energy, like a boxer before a fight. Riker was calm, methodical, already studying the materials on the table. Mason looked nervous, his knee bouncing under the table. Hawke sprawled in his chair with false casualness, but his eyes were sharp. Draven sat perfectly still, observing. Holt's hands were steady on the table. Bishop was checking his watch, calculating timelines. Keller was already at the side wall, setting up equipment with surgical precision.

"Alright," Ward said, his voice tight with caffeine and focus. "Let's talk about how we're going to execute these motherfuckers."

Keller was setting up equipment along the side wall. Night vision goggles, AN/PVS-5s, the best the military had in 1985, though they were bulky and the image quality was grainy green. Encrypted radios. Keller went with the British PRC-319s, He chose these for their burst transmission capability and text messaging function. Surveillance equipment, cameras, recording devices, directional microphones.

He handled each piece with the calm precision of a surgeon, checking connections, testing battery levels, making notes in a small notebook with mechanical pencil.

Ward spread a large-scale map of Nicaragua across the table, then layered satellite photographs over it. Hayes had obtained them from the National Reconnaissance Office. Recent imagery, high-resolution, taken by a KH-11 satellite that officially didn't exist.

The photos were so detailed.

Cole could see individual vehicles, guard positions, even the shadows cast by walls and buildings. The kind of intelligence that cost taxpayers millions and that most people would never know existed.

"Reyes first," Ward said, tapping the map with a pen, "because he's the complicated one." He pointed to a compound northeast of Managua. "This is his primary residence. Walled estate, approximately four acres. Main house here," he indicated a large structure. "Guest house here, barracks for his security detail here. Intelligence estimates put his personal guard at twenty to thirty men, rotating in eight-hour shifts."

Ward pulled out a detailed breakdown, typed on a manual typewriter, single-spaced. "Shift change at 0600, 1400, and 2200 hours. Guard force composition: former Nicaraguan Army, some with special operations backgrounds. At least three served with the Batallón de Lucha Contra Bandidos, counterinsurgency specialists. They know what they're doing."

"Loyal?" Torres asked, leaning forward with the aggressive energy he always had when planning violence.

"To the money," Ward said. "Reyes pays three times what the army does. But they're professionals. They're not going to panic, and they're not going to run. If we hit him at the compound, we're looking at a sustained firefight with trained personnel who know the terrain."

Cole studied the photographs.

The compound sat on elevated terrain with clear sight lines in all directions. The walls were twelve feet high, topped with broken glass embedded in concrete.

Guard towers at each corner, elevated platforms with sandbag protection. A single access road that could be covered from multiple positions. The main house was two stories, reinforced construction.

The barracks could hold thirty men easily.

Draven pulled one of the satellite photos closer, his eyes scanning the terrain with the patience of someone who understood high ground and fields of fire. His finger traced the approaches. "Those guard towers have overlapping fields of fire. Anyone approaching from the access road is fucked. Even if we came in from the sides, we'd be exposed for at least two hundred meters. And look here," he tapped the photo, "they've cleared the vegetation around the perimeter. No cover, no concealment."

"Right," Ward said. "Hitting him there is a shitshow waiting to happen. We'd need a full assault element, air support, and a lot of luck. Even then, casualties would be high. We'd be looking at a minimum of twelve operators, probably more. And we'd have to extract under fire, which means helicopters, which means noise, which means the entire Nicaraguan military knows we're there."

"So, we don't hit him there," Vail said.

"Exactly." Ward pulled out another set of photographs, these showing a residential neighborhood. "Reyes has a mistress. Maria Sanchez, twenty-six years old, former model. Lives in a neighborhood called Los Robles, about twenty minutes from his compound. He visits her every Thursday night, arrives between 2100 and 2130 hours, stays until Friday morning. Takes a three-vehicle convoy, lead vehicle, his vehicle, trail vehicle.

But the security is lighter. Six to eight men instead of thirty."

"How solid is this intel?" Cole asked. He needed to know the confidence level. Ninety percent wasn't good enough if the ten percent got them killed.

Ward flipped through his notes. "Source is a local asset, been on S.A.Ds payroll for eight months. He's a driver for one of Reyes's business associates, has access to scheduling information.

We've confirmed the pattern through independent surveillance. Hayes' people have been watching the mistress's house for the past three weeks. Reyes has shown up every Thursday, same time window, same security posture. Source reliability is rated at ninety-nine percent."

Torres sat up straighter. "What's the wall situation?"

"Eight feet, concrete block, no guard towers. Single gate, opens inward." Ward pointed to the photos. "The house is two stories, approximately 2,400 square feet. Courtyard in front where he parks his vehicles. Most of his security stays outside with the vehicles. Only two bodyguards go inside with him."

"Breach points?" Holt's voice had that edge it got when he was thinking about breaching with shape charges or water impulse charges. He loved this shit

Ward pointed to the photos. "Gate is primary. It's steel,

but it's not reinforced. We can breach it with a hydraulic spreader or a vehicle ram if necessary. But there's a section here on the east wall where the concrete's degraded, you can see the discoloration in the photo. Holt could put a shape charge there if we need a secondary entry point."

Holt nodded from his seat, his steady presence a counterweight to Torres's intensity. "Linear shape charge, minimal noise. I can use a water impulse charge, basically a water-filled tube with det cord. Thirty seconds to place, ten seconds to blow. Cuts through concrete like butter, and the water dampens the sound. Neighbors might hear it, but it won't sound like an explosion. More like a car backfiring."

"According to Hayes' people he never changes his routine He's predictable as fuck. Same route every time. He takes Avenida Bolívar to Carretera Sur, then into Los Robles. Same time, same security posture. Three vehicles, six to eight men total."

"No respect for security protocols," Cole said.

"That works in our favor and definitely not his." He leaned forward, studying the photos. "This shitbag wants to hunt us but has no fear of us hunting him. This dickhead has no idea who he is fucking with."

Chapter Ten

Ward spread out more photos of the residential street. Two-story houses behind walls, but nothing like the fortress of Reyes's compound. Trees lined the street. Streetlights every fifty meters. "The mistress's house is here. Walled, but the walls are eight feet, as I mentioned earlier, no guard towers, no hardened positions. He parks his vehicles in the courtyard, leaves most of his security outside. They smoke, they talk, they get complacent."

"How many inside with him?" Price asked.

"Two. Personal bodyguards. Both carry sidearms, Browning Hi-Powers, and AK-47s. They stay in the front room while he's upstairs with the woman. We've observed them through windows. They sit, they watch TV, they drink. They're not expecting trouble."

Mason leaned forward, and Cole could see the nervous energy in his shoulders, the way his hands kept moving. Mason was always like this before contact, anxious, asking questions, second-guessing. But once the shooting started, he was fearless.

"What about neighbors? If it goes hand-to-hand, noise discipline goes to shit."

"Houses on either side are occupied," Ward said. "But the walls are solid concrete block, and the houses are set back from the property lines. Suppressed weapons, quick in and out, nobody hears shit.

We've measured the distances; the nearest house is twenty meters away with a solid wall between.

A suppressed gunshot inside the target house won't be audible to the neighbors."

"Exfil route?" Torres asked.

Ward traced a line on the map with his finger. "Two blocks south, we have a vehicle staged, a Toyota pickup, common as dirt in Managua. Four-minute drive to a safe house in Altamira, then we move to a secondary location before extraction. The safe house is owned by one of Harrow's assets, a businessman who imports agricultural equipment. It's clean, it's secure, and it has a garage where we can switch vehicles."

"And if someone does?" Mason pressed. "If a bodyguard gets close before we drop him? If we have to go hands-on?"

"Then you fucking handle it," Cole said, his voice flat. Mason needed the certainty, needed to know Cole believed in him. "You're faster than anyone in this goddamn room when it's close. You know that."

Mason nodded, some of the tension leaving his shoulders. He gave a slight grin to Cole.

Cole looked at the photos, running the scenario in his head like a film. Breach the wall at 2145 hours. or walk through the front gate, whichever is best. Neutralize the exterior security. A six man, maybe eight. Suppressed weapons, double-tap each target. Hit the house.

Two bodyguards in the front room. Reyes upstairs with the woman. Kill the bodyguards first, then move upstairs.

Reyes dies in the bedroom. The woman, they'd have to control her, keep her quiet, but she lives. Exfil before anyone knows what happened.

Four minutes to the vehicle. Ten minutes to the safe house. It was doable. Tight, but doable. Draven studied the map, his finger tracing sight lines and elevation changes.

"What about observation posts? I want eyes on the target house before we move. Rooftop here." He tapped a building two blocks away. "It gives us line of sight on the front gate and the street approach. I can see vehicles coming and going, count personnel, confirm Reyes is inside before we commit."

"Good," Cole said. "You'll set up there at 1900 hours, three hours before we move. Gives you time to get settled, observe the pattern. Keller will have comms with you."

Keller looked up from the radio equipment he'd been examining. The PRC-319s were spread out on the table, and he was checking each one methodically. "I'll need a relay if Draven's that far out. These encrypted British PRC-319 radio sets have shit range in urban terrain, maybe two kilometers line of sight, less with buildings in the way.

His voice was precise, mathematical. "I can set up a repeater on this building here." He pointed to a structure between Draven's position and the target house. " It gives us coverage for both the observation post and the assault element. I'll use a BID/250 it uses frequency hopping, super secure, as the repeater, set it to automatically retransmit on a frequency. That gives us a range of about five kilometers total."

"Do it," Cole said.

He watched Keller's hands as he made notes in his notebook. Steady, controlled. Keller was holding together, but Cole knew the man's mind could fracture under the wrong kind of pressure.

The math helped him. Planning was good for him. Numbers, frequencies, protocols. It kept him grounded, gave him something concrete to focus on.

"What about the woman?" Riker asked.

"Maria Sanchez," Ward said flatly. "Twenty-six, no political affiliations, no military connections. She's collateral. If she sees us, she dies. No witnesses. She has no kids, no parents, no one would miss her."

The room was quiet for a moment. Cole felt the weight of it, the casual way Ward had just written off a human life. He understood the logic, no witnesses meant no investigation, no manhunt, no complications. But there was a line, and Cole wasn't going to cross it.

"We don't ever execute the innocent, ever," Cole said, his tone all command, no bullshit. "Figure out another way. That's non-negotiable."

Ward nodded in understanding, as did the rest of the group. When Cole used that tone, they knew better than to challenge him. "You use Baklavas to cover your faces, knock her out by the time she wakes up, or someone finds her, we're long gone."

"Better," Cole said. "We're not murderers. We eliminate people who need to be eliminated. She's not one of them."

"Next Thursday," Ward continued. "Six days from now. That gives us time to get into country, establish surveillance, confirm the pattern, and execute."

"Alpha element," Cole said, looking around the table.

"Me, Riker, Torres, Hawke, Mason, Holt, Bishop, Keller, and Draven. Nine men.

We'll handle Reyes. That leaves you three to take care of Lawson. Price you are Bravo actual. You good with that?"

"Five by boss." Price said in a calm neutral voice

Ward nodded and pulled the Nicaragua maps aside, replacing them with street maps of Washington, D.C. The maps were detailed, showing Georgetown, the street grid, building layouts.

"Now let's talk about Lawson."

Torres glanced at Cole, and Cole saw the question in his eyes. Torres needed to know Cole would be there, close enough to keep him anchored, to keep him from going too far. Cole gave him a slight nod. Torres relaxed, his shoulders dropping slightly.

Vail stretched in his chair, restless energy barely contained. "What's the weapons loadout? Are we going loud or quiet?"

"Quiet until it's not," Cole said. "Suppressed CAR-15s with Aimpoint red dot optics, suppressed Berettas. But I want you carrying backup firepower. If it goes sideways, I want options."

"Now you're talking," Vail said with a grin.

Chapter Eleven

Hayes stepped forward, and Cole saw the guilt written all over his face. The man looked like he hadn't slept since the briefing. His eyes were bloodshot, his hands shaking slightly. He'd been the one to give Lawson information, not knowing what Lawson would do with it. Now Hayes was trying to fix it, trying to make it right.

"Lawson lives in Georgetown," Hayes said, his voice tight. "Townhouse on N Street Northwest, between 30th and 31st. Three stories, brick construction, built in the 1920s. He lives alone. Divorced, no kids. Housekeeper comes twice a week, Tuesdays and Fridays, arrives at 0900, leaves by 1400."

He spread out surveillance photos. Lawson leaving his house in a suit, briefcase in hand. Lawson getting into a car, a dark blue Volvo sedan. Lawson at a restaurant, sitting alone, drinking. The photos were recent, taken over the past week.

"His routine is consistent," Hayes continued. "Leaves for

Langley at 0645 every morning, returns between 1900 and 2000 hours. He has a security detail during the day, two men, armed, they follow him to and from work. But they don't follow him home. Agency policy, senior officials are considered low-risk on domestic soil."

"Dumb fucking policy," Vail muttered.

"Works in our favor," Price said. "What's the interior layout?"

Hayes pulled out architectural drawings, original blueprints from the 1920s, obtained from D.C. building records. "Ground floor is living room, kitchen, study. Hardwood floors, original construction.

Second floor is bedroom, bathroom, office. Third floor is storage, mostly unused. Basement is finished, he's got a home gym down there, treadmill, weights, nothing fancy."

Draven studied the drawings with the same careful attention he'd given the Nicaragua maps. "Windows on the second floor, what's the sight line from the street?"

"Partially obscured by trees," Hayes said. "But we're not going in through windows. Too visible, too much risk of being seen by neighbors or passersby."

"I'm not talking about entry," Draven said. "I'm talking about observation. I want him watched. You should have his pattern for at least two nights before you move. Make sure nothing's changed, make sure he's alone, make sure there are no surprises."

"Good," Price said. "Vail will handle overwatch. Set up across the street, observe for two nights, confirm the pattern."

"Alarm system?" Torres asked.

"Standard residential," Hayes said. "ADT system, installed in 1982. Motion sensors on the ground floor, door and window contacts. Control panel is in the front hallway, just inside the door. We can bypass it."

"How?" Ward asked.

Hayes pulled out technical specifications. "The system uses a phone line to communicate with the monitoring station.

We cut the phone line before entry; the system can't call out.

The control panel will beep when we open the door, but we'll have thirty seconds to enter the code before the alarm sounds. If we can't get the code, we just cut the power to the control panel. It's not a sophisticated system."

Torres leaned forward. "What about interior doors? Locks?"

"Bedroom door doesn't lock," Hayes said. "Study has a keyed lock, but he doesn't use it, we've observed him going in and out, never locks it. Basement door locks from the inside when he's working out, but he'll be asleep when we hit him."

"Neighbors?"

"Townhouses on either side, but the walls are thick, original brick construction, fourteen inches thick. Suppressed weapon, nobody hears anything. The neighbors on the left are a retired couple, both in their seventies, they go to bed early. The neighbors on the right are a young couple, both work long hours, usually not home until late."

Cole studied the drawings, visualizing the approach. "How does Price make it look like suicide?"

Hayes pulled out another folder, this one containing psychological profiles and personal information. "Lawson's been under stress. The Agency knows it. He's been drinking more; we've observed him buying liquor three times in the past week. He's sleeping less, lights in his bedroom stay on until 0200 or 0300 most nights. His ex-wife took him to the cleaners in the divorce; he's paying alimony and child support even though the kids are grown.

He's got financial problems, career problems. A suicide wouldn't surprise anyone."

"Weapon?" Price asked.

"His own," Hayes said. "He keeps a Colt 1911 in his desk. We've confirmed this through a source who was in his house last month. We use that, put it in his hand, gunshot to the right temple. He's right-handed, so the angle will be correct."

"Note?" Vail asked.

"Already drafted," Hayes said, pulling out a handwritten page. "I've studied his handwriting; I have samples from documents he's signed. This will pass forensic analysis. It's vague enough to be believable, stress, regret, can't go on. Nothing specific about Ghostline or Nicaragua. Just a man who's reached the end."

Cole read the note. The handwriting was shaky, emotional. *I can't do this anymore. The weight is too much. I'm sorry.* It was good. Depressed, defeated, the kind of thing a man might write before eating a bullet.

Ward shifted in his seat. "What if he wakes up? What if we have to control him before we can stage it?"

"Then you control him," Price said. "Quiet, quick. Rear naked choke, cut off the blood flow to the brain, he's unconscious in eight seconds. Then we stage it. But he's not going to wake up. We're hitting him at 0300 hours; he'll be deep in REM sleep. The human body is most deeply asleep between 0200 and 0400. His reaction time will be slow, his cognitive function impaired. We'll be on him before he knows what's happening."

"How do we get in?" Price asked.

"Back door," Hayes said. "It's a standard residential lock, Schlage deadbolt. I can pick it in under a minute. No forced entry, no signs of break-in.

We go in after midnight, he's asleep. Quick and quiet."

Ward pulled out a detailed timeline, written in his precise handwriting. "0225 hours: Vail confirms Lawson is home, lights are out. 0245: Price, Ward, and Vail approach from the alley behind the house. 0250: Pick the lock, disable the alarm. 0259: Enter the house, move to the second floor. 0301: Reach the study. 0303: Enter the study, control Lawson, stage the suicide. 0306: Exit the house. 0320: Exfil complete. Total time inside the house: seven minutes."

Price looked at Vail and Ward. "Bravo element. Three of us. In and out in ten minutes."

"Make it five," Cole said. "Longer you're there, more chance something goes wrong. More chance a neighbor sees something, more chance a cop drives by, more chance Lawson wakes up."

"Five," Price agreed.

Harrow stood up from where he'd been leaning against the wall, arms crossed, watching the planning unfold. "Let me talk logistics." He moved to the table and pulled out a different map, Central America, with markings in red ink. "I've got contacts in Nicaragua from the old days. People who owe me favors, people who know how to keep their mouths shut." He pointed to Managua. "Safe house here, in the Altamira district. Owned by a local businessman who's on our payroll. You'll have weapons, equipment, vehicles, everything you need."

"What kind of weapons?" Torres asked.

"CAR-15 carbines, suppressed," Harrow said. "Colt 9mm suppressors, subsonic ammunition. Beretta 92s also suppressed. AK-47s if you need deniability.

If shit goes sideways and you have to leave weapons behind, they trace back to Soviet supply lines, not us.

We've got a mix of weapons so you can choose what works best for the mission."

"Night vision?" Cole asked.

Hawke grinned. "I want one of those AKs. Reliable as fuck."

"You'll have options," Harrow said.

Bishop spoke up from where he'd been working on equipment. He was the team medic, the one who kept them alive when things went wrong. "Gen 2-night vision, best we've got. AN/PVS-5s. Not perfect, but they'll do the job." He held up one of the goggles, checking the lens for scratches or defects. "Image intensification, about 20,000x amplification. You'll see in starlight, but they're heavy, about two pounds on your head. And the field of view is narrow, about forty degrees. You'll have tunnel vision, so keep your head on a swivel."

He set the goggles down and picked up a radio. "I'm also setting you up with encrypted radios, PRC-319s, like Keller said. They're bulky as fuck, but they're secure. Surveillance gear for reconnaissance, cameras, Nikon F3s with telephoto lenses, recording equipment, Sony cassette recorders with parabolic microphones."

Keller moved over to examine the radios, his hands moving over them with practiced precision.

"Frequency range?"

"VHF, 30 to 88 megahertz," Bishop said. "Encrypted with rolling codes. I'll program them before you deploy.

Each radio will have a unique encryption key that changes every twenty-four hours. Even if someone intercepts the transmission, they won't be able to decrypt it."

"Good," Keller said. "I'll need to test the encryption protocols.

Make sure there's no signal bleed, no interference from other frequencies."

"Already done," Bishop said. "But you can verify if it makes you feel better."

"It does," Keller said.

Chapter Twelve

Bishop pulled out a large medical kit and set it on the table. It was a Pelican case, waterproof, filled with trauma supplies. "Trauma kits for both elements. Tourniquets, CAT tourniquets, the new ones, they work better than the old rubber ones. an experimental not yet FDA approved Hemostatic gauze, QuikClot, according to the man who was developing it Frank Hursey, it stops bleeding fast. Chest seals for sucking chest wounds. Morphine syrettes for pain. IV supplies, saline, antibiotics. If someone takes a hit, you've got what you need to keep them alive until exfil."

"Let's not take any hits," Torres said.

"Let's plan like we will," Bishop replied calmly. "Hope for the best, prepare for the worst. Everything I learned in training says people die without quick, precise medical trauma care. The difference between making it home and bleeding out in some jungle is having the right equipment and knowing how to use it under pressure. We're not going to be the ones who find that out the hard way."

Torres fist bumped Bishop in recognition of his statement.

"Passports?" Vail asked.

Harrow nodded. "You're agricultural equipment consultants for a company called Brazos Agricultural Solutions out of Houston, Texas. It's a real company; we own it through a shell corporation.

You've got business cards, letterhead, supporting documentation. If anyone checks, it holds up. The company has a real office, a real phone number, a real secretary who'll answer and confirm your employment."

"Cover story?" Mason asked, his nervousness showing again in the question.

"You're surveying potential markets for irrigation equipment," Harrow said. "Nicaragua's trying to rebuild its agricultural sector after years of war, so it's plausible. You'll have meetings scheduled with local officials, you won't actually go to them, but they're on the books. If someone checks your story, they'll find appointments, correspondence, everything that makes you look legitimate."

"Exfil?" Cole asked.

"Multiple routes," Harrow said. "Primary is a rigid hull inflatable boat pickup from the coast. The USS *Constellation* will be operating in international waters off Nicaragua. They'll have the RHIB standing by to pick you up from the beach and take you to the carrier. Secondary is overland to Honduras, then a flight out of Tegucigalpa. We've got vehicles staged along the route, safe houses every fifty kilometers. Tertiary is a charter flight out of Managua to San José, Costa Rica. We've got a plane standing by pilot's on our payroll."

"And if all that goes to shit?" Riker asked.

"Then you walk to the embassy, and we burn the whole

program," Harrow said flatly. "But that's not going to happen. We've planned for every contingency."

Ward pulled out a timeline, written in his precise handwriting.

"Alpha element deploys to Managua in seventy-two hours. You'll have three days on the ground for reconnaissance and final planning before the Thursday night hit. Bravo element stays here until Wednesday, then moves on Lawson early Friday morning at 0303 hours local, approximately four hours after Reyes is handled."

"Why the gap?" Hawke asked.

"Because we need confirmation," Cole said. "We hit Reyes at 2200 Managua time; that's 2300 Thursday night D.C. time. Keller monitors the operation and confirms the neutralize. Once we verify Reyes is down and Alpha element is clear, Bravo gets the green light. Lawson goes down at 0303 Friday morning, roughly four hours later. That gives us time to confirm the first hit was clean and ensures Lawson hasn't been alerted if something goes sideways in Nicaragua."

"Time zones complicate it," Ward added. "Nicaragua is Central time, D.C. is Eastern. But the operations are coordinated. Reyes first, then Lawson. Sequential, not simultaneous. If anything goes wrong in Managua, Bravo aborts."

"Exactly," Ward said.

Hayes cleared his throat. "I'll be your contact for Lawson's movements. If anything changes in his routine, I'll know immediately. I've got access to his schedule, his calendar, his movements. I'll relay through encrypted channels. We'll use a one-time pad system, unbreakable."

Keller looked up from the radio equipment. "I'll need to coordinate timing between both elements.

If we're executing them sequentially with a four-hour

gap, I need real-time comms to confirm the Nicaragua hit before Bravo moves. If I can set up a satellite uplink, it gives us real-time coordination between Nicaragua and D.C. with almost no delay."

Hayes spoke up. "I have a friend at the NRO that owes me a big favor. I will get the uplink established, if you want?"

"Do it," Harrow said.

"We are both burning through IOUs. But this is worth it."

"You're putting your ass on the line," Vail said to Hayes.

"I know," Hayes met his eyes. "I fucked up. I gave Lawson information without knowing what he'd do with it. This is me fixing it. This is me making it right."

The room was quiet for a moment. Then Cole nodded. "Alright."

Harrow moved to the center of the table, his presence commanding attention. "Before we go further, I need to be clear about something. This mission is not authorized at any level. I mean any. The kind of level where there's no paperwork, no record, no trail. If it goes right, nobody ever knows it happened. If it goes wrong, we all disappear."

"Disappear how?" Draven asked quietly.

"However, they decide," Harrow said. "Prison, maybe. More likely a bullet.

They'll call us rogue operators, disavow everything, and make sure we can't talk. The President won't save you. The Agency won't save you. I won't be able to save you. You'll be ghosts, and not the good kind."

"So, business as usual," Torres said.

A few people smiled, but it was the kind of smile that didn't reach the eyes.

"I need to know you're all in," Harrow said. "Because

once we start, there's no stopping. We're going to neutralize a CIA Deputy Director and a Nicaraguan military commander. That's not something you walk back from. That's not something you retire from. This will follow you for the rest of your lives."

Cole looked around the table. Every man met his eyes and nodded. He saw determination in Riker's face, controlled violence in Torres's eyes, nervous energy in Mason's posture, calm acceptance in Holt's expression. They were all in. They'd been in since the moment they learned about the betrayal.

"We said it before, Nate, we're in," Cole said.

Harrow studied them for a long moment, then nodded. "Alright. Ward, finalize the operational plans. I want detailed timelines, contingency plans, backup plans for the backup plans. Bishop, get the equipment ready. I want everything tested, everything verified. Keller, set up the comms infrastructure. I want redundant systems, multiple frequencies, backup radios. Price, coordinate with Hayes on Lawson's schedule. I want real-time updates, any changes, anything unusual. Cole, get your element ready to deploy. Weapons training, rehearsals, everything."

He pulled out a secure phone, a STU-II, one of the new encrypted phones the government was rolling out and set it on the table. He plugged it into an open phone line port on the wall. "I need to make some calls. You've got seventy-two hours. Use them."

The team stood and started filing out, already breaking into smaller groups to handle their pieces of the mission. Torres stayed close to Cole, and Cole saw Holt move to Torres's other side. Good. Holt's steady presence would help keep Torres balanced, keep him from going too far.

Bishop and Keller moved to the equipment, already

deep in a technical discussion about radio frequencies and encryption protocols. Keller's hands were steady as he handled the gear, his mind focused on the mathematics of communication. Bishop was checking medical supplies, making lists, calculating dosages.

Draven and Ward were studying the maps together, Draven pointing out observation positions and sight lines while Ward made notes in his precise handwriting. Price just watched and learned. He knew that being part of a team meant learning what everyone else did. He might have to take over one day if one of his teammates didn't come back or were injured.

Mason, Hawke, Vail, and Riker were talking weapons, Hawke's restless energy a contrast to Mason's nervous questions. But they balanced each other out Hawke's chaos and Mason's controlled aggression. Vail and Riker were checking the M24 and M40 sniper systems, discussing ranges and wind calculations. Cole stayed behind with Harrow, waiting until most of the room had cleared.

Harrow picked up the phone and started dialing. Cole listened as he spoke in Spanish, his voice low and careful. Old contacts, old favors being called in. The kind of network that took decades to build and could disappear in a day if someone talked. Harrow was calling in markers, making promises, arranging logistics. Safe houses, weapons, vehicles, extraction routes. The infrastructure of a covert operation. When Harrow hung up, he looked at Cole. "Safe house is set. Weapons will be there when you arrive. Local contact is a man named Ruiz; he'll get you whatever else you need. He's been on our payroll since '79, helped us with operations during the revolution. He's solid."

"Reliable?"

"As reliable as anyone in this business. Like I said he's been on our payroll since '79. Hasn't fucked us yet."

Cole nodded. "What about Lawson? You really think we can hide that it was us?"

"They will know it was someone on the inside, if the Suicide set up doesn't pass muster" Harrow said. "But they do not know that much about us. Ghostline is compartmented, need-to-know only. The President may suspect us but would never ask. It allows him plausible deniability. And presidents love plausible deniability."

Cole hated politicians. They cared only for themselves and their next election. They used people like Cole and his team as tools to expand their own goals, then threw them away when they became inconvenient.

Let them find out it was us, Cole thought. *Let them come after us. I will burn their world down before I go to my grave.*

"You good with Price leading Bravo?" Harrow asked.

Cole shook himself from his thoughts and responded. "Yeah. He's solid. Vail will keep him honest, and Ward's good in tight spaces. Patient. They'll get it done."

"And you're good with killing Reyes yourself?"

"That's the job you trained me to do."

Harrow studied him, his eyes searching Cole's face for something. "You know what bothers me about you, Cole? It's not that you're willing to end life. It's that you don't seem to feel anything about it."

"Would you rather I felt bad?"

"I'd rather you felt something. Anything. Because the day you stop being human is the day you become the same as the people we're hunting."

Cole didn't respond. There was nothing to say that Harrow would understand. Cole could not explain it to himself, how was he going to explain it to anyone else. All he knew was that when he and the team went kinetic, he felt at home. As a very young child, violence was not something he had been drawn to. It wasn't until his older brother made him fight that he realized he was not only good at it, but he also liked it. The adrenaline he felt became an addiction. He never went looking for a fight, but he never again ran from one. He went into it like he was made for it. He left the planning room and walked down the corridor to where the rest of Alpha element was gathering gear. Riker was checking magazines, tapping them in his palm to seat the rounds, making sure the springs were properly tensioned. Torres was cleaning his CAR-15 suppressed assault rifle with the focused intensity he always had before a mission.

Running a bore brush through the barrel, checking the gas system, testing the suppressor's baffles. He was taking these weapons he was just keeping focused on anything he could.

Mason and Hawke were going over maps, Hawke pointing out potential chaos points while Mason asked questions about contingencies.

Holt was methodically organizing demolitions equipment, his steady hands sorting detonators and breacher charges, checking expiration dates on the explosives, testing firing circuits with a multimeter. Draven sat nearby, studying the satellite photos with the patience of someone who understood that observation was its own kind of weapon. If he could get a line of sight, he could neutralize whatever drifted into that line of sight.

"Are we good?" Riker asked.

"We're good," Cole said. "Seventy-two hours, then we're wheels up."

"About fucking time," Torres muttered, and Cole saw the controlled violence in his eyes. Torres needed this. Needed the mission, needed the action. He, like Cole, was at home in violence. He also needed Cole nearby to keep him from going too far.

Cole pulled out the photos of Reyes's mistress's house and spread them on the table. "Let's walk through it. Every step, every contingency. When we hit that house, I want it to be muscle memory." Cole looked them all in the eye around the table and spoke. "We all come home or none of us do. Do you understand?" They all nodded agreement.

They gathered around, and Cole started talking through the plan. Breach point, entry sequence, room clearing, target elimination, exfil. They'd done it a hundred times in training, but this time it was real. This time the bullets were real. This time, they were hunting a man who thought he was untouchable. He was wrong, Cole thought to himself.

Torres leaned in, asking questions about angles and fields of fire.

Holt confirmed breach charges and backup demolitions. Mason worked through hand-to-hand scenarios, his nervousness channeling into preparation. Hawke grinned at the chaos points, already thinking three moves ahead. Riker studied the photos, finding the high ground, the observation posts, the places where patience would give them the advantage. In six days, Tomás Reyes would be dead, Deputy Director Lawson would be found in his Georgetown townhouse with a bullet in his head and a note on his desk.

Cole looked at his team and felt pride. He didn't feel fear, nor excitement, or even doubt. Just the cold certainty that they would do what needed to be done. Because that's what they did. They eliminated targets, and they vanished.

And nobody ever saw them coming.

Chapter Thirteen

The final briefing started at 0430 hours in the bunker. Harrow stood at the head of the table with a pot of coffee that smelled like it had been brewed sometime during the Carter administration. The fluorescent lights hummed overhead. Outside, Fort Bragg was still dark.

"Last chance to ask questions," Harrow said. "Once you're wheels-up, you're on your own until exfil."

Cole looked around the table. His team looked back, tired, focused, and ready. They'd been over the plan so many times they could run it in their sleep. But Harrow was right to ask. This was the moment when doubt crept in, when the reality of what they were about to do became impossible to ignore.

"Comms protocols?" Keller asked.

"Encrypted burst transmissions only. Thirty seconds maximum. Keller, you'll have the satellite uplink at the safehouse. If you need to reach us, go through the relay station at Palmerola Air Base in Honduras. They'll forward to Bragg."

"What if the relay goes down?"

"Then you're dark until exfil. Use your judgment."

Torres shifted in his seat. "Rules of engagement?"

"Reyes is the primary target. His bodyguards are secondary.

The mistress is a non-combatant, avoid, if possible, control if necessary. Anyone else you encounter is a judgment call.

But remember, this is a covert operation. Bodies draw attention. Attention gets people killed."

"What about Lawson?" Price asked from the other end of the table.

"Same rules. Primary target only. Harrow's expression hardened. "And make damn sure it looks like a suicide. If anyone suspects murder, this whole thing could unravel."

Price nodded. Vail and Ward sat on either side of him, stone-faced.

"Cover documents," Harrow continued. He slid a manila envelope down the table to Cole. "Passports, business cards, company letterhead, sales records going back two years. Your legend is solid. David Richardson, agricultural equipment consultant. You've got a hotel reservation at the Intercontinental in Managua, meetings scheduled with three different agricultural cooperatives, and a rental car waiting at the airport."

Cole opened the envelope. The passport looked worn, like it had been through a dozen border crossings. The business cards were slightly bent at the corners. The sales records showed transactions in Guatemala, El Salvador, Honduras. Someone had put real work into this.

"Memorize your legend," Harrow said. "Know it cold. If customs asks you a question and you hesitate, you're fucked."

"What about weapons?" Holt asked.

"Nothing on the flights.

You're clean until you reach the safehouse.

Carlos will have everything waiting. CAR 15s, Barretta's, AKs, pistols, explosives, not all foreign manufacture, but I know what you guys like to use. None that traces back to us."

"What if we get searched at customs?"

"Then you're a businessman with catalogs and order forms. Smile, be boring, and get through. If they detain you, the cover will hold for twenty-four hours. After that, we disavow and you're on your own."

The room went quiet. Everyone understood what that meant.

Harrow looked at his watch. "Price, your flight leaves RDU at 0800. Cole, yours leaves at 0930. Different airlines, different routes, different arrival times. You don't know each other. You don't acknowledge each other. You're strangers until you reach the safehouse."

"Understood," Cole said.

"One more thing." Harrow's voice dropped. "What you're about to do is illegal. It violates the Boland Amendment, the War Powers Act, and about a dozen international treaties. If you get caught, the President will deny knowledge. The Agency will deny knowledge. I will deny knowledge. You'll be tried as criminals or handed over to the Nicaraguans. Either way, you're fucked." He was looking directly at Cole.

He let that sink in.

"So, we don't get caught." Cole said dryly

Price, Vail, and Ward left Fort Bragg at 0600. They headed north toward Washington in a rental sedan with Virginia plates. They'd handle Lawson. Cole watched them go from the tarmac, then turned back to his own team. Nine men. One mission. A foreign country where Americans weren't particularly welcome in January 1985. The Sandinista-controlled government was fighting the rebel Contras, and the rebels were backed by the United States. That made Nicaragua hostile territory for anyone with an American passport.

They split into three groups for the commercial flights. Cole, Riker, and Torres on American Airlines through Miami.

Bishop, Holt, and Mason on Eastern through Houston. Hawke, Draven, and Keller on Pan Am through Mexico City. Different flights, different times, different routes. If one group got flagged, the others would still make it through.

"Alright," Cole said. "Let's go execute a piece of shit general."

Cole's passport said his name was David Richardson, agricultural equipment consultant for Brazos Agri-Solutions out of Houston. The passport was real, issued by the State Department through channels that didn't ask questions. The company was real too, at least on paper, incorporated in Texas, registered with the IRS, with a phone number that rang to an answering service in Dallas. Harrow's people had built the cover deep enough that it would hold up to anything short of a full investigation.

Cole wore khakis, a short-sleeve button-down, and a tie that felt like a noose. He fucking hated wearing a tie. He carried a briefcase with product catalogs, order forms, and a calculator. He looked like every other businessman trying to sell something to a third-world country that didn't have money to buy it.

He felt naked without his Sig P226. No weapon. No

body armor. No radio. No night vision. No medical kit. Just a briefcase full of paper and a cover story that would fall apart the moment someone looked too closely. This was the part of the job Cole hated most the vulnerability of commercial travel. On a military op, he controlled the variables. He had his team, his weapons, his training. But on a commercial flight, he was just another passenger. If something went wrong, he had nothing.

Torres wore the same uniform, though he looked less comfortable in it. His tie was crooked and his jaw was tight. He kept adjusting his collar like it was strangling him.

Riker, on the other hand, looked natural, like he'd been born in business casual.

He even had reading glasses that he didn't need, perched on his nose while he read *The Hunt for Red October*, a Tom Clancy novel.

"You look like a fucking accountant," Torres muttered as they waited at the gate.

"That's the idea," Riker said without looking up from his book.

He looked like he was actually reading it, Cole thought. Then asked him with a laugh, "You mean you can actually read?"

Riker shot Cole a middle finger and went back to reading.

Cole scanned the terminal. Raleigh-Durham International Airport was busy for a Thursday morning, business travelers, families, college students heading back to school. No one paid attention to three men in khakis waiting at Gate C7.

That was good. Invisible was good.

American Airlines Flight 447 to Miami boarded at 0915. Cole was in seat 14A, window. Torres was in 18C, aisle. Riker was in 22F, middle. They'd deliberately chosen separate seats. If someone was watching, three men traveling together would draw attention. Three men scattered through coach looked like strangers. The flight attendant smiled as Cole boarded. "Welcome aboard."

"Thanks."

He found his seat, stowed his briefcase in the overhead bin, and sat down. The seat next to him was empty. The seat next to that was occupied by a woman in her fifties reading a romance novel. She didn't look up. Cole buckled his seatbelt and looked out the window. The tarmac was wet from overnight rain. A baggage cart rolled past, followed by a fuel truck. Everything looked normal.

The plane filled up slowly. A businessman in a suit sat down next to Cole, opened a newspaper, and started reading. Cole glanced at the headline: *Monroe Defends Contra Aid Despite Congressional Ban.* The irony wasn't lost on him.

The flight attendant went through the safety briefing. Cole didn't listen. He'd heard it a thousand times. Instead, he watched the other passengers. Looking for anything out of place. Anyone paying too much attention. Anyone who didn't belong.

Nothing.

The plane pushed back from the gate at 0928. Two minutes early. The engines spooled up and they taxied toward the runway. Cole felt the familiar pressure as the plane accelerated, then the lurch as the wheels left the ground. They were airborne. No turning back now. The flight to Miami was uneventful. Cole spent most of it staring out the window, watching the landscape pass below. North Carolina gave way to South Carolina, then Georgia, then Florida. Somewhere down there, people were living normal lives. Going to work. Raising families. Worrying about mortgages and car payments and what to have for dinner.

And Cole, well he was going to Nicaragua to kill a man.

He felt nothing about that. No guilt, no excitement, no fear. It was just a job. A necessary job. Reyes was a piece of shit who'd sold out his country to the Soviets. He deserved what was coming.

The plane landed in Miami at 1147. Cole deplaned, walked through the terminal, and found his connecting gate. Flight 923 to Managua didn't leave until 1430, so he had time to relax. He bought a sandwich at a kiosk and sat down in the gate area. Torres was already there, sitting three rows away, reading a newspaper. They didn't acknowledge each other. Riker showed up ten minutes later, still reading his Clancy novel.

The gate area filled up slowly.

Mostly Nicaraguans heading home, families with children, old women in traditional dress, young men who looked like they might be Contras or Sandinistas or just trying to survive. A handful of Americans. Mostly journalists with cameras, aid workers with earnest expressions, businessmen with briefcases. Cole watched them all. Looking for surveillance. Looking for threats. Looking for anyone who might be more than they appeared.

Nothing.

Chapter Fourteen

Monday, March 18th, 1985

At 1415, they started boarding. Cole was in Group 3. He waited until his group was called, then walked down the jetway and onto the plane. This one was smaller, a Boeing 727, half-empty. Cole's seat was 12F, window. The seat next to him stayed empty. Across the aisle, a Nicaraguan woman was trying to calm a crying baby. The plane pushed back at 1432. The engines roared and they climbed into the Florida sky. Cole watched Miami disappear below, then the Florida Keys, then nothing but blue water.

The Gulf of Mexico.

Somewhere down there, the Navy had vessels on station, destroyers, frigates, maybe a carrier group. If everything went to shit, that's where they'd run. Assuming they made it to the coast. Assuming they weren't already dead. He felt nothing about that possibility either. It was just another variable in the equation. The flight attendant came by with drinks. Cole ordered a Coke. The woman across the aisle ordered nothing, she was too busy with the baby. The baby kept crying. High-pitched wails that cut through the engine noise.

Cole closed his eyes and tried to rest. He'd need to be sharp when they landed. Sharp and alert and ready for anything. Two hours later, the plane began its descent. Cole opened his eyes and looked out the window. The plane was descended through clouds and Cole got his first look at Nicaragua from altitude. Green jungle, brown rivers, scattered villages connected by dirt roads. It wasn't that long ago he was in that jungle on the team's first mission.

The reason he was heading back into Nicaragua. Of course, last time he'd come in by boat and hadn't bothered with the country's customs department.

Managua sprawled along the southern shore of Lake Managua, a city that had been destroyed by an earthquake in '72 and never fully rebuilt. From the air it looked like a wound that hadn't healed right. Whole neighborhoods were just empty lots. The city center was a ghost town. What buildings remained looked fragile, temporary, like they might collapse at any moment.

The plane banked and lined up for final approach. Cole could see the airport now, a single runway, a small terminal, military aircraft parked on the far side of the field. Soviet-made helicopters. Cuban transport planes. This wasn't just an airport. It was a forward operating base. The wheels touched down with a screech. The plane decelerated hard, engines reversing. They taxied toward the terminal and came to a stop.

"Welcome to Managua," the flight attendant said over the intercom. "Local time is 1547. Please remain seated until the captain has turned off the seatbelt sign." She then said it again in Spanish

Cole waited. The seatbelt sign went off.

Passengers stood and started pulling luggage from the overhead bins. Cole grabbed his briefcase and joined the line shuffling toward the exit. The jetway smelled like jet fuel and humidity. Cole walked into the terminal and immediately started cataloging details. Augusto C. Sandino International Airport was smaller than Cole expected. The terminal was concrete and glass, functional but worn. The floor was scuffed linoleum. The ceiling tiles were water-stained. The air conditioning was either broken or nonexistent. The temperature inside was barely cooler than outside.

Revolutionary posters covered the walls. Sandinista slogans in Spanish.

Images of workers and soldiers raising fists. Anti-American rhetoric that Cole could mostly understand. Patria Libre o Morir. Free homeland or death.

Yanqui Go Home.

Nicaragua No Es Vietnam.

"Friendly," Torres muttered as they walked toward customs. He was three people behind Cole in line, close enough to hear but far enough to maintain the fiction that they didn't know each other.

The customs line moved slowly. Cole counted six soldiers in olive drab fatigues standing at intervals along the wall. All of them carried AK-47s slung across their chests. They were young, most of them eighteen, maybe twenty. But they had the eyes of people who'd seen combat. Nicaragua had been at war for years. First the revolution against Somoza, then the Contras. These kids had grown up with violence. Cole watched them. Noted their positions. Noted their weapons. Noted which ones looked alert and which ones looked bored. Two were alert. The rest were just putting in time.

The customs officer stations were manned by older men in uniform. They looked tired. Bureaucrats doing a job they'd done ten thousand times. But tired didn't mean careless. Cole had seen tired customs officers catch smugglers because something didn't feel right. He ran through his legend one more time. David Richardson. Agricultural equipment consultant. Brazos Agri-Solutions. Houston, Texas. Here to establish a distribution network for irrigation systems and tractors. Meetings scheduled with three cooperatives, one in Managua, one in León, one in Granada. Staying at the Intercontinental Hotel. Leaving in five days.

Simple. Boring. Believable.

Cole's turn came.

He stepped up to the counter and handed his passport to the customs officer, a middle-aged man with a mustache and tired eyes. The man's uniform was clean but worn. His name tag said MORALES. Morales opened the passport and studied the photo. Then he looked at Cole's face, comparing. His eyes were sharp despite the fatigue. Tired or not, this man was good at his job.

"Purpose of visit?" Morales asked in accented English.

"Business," Cole said. He kept his voice neutral, slightly bored. "Agricultural equipment sales."

"What kind of equipment?"

"Irrigation systems, tractors, harvesting machinery."

Cole opened his briefcase and pulled out a catalog. The catalog was real, printed by CASE IH, a legitimate manufacturer. It had pictures of the CASE IH 585 tractor and the CASE 94 series four-wheel drive models. Prices in US dollars. Technical specifications. Everything a real salesman would carry.

"We're hoping to establish a distribution network in

Central America. Nicaragua has excellent agricultural potential."

Morales took the catalog and flipped through it without really looking. He was more interested in Daid Richardsons passport. He turned to the visa page, checked the stamp, then turned to the back pages and looked at the entry and exit stamps. It had stamps from Guatemala, El Salvador, Honduras, Costa Rica. All from the past two years. All part of the legend. All real. Morales looked up. "You travel to Central America often?"

"Three or four times a year. It's a growing market."

"And you are staying where?"

"The Intercontinental Hotel. I have a reservation."

"How long?"

"Five days. I have meetings scheduled with agricultural cooperatives in Managua, León, and Granada."

Morales studied Cole's face for a long moment. Cole kept his expression neutral, bored, like a man who'd been through a hundred customs inspections and expected to go through a hundred more. Like a man who had nothing to hide because he was exactly what he appeared to be, a salesman trying to make a living in a difficult market.

Finally, Morales stamped the passport and handed it back. "Welcome to Nicaragua, Mr. Richardson."

"Thank you."

Cole took the passport, closed his briefcase, and walked toward baggage claim. His heart rate hadn't changed. His breathing was steady. He'd passed the first test.

Torres came through next, then Riker. Cole didn't watch them. He collected his luggage, one suitcase, nothing that would draw attention, and walked toward the exit. The automatic doors opened and Cole stepped out into the humid Managua afternoon. The air hit him like a wall. The temperature was in the mid-eighties, but the humidity made it feel like a hundred. Cole's shirt was already sticking to his back. The humidity was worse than North Carolina's, thick and oppressive, like breathing through a wet towel.

The air smelled like diesel exhaust and rotting vegetation. Somewhere nearby, someone was burning trash. Car horns honked. Voices shouted in Spanish. The chaos of a third-world city. Cole scanned the area. Taxi drivers were calling out to passengers. Families were reuniting. Soldiers were watching from the terminal entrance. Everything looked normal.

Chapter Fifteen

A man stood near the taxi stand holding a sign that said BRAZOS AGRI-SOLUTIONS. He was in his fifties, lean and weathered, with the look of someone who'd spent his life in places where comfort was a luxury. He wore jeans, a guayabera shirt, and sunglasses that hid his eyes. His hands were calloused. His face was lined by sun and wind.

This was Carlos Rivera. Their local contact. The man who would provide logistics, transportation, and weapons.

"Mr. Richardson?" he asked as Cole approached.

"That's me."

"I'm Carlos. I'll be your driver and translator during your visit. "His English was perfect, barely accented. Educated. Probably middle-class before the revolution. "Your colleagues arrived earlier. They're already at the hotel."

"Good." Cole said with a smile and then thanked the man.

Carlos took Cole's suitcase and led him to a Toyota Land Cruiser parked in the lot. The vehicle was at least ten years old, dented and scratched, with Nicaraguan plates. The kind of vehicle that wouldn't draw a second glance.

They loaded the luggage and climbed in. The interior smelled like cigarettes and stale bread. Carlos started the engine and pulled out of the lot.

"First time in Managua?"

Carlos asked as he navigated toward the exit.

"First time in Nicaragua," Cole said. It was a lie, of course, but Carlos wasn't cleared for that information. Cole wasn't sure what Carlos knew or didn't know. Harrow had said Carlos was reliable, but reliable didn't mean fully briefed.

"It's not what it used to be," Carlos said. "The earthquake destroyed the old city center. Then the revolution. Then the war." He shrugged. "But we survive. We always survive." Carlos drove like he knew the city, navigating traffic that seemed to have no rules. Motorcycles weaved between cars. Buses belched black smoke. Pedestrians crossed wherever they felt like it. Hawke was loving this chaos, Cole thought.

The city was a study in contrasts. Modern buildings stood next to empty lots where earthquake rubble had never been cleared. Revolutionary murals covered walls, images of Sandino, of workers with rifles, of children reading books. Soldiers manned checkpoints at major intersections, stopping vehicles at random. Poverty was everywhere, in the crumbling infrastructure, the barefoot children selling cigarettes on street corners, the desperate eyes of people trying to sell whatever they could. Cole cataloged it all. Checkpoint locations. Patrol patterns. Traffic flow. Escape routes. They passed through a checkpoint at the intersection of two main roads. A soldier waved them through without stopping. Carlos didn't slow down.

"They're looking for Contras," Carlos said. "Not businessmen."

"Good to know."

They drove through a neighborhood of small shops and street vendors. Then into a residential area with larger homes behind walls. The streets were quieter here. Trees provided shade. The houses looked middle-class, not wealthy, but comfortable.

"This is Altamira," Carlos said. "Middle-class neighborhood. Quiet and safe."

The safehouse was on a quiet street lined with modest homes behind walls and gates. The house itself was unremarkable, single story, white stucco, red tile roof, a small courtyard with a mango tree. Bars on the windows. A solid wooden gate. The kind of place that wouldn't draw a second glance. Carlos pulled into the driveway and killed the engine. "Your colleagues are inside. I'll be back tomorrow morning at 0800 to take you to your appointments."

"No need we will use the vehicles you acquired for us. Stay available in the event we need you"

"If that need should arise, there's a phone inside. The number for my pager is on the refrigerator."

"Got it. Thanks again"

Carlos helped Cole with his suitcase, then got back in the Land Cruiser and headed down the street, back to the airport.

Cole stood in the driveway for a moment, looking at the house. The walls were eight feet high, topped with broken glass. The gate was solid wood with a heavy lock. The windows had bars. Good security for a middle-class home. Not good enough to stop a determined assault, but good enough to slow someone down. He walked to the front door and knocked twice, paused, then knocked once. The signal they'd agreed on. The door opened. Bishop stood there, looking relaxed. "Welcome to Nicaragua." He said in his best Spanish accent.

"Gracias."

Cole stepped inside. The house was sparse but functional. Concrete floors. Minimal furniture. A couch, a table, a few chairs, bars on the windows. A small kitchen with a two-burner stove and a refrigerator that hummed loudly. Three bedrooms, one bathroom. Everything clean but worn. The other teams had already arrived.

Holt was in the living room, checking the doors and windows, assessing security. Hawke was in the kitchen, drinking water from a bottle. Draven was studying a map spread out on the table. Mason sat on the couch, looking nervous. Keller had claimed the back bedroom and was already setting up equipment. Cole could see him through the open door with a satellite dish disguised as a TV antenna, encrypted radios, and other tech gadgets that probably cost more than the house.

"How was your flight?" Bishop asked.

"Long," Cole said. "Everyone make it through customs?"

"No problems. Fake IDs held up fine."

Bishop pulled out a trauma kit and started organizing supplies on the kitchen counter. "I've got enough here to handle gunshot wounds, shrapnel, burns. If someone goes down, I can keep them alive long enough to get to exfil."

"Let's hope we don't need it." Draven said.

"That's the plan, dumbass." Came Bishops retort

Torres and Riker arrived twenty minutes later. Carlos dropped them off and drove away without coming inside. Smart. The less he knew, the better.

Carlos sat in the Land Cruiser for a moment after the Americans went inside, his hands still on the steering wheel. Through the window, he could see them moving around, unpacking equipment, checking weapons, setting up whatever it was they needed to do their work. Their work. That was the polite way to think about it. He'd been doing this for three years now. Ever since the CIA contact had approached him at his cousin's restaurant and asked if he wanted to make some money. Real money. American dollars. All he had to do was provide logistics. Transportation. Safe houses. Introductions to people who could acquire certain items.

He'd said yes before the man finished talking. The money was good. Better than anything he could make legitimately in Managua, where the economy was strangled by war and sanctions and corruption. But the money wasn't why he kept doing it.

His brother Miguel had been a teacher. Not political. Not a revolutionary. Just a man who taught mathematics to children and came home every evening to his wife and daughter. But he'd been in the wrong place at the wrong time. A protest that turned violent, a Sandinista crackdown that didn't distinguish between agitators and bystanders.

Miguel had died on a Managua street with a bullet in his chest, bleeding out while soldiers stood guard and prevented anyone from helping him. That was two years ago. Carlos had buried his brother. He'd held Miguel's widow while she sobbed. He'd watched his niece, only seven years old who had asked when her papa was coming home.

So, when the CIA came calling, Carlos said yes.

He watched the Americans through the window. Some of them looked young. Too young. The one called Mason couldn't be more than seventeen, eighteen. Fresh-faced despite the hard eyes. The others looked older, harder, moving with the kind of economy that came from years of practice. He would have been surprised to realize that they were all eighteen or nineteen and had been doing this less than six months.

Carlos had helped teams like this before. Some succeeded. Some disappeared. He never asked what happened to the ones who disappeared. He knew what they were here to do. He didn't know the target; they never told him that. But he knew the pattern. Surveillance. Planning. Then one night they'd go out and someone would die. Someone important. Someone the Americans wanted gone.

Sometimes Carlos wondered if that made him a patriot or a traitor. The Sandinistas would call him a traitor, certainly. A collaborator. A tool of American imperialism.

If they ever found out what he did, they'd put him against a wall and shoot him. But the Sandinistas had murdered his brother. They'd turned Nicaragua into a prison. They'd invited the Soviets and the Cubans to set up shop, turning his country into a Cold War battlefield. So maybe he was a patriot after all. Or maybe he was just a man who'd lost his brother and wanted someone to pay for it.

Carlos started the engine and backed out of the driveway. Tomorrow morning he'd return with the Items they'd requested. Food, mostly. But he was prepared to get more ammunition or other types of weapons if needed. He had a contact in the Contra army. He would play his part. Smile and nod and pretend he was just a driver. And then, maybe tomorrow night, maybe the night after, someone in Managua would die. Someone important. Someone who probably deserved it, though Carlos would never know for sure. He'd read about it in the newspaper. Another casualty of the war. Another body. And part of that would be on him.

Carlos drove through the darkening streets, past checkpoints and soldiers and walls covered in revolutionary slogans. Patria Libre o Morir. Free homeland or death. They were everywhere, on buildings, on buses, on billboards. The revolution's promise repeated endlessly until it lost all meaning. He wondered which one Nicaragua would get. He wondered if his brother would be proud of what he was doing, or ashamed. He wondered if it mattered. By the end of the week, someone would be dead. And Carlos would collect his money and try not to think about it. That was the job.

That was survival.

Chapter Sixteen

Back in the safehouse, Cole responded to Bishop, "If everyone does their job right, no one is going to get hurt on our side."

"Hoorah," Bishop said, a little smile on his face.

Hawke came out of one of the bedrooms, grinning. "This place is a shithole. I love it."

"It's got running water and electricity," Draven said from where he was studying a map. "That's more than some places we've been."

"Fair point."

Keller emerged from the back bedroom, trailing antenna cable. "I need someone on the roof to mount this dish. Needs to point northeast, elevation about forty degrees."

"I'll do it," Draven said. He took the cable and disappeared outside.

Cole watched him go. Draven moved with the same calm patience he brought to everything. Five minutes later he was on the roof, invisible from the street, mounting the satellite dish with the precision of someone who'd done it a hundred times. Cole was positive he had only done it three times, and those were in training.

"Let's see the weapons," Cole said.

Holt led them to the master bedroom. He'd already found the cache, hidden under the floorboards beneath the bed. He pulled up the boards to reveal a small arsenal wrapped in oilcloth.

Four CAR-15s with suppressors attached, and the new Aimpoint 1000 reddot. American manufacture, 5.56mm. Serial numbers filed off. The stocks were collapsible; the barrels shortened for close-quarters work. Cole picked one up, checked the action. Smooth. He pulled the charging handle back and looked down the barrel. Clean. No pitting, no rust. Someone had taken care of these weapons.

"When's the last time these were fired?" Torres asked, picking up another CAR-15.

"Recently, from the smell," Holt said. "They're clean, oiled, ready to go."

Cole set the CAR-15 down and picked up one of the pistols. Beretta 92, 9mm, with a suppressor. Also, with the serial number filed off. He dropped the magazine, fifteen rounds, and checked the chamber. Empty. He worked the slide. The action was smooth.

"I want to test-fire these and zero the reddots, before the operation," Torres said.

"We will," Cole said. "Tomorrow night, outside the city. Carlos will take us somewhere remote."

There were four Berettas total, all suppressed. All American manufacture, which was interesting. Someone had gone to the trouble of acquiring American weapons for a covert op in Nicaragua. That suggested CIA involvement at a higher level than Carlos. Holt pulled out more items from the cache. Three AK-47s, Romanian manufacture, serial numbers filed off. Backup weapons if they needed something that looked local. Four Soviet RGD-5 fragmentation grenades. Two blocks of C-4 with detonators. A coil of det cord. Blasting caps. Everything they'd need for a direct-action mission.

"And the night vision?" Cole asked.

Holt reached deeper into the cache and pulled out four sets of PVS-5-night vision goggles, Gen 2. American military issue, also with serial numbers removed. The rubber eyepieces were worn but the optics looked clean.

"Harrow's contact came through," Holt said. "Everything's here."

"What about comms?" Cole asked.

Keller came back into the room, wiping his hands on his pants. "Comms are up. I've got satellite uplink, encrypted radio net, and I'm monitoring local police and military frequencies."

"What are they saying?" Cole asked.

"Routine traffic mostly. Checkpoint reports, patrol schedules. Nothing about us." Keller's hands were steady now, his focus absolute. When he had a technical problem to solve, the rest of the world disappeared. "I'm using a KY-57 for encryption. Burst transmissions only, thirty seconds maximum. If we need to reach Bragg, I'll relay through Palmerola."

"Good. What about local frequencies?"

"Police use VHF, military uses UHF.

I've got both covered. If they start talking about Americans or suspicious activity, we'll know immediately."

"Keep monitoring."

"Copy."

Bishop finished organizing his medical station in one of the bedrooms. He'd spread everything out on the bed, trauma supplies, IV fluids, antibiotics, surgical instruments. Everything they'd need if someone took a bullet and they couldn't get to a hospital.

"I've got four units of O-negative blood," Bishop said. "Plasma expanders, morphine, field surgical kit. If someone takes a hit, bring them here. I can stabilize anything short of a head shot."

"Let's not test that," Hawke said.

"Let's not."

Torres paced the living room, his energy barely contained. "When do we start surveillance?"

"After dark," Cole said. "We establish our cover first.

During the day, we're businessmen. We visit agricultural sites, we meet with potential clients, we act like we're here to sell tractors."

"And at night?"

"At night we find Reyes and figure out how to neutralize him."

Cole pulled out the satellite photos and spread them on the table.

The team gathered around. The photos showed a two-story house in a neighborhood called Los Robles. Yellow stucco, red tile roof, small balcony on the second floor. Eight-foot wall topped with broken glass. Single gate for vehicle access. "This is the mistress's house," Cole said. "Reyes visits every Thursday night, arrives around 2100, leaves around 0200. He travels with two bodyguards in a three-vehicle convoy, lead car, Reyes in the middle, trail car. All three vehicles are armored."

"Security inside?" Holt asked.

"Two bodyguards stay with him. Both carry Browning

Hi-Powers and AK-47s. The mistress has a maid who doesn't live on the property. No other staff."

"What about neighbors?"

"Middle-class neighborhood. Houses on both sides, but the walls provide privacy. Street lighting is minimal. Traffic is light after dark."

Draven studied the photos. "We need eyes on the house. Confirm the pattern, identify vulnerabilities, time the guard rotations."

"Agreed. Draven, you'll set up an observation post.

Find a building with line of sight to the target house. I want photos, timings, everything."

"How long do I watch?"

"Seventy-two hours minimum. We need to confirm Reyes's schedule and make sure there are no surprises."

"What about the rest of us?" Torres asked.

"We establish our cover. Tomorrow morning, we will take the Land cruisers Carlos acquired to meet with agricultural cooperatives. We act like businessmen. We smile, we shake hands, we talk about tractors. We make ourselves visible and boring."

"And at night?"

"At night we scout the neighborhood. Different routes in and out. Identify choke points, escape routes, places where we can stage vehicles. We do it on foot, casual, like we're just walking around."

Mason sat on the couch, his leg bouncing. He'd been quiet since they landed, his usual pre-contact anxiety showing through. Cole sat down next to him.

"You good?" Cole asked quietly.

"It's always different when it's real. But you've trained for this. You know what to do."

"Yeah. Just... it's different when it's real, you know?"

"What if I freeze?"

"You won't."

"How do you know?"

"Because when it starts, you won't have time to think. Your training takes over. You've done this a thousand times in training. Your body knows what to do." Cole kept his voice level, matter-of-fact. "And if you do freeze, someone else will handle it. That's why there's nine of us."

Mason nodded slowly. "Okay."

"You're good at hand-to-hand. Better than most of us. If it goes close-quarters, I want you there."

That seemed to help. Mason's leg stopped bouncing. Cole stood and walked back to the table. The team was still studying the photos, asking questions, identifying problems.

"What's our exfil pace (Primary, Alternate, contingency, and emergency)?" Hawke asked.

"Primary exfil is by vehicle. We drive to the coast, meet a boat at a predetermined location, and get picked up. Alternate is overland to Honduras. Contingency is We ride to the airport and catch the charter flight. Emergency plan is to walk into the American Embassy and burn the program and us."

"How long until the boat arrives?"

"Seven hours after we call it in. That means we need to be at the coast by dawn."

"That's a lot of down time."

"It's what we've got."

They went over the plan again. Entry sequence. Target elimination. Exfil routes. Contingencies. Everyone asked questions. Everyone identified potential problems. This was how they worked, collaborative, thorough, leaving nothing to chance. By 1900 hours, they had a solid plan. Not perfect, but solid. They'd refine it over the next three days as they gathered more intelligence.

"Alright," Cole said. "Let's get some rest. Tomorrow, we start playing businessman."

Chapter Seventeen

Tuesday, March 19th, 1985

The next morning, they got up, dressed in Business casual civilian clothes and did business with the locals. Draven almost sold a unit, which would have added to their slush fund, but the dude would never get his tractor. Draven had told him that the one he wanted would take a year as it was not ready to ship. The man bought the excuse and took a pamphlet to look over.

That night, they changed into civilian clothes, jeans, t-shirts, nothing that would stand out. Then they split up. Cole, Riker, and Torres went to scout the mistress's neighborhood. Bishop and Mason stayed at the safehouse to organize equipment. Hawke and Holt walked the streets, getting a feel for the city, identifying routes and choke points. Draven grabbed his surveillance kit, binoculars, camera with telephoto lens, notebook, and Keller. They headed out to find an observation post.

The mistress's house was in a neighborhood called Los Robles, about three kilometers from the safehouse. Middle-class, tree-lined streets, houses behind walls. The target house was pale yellow, two stories, with a red tile roof and a small balcony on the second floor. The wall around it was eight feet high, topped with broken glass. A single gate provided access. Cole, Riker, and Torres walked past it twice, not stopping, not staring, just three men out for an evening walk. They noted the sight lines, the neighboring houses, the street lighting. Everything matched the satellite photos.

"Gate's the weak point," Torres said quietly as they turned the corner. "We go over the wall, we're exposed. We go through the gate; we control the approach."

"Then it looks like we go through the gate," Cole agreed.

"What about the neighbors?"

"House on the left is dark. Looks empty. House on the right has lights on, but the wall blocks line of sight."

"Street lighting?"

"Minimal. One streetlight at the corner, another one halfway down the block. Plenty of shadows."

They walked the perimeter, noting everything. Escape routes. Choke points. Places where they could stage vehicles. Places where they could set up overwatch. By the time they got back to the safehouse, Draven had already found his observation post, a second-floor apartment three blocks from the target house. The tenant was visiting family in León. Carlos had arranged it with cash and no questions asked.

"Good line of sight," Draven said. "I can see the front gate and most of the courtyard. I'll set up tomorrow morning and start logging activity."

"Good. Keller, you monitor comms. If anything changes, I want to know immediately."

"Copy."

After the surveillance debrief, they all went to relax.

Keller, however, was hunched over his radio equipment, headphones on, listening to the local frequencies. He'd filled a notebook with times, call signs, patrol patterns.

"Anything?" Cole asked walking into the comms room.

"Police checkpoint on the Pan-American Highway stopped a truck full of Contra weapons. Military patrol in Barrio Martha Quezada broke up a black market. Nothing about us."

Keller looked up. "Reyes's motorcade was spotted heading into Managua this afternoon. Three vehicles, heavy security. He's at his main compound now."

"When's he scheduled to visit the mistress?"

"Thursday night, according to Harrow's intel. That gives us three days to confirm the pattern and finalize the plan."

Cole nodded. Three days to watch, to wait, to prepare. Three days until they killed a man who thought he was untouchable. "We're close," Cole said quietly to Torres, who was pacing again. "Stay focused."

Torres took a breath, nodded. "I'm good."

"I know you are."

That night, they ate rice and beans that Bishop cooked on the small stove. They went over the plan again, refining details, identifying contingencies. Draven showed them photos he'd taken during the reconnaissance. The target house from multiple angles, the neighboring houses, the street approaches. Everything matched the intel.

Keller monitored the radio traffic, translating the Spanish chatter, building a picture of the security situation. The Sandinista military was focused on the Contras, not on a group of American operators hiding in plain sight. Mason's anxiety had settled. He cleaned his weapons with steady hands, his training taking over. Hawke adapted to the chaos of Managua like he'd been born there, already planning how to use the crowded streets and unpredictable traffic to their advantage during exfil.

Cole sat on the couch and felt nothing. No fear, no excitement, no doubt. Just the cold certainty that in three days, Tomás Reyes would be dead. And he and the team would disappear back into the shadows where they belonged.

Chapter Eighteen

W*ednesday, March 20th, 0400 hours*
Managua, Nicaragua

The stairs to the second-floor apartment creaked under Draven's weight. He froze. Listened. Nothing. Just the ambient noise of a city still mostly asleep, distant dogs barking, the hum of a generator two blocks over, the occasional vehicle passing on the main road. Keller was behind him, carrying the equipment bag. Forty pounds of optics, camera gear, and surveillance equipment. He moved carefully, distributing his weight to minimize noise. Carlos had given them the key three hours ago. The tenant, an elderly woman named Rosa, was visiting family in León for two weeks. Carlos had paid her three hundred dollars American. No questions asked. No paperwork. Just cash and a promise that nothing would be damaged. The apartment door was at the end of the hallway. Draven inserted the key slowly, feeling for the tumblers. The lock turned with a soft click.

They slipped inside and closed the door behind them. The apartment was small. One bedroom, a cramped kitchen, a living room with a single window that faced south. The furniture was old but clean. Religious icons on the walls. A photograph of Rosa with her grandchildren on the mantle. Draven moved to the window and pulled back the curtain an inch. Perfect sight line.

Three blocks away, the mistress's house sat on a corner lot in the Los Robles neighborhood. Two-story. Yellow stucco with a red tile roof. Eight-foot walls surrounding the property. Single gate at the front. Small courtyard visible through the wrought iron bars.

"We're good," Draven said quietly.

Keller set the equipment bag on the floor and unzipped it. He pulled out a Leupold Mark 4 spotting scope, 20-60x magnification, mil-dot reticle, nitrogen-purged to prevent fogging in the humidity. He mounted it on a lightweight tripod and positioned it two feet back from the window, angled through the gap in the curtains. Draven knelt behind the scope and adjusted the focus. The target house jumped into clarity. He could see the front gate, most of the courtyard, the ground-floor windows, and part of the second-floor balcony. The northeast corner bedroom was partially visible through the wrought iron railing.

"Range?" Keller asked.

Draven used the mil-dot reticle to estimate.

"Three hundred twenty meters. Give or take."

Keller pulled out a Nikon F3 camera with a 600mm telephoto lens. He set it on a second tripod beside the spotting scope, adjusted the focus, and took a test shot of the house. The shutter clicked softly. He checked the frame. Clear. Sharp. Good depth of field. "We're set," Keller said.

Draven glanced at his watch. 0412 hours.

Keller opened a small notebook and made the first entry in the surveillance log: 0412 - OP established. Target house visible. No movement. Neighborhood quiet. They had water bottles, a dozen Tiger Milk bars, a bucket to piss in, and enough 35mm film to document a week of activity. The apartment had no air conditioning. By noon, it would be sweltering.

But that was the job.

Draven settled in behind the scope. Keller sat beside him with the camera and the log. They waited. The city woke slowly around them.

At 0523, the first light appeared in the eastern sky. A pale gray that gradually turned orange. Street vendors began setting up on the corner two blocks away. A man with a cart selling fruit. A woman with a portable grill preparing breakfast tamales.

The smell of cooking meat drifted through the open window. Draven's stomach growled. He ignored it.

At 0547, the front door of the target house opened.

"Movement," Draven said.

A woman stepped into the courtyard. Mid-thirties. Dark hair pulled back. Wearing a light blue robe. She walked to the gate, spoke briefly with someone inside, probably the maid, then returned to the house.

"That's Maria," Keller said, snapping photos. Click. Click. Click. "Matches the description from the intel packet."

"Mark it."

Keller wrote in the log: 0547 - Female subject (Maria) exits house. Brief conversation at gate. Returns inside. Wearing robe. No visible security.

At 0638, the sun broke over the horizon. The temperature in the apartment began to climb.

At 0730, a woman in her fifties arrived at the gate. She

rang the bell. Maria answered, let her in. The woman carried a cloth bag, probably cleaning supplies.

"Maid," Draven said.

Keller photographed her. 0730 - Maid arrives. Female, approx. 50-55 years old. Cloth bag. Admitted by Maria.

At 0815, a man arrived on a bicycle. Older. Wearing work clothes and a straw hat. He carried gardening tools.

"Gardener," Keller said, taking more photos.

0815 - Gardener arrives. Male, approx. 60-65 years old. Bicycle. Tools. Admitted through gate.

By 0900, the temperature in the apartment was approaching ninety degrees. Sweat soaked through Draven's shirt. He drank water slowly, rationing it.

Keller wiped his face with a bandana and kept writing.

At 0920, Maria appeared in the courtyard. She wore a sundress now. She carried a cup of coffee and a watering can. She moved among the potted plants along the courtyard wall, watering them methodically.

"Subject visible," Draven said. "Courtyard. Alone."

Keller took a series of photos. Through the 600mm lens, Maria looked close enough to touch. He could see the pattern on her dress. The steam rising from her coffee cup.

"Eight-foot walls," Draven said, studying the property through the scope. "Single gate. No guard towers. No visible cameras. Lighter security than the compound."

"That's why we're hitting it here," Keller said.

They logged everything.

At 1047, Maria went back inside.

At 1135, the maid came out to shake a rug.

At 1214, the gardener trimmed hedges near the front gate.

At 1400, the maid left. She walked out through the gate, carrying her cloth bag, and disappeared down the street.

1400 - Maid departs. On foot. Southbound.

At 1530, the gardener left. He rode his bicycle north toward the commercial district.

1530 - Gardener departs. Bicycle. Northbound.

By 1600, the house was quiet again. Just Maria inside.

Draven and Keller took turns on the scope. One watched. One rested. Every thirty minutes, they switched. The heat was oppressive. The apartment felt like an oven. Draven's shirt was soaked through. His eyes burned from staring through the scope for hours. But he didn't complain. Neither did Keller. This was surveillance work. Tedious. Uncomfortable. Essential. At 1800, the sun began to set. The temperature dropped slightly. Draven felt the first hint of relief.

Keller keyed the radio. "OP to base. Staff's gone for the day. House is clear except for the woman."

Cole's voice came back through the encrypted channel. "Copy.

Draven stayed on the scope. Keller reloaded the camera with fresh film. They waited.

Chapter Nineteen

Thursday, March 21st, 0630 Hours
Reyes Compound, Managua

Tomás Reyes woke to the smell of coffee and the sound of his daughter singing off-key in the kitchen. He smiled before he opened his eyes. Isabela only sang when she was happy, and lately that had been rare. The country was tearing itself apart, and twelve-year-olds understood more than people gave them credit for. She heard the news. She saw the soldiers in the streets. She knew her father's work was dangerous.

But this morning, she was singing.

Reyes lay in bed for a moment, listening. The song was something from the radio, American pop music that had made its way south. Isabela's Spanish accent mangled the English lyrics, but she didn't care. He could hear Sofia in the kitchen too. The clatter of dishes. The hiss of the stove. Normal sounds. Safe sounds. Reyes pushed himself out of bed and walked to the bathroom. He splashed cold water on his face and looked at himself in the mirror.

Forty-three years old. Gray creeping into his hair. Lines

around his eyes that hadn't been there five years ago. He looked tired. He was tired. He dried his face and walked to the kitchen. Sofia stood at the stove, her dark hair pulled back in a loose bun. She wore her robe; the blue one he'd bought her for her birthday two years ago. She was frying eggs and heating tortillas on the comal.

Isabela sat at the small kitchen table, her math homework spread out in front of her. She had a pencil tucked behind her ear and another one tapping against her teeth as she studied a problem.

"Buenos días," Reyes said, kissing Sofia's cheek.

She turned and smiled. "You're up early. I thought you'd sleep in."

"Couldn't. Too much to do."

Isabela looked up from her homework. "Papá, I don't understand this problem."

Reyes sat down next to her and looked at the textbook. Algebra. Quadratic equations. He'd been good at math once, before politics and war had consumed everything. "Show me what you've tried," he said. She walked him through it. Her logic was sound until the third step, where she'd transposed a number. He pointed it out gently, and her face lit up.

"Oh! I see it now. I'm so stupid."

"You're not stupid," Reyes said. "You're smarter than I was at your age."

"That's not true."

"It is. Your mother will confirm it."

Sofia brought him coffee, strong and black, the way he liked it, and set a plate of eggs and beans in front of him. "He's right. You're much smarter."

Isabela grinned and went back to her homework. They ate together, the three of them, talking about nothing important. Isabela's upcoming school trip to Granada. Sofia's sister who was visiting next month from Managua. The garden that needed weeding.

Normal things.

For twenty minutes, Tomás Reyes wasn't a senior commander in the Nicaraguan military. He wasn't a man making impossible choices in an impossible situation.

He wasn't coordinating with Soviet advisors or negotiating with American intelligence officers in secret courtyards. He was just a father. A husband. It was the best part of his day.

But it couldn't last.

At 0830, he kissed Sofia goodbye. He hugged Isabela and told her to finish her homework. Then he walked out to the car where his driver was waiting.

Chapter Twenty

Thursday March 21st, 0845 Hours

The compound was fifteen minutes away. The driver confirmed the destination, Reyes just nodded his head

The meeting started at 0930. Six officers sat around the conference table in Reyes's office. All of them looked to him for answers he didn't have. Colonel Mendoza spoke first. He was fifty-two, a career officer who'd fought in the revolution and stayed loyal to the Sandinista government. "The Soviets are pushing for more aggressive operations in the north. They want us to move against the Contra supply lines coming through Honduras." Major Ortega leaned forward. He was younger, thirty-eight, and more cautious. "And if we do that, the Americans will escalate. We'll have CIA paramilitaries operating openly inside our borders."

"They're already here," Mendoza said. "We're just pretending they're not."

Reyes listened. He always listened first. Captain Ruiz, the intelligence officer, nodded. "We've confirmed at least three American-backed operations in the last month. Sabotage. Assassinations. They're not even trying to hide it anymore." The room was hot. The air conditioning had been broken for two weeks. A fan in the corner pushed warm air around uselessly.

"What do you recommend?" Reyes asked Mendoza.

"Limited operations. Targeted strikes against Contra logistics. Enough to satisfy the Soviets without provoking a full American response."

"And you think the Americans will see it that way?"

Mendoza hesitated. "No. But what choice do we have?"

That was the question, wasn't it? What choice did any of them have? Nicaragua was caught between two empires. The Soviets wanted them to fight. The Americans wanted them to collapse. And men like Reyes were expected to navigate a path that didn't exist. Every decision was wrong. Every compromise was a betrayal of someone. He thought about Lawson. About their conversation in the courtyard three months ago. About the deal they'd made.

Hypothetically.

Reyes had told himself it was pragmatic. That it was the only way to protect his country from being torn apart. If the Americans were going to operate here anyway, better to have some control over it. Better to know what was coming. Lawson had been careful with his words. Never explicit. Never direct. But the message had been clear: If you help us, we'll help you. If you don't, we'll destroy you. But late at night, when Sofia was asleep and the house was quiet, he wondered if he'd made a deal with the devil. He wondered if there was any difference anymore.

"We'll proceed with limited operations," Reyes said finally. "But carefully. I want every strike approved by me personally. No independent action."

The officers nodded. The meeting continued for

another hour. Supply issues. Personnel rotations. Intelligence reports from the field. By the time it ended, Reyes had a headache that wouldn't quit. He stayed late at the office, reviewing reports, signing orders, making decisions that would get people killed. Young men. Soldiers. Some of them not much older than Isabela.

It was 1730 when he finally left the compound. Tonight, he would go to Maria's house in Los Robles. Away from the compound. Away from the constant pressure of command. Away from Sofia's disappointed silences.

His driver took him to Marias house. And Reyes went inside.

Just for a few hours, he could pretend to be someone else.

Chapter Twenty-One

Thursday, March 21st, Eight and a half hours earlier
Managua, Nicaragua

Cole sat in the passenger seat of the Land Cruiser, a folded map on his lap and a stopwatch in his hand. Riker drove. Torres sat in back, taking notes. They were mapping exfiltration routes one final time. No business meetings today. "Start the clock," Cole said.

Riker pulled away from the curb two blocks from the mistress's house. He drove south on Calle Principal, then turned west onto Avenida Roosevelt. Light traffic. A few pedestrians. Nothing unusual. Cole watched the stopwatch. "First checkpoint is the intersection at Avenida Bolívar. How long?"

"Three minutes, forty seconds," Riker said.

Cole marked it on the map. "Continue."

They drove through a residential neighborhood. Single-story houses. Modest. Quiet. A woman swept her front steps. A man worked on a car in his driveway. "Turn here," Cole said, pointing to a side street. Riker turned. The street narrowed. Fewer houses. More trees. "This is the primary route to the coast," Cole said. "Residential, then commercial, then highway west. Forty-eight minutes to the beach in light traffic. Seventy in heavy." Torres wrote it down.

They drove the route twice more, varying the speed, noting landmarks. A gas station on the corner. A church with a blue door. A bodega with faded Coca-Cola signs. The highway junction where they'd turn toward the Pacific.

"Navy pickup is at grid coordinates we'll get day-of," Cole said. "RHIB comes in, we load up, they take us to the Constellation in international waters. Fastest exfil, cleanest break."

"If the coastal route is compromised?" Torres asked.

"Secondary is overland to Honduras," Cole said. "Riker, take us north. "Riker turned onto the Pan-American Highway, heading toward the border. The landscape changed. More rural. Fewer checkpoints but longer distances between safe points. They passed a military convoy heading south. Five trucks. Soldiers in the back, rifles across their laps.

"Checkpoint at kilometer eighteen," Cole said. "Mark it." Torres wrote: Secondary route - checkpoint at km 18. Military presence. Medium security. "This route takes us to the border crossing at Las Manos," Cole said. "We've got vehicles staged on the Honduras side. From there it's a straight shot to Tegucigalpa, then a flight out."

"How long?" Riker asked.

"Six hours to the border if we're moving fast. Another four to Tegucigalpa. But it's the safest option if the coast is hot." They drove north for another twenty minutes, timing the route, noting the terrain and potential ambush points. "Tertiary route," Cole said. "Back to Managua." Riker turned the Land Cruiser around and headed back toward the city.

They took surface streets, avoiding the main highways.

"If both primary and Alternates are compromised, we go to Augusto C. Sandino International," Cole said. "Charter flight to San José. Pilot's on Hayes' payroll; plane's fueled and ready."

"That's a lot of exposure," Torres said.

"It is. But if we're using tertiary, we're already fucked.

At that point it's about speed, not stealth." They drove past the airport once. Security was light. A few guards at the gates. Nothing that would stop a determined team.

"And if we're really fucked?" Torres asked.

"Then head to the embassy and see what's what. Maybe jail either here or in the U.S. As long as Reyes is dead, I am good with that."

Torres nodded. He didn't ask what happened if someone didn't make it to the rendezvous.

They all knew the answer.

They drove past the mistress's house twice during the route mapping. Never slowing. Never looking directly at it. Just three more foreigners in a city full of them. Riker noted the sight lines, the cover, the places where things could go wrong. "Gate's the choke point," he said. "We go through there, we're committed."

"That's why we go fast," Cole said. They returned to the safe house by 1100 hours.

Back at the safe house, Bishop sat at the kitchen table with the radio equipment spread out in front of him. He wore headphones, monitoring multiple frequencies. Military channels. Police channels. Civilian emergency services. Most of it was routine chatter. Patrol reports. Traffic accidents. A domestic disturbance on the east side. But Bishop listened to all of it, building a picture of the security situation in real time.

Hawke and Mason were in the driveway, prepping the

vehicles. Hawke checked the tire pressure on the Land Cruiser, 32 PSI all around. He topped off the fluids. Oil. Coolant. Brake fluid. Everything had to be perfect. Mason stashed extra magazines in the door panels and under the seats. Thirty-round mags for the AKs. Fifteen-round mags for the Berettas.

He wrapped them in cloth to prevent rattling. "How's it look?" Cole asked, walking over.

"Good," Hawke said. "Tires are solid. Fluids are topped off. Full tank of gas. We're ready for a fast exfil."

Cole nodded. "Good work."

Inside, Bishop pulled off his headphones. "Radio traffic from DC. Price is checking in."

Cole walked over and picked up the handset. "Go ahead."

Price's voice crackled through the encrypted channel. "Target departed for work at 0742 local time. Routine so far. He's at Langley now. We're maintaining surveillance on the townhouse."

"Copy. Any changes to his pattern?"

"Negative. Same routine. Same schedule. He's acting like a man with nothing to hide."

"Good. Maintain position. We'll update you after tonight."

"Roger. Price out."

Cole set down the handset.

Keller's voice came through next from the observation post. "OP to base. Mistress's house is quiet. Staff departed at 1530. No security visible."

"Copy that," Bishop replied. "Report any movement."

Cole walked over to the wall where they'd pinned a large-scale map of Managua. Red pins marked the mistress's house. Blue pins marked their safe house. Green lines traced the three exfiltration routes.Everything was coming together.

The team spent the afternoon going over the plan one more time.

Equipment checks. Contingencies. Timing.

At 1600, they ate an early meal. Rice and beans that Bishop cooked on the small stove. Nobody talked much.

At 1700, they began final preparations.

Chapter Twenty-Two

Thursday, March 21s, 1430 Hours EDT

Langley, Virgina

Deputy Director of Operations Marcus Lawson sat in the Deputy Director of Intelligence's office and tried not to look at his watch. The office was on the seventh floor of the Original Headquarters Building. Large windows overlooked the Virginia countryside. The walls were lined with framed photographs, DDI Carmichael shaking hands with senators, standing beside the Director, receiving awards.

Carmichael sat behind his desk, a folder open in front of him. "We have a problem," Carmichael said. He was younger than Lawson by five years, with the kind of smooth confidence that came from never having worked in the field. "Nicaragua."

Lawson waited.

"Three Soviet advisors dead in the past six weeks," Carmichael continued. "All of them precision neutralizes. No witnesses. No evidence. Professional work."

"The Contras are getting better trained," Lawson said. "We've been working with them for..."

"This isn't the Contras." Carmichael opened the folder. Inside were photographs.

Satellite images. Intelligence reports. "The Contras use ambushes. IEDs. Mass casualties. This is something else. Surgical strikes. In and out. No collateral damage."

Lawson studied the photos without touching them. "What are you suggesting?"

"I'm suggesting someone in your directorate is running operations without proper oversight."

"That's a serious accusation."

"It's a serious problem." Carmichael leaned back in his chair. "The Senate Intelligence Committee is already asking questions about Central America. If they find out we're conducting unauthorized operations..."

"We're not," Lawson interrupted. "Everything my directorate runs goes through proper channels. You know that."

"Do I?"

Lawson met his eyes. "If you have evidence of unauthorized operations, present it. Otherwise, you're wasting my time."

Carmichael studied him for a long moment. "There are rumors. Whispers. About a team. Military operators conducting missions that aren't on any books."

"Rumors aren't intelligence."

"No. But they're worth investigating."

Lawson stood. "If there are rogue elements operating in Central America, I want to know about it. That's a threat to operational security. To the Agency. To everything we're trying to accomplish down there."

"So, you'll look into it?"

"I'll make inquiries. Quietly. If someone's running unauthorized operations, they need to be shut down."

Carmichael nodded slowly. "Keep me informed."

"Of course." Lawson walked out. The hallway was quiet. Fluorescent lights hummed overhead. The carpet muffled his footsteps. His hands were shaking slightly. He shoved them in his pockets. He'd been careful. So careful. The meeting in Managua. The information passed through cutouts. The careful cultivation of Soviet contacts who believed he was motivated by ideology rather than money. But Carmichael was smart. Ambitious. The kind of man who built his career by exposing problems. If he kept digging, he might find something. Not the whole truth. Lawson had been too careful about that. But enough to raise questions. Enough to trigger an investigation. And investigations had a way of uncovering things you didn't expect. Lawson walked to his office and closed the door. He sat at his desk and stared at the phone.

The team that was in Nicaragua in November and December, whoever they were, would go back at some point, and when they did, they would be met with men who are ready to take them down. He was sure of that. They had no clue that they were a known quantity. Everything would continue as planned. He picked up the receiver and dialed his ex-wife's sisters house number in Connecticut.

It rang four times before she answered.

"Hello?"

"Hey. It's me."

"Marcus." Her voice was flat. No warmth. No surprise. "What do you want?"

"I just... I wanted to call."

"It's Thursday, Marcus. Not our anniversary. Not my birthday. Just Thursday."

He'd forgotten what day it was. "I know. I just wanted to hear your voice."

There was a long pause. He could hear the television in the background. A game show. Canned laughter.

"You sound tired," Margaret said finally.

"I am tired."

"Then go home. Get some rest."

"Margaret..."

She hung up. Lawson sat there with the phone in his hand, listening to the dial tone. Twenty-three years of marriage. Two children who barely spoke to him. A wife who'd stopped believing his promises years ago. He'd told himself it was worth it. That he was protecting something. That the system was broken and someone had to fix it. But sitting in his office at Langley, listening to the dial tone, he couldn't remember what he'd been trying to protect. He hung up the phone and looked at his watch. 1520 hours. He had paperwork to finish. Reports to file. A meeting at 1600 with the Latin America desk. Just another Thursday at Langley.

He had no idea that in Managua, nine operators were preparing to neutralize Tomás Reyes. He had no idea that in Georgetown, three operators were watching his townhouse, logging his movements, planning his death.

He had no idea that tonight, everything would change.

Chapter Twenty-Three

T*hursday, March 21st, 1800, hours*
Managua, Nicaragua

Draven's voice crackled over the radio. "We've got movement. Black sedan, six bodyguards, approaching from the north."

Cole moved to the radio at the safe house. "Is it him?"

"Stand by."

Through the spotting scope, Draven watched the sedan slow as it approached the target house. A Mercedes. Black. Diplomatic plates. Two bodyguards got out first. Then the other four. They wore civilian clothes but moved like military. They scanned the street. Professional. Alert. Then the rear door opened. Tomás Reyes stepped out. He wore slacks and a guayabera shirt. No uniform. He looked around quickly, then moved toward the gate. "Confirmed," Draven said quietly into the radio. "That's Reyes. He's entering the house now."

Keller snapped photos. Click. Click. Click.

Through the scope, Draven watched Reyes approach

the front door. Maria opened it before he could knock. She smiled. Kissed him. They disappeared inside with two Bodyguards in tow. The other four bodyguards stayed outside in the front courtyard, visible through the gate. One lit a cigarette. The other leaned against the wall. The other two just walked around the car, Relaxed but watchful.

"Four bodyguards outside," Draven reported. "Reyes is inside with the woman. Two guards went inside with Reyes"

"Same pattern as the intel briefing," Keller added, writing in the log. 1847 - Target arrives.

Black Mercedes. four bodyguards. Enters house. Greeted by Maria. Two guards went inside.

"Creature of habit," Draven said.

"That's what gets you killed."

Cole checked his watch at the safe house. 1852 hours. "Stay on him," Cole said. "I want to know when he settles in."

Twenty minutes later, Keller reported back. "Lights on upstairs. Second floor, northeast corner. That's the bedroom. Reyes is with the woman."

"Roger."

"Security?"

"Four bodyguards in the front courtyard. They're smoking, relaxed. Not expecting trouble. Two inside, no idea what they are doing. No visual"

Cole checked his watch. 1912 hours. Reyes would be there for hours. The intelligence had been clear, he usually stayed until late, sometimes past midnight.

"Good. Maintain position. Log everything."

"Copy."

Thursday, March 21st, 1830, Hours
Observation Post

Cole's voice crackled over the radio. "Keller, pack it up. Head back to the safe house. Draven can maintain the OP solo." Keller looked at Draven, who nodded without taking his eye from the spotting scope.

"Copy," Keller said into the radio. "RTB in five."

He gathered his gear, notebook, camera, radio, and stuffed them into a small pack. The surveillance log went into a waterproof pouch. He left the PRS-319 radio with Draven along with extra batteries.

"You good here?" Keller asked.

"Yeah. Pattern's confirmed. He's not going anywhere."

Keller slung the pack over his shoulder and moved to the door. "See you when it's done."

"Stay sharp."

Keller descended the stairs quietly, checked the street through a gap in the boards, then slipped out the back. The walk to the safe house took eight minutes. He moved casually, just another local heading home in the evening. At 1900 hours, he entered the safe house through the rear entrance. Cole looked up from the map table. "Set up comms. I want continuous contact with Draven until we move." Keller nodded and went to work setting up the radio station in the corner of the living room.

Thursday, March 21st, 1905 Hours
Managua Safehouse

The team gathered in the living room. Cole spread the surveillance photos across the table. Reyes arriving at the mistress's house. Reyes walking through the gate. The bodyguards in the courtyard, smoking. Maria opening the door. "He's there now," Cole said.

"Arrived at 1800. Went upstairs with the mistress at 1905. four guards outside in the courtyard, two in the house."

"When's the window?" Riker asked.

"Tonight. We hit him at 2200 hours. He'll be upstairs, isolated. It's as vulnerable as he gets."

Torres leaned over the photos. "What about Lawson?"

"Price, Ward, and Vail are already in position in DC. They've had him under surveillance since Tuesday. He's at his Georgetown townhouse now, got home from Langley at 1730 their time."

"When do they take him?"

"0300 hours Friday morning. When he's in REM sleep. Deepest part of the sleep cycle. He'll never know what happened."

Bishop looked up from the radio equipment. "So, we hit Reyes tonight, they hit Lawson five hours later?"

"Correct. Coordinated but separated. By the time Lawson's body is discovered Friday morning, we'll already be out of Nicaragua. No connection between the two hits."

Draven's voice came over the radio. "OP to base. Target is still upstairs. Lights on in the bedroom. Guards outside are settled in. Same positions."

"Copy," Cole said into the radio.

Then to the team: "We move in fifteen minutes. That gives us two and a half hours to prep and get into position.

Draven maintains overwatch from the OP. The rest of us go through the gate. Fast and quiet, and out in five minutes."

"Rules of engagement?" Mason asked.

"Anyone who sees us dies. No witnesses. No survivors except the mistress, we leave her alive if we can, to discover the body and call it in."

Cole looked at each of them. Mason's hands were steady. His earlier anxiety had burned off. Now he was focused. Torres's energy was controlled. Channeled. Riker was calm. He always was. Hawke was ready. He'd been ready since they landed.

They were all ready.

"Gear up," Cole said. "We move in two hours." The team dispersed to their equipment. Suppressors were attached to pistols. Magazines were checked one final time. Gloves were pulled on. Knives were clipped inside waistbands. Cole walked over to the table where his Beretta 92 lay disassembled. He reassembled it methodically. Slide. Barrel. Recoil spring. Magazine. He press-checked the chamber. Empty. He loaded a fifteen-round magazine and chambered a round. Fourteen in the mag. One in the pipe. He attached the suppressor, a custom-built unit that added six inches to the barrel but reduced the report to a whisper. He holstered the weapon and checked his watch.

1945 hours. Fifteen minutes until they loaded into the vehicles. Cole sat on the couch and felt nothing. No fear. No excitement. No doubt. Just the cold certainty that in two and a half hours, Tomás Reyes would be dead. And five hours after that, Robert Lawson would follow him.

At 1955 hours, they would load into the vehicles.

At 2000 hours, they would move into position.

In DC, Price, Ward, and Hawke were already in position outside Lawson's Georgetown townhouse. Waiting. Patient. They had five hours until 0300.

Here in Managua, Cole had about two hours until 2200. "Final comms check," Cole said into the radio.

"OP is set," Draven replied. "Clear sight lines on the target house."

"Assault element is ready," Torres said from the back seat.

"Copy all," Cole said. "We hit him at 2200. Stay sharp."

He set down the radio and looked at his team.

Two hours. And then they would go to work.

Chapter Twenty-Four

T*hursday, March 21st, 1955, Hours*
Managua, Nicaragua

Cole turned away from the window and looked at his team. "Load up," he said. They moved with practiced efficiency. Riker holstered his Beretta and grabbed a light jacket to conceal it. Hawke pocketed his spare magazines and pulled on a pair of thin leather gloves. Torres clipped his knife inside his waistband and checked his watch. Mason slung a small backpack over his shoulder, inside were zip ties, duct tape, and a few items they'd need for staging the scene. Holt was already outside, starting the Land Cruiser. The engine turned over with a low rumble, then settled into a steady idle. Cole did a final check. Weapon. Suppressor. Optics. Spare mags. Gloves. Radio. Everything was in place.

"Bishop, Keller, you're staying here," Cole said. "Monitor comms. If we call for exfil, you move immediately." From his pack, he pulled out a black balaclava and tucked it into his jacket pocket. Around him, the others did the same. Standard procedure. No faces. No identities.

If Maria Sanchez woke up during the operation, if a neighbor looked out a window at the wrong moment, if any surveillance caught them on the property, they'd see nothing but shadows in black masks. Riker rolled his balaclava and stuffed it into his waistband. Torres folded his carefully and slipped it inside his jacket. Mason and Hawke pocketed theirs without comment. It was routine. Part of the checklist. Like loading magazines or checking comms.

"Copy," Bishop said.

"If we don't check in by 2230, assume compromise and execute contingency three."

"Understood."

Contingency three meant abandon the safe house, destroy all evidence, and head for the coast independently. It meant the operation had failed and the team was scattered. Cole didn't plan on using contingency three. He walked to the door and looked back at his team one last time. Riker. Hawke. Torres. Mason. Holt outside in the vehicle.

"Let's go to work," Cole said.

They filed out into the humid night.

Thursday, 21 March 2000 Hours CST

The Land Cruiser pulled away from the safe house and merged into traffic. Holt drove with careful precision, maintaining exactly the speed limit, signaling every turn, doing nothing that would attract attention. Cole sat in the passenger seat, watching the streets. Managua after dark was a different city. The daytime chaos, vendors, pedestrians, honking horns, had given way to something quieter but no less alive. Bars and restaurants were open, their lights spilling onto the sidewalks. Groups of young men stood on corners, smoking and talking. A few cars moved through the intersections, headlights cutting through the darkness. In the back seat, Riker, Hawke, Torres, and Mason sat in silence. They looked like five men heading out for the evening. Nothing unusual. Nothing suspicious.

That was the point.

Cole's mind was already at the target house, running through the sequence. Approach. Neutralize the exterior guards. Enter. Clear the ground floor. Move upstairs. Execute Reyes. Stage the scene. Exfil.

Three minutes from start to finish. Maybe four if they had to adapt.

"Traffic's light," Holt said quietly.

"Good."

They passed a police checkpoint at the intersection of Avenida Bolívar and Calle 27. Two officers stood by a barricade, checking vehicles at random. Holt slowed as they approached, but the officers waved them through without stopping.

Cole exhaled slowly. One less variable.

"OP, this is Alpha," Cole said into the radio. "We're mobile. ETA to staging area is twenty minutes."

"Copy, Alpha," Draven replied. "Target is still inside. No change in security posture. Four guards outside, two inside."

"Copy. Keep us updated."

"Will do."

Cole checked his watch. 2024 hours. They had been in position for four minutes. They had an hour and thirty-six minutes until execution. The streets grew quieter as they sat in the residential neighborhood. Fewer cars. Fewer people. The houses here were modest but well-maintained, with small yards and iron gates. Lights glowed in some windows. Others were dark. Holt had taken the route they'd mapped during reconnaissance. Left on Calle 15. Right on Avenida Roosevelt. Straight for six blocks, then left again. No checkpoints. They had arrived with no complications.

At 2020 hours, he pulled over two blocks from the target house and shut the engine down. "We're in position," Cole said into the radio.

"Copy," Draven replied. "Target is still inside. Security unchanged."

Cole checked his watch. 2021 hours. One hour and thirty-nine minutes until execution.

"Now we wait," he said.

Thursday, March 21st, 2045, Hours CST

The team sat in silence. Riker stared out the window. Hawke checked his watch every few minutes. Torres breathed slowly, steadily, the way he always did before an operation. Mason had his eyes closed, but Cole knew he wasn't sleeping. Cole's mind ran through contingencies again. What if a civilian walks by during the hit? They'd have to control the situation. Detain the civilian until the team exfils. Non-lethal if possible. What if Reyes leaves before 2200? Then they follow. Adapt. Find another opportunity. What if the guards are more alert than expected? Then they move faster. Suppress them before they can react. Cole had learned that the key to successful operations wasn't eliminating risk, it was managing it. You couldn't control everything. But you could prepare for most things. And when something unexpected happened, you adapted.

That's what separated good operators from dead ones.

At 2103 hours, the radio crackled. "Alpha, this is OP," Draven said. "Update. Target is still inside. Lights on in the upstairs bedroom. Guards are relaxed. Two of them are smoking by the vehicles. The other two are talking near the gate."

"Copy. Any change in the interior?"

"Negative. Two guards in the front room. Haven't moved in the last hour."

"Copy. Keep watching."

"Will do."

Cole looked at his watch. 2104 hours. Fifty-six minutes.

Thursday, 21st, March 2130 Hours CST

The neighborhood was quiet. A car had driven past ten minutes ago, but otherwise, the street was empty. A dog barked somewhere in the distance. A television flickered in a window across the street. Cole checked his watch. 2131 hours. Twenty-nine minutes. "Gear up," he said quietly. Then radioed Bravo team

"Bravo, this is Alpha," Cole's voice said. "We are in position to hit the target. Stand by for confirmation when we are clear"

"Copy, Alpha. Standing by."

Price set the radio down and exhaled slowly. Price settled back in his seat and watched the townhouse. Lawson was inside. Alone. His ex-wife was in Connecticut living with her sister. The man was vulnerable, isolated, and completely unaware that three Ghostline operators were sitting outside his home, waiting for the order to neutralize him.

Managua, 2145

The team moved in silence. Riker pulled on his gloves. Hawke checked his suppressor one last time. Torres adjusted the knife clipped inside his waistband. Mason opened his backpack and confirmed the contents, zip ties, duct tape, a small pry bar, a handful of cash and jewelry they'd use to stage the robbery. Cole pulled on his own gloves and performed a final press check on his Beretta. Chambered round. Safety off. Ready.

"OP, this is Alpha," Cole said into the radio. "Status?"

"Target is still inside," Draven replied. "Upstairs bedroom. Lights still on. Guards unchanged. Four outside, two inside."

"Copy. We're moving in fifteen minutes."

"Copy. Good hunting."

Cole set the radio down and looked at his team.

"Rules of engagement," he said quietly. "Suppress all guards. No survivors. Reyes is the primary target. The woman is secondary, if she can identify us, she's a liability. We stage it as a robbery gone wrong. Grab some cash and jewelry but leave the expensive pieces. Amateurs would panic and run. We make it look sloppy but believable." The team nodded. "Exfil is in pairs. Cole and Riker south. Hawke and Torres east. Mason circles back to meet Holt. We walk; we don't run. Four blocks to the pickup points. Holt will rotate between locations. Everyone clear?"

"Clear," Riker said.

"Clear," Hawke said.

Torres and Mason nodded.

Cole checked his watch. 2144 hours.

Sixteen minutes.

"Let's get ready to move," he said.

Georgetown, 2050 Hours

Price checked his watch. 2050 local time. In Managua, it was 2150. Cole's team would be moving now and hitting the house in ten minutes. The plan was simple: Nicaragua first, then DC. If the Reyes hit went sideways, if the team got compromised, if anything went wrong, the Lawson operation would abort. They couldn't risk two high-profile assassinations on the same night if one of them had already blown up. So, they waited. And listened to the radio traffic from Alpha team.

They would know when the hit went down and if there were any complications. Price looked at his team. "You guys ready?"

"I'm good." Ward said.

"Vail?"

"Ready."

Managua, 2150

Alpha team was moving. They got out of the Land Cruiser and split into pairs. Cole and Riker walked together, moving at a casual pace. Hawke and Torres followed thirty seconds behind, taking a parallel route. Mason trailed another thirty seconds back, watching their six. The neighborhood was quiet. Residential. A few lights in windows. A dog barking somewhere. The air was thick and humid, carrying the smell of cooking food and diesel exhaust. Cole's hand rested near his concealed weapon, but he kept his posture relaxed. Just two men out for an evening walk. Nothing unusual. Nothing suspicious. They turned a corner and moved down a side street. The houses here were dark. No cars. No pedestrians. Cole's tactical mind was working constantly, cataloging details. Exit routes. Cover positions. Potential witnesses. The layout of the street. The distance to the target house. Two blocks ahead, he could see the glow of lights from Reyes's mistress's house.

"OP, this is Alpha," Cole said quietly into his radio. "We're one block out."

"Copy," Draven replied. "Target is still inside.

Guards are in position. You're clear to approach."

"Copy."

Cole and Riker reached the corner across from the target house and stopped. Hawke and Torres arrived fifteen seconds later, approaching from a different angle. Mason took up a position thirty meters back, watching the street.

Cole checked his watch. 2155 hours.

Five minutes. He looked at Riker. At Hawke. At Torres. At Mason in the distance. They were ready.

The target house sat behind a low wall with an iron gate. The courtyard was visible through the bars, two vehicles parked inside, four guards standing near them, talking and smoking. The front door of the house was closed. Lights glowed in the windows. Cole's heart rate was steady. His breathing was controlled. His mind was clear. This was what he'd trained for. What he was built for. At 2159 hours, he keyed his radio. "All elements, this is Alpha. We are going in sixty seconds. Execute on my mark."

"Copy," Draven said from the OP.

"Copy," Mason said from his position down the street.

Cole looked at his team.

Riker's face was calm, focused. Hawke's jaw was set. Torres's eyes were locked on the target house.

Cole checked his watch.

2200 hours.

"Execute," he said.

Georgetown, 2100 Hours

Price heard the execute command from Cole.

Alpha team was moving on Reyes. Approximately five hours until Price's team moved on Lawson. He said a silent prayer for his brother in Nicaragua. They are in the fight now.

Chapter Twenty-Five

M*anagua, 2200 Hours*

Hawke moved first. He crossed the street at a casual pace, hands in his pockets, looking like a man heading home after a long day. The four guards in the courtyard didn't even glance at him. That was their first mistake. Hawke's hand came out of his pocket holding the suppressed Beretta. He raised it smoothly, acquired the first target, and squeezed the trigger. The suppressor made a sound like a sharp cough. The first guard dropped, a neat hole in his forehead, before his brain could register what had happened, it was all over the parked car he was standing by.

Cole and Riker were already moving. They crossed the street in three long strides, weapons up, moving fast. The second guard turned, his eyes widening as he saw Hawke's weapon. He reached for his own pistol. Riker shot him twice. Center mass. The man staggered backward and collapsed against one of the vehicles. Torres was through the gate now, his Beretta tracking to the third guard. The man opened his mouth to shout. Torres put a round through his throat. The shout became a wet gurgle. The guard fell to his knees, clutching his neck, blood pouring between his fingers.

The fourth guard finally reacted. He yanked an AK-47 off his shoulder and tried to bring it up. Mason shot him three times. Chest. Chest. Head. The guard crumpled. Four guards down in eight seconds. They all policed up their brass, so there was no evidence.

Cole moved to the front door. It was unlocked, Reyes felt safe here, in his mistress's house, surrounded by his men. The last mistake he would ever make.

Cole pushed the door open and moved inside, weapon up, scanning for threats. The front room was small. A couch. A television. A coffee table. Two bodyguards sat on the couch, their weapons leaning against the wall.

They turned, reaching for their AK-47s. Riker shot the first one in the side of the head.

The suppressed round punched through his temple and exited the other side, spraying blood and brain matter across his partner's face. The second guard froze for a split second, his face covered in his friend's blood, his mind trying to process what had just happened. Cole used that split second. He placed the red dot on the man's forehead and fired. Another cough from the suppressor. The round went through the man's forehead clean and the hollow point round mushroomed in his brain cavity and exploded out the backside of his head, then two more in his chest as he moved past the body.

"Clear they all reported with a whisper".

"Ground floor secure," Cole said quietly into his radio.

Hawke and Torres moved through the front door, weapons up, covering the entry. Mason stayed outside, watching the street. Cole moved to the stairs. Riker was right behind him, covering his six. Cole pulled the black balaclava up over his face, the fabric settling into place, covering everything but his eyes. Riker did the same, then Torres and Hawke.

Four operators, faces completely concealed.

The staircase was narrow. The walls were painted a faded yellow. A picture frame hung crooked on the wall, a beach scene, generic and cheap. Cole moved up the stairs, his weapon tracking ahead of him, his footsteps silent on the worn carpet. At the top of the stairs, a hallway stretched to the left. Three doors. Two were closed. One was open, a bathroom, dark and empty.

The door at the end of the hall showed light underneath. Cole moved forward, his breathing controlled, his finger resting on the trigger guard. At the door, he paused. Listened. Voices inside. A man and a woman. The man's voice was low, relaxed. The woman laughed. Cole looked at Riker. Riker nodded.

Cole kicked the door open. The door slammed inward, the frame splintering. Cole moved through the doorway, weapon up, acquiring targets. Reyes was on the bed, half-dressed, his shirt unbuttoned. The woman was next to him, wearing a silk robe. Her eyes went wide. She screamed.

Reyes lunged for a pistol on the nightstand. Cole shot him twice. Center mass. He loved these new redots. The rounds punched through Reyes's chest, and he jerked backward, his hand falling short of the weapon. Cole walked forward and put a third round through Reyes's forehead. The man had collapsed onto the bed, blood spreading across the white sheets. Brain matter splattered the headboard.

The woman kept screaming.

"Cállate," Cole said in Spanish. Quiet.

She went silent, her eyes wide with terror, her hands clutching the robe.

Torres and Mason came through the door, moving fast. Torres grabbed Reyes's body and pulled him upright, checking for a pulse. There wasn't one. Mason moved to the dresser and started staging the scene. He knocked over a lamp. Scattered jewelry across the floor. Pulled open drawers and rifled through them, making it look like someone had been searching for valuables. Riker stood near the door; his weapon trained on the woman, Maria Sanchez. She was staring at Cole, her mouth open, her body trembling. Riker looked at Cole. Cole looked at the woman. She was staring at masked men. Black balaclavas. No faces. No features she could describe. Just dark shapes with weapons.

She couldn't identify them. Couldn't tell the police anything useful beyond "masked men" and "robbery." But the robbery scenario would work better with a witness who'd been knocked out during the struggle. Someone who woke up hours later, traumatized, unable to recall details clearly beyond those basics. It made the cover story more authentic than having no witness at all, more believable that thieves had panicked, struck her, and fled.

Cole made the decision. He nodded to Torres. Torres moved quickly. Maria started to scream again, but Torres was already behind her. He struck her at the base of the skull with controlled force, enough to render her unconscious, not enough to cause permanent damage. She slumped forward onto the bed beside Reyes, unconscious but breathing.

"Check her pulse," Cole said.

Torres pressed two fingers to her neck. "Strong and steady. She'll be out for a while."

Mason grabbed cash from Reyes's wallet on the nightstand, about two hundred córdobas. He took a cheap watch from the dresser but left the expensive jewelry. Amateurs would panic and grab everything. Professionals would know what to take and what to leave. Torres positioned Reyes's hand near the nightstand, making it look like he'd tried to reach his weapon. Which he had. It just didn't look natural since Cole decided to put the round in Reyes' head

Cole checked his watch. 2203 hours. Three minutes from entry to completion. "Police the brass it's time to move," he said. They filed out of the bedroom, down the hallway, down the stairs. Past the bodies in the front room. Through the courtyard, stepping over the dead guards. Mason pulled the gate closed behind them.

The street was empty. They split up. Cole and Riker headed south, walking at a normal pace. Hawke and Torres went east. Mason circled back toward the staging area where Holt was waiting.

No running. No panic. Just five men disappearing into the night. Cole's heart rate was steady. His breathing was controlled. His mind was already on the next phase, exfil, rally point, extraction. Behind them, the house was silent. Four bodies inside. Four more in the courtyard. In an hour, maybe two, someone would find them. The police would investigate. They'd find a robbery, a struggle, a senior Sandinista commander murdered in his mistress's home.

They'd never find the team.

Cole made the call.

"Bravo this is alpha we are clear of the house. Confirm?"

"Confirmed." Price acknowledged.

Chapter Twenty-Six

Managua, 2207 Hours

Cole and Riker walked four blocks south before Holt picked them up in the Land Cruiser. They climbed in without a word. Holt pulled away from the curb and drove at exactly the speed limit.

"Status?" Holt asked.

"Clean," Cole said. "Target is down. No complications."

"Copy."

Cole keyed his radio. "Keller, this is Alpha. Call the ship for exfil and then break down the safehouse and prepare for pickup. ETA five minutes."

"Copy, Alpha," Keller's voice came back. "Breaking down now."

Three minutes later, they picked up Hawke and Torres at the designated corner. Both men climbed into the back without a word. The Land Cruiser was full now, Holt driving, Cole in the passenger seat, Riker, Hawke, and Torres in the back.

In the second vehicle, the driver, Mason swung by the safehouse. Keller and Bishop were waiting outside with their gear already packed. They loaded quickly and the vehicle pulled away. Two minutes later, they picked up Draven at the rally point. He had broken down the observation post solo and was waiting with his equipment, and they headed west toward the Pacific.

By 2218 hours, the whole team was mobile, heading west toward the Pacific. Cole sat in the passenger seat and keyed his radio.

"Bravo, this is Alpha. We are moving to exfil. Operation complete. You are clear to proceed."

There was a pause. Then Price's voice came through, calm and professional. "Copy, Alpha. Proceeding with Bravo. Good work."

"Keep your head on a swivel, Alpha."

"Will do. Alpha out." Cole set the radio down and looked out the window. Managua was sliding past, its lights fading behind them. The streets were quiet. No sirens. No pursuit. No indication that anyone had noticed what had just happened. In approximately five hours, Price's team would hit Lawson in Georgetown.

Cole checked his watch. 2221 hours.

Georgetown, 2318 Hours

Price sat in the Ford sedan and listened to Cole's transmission. "Copy, Alpha. Proceeding with Bravo. Good work. Keep your head on a swivel."

"Will do." Came Cole's reply

He set the radio down and looked at Ward. "We're go," Price said. Ward nodded. In the back seat, Vail checked his weapon. Price checked his watch. 2319 local time. They had three hours and forty-one minutes until execution. He settled back in his seat and watched Lawson's townhouse. The man had no idea what was coming.

Nicaragua, 2240 Hours

The highway west was dark and mostly empty. Holt drove at exactly the speed limit, his hands steady on the wheel, his eyes scanning the road ahead. Cole watched the side mirrors. No headlights behind them. No pursuit. In the back seat, Hawke, Torres, and Riker sat in silence.

The adrenaline was fading now, replaced by the familiar exhaustion that came after an operation.

"OP, this is Alpha," Cole said into the radio. "What's your status?"

"We're ten minutes behind you," Draven replied. "No complications. We're clear."

"Copy. Rally point is two hours out. We'll wait for you there."

"Copy."

Cole set the radio down and looked out the window. The city lights were gone now, replaced by darkness and the occasional glow of a small village. The air coming through the vents was warm and humid, carrying the smell of the ocean. In an hour, someone would find Reyes. The police would investigate. They'd find a robbery, a struggle, a senior commander murdered in his mistress's home.

The team was like smoke in the wind, gone.

Cole thought about Lawson. In 3 hours and 20 minutes, Price's team would move. By dawn, both targets would be dead. Shoot, Move, and disappear. That's what Ghostline did. They found the people who needed to die. And they made it happen. Cole checked his watch. 2251 hours. The coast was an hour and nine minutes away. The Navy vessel was waiting in international waters, ready to extract them. They weren't safe yet.

But they were close.

Chapter Twenty-Seven

R*ally Point, 2340 Hours CST*
Nicaragua

The rally point was a dirt road three kilometers from the coast, hidden by dense vegetation and far from any towns. Holt pulled off the highway and followed the narrow track until they reached a small clearing. He cut the engine. The team sat in silence, listening. Nothing. Just the sound of insects and the distant crash of waves. "We wait here," Cole said. "Draven's team should be here in ten minutes." The team got out and stretched. Riker lit a cigarette. Hawke checked his weapon. Torres walked to the edge of the clearing and stared into the darkness. Cole stood by the Land Cruiser and thought about the operation. The approach. The execution. The exfil. Everything had gone according to plan. No complications. No casualties. No witnesses.

Clean.

At 2351 hours, headlights appeared on the dirt road. Draven's vehicle pulled into the clearing and stopped. Draven, Keller, Bishop, and Mason climbed out.

"Everyone good?" Cole asked.

"We're good," Draven said.

"No pursuit. No complications."

"Copy."

Cole checked his watch. 2359 hours. In three hours, Price's team would hit Lawson. By dawn, both operations would be complete.

"Let's move to the coast," Cole said. "The Navy's coming." The team loaded back into the vehicles and drove the final three kilometers to the beach. The ocean stretched out before them, dark and endless. Somewhere out there, beyond the horizon, a Navy vessel was waiting.

Cole stood on the beach and looked at his team. They'd done their job. They'd executed the mission. They'd eliminated a target that threatened American interests. And tomorrow, they'd do it again. That's what they did. They were the shadows. The ghosts. The operators who didn't exist. And they were very, very good at their job. Cole checked his watch one last time. 0012 hours. In two hours and fifty-one minutes, Robert Lawson would be dead. And Ghostline would head back to Bragg and find out what was next.

Chapter Twenty-Eight

Friday, March 22nd, 0225 Hours EDT
Georgetown, Washington DC

Price sat in the Ford sedan three blocks from Lawson's townhouse and felt the encrypted radio vibrate against his chest. He pulled it out. Cole's voice came through clean and professional despite the distance.

"Alpha is clear. Awaiting exfil."

Price keyed the transmit button twice. Acknowledgment without words. He set the radio on the center console and looked at Vail in the passenger seat, then back at Ward in the rear.

"We're still green," Price said.

Vail nodded once. Ward checked his watch, 0226 hours, and said nothing.

Price had been on two previous operations. This was his third and he was in charge this time. Nicaragua had been his first kill, a Sandinista officer in the jungle outside Managua. The second had been during the Night Arrow mission, a quick hit on a kill team member. Both times, he'd done his job. Both times, he'd compartmentalized and moved on. But this was different. This was Washington DC. The nation's capital. And the target was a CIA official.

The Pressure of that sat heavy in his chest. He pushed it down. Compartmentalized. Focused on the mechanics.

They'd been parked here for ninety minutes, watching Lawson's townhouse from a safe distance. The neighborhood was quiet. Upscale. Tree-lined streets, brick sidewalks, wrought-iron fences. Mercedes and BMWs parked at the curb. The kind of place where people paid six figures in property taxes and didn't ask questions about their neighbors. Perfect for what they were about to do. Price reached under his seat and pulled out the suppressed Ruger Mark II. .22 caliber. Subsonic rounds. The weapon was small, almost toy-like, but lethally effective at close range.

Contingency only. If the plan went sideways and they needed a quiet kill. The primary plan was simpler: use Lawson's own Colt .45. Make it look like he'd eaten his gun. No forced entry. No evidence of a struggle. Just a depressed CIA official who couldn't live with his guilt.

Price checked the Ruger's magazine anyway. Ten rounds. More than enough if they needed it. Vail had an identical weapon. So did Ward. They also carried lock picks, latex gloves, and a typed suicide note sealed in a plastic bag. Everything they needed to make murder look like self-inflicted tragedy.

"Run it one more time," Price said.

Vail spoke first. "Back entrance through the garden gate. I pick the lock on the rear door. We clear the first floor, move to the second. Lawson's in the study. We control him, execute with his own Colt .45, stage the scene."

"Timing?" Price asked.

"Three minutes from entry to exit," Ward said. "No more."

"Staging?"

"Colt in his right hand," Vail said. "Single shot to the right temple. Powder burns on the skin. Blood spatter consistent with self-inflicted wound. Suicide note on the desk. We wipe every surface we touch, remove any trace of forced entry."

"Exfil?"

"We separate," Ward said. "Different directions. No radio contact until we're at the rally point." Price nodded. They'd rehearsed this a dozen times. Talked through every contingency. But talking and doing were different things.

"What could go wrong?" Price asked. It was the question Cole always asked. The question that kept operators alive.

Vail answered without hesitation. "Lawson's not alone. Someone's visiting. A neighbor sees us. Police patrol drives by at the wrong time. The door's reinforced and we can't pick it. Alarm system we didn't know about. Lawson fights back and we have to control him physically. Blood spatter doesn't match suicide. Forensics finds something we missed."

"Solutions?"

"If he's not alone, we abort," Vail said. "If someone sees us, we're just pedestrians. If police show up, we walk away. If the door's reinforced, we go through a window. If there's an alarm, we move fast and get out before response arrives.

If he fights, we control him quietly. If forensics finds something, we're already gone and there's no trail back to us."

Price looked at Ward. "Anything else?"

"Yeah," Ward said. "We could get caught. We could get killed. We could start a shitstorm that ends with all of us in prison or dead."

"Then let's not get caught," Price said.

He checked his watch. 0230 hours. Time to move.

0230 Hours, Georgetown

Price started the engine and pulled away from the curb.

He drove slowly, carefully, exactly at the speed limit. No reason to attract attention. Georgetown at night was quiet but not empty. A couple walked their dog on the side-walk. A taxi passed going the opposite direction. Lights glowed in windows, people watching television, reading books, living normal lives.

Price turned left onto Lawson's street and drove past the townhouse without slowing. The lights were on in the second-floor study. Same as they'd been for the past three nights. Lawson was a creature of habit. Came home at 1830. Ate dinner alone. Worked in his study until midnight. Went to bed. Predictable. That predictability was going to be his undoing. Price turned right at the next inter-section and circled the block. He parked two streets over, cut the engine, and checked his watch again.

0238 Hours.

"Vail, you're up," Price said. Vail pulled on latex gloves, tucked the suppressed Ruger into his waistband under his jacket, and stepped out of the car. He walked east, hands in his pockets, looking like any other Georgetown resident heading home after a late dinner. Price waited sixty seconds, then looked at Ward. "Go." Ward exited the vehicle and walked west. Different direction. Different route. Same destination.

Price sat alone in the sedan and felt his heart rate slow. This was the moment. The point of no return. Once they entered that house, there was no going back. He thought about Lawson. Thought about the man's file. Forty-seven years old. Divorced. No kids. Twenty-three years with the

Agency. Deputy Director of Operations. A man who'd spent his career in the shadows, running agents, managing covert programs, making decisions that affected national security.

A man who'd been compromised. Whose righteous indignation had put him and Ghostline into this situation.

Who'd become a threat to everything Ghostline was trying to protect. Price didn't feel good about executing him. But he didn't feel bad either. It was just the job. He checked his watch. 0244 hours. Time to move.

March 22nd, 0245 Hours EDT

Price walked south on 31st Street, moving at an easy pace. The night air was cold and damp. His breath misted in front of him. Streetlights cast long shadows across the brick sidewalks. A car passed. Price didn't look at it. He turned into the alley that ran behind Lawson's townhouse. The alley was narrow, lined with wooden fences and garden gates. Trash cans sat at intervals. A cat darted across his path and disappeared into the darkness.

Fifty meters ahead, he saw Vail and Ward standing near Lawson's gate. They looked like two friends having a conversation. Casual. Unremarkable. Price approached and stopped beside them. "Status?" he asked quietly.

"Clear," Vail said. "No movement in the alley. No lights in the neighboring houses. Lawson's still in the study." Price looked at the gate. It was wooden, about six feet tall, with a simple latch lock. Ward already had his pick set out.

"Do it," Price said.

Ward knelt and worked the lock. It took him fifteen seconds. The latch clicked open. They moved through the gate into Lawson's back garden.

0259 Hours

The garden was small but well-maintained. Brick patio. Potted plants. A wrought-iron table with two chairs. The back of the townhouse loomed above them, three stories of red brick and white trim.

Light spilled from the kitchen window on the first floor. Price moved to the back door and tested the knob. Locked. He stepped aside and let Vail work. Vail knelt and examined the lock with a small penlight. "Schlage deadbolt. High quality. This will take a few minutes."

"Make it ninety seconds," Price said.

Vail inserted his tension wrench and pick. He worked methodically, feeling for the pins, applying pressure, listening for the clicks. Price and Ward stood on either side of the door, watching the windows, watching the alley, watching for any sign of trouble.

Sixty seconds passed.

Eighty.

At ninety-two seconds, the deadbolt turned with a soft metallic click. Vail stood and pocketed his tools. "We're in."

Price pulled on his latex gloves. So did Ward. They drew their suppressed Ruger's and held them low, along their legs, out of sight. Price turned the knob and pushed the door open. They entered the kitchen.

0301 Hours

The kitchen was exactly what Price expected. Marble counters. Stainless steel appliances. Hardwood floors. Everything clean and organized. The hum of the refrigerator was the only sound. A coffee maker sat on the counter, half-full. The smell of old coffee hung in the air.

Price moved through the kitchen into the dining room. Empty. A table with six chairs. A chandelier overhead.

Framed artwork on the walls. He cleared the living room next. Leather furniture. Bookshelves. A fireplace. No one there. Vail checked the powder room under the stairs. Empty. Ward covered the front door, making sure no one came in behind them.

Price moved to the staircase. It was carpeted. Good. Their footsteps would be silent. He started climbing. The second-floor hallway was dark except for a line of light under one door. The study. Price could hear faint music, classical, something with strings. He stopped outside the door and looked back at Vail and Ward. They were right behind him, weapons ready. Price took a breath. Let it out slowly. This was it.

He reached for the doorknob.

0303 *Hours*

Price turned the knob and pushed the door open. Robert Lawson sat at his desk, reading a file. He looked up, startled, and his eyes went wide. For a moment, nobody moved. Lawson's mouth opened. He started to say something, a question, a protest, a plea, but Price was already moving. He crossed the room in three steps and raised the suppressed Ruger, aiming it at Lawson's face.

"Don't," Price said quietly.

Lawson froze. His hands were on the desk, palms down. His breathing was rapid, shallow. Fear in his eyes.

"Stand up," Price said. "Slowly." Lawson stood. His legs were shaking. "Turn around. Face the wall."

Lawson turned. Price moved behind him, keeping the Ruger trained on the back of his head. Ward entered the room and closed the door.

"Vail," Price said. "Desk drawer. Right side."

Vail moved to the desk and pulled open the drawer. Inside was a Colt 1911, .45 caliber, standard military issue.

Lawson's personal sidearm. Vail picked it up, checked the chamber. Loaded. "Got it," Vail said.

"Good," Price said. "Lawson, on your knees." Lawson hesitated.

"Now."

Lawson knelt. His hands were trembling. He was breathing hard, trying to control the panic. Price stepped back. Ward moved in from the side, positioning himself behind Lawson.

"Please," Lawson said. His voice was hoarse. "Please, I can..."

"Quiet," Price said.

Ward took the .45 from Vail and knelt behind Lawson. He wrapped Lawson's right hand around the grip, positioning the fingers carefully. Thumb on the safety. Index finger on the trigger.

Lawson tried to pull away, but Ward held his wrist firm. "Don't move. You fucked with the wrong team" Ward said. He pressed the muzzle of the .45 against Lawson's right temple. Contact shot. The barrel was cold against skin. Lawson was crying now. Quiet, desperate sobs. Ward's hand covered Lawson's hand. His finger pressed down on Lawson's finger.

The .45 fired.

The sound was loud in the small room, a sharp crack that echoed off the walls. Lawson's head snapped sideways. His body went limp and collapsed to the floor. Blood pooled on the hardwood, spreading slowly. The entry wound was clean, surrounded by powder burns. The exit wound had taken bone and brain matter with it, spattering the wall behind the desk. Price knelt and checked for a pulse. Nothing. Lawson's eyes were open, staring at nothing.

"Clear," Price said.

Ward set the .45 on the floor next to Lawson's right hand, positioning it so it looked like it had fallen from his grip.

Careful not to disturb Lawson's prints. Vail moved to the desk and pulled out the suicide note. It was typed on plain white paper, sealed in a plastic bag to avoid contamination. He removed it carefully and placed it on the desk, positioning it so it looked like Lawson had been writing it before he died. The note was simple. Apologetic. It mentioned career stress, financial problems, the divorce. It said he couldn't go on. It said he was sorry.

Price examined the scene. The entry wound showed powder burns, consistent with a contact shot. The angle was right for self-infliction. The blood spatter on the wall matched what you'd expect. The .45 was Lawson's own weapon, registered to him, with his prints on it. It was bullshit. But it would be enough. It would pass. "Staging looks good," Price said. "Let's clean up."

They moved quickly. Vail wiped down every surface they'd touched, the doorknob, the desk, the chair. The problem with latex gloves in the powder residue they leave behind. Ward checked the hallway, the stairs, the kitchen. Price examined the back door, making sure there were no signs of forced entry.

At 0306 hours, they were done. Three minutes. Just like they'd planned. "Let's move," Price said. They exited through the back door, closed it behind them, and moved through the garden to the alley. The neighborhood was still quiet. No sirens. No lights. No indication that anyone had heard or seen anything. They walked to the gate, passed through it, and separated without a word. Vail went east. Ward went west. Price went south. Three men. Three directions. No connection between them. By the time anyone found Lawson's body, they'd be gone.

0320 *Hours*

Price walked four blocks before he allowed himself to relax.

His heart rate was elevated but steady. His hands were calm. The adrenaline was there but controlled. He'd not done this before. But knew He'd do it again. He reached the Ford sedan, climbed in, and started the engine. He drove carefully, obeying every traffic law, blending into the sparse late-night traffic. At 0335 hours, he pulled into the parking garage of a Holiday Inn in Arlington. He took the elevator to the third floor and walked to room 312. He knocked twice. Paused. Knocked once. The door opened. Ward stood there, already changed into clean clothes. Vail was sitting on one of the beds, watching the news on mute.

"Status?" Price asked.

"Clean," Ward said. "No tail. No complications."

"Same," Vail said.

Price nodded and closed the door. He pulled off his jacket and gloves, stuffed them into a plastic bag, and sealed it. Ward would dispose of everything later, burn it, bury it, make it disappear. He sat on the edge of the bed and checked his watch. 0341 hours.

In Nicaragua, Cole's team was probably at the coast by now. Waiting for the Navy pickup. The Reyes hit was done. Clean. Professional. Now Lawson was done too. Two targets. Two hits. Both successful. Price pulled out the encrypted radio and keyed the transmit button.

"Bravo to Alpha. Lawson is done. Clean exit. No complications."

Cole's voice came back immediately. "Copy. Good work. What's your exfil plan?"

"Commercial flight out of Reagan at 1100. We'll be back at Bragg by 1400."

"Copy. We'll see you there."

"Stay safe, Alpha One."

"Will do."

Price set the radio down and looked at Vail and Ward. They were exhausted. Wired. Coming down from the adrenaline. But they were alive. And the job was done. "Get some sleep," Price said. "We've got less than six hours before we need to be at the airport."

Ward nodded and stretched out on one of the beds. Vail turned off the television and closed his eyes. Price sat in the chair by the window and looked out at the Arlington skyline. Somewhere out there, in Georgetown, Robert Lawson's body was cooling on the floor of his study. In a few hours, someone would find him. The police would be called. An investigation would begin. And it would lead nowhere. Because Ghostline didn't leave trails.

Only bodies.

Chapter Twenty-Nine

F*riday March 22nd, 0900 Hours*
Arlington, Virginia

Price's watch alarm vibrated against his wrist. He opened his eyes and checked the time. 0900 hours. "Let's move," he said quietly. Ward and Vail were already awake, packing their bags in silence. They wiped down the hotel room, doorknobs, light switches, bathroom fixtures, removing any trace they'd been there.

At 0920, they checked out. The desk clerk barely looked at them. Just another group of business travelers leaving early. They drove to Reagan National Airport and returned the rental car. The attendant logged the mileage and handed Price a receipt. No questions. No problems.

At 0950, they checked in for their 1100 flight using false identification, business consultants returning to North Carolina after meetings in DC. The airport security agent glanced at their IDs and waved them through.

They found a quiet corner of the terminal and waited. Price bought coffee. Ward read a newspaper. Vail sat with his eyes closed, looking like any other exhausted businessman.

At 1045, they boarded the flight. Price took a window seat.

Vail sat beside him. Ward sat three rows back. The plane taxied to the runway and lifted off at 1103 hours.

Price looked out the window and watched Washington DC disappear below him. Somewhere down there, police were surrounding Lawson's townhouse. Investigators were photographing the scene.

A medical examiner was documenting the wound. And they were concluding it was suicide. Because that's what it looked like. That's what it was supposed to look like. Price closed his eyes and felt nothing. No guilt. No satisfaction. Just the hollow awareness that he'd done his job.

That's what they did. They eliminated threats. They protected national security. They operated in the shadows where the law couldn't reach.

And then they disappeared.

The flight landed at Fayetteville Regional Airport at 1310 hours. They collected their bags, rented a car, and drove to Fort Bragg. By 1500 hours, they were back on base.

Chapter Thirty

Friday, March 22nd, 0415 CST

Nicaraguan coast

Cole stood on the beach and felt the encrypted radio vibrate. He pulled it out and keyed the receive button.

"Bravo to Alpha. Lawson is done. Clean exit. No complications."

Cole checked his watch. 0415 Managua time. 0315 in DC. Right on schedule.

"Copy. Good work. What's the exfil plan?"

"Commercial flight out of Reagan at 1100. We'll be back at Bragg by 1400."

"Copy. We'll see you there."

"Stay safe, Alpha One."

"Will do."

Cole set the radio down and looked at his team. They were spread out along the beach, waiting for the Navy pickup. Riker sat on a piece of driftwood, field-stripping his Beretta. Torres stood at the water's edge, staring at the horizon. Hawke, Holt, Mason, Bishop, Draven, and Keller were checking their gear one last time. Nine men. Two operations. Both successful.

"Lawson's done," Cole said.

Nobody responded.

They'd known it was coming. Now it was confirmed. Two targets eliminated. Reyes in Managua. Lawson in Georgetown. Both hits clean. Both staged to look like something else. Nobody would connect the dots. Nobody would know the truth.

That was the point.

Cole checked his watch. 0420 hours. The Navy boat was due in one hour. Behind them, Managua was waking up. Police were surrounding the house in Los Robles. Investigators were photographing bodies. Someone was calling it a robbery.

In Georgetown, someone was about to discover Lawson's body. Police would be called. An investigation would begin. Someone would call it suicide. And by the time anyone thought to connect the two deaths, Ghostline would be gone.

"Radio check," Cole said quietly.

"Two is good," Draven replied from down the beach.

"Three is five by five," Bishop said.

"Bravo is good," Price's, Thanks for waking me up voice came through from DC, faint but clear.

Cole looked at the ocean. The water was black and endless. Somewhere out there, beyond the horizon, a Navy destroyer was waiting. They'd done their job. They'd executed the mission. They'd eliminated two threats to national security. And now they were going home.

0500 Hours

Cole's radio crackled. "All units, be advised, Nicaraguan

police bands are active. They found Reyes." Keller's voice was steady.

He was monitoring local communications from the vehicle parked fifty meters up the beach. "No mention of suspects. Sounds like they're treating it as a robbery."

"Copy," Cole said.

Riker looked up from the Beretta. "They buying it?"

"For now." They sat in silence for another twenty minutes. Cole could smell the ocean, salt and fish and wet sand. It reminded him of Coronado, of Surfing and beach parties as younger man, before the recruitment, of a time when things were simpler. That felt like a lifetime ago.

At 0519 hours, Keller spoke again. "I've got engine noise. Offshore." Cole moved to the water's edge and pulled out a small infrared strobe. He activated it and held it at waist level, pointed toward the ocean. Two minutes later, a rigid-hull inflatable boat or RHIB as they called it, materialized from the darkness. No running lights. Just the low rumble of an outboard motor and the white foam of its wake. The boat grounded on the sand.

A Navy petty officer in black fatigues nodded at Cole. "You Delta?"

"Yeah, something like that."

"Oookay then, Let's go." the petty officer, a Navy Seal understood not to ask any more questions. The team waded into the surf and climbed aboard. The petty officer just sat quietly, and counted heads, confirmed nine, and pushed off.

The outboard roared to life and they were moving, bouncing over the waves toward open water. Cole looked back once. The beach was already invisible, swallowed by darkness. At 0600, they reached the Navy vessel, a destroyer part of the carrier group, sitting dark and quiet in international waters. They climbed aboard via a rope ladder. A lieutenant met them on deck.

"Welcome aboard. You're secure."

Cole nodded. "Appreciate it."

The lieutenant gestured toward a hatch. "We've got bunks below. Food if you want it. We'll have you back in the States by tomorrow night." The team filed below deck. Nobody spoke until they were in the berthing area, door closed, alone. Then Riker sat down heavily on a bunk and let out a long breath. "Fuuuuck."

"Could not have said it better." Torres said.

Holt pulled off his boots. Mason checked his weapon one more time before setting it aside. Bishop sat with his back against the bulkhead, finally relaxing. Draven and Keller exchanged a look that didn't need words. Cole sat on the edge of a bunk and felt the tension drain out of his shoulders.

They'd done it and had no friendly or collateral casualties. He pulled out the radio one last time. "Price, Cole, you good?"

"We're good," Price replied. "Wheels up in seven hours. See you at Bragg."

"Copy."

Cole set down the radio and looked at his team. They were exhausted, wired, coming down from the adrenaline. Without the adrenaline the soreness started to creep in. But they were alive. "Good work," he said quietly. Riker nodded. Holt gave a slight smile. Torres closed his eyes. They'd done what they came to do.

In Managua, police surrounded the house in Los Robles. Investigators photographed the bodies, documented the scene, searched for evidence that would lead nowhere. The official report would call it a robbery. A tragedy. A senior commander murdered by common criminals. Nobody would mention America. Nobody would know the truth.

In Georgetown, a housekeeper arrived at 0800 hours and found Robert Lawson's body in his study. She screamed. She called 911. Police arrived within minutes. The scene was exactly what it appeared to be. A man alone in his study. A gun in his hand. A suicide note on the desk. Blood on the wall. The medical examiner would confirm it. Self-inflicted gunshot wound. No signs of struggle. No evidence of foul play. The official report would call it suicide. A tragedy. A man overwhelmed by career stress and personal problems. Nobody would mention treason. Nobody would mention Ghostline.

By morning, both stories would be buried under other news. Another casualty in Nicaragua. Another suicide in Washington. Tragedies, yes, but not unusual. And somewhere in the Atlantic, nine men slept the dreamless sleep of soldiers who'd completed their mission. This job was done.

But there would be another soon.

Chapter Thirty-One

F*RIDAY 0800 HOURS*
GEORGETOWN, WASHINGTON DC

Mrs. Patricia Morrison had worked for Robert Lawson for eight years. She knew his routines, his preferences, the way he liked his coffee. She knew when he was stressed, which was often, and when he needed space. She arrived at the Georgetown townhouse at precisely 0800 hours, same as always. Friday mornings were for deep cleaning. She had her own key. The front door was locked. Normal. She let herself in, set her purse on the entry table, and called out. "Mr. Lawson? It's Patricia."

No answer.

She walked through the first floor. Kitchen clean. Living room undisturbed. Everything in its place. His briefcase sat by the stairs where he always left it. She climbed to the second floor, her knees protesting. Getting old. She'd need to retire soon, maybe move closer to her daughter in Baltimore.

The study door was closed. "Mr. Lawson?" She knocked. Waited. Nothing. Patricia opened the door.

The scream came before she could stop it. High and sharp and full of a terror she'd never felt before. Her hand flew to her mouth. Her legs went weak.

Robert Lawson sat slumped in his desk chair, head tilted back, eyes open and empty. Blood on the wall behind him. Blood on the desk. A Colt Automatic in his right hand, finger still inside the trigger guard.

She stumbled backward into the hallway, fumbling for the phone on the desk. Her hands shook so badly she could barely dial. "911, what's your emergency?"

"He's—oh God—he's dead. There's blood. There's so much blood."

"Ma'am, I need you to stay calm. What's your location?"

Patricia gave the address, her voice breaking. The operator kept talking, kept asking questions, but Patricia couldn't focus. She could only see Mr. Lawson's face. The way his eyes stared at nothing.

Georgetown Police arrived at 0809 hours. Officers Hendricks and Martinez took the stairs two at a time, hands on their weapons. Hendricks cleared the study first. One look told him everything he needed to know. He'd seen suicides before. This one fit the pattern.

"Secure," he called down.

Martinez stayed with Mrs. Morrison in the living room while Hendricks examined the scene. He didn't touch anything. Just observed. Documented. Automatic pistol in the victim's hand. Military issue M1911 Colt .45 caliber. Contact wound to the right temple. Powder burns on the skin. Blood spatter consistent with self-inflicted gunshot. Typed suicide note on the desk, partially obscured by blood.

Hendricks read the note without touching it.

I can't do this anymore. The pressure. The lies. I'm sorry.

Short. Simple. Authentic.

By 0830 hours, the house was full of people. Crime scene techs. A medical examiner. Detectives from the Second District. And then, at 0847 hours, the FBI arrived.

Special Agent Catherine Marks showed her credentials to the detective in charge. "This is a federal matter. CIA employee. We're taking over." The detective didn't argue. Nobody argued with the FBI. Marks walked through the scene with the calm efficiency of someone who'd done this a hundred times. She examined the body, the weapon, the note. She asked questions. Took photographs.

"Who found him?"

"Housekeeper. Patricia Morrison. She's downstairs."

"Anyone else have access to the house?"

"Ex-wife, but they've been divorced for six months. She's in Connecticut with her sister."

Marks nodded. She pulled on latex gloves and carefully lifted the suicide note, reading it fully. Then she moved to Lawson's desk, opening drawers, examining files. Financial records showed mounting debt. Credit cards maxed out. Mortgage payments behind. Divorce settlement had cleaned him out. She found the divorce papers in the bottom drawer. Signed three months ago.

Custody battle over the kids. Messy. Expensive. Everything pointed to a man under unbearable pressure.

Medical Examiner Dr. Robert Chen arrived at 0915 hours.

He examined the body with clinical precision. Contact wound. Powder burns.

Stippling around the entry point. Trajectory consistent with self-inflicted injury. Rigor mortis just beginning. Time of death approximately 0200-0300 hours the previous night.

"Suicide," Chen said. "No question."

Marks interviewed Mrs. Morrison. The housekeeper was still shaking, still crying. She confirmed that Lawson had been depressed. Stressed. Drinking more than usual. She'd worried about him.

"Did he seem suicidal?"

"I don't know. Maybe. He was so sad all the time."

By 1145 hours, the FBI had everything they needed. Marks filed her preliminary report. Suicide. No signs of foul play. No evidence of forced entry. No indication of third-party involvement.

The case was closed by noon.

The Washington Post ran a small story on page six the next morning. CIA Official Dies in Apparent Suicide. Three paragraphs. No details. No speculation.

Just another tragedy in a city full of them.

Chapter Thirty-Two

Friday, 1320 Hours

Altamira Neighborhood, Managua

Maria Sanchez woke to pain. Her head throbbed. Her mouth tasted like copper. The light coming through the bedroom window was too bright, too harsh, and she squeezed her eyes shut against it.

Something was wrong.

She tried to remember. Tomás had come over Thursday night. They'd had wine. They'd talked. He'd been tense, distracted. Something about work. Something he couldn't discuss.

Then... nothing.

Maria opened her eyes slowly. The ceiling came into focus. Her ceiling. Her bedroom. She was lying on the floor beside the bed; her cheek pressed against the rug.

Why was she on the floor? She tried to sit up. The room spun. Her stomach lurched. She pressed a hand to the side of her head and felt a tender spot above her left ear. Not bleeding. Just sore. What happened? She pushed herself up to her knees, breathing hard, fighting the nausea. The bedroom looked wrong. Drawers pulled open. Jewelry box overturned on the dresser. Her things scattered across the floor.

"Tomás?"

Her voice came out hoarse. Weak. That's when she saw him. Commander Tomás Reyes lay on the floor three feet away, on his back, his eyes open and staring at nothing.

Two dark holes in his chest, one in the center of his forehead. Blood soaked into the rug beneath him, dried now, dark and thick.

Maria's breath caught. "No."

"Noooo." She crawled toward him, her hands shaking. "Tomás? Tomás, wake up. Please wake up."

She touched his face. Cold. Stiff.

Dead.

Maria pulled her hand back like she'd been burned. Her mind raced, trying to piece it together. The wine. The conversation. Then... darkness. Someone had been here. Someone had...

They'd knocked her out.

She looked around the bedroom again, seeing it differently now. The drawers weren't just open; they had been searched. Methodically. Professionally. The jewelry box wasn't just overturned, it was empty. Her watch was gone. The cash she kept in the nightstand. Everything valuable.

Staged.

The word came to her unbidden. This wasn't a robbery. This was made to look like a robbery.

Maria's stomach heaved.

She turned away from Tomás's body and vomited on the floor, her whole body shaking. When she could breathe again, she looked at him one more time. His shirt was half-unbuttoned. His hand was near the nightstand, like he'd been reaching for something. The gun he kept in the drawer.

He'd tried to fight.

And they'd killed him. Maria started screaming.

Captain Hector Morales of the Nicaraguan National Police arrived at 1355 hours with four officers and a forensics team. A neighbor had called it in, screaming from the Sanchez house. Hysterical screaming that wouldn't stop.

When Morales entered the bedroom, he found Maria Sanchez sitting against the wall, her knees pulled to her chest, rocking back and forth. Her eyes were red. Her face was pale. She kept saying the same thing over and over.

"They shot him. They shot him. They shot him."

Commander Tomás Reyes lay on the floor beside the bed, two bullets in his chest, one in his head. Dead for hours. Rigor mortis fully set in. Time of death sometime between 2200 and 2400 hours the previous night. Four bodyguards were dead throughout the house. Rounds center mass. Very Professional.

The safe in the study was open. Cash gone. Jewelry gone. Watches, rings, anything valuable.

"Robbery," one of the officers said.

Morales wasn't so sure. The scene was too clean. Too efficient. Robbers didn't move like this. Didn't kill like this. But orders were orders.

By 1600 hours, the house was swarming with investigators. Military intelligence. Sandinista officials. Everyone wanted answers. Everyone wanted someone to blame. Morales walked through the scene again. The bodyguards had been taken by surprise. No signs of struggle. No defensive wounds. Just quick, efficient executions. The bedroom showed more violence. Reyes had reached for a weapon on the nightstand. Hadn't made it. The woman, his mistress,

Maria Sanchez, had been incapacitated. Blunt force trauma to the head. Not fatal. Just enough to keep her unconscious while they worked.

"Find me suspects," a colonel told Morales. "By tonight."

Morales knew what that meant. Find someone. Anyone. Make the problem go away. By 1800 hours, they had three names. Local criminals with records. Burglary. Assault. Armed robbery. They'd been planning a job across town, a jewelry store, but couldn't prove it. No alibi. No witnesses.

Close enough.

The arrests happened at 2030 hours. Three men dragged from their homes, protesting their innocence. Nobody listened. Nobody cared. By Saturday morning, the case was officially solved. Three criminals. A robbery gone wrong. A tragedy, but not unusual in a country at war. The official report made no mention of nefarious actions.

Just another crime in a city full of them.

Chapter Thirty-Three

Friday, 1045 Hours

Reagan National Airport, DC

Price walked through the terminal like any other businessman. Dark suit. Leather briefcase. Wall Street Journal under his arm. He'd shaved in the hotel, showered, changed clothes. Nothing about him suggested he'd executed a man six hours ago.

He checked in for his flight to Charlotte. The gate agent smiled. "Have a nice flight, Mr. Patterson."

"Thank you."

He found a seat near the window and opened the newspaper. The Lawson story wasn't in it yet. Too soon. By tomorrow, maybe. A small article. A footnote. Price thought about the operation. The approach through the garden. The lock on the back door. The carpeted stairs. Lawson's face when he'd turned around. The recognition. The terror. Lawson's own Colt .45 had been loud, louder than Price would have preferred, but the concrete walls had done their job. The sound was muffled, contained. Lawson had dropped like a puppet with cut strings.

Staging the scene had taken three minutes. The Automatic in hand. Suicide note positioned. Blood spatter managed. Every detail perfect. Price had never assassinated a man before. He was good with it; he had to be.

He was sure he would have to do it again, hopefully not another American He looked around the terminal.

Families, businessmen, and students. Normal people living normal lives. None of them knew what he'd done. None of them would ever know.

That was the job.

His flight boarded at 1050 hours. The plane departed at 1110 a late departure, climbing into the gray March sky. Two hours later, they touched down at Fayetteville Regional Airport. Vail and Ward were doing the same thing. Different flights. Different routes. All of them converging on Fort Bragg by 1400 hours.

Price landed at 1310 hours. An unmarked sedan was waiting in the parking lot. No conversation. Just a silent drive to the base. He thought about Cole and the Nicaragua team. Wondered if they'd made it out clean. Wondered if the operation had gone as planned.

He'd know soon enough.

The sedan pulled through the Pope AFB gate at 1407 hours. Vail's car was already there. Ward arrived ten minutes later. They didn't speak. Didn't acknowledge each other. Just waited for the Nicaragua team to arrive. The job wasn't done until everyone was home. Time to clean up and get some rest.

Chapter Thirty-Four

Sunday March 24th, 1440, Hours EDT

Pope Air Force Base, North Carolina

The C-130 touched down at Pope Air force Base. Cole felt the wheels hit, felt the aircraft shudder as the pilot reversed thrust. Through the small window, he could see the familiar landscape of Fort Bragg. Home.

The ramp dropped. Cold North Carolina air rushed in. Cole stood, grabbed his gear, and walked down the ramp into the gray afternoon. The rest of the team followed. An unmarked truck waited on the tarmac for them. No markings. No escort. The driver didn't speak. He just drove them back to Fort Bragg through the late afternoon traffic. The base was quiet. Friday afternoon. Most soldiers were thinking about the weekend. About beer and football and time away from the grind. Cole watched the familiar buildings pass by and felt nothing. No relief. No satisfaction. Just the hollow awareness that they'd crossed a line that couldn't be uncrossed.

The truck stopped outside a nondescript building on the edge of the Delta compound. They filed inside, carrying their gear, moving with the mechanical efficiency of men who'd done this a hundred times. The armory was first. Weapons had to be cleaned, inspected, logged. Cole field-stripped his Beretta, cleaned every component, reassembled it. The ritual was calming. Familiar. Hawke turned in his rifle. Riker his sidearm. One by one, the team processed through.

"Any issues?" the armorer asked.

"None," Cole said. "Everything functioned perfectly these need to be destroyed."

The armorer nodded his understanding.

Next was gear sanitization. Mission-specific items had to be destroyed. The suppressor Cole had used. The lock picks. The gloves. Anything that could be traced back to Nicaragua.

They burned what was flammable in a barrel behind the building and crushed everything else and then had it buried or thrown into McKeller Lake.

Medical checks were last. Bishop examined each operator. Blood pressure. Heart rate. Visual inspection for injuries.

"You're good," Bishop said to Cole. "No issues."

"Thanks."

By 1645 hours, they were done. Everyone accounted for. Zero casualties. Zero complications. The Nicaragua team and the DC team gathered in a staging area. Price nodded at Cole. Cole nodded back. No words necessary. Both teams mission complete. Now came the debrief.

Sunday, 1700 Hours

Fort Bragg, North Carolina

Harrow was waiting in the briefing room with coffee and folders.

He looked tired. Older than he had a week ago. Running black operations aged you fast. "Sit," he said. They sat. Twelve men. Alpha team and Bravo team. All of them exhausted. All of them processing what they'd done. Harrow opened the first folder. "Reyes is officially a robbery victim.

Nicaraguan police have three suspects in custody, local criminals with priors. They'll probably convict someone by the end of the month. The Sandinistas are satisfied. The Soviets are suspicious but have no proof."

He opened the second folder. "Lawson is officially a suicide. Single gunshot to the right temple, his own weapon. Suicide note was found. The FBI investigated. Medical examiner confirmed self-inflicted wound. The Agency is treating it as a personal tragedy, career stress, divorce, financial problems. His ex-wife is devastated. They're planning a quiet funeral next week." Cole nodded. Riker stared at the table. Torres drank his coffee. Price sat perfectly still, his face unreadable.

"Any complications during the ops?" Harrow asked.

"No sir," Cole said. "Everything went as planned."

"Injuries?"

"None."

"Equipment issues?"

"None."

"Witnesses?"

"None that matter," Price said. "Scene was clean."

Harrow studied them for a long moment.

The silence stretched. Outside, a helicopter flew over. Inside, nobody moved. "You did good work," Harrow finally said. "Clean, professional, no trace. That's what this unit is supposed to be. That's what Ghostline is."

Nobody responded.

Harrow leaned back in his chair. "I know what you're thinking. You executed two men who weren't shooting at you. Men who didn't know you were coming. That sits different than combat."

"That sits different than anything you've done before."

"We're good, sir," Riker said quietly.

"I know you are. But I also know what this costs." Harrow looked at each of them in turn. "You didn't sign up for this. You guys were recruited to take out Cartel leadership and drug pipelines. You knew what it was. But knowing and doing are different things.

Knowing you can kill a man in his bedroom is different than actually doing it. Knowing you can stage a suicide is different than actually pulling the trigger."

Cole met his eyes. "We did the job."

"You did." Harrow closed the folders and stood, walking to the window. He stared out at the compound for a long moment before turning back. "And now I need to tell you something. Something that changes the game."

The room went still.

Harrow walked back to the table. "When we started this, Ghostline was blacker than black.

Nobody knew you existed, not Congress, not the Joint Chiefs, not even most of the intelligence community. You were a ghost story that didn't exist on any organizational chart or budget line."

He paused. "That's changed. You're not completely black now. Two people know you exist: the National Security Advisor and Deputy Director of Intelligence Carmichael. They don't know your names, your faces, or operational details. But they know there's a unit."

"They know what you can do. Out of the black and into the grey"

"Who controls us?" Price asked, his voice careful.

"I do," Harrow said flatly. "They provide resources and intelligence. They advise the President. But they don't approve missions. They don't task you. I do. That hasn't changed."

Cole felt something heavy settle in his chest. "We're not a hundred precent deniable anymore?"

"Publicly, you don't exist. If you get caught, we disavow. If you are KIA, we deny. That hasn't changed." Harrow's knuckles went white on the table edge. "But internally, at the highest levels, you're known. And that's dangerous."

"How?" Vail asked.

“People in Washington talk. They leak. They have agendas. If someone decides you're a liability or a bargaining chip, they can burn you. They can't prove you exist, but they know."

The gravity of that settled over the room.

"This wasn't supposed to happen," Harrow continued.

"Ghostline was supposed to stay black. But after Nicaragua and Lawson, people started asking questions. They wanted to know what capability eliminated those threats so cleanly. Eventually, they got answers."

"Who told them?" Riker asked.

"Doesn't matter.' Came Harrows repl. “What matters is the rules have changed."

"What does this mean for operations?" Price asked.

"More of them. A lot more. When there's a problem that can't be handled through normal channels, Washington knows there's a solution. They'll try to use you frequently. Could be once a month. Could be once a week. Could be multiple operations simultaneously.

I won’t let you get burnt out. I can tell them to pound

sand. I cannot tell the President that. If he wants it, we do it."

Hawke leaned forward. "What kind of problems?"

"The kind that threaten American interests. The kind that need to disappear." Harrow straightened. "You're not soldiers anymore. You're a whisper. You appear, eliminate the target, disappear. No trace. No connection to the United States government."

"And if we want out?" Mason asked.

Harrow's expression went hard. "You can get out. Leave the military, transfer to the conventional Army, your choice. If you're wounded beyond operational capacity, same options, transfer out or medical discharge. But understand this: you know too much. You've done too much. If you walk away and become a problem, if you talk, if you leak information.

If you compromise what we do, you become a target. There are other units. Other capabilities. None as good as you guys. You know that."

The silence was absolute. Cole understood. They'd crossed a threshold. They were grey, acknowledged internally, denied publicly. It gave them resources but made them vulnerable. Being known, even in the shadows, was dangerous.

Harrow picked up the folders. "Take seventy-two hours. Clear your heads. Stay on base or go wherever. When you come back, we'll start planning the next one. There's already a target list. Washington is very pleased with your work. They want more." He walked out, leaving them alone in the briefing room.

For a long moment, nobody spoke. Then Riker stood up. "Seventy-two hours. I'm gonna sleep for about forty-eight of them."

"Yeah," Torres said. "And drink through the other twenty-four."

A few people smiled, but it was the kind of smile that didn't reach the eyes. They filed out one by one. Price, Vail, and Ward headed to the armory to turn in their remaining gear. Mason and Holt went to debrief with Bishop about the medical equipment. Draven and Keller disappeared toward the communications building.

Cole stayed in the briefing room, staring at the empty table. He thought about Reyes in the bedroom, reaching for the weapon on the nightstand. The way his body had jerked when the bullet hit. The sound of him hitting the floor. He thought about Lawson in his Georgetown townhouse. The staged suicide. The gun in his hand. The note on the desk. Price's cold efficiency.

Two men. Erased because they leaked information and tried to eliminate his team. Cole didn't feel guilty. He felt aware. This was what they did now.

This was what they were.

Chapter Thirty-Five

Sunday, 1830 Hours

Fort Bragg, North Carolina

The team dispersed like smoke. Riker and Torres headed to the NCO club. They needed beer and noise and the company of other soldiers who didn't ask questions.

"First round's on me," Torres said.

"First five rounds are on you," Riker replied. "I just helped Murder a guy in his bedroom in a foreign country. I need to get drunk."

"Fair enough."

They found a corner booth and ordered whiskey. Didn't talk much. Just drank and watched the other soldiers laugh and joke and live their normal lives.

"You think about it?" Torres asked after the third drink.

"About what?"

"What we did."

Riker stared at his glass. "Yeah. I think about it."

"And?"

"And I don't know what I think. I did the fucking job. That's all."

Torres nodded. That was enough.

Mason and Bishop went to the gym. They needed to move. Needed to sweat. Needed to burn off the adrenaline that still hummed in their veins. Mason hit the heavy bag. Hard. Fast. Methodical. Each punch a release. Bishop ran on the treadmill. Mile after mile. Pushing until his legs burned and his lungs screamed. Neither of them talked. They didn't need to.

Hawke sat in his barracks room and wrote a letter home. Carefully vague. Craftily edited.

Dear Dad,

Training is going well. Can't talk about specifics, but I'm learning a lot. The team is solid. Good guys. We look out for each other.

I'm safe. Don't worry about me. I'll call when I can.

Love, Trevor

He sealed the envelope and set it aside. His Father would read between the lines. He always did. But he wouldn't ask questions. He knew better.

Price sat alone in his quarters, staring at the wall. He'd shot men before. Not often. But enough to know the weight of it. Killing in combat was one thing. The enemy was shooting back. It was survival. It was war. This was different. This was execution. This was murder dressed up as necessity. Price didn't regret it. Lawson had been a threat.

A leak. A problem that needed solving. But he felt it.

The pressure of it. The knowledge that he'd crossed a line most people never even saw. He thought about his Pastor. The talk that they had. Was he becoming what the pastor suggested he become, he thought, or was he becoming something unthinkable. Would he be proud? Would he understand?

Price didn't know. Didn't matter. The job was done.

Sunday, 2100 Hours

Keller and Draven sat in the communications room, monitoring traffic. Radio intercepts. Satellite feeds. The endless flow of intelligence that kept operations running.

"Soviet embassy in Managua is lighting up," Keller said, adjusting his headset. "Increased radio traffic. Encrypted, but the volume is way up."

Draven pulled up the intercept logs. "They're requesting additional security. Major Federov, remember him from the briefing? He's asking for more personnel. More weapons. More surveillance."

"They know something happened."

"They suspect. But they don't know. Not for sure."

Keller switched frequencies. Nicaraguan military channels. More chatter. More activity. Units on alert. Patrols increased.

"They're spooked," Draven said.

"Good. They should be fucking spooked."

A secure message came through from Langley. Keller decoded it, read it twice, then handed it to Draven.

"CIA assessment: Soviets suspect American involvement but have no proof.

Nicaraguan government satisfied with robbery explanation. Operation considered successful. No blowback expected."

Draven nodded. "Washington's happy."

"Washington's always happy when problems disappear."

Another message came through. This one marked EYES ONLY - HARROW.

Keller printed it and walked it down the hall to

Harrow's office. The colonel was still there, still working, still planning. "Colonel. From Langley."

Harrow read the message. His expression didn't change. He just nodded and filed it away. "Thank you, Keller."

"Roger that."

Keller left. Harrow sat alone in his office, staring at the message. Next target identified. Briefing materials to follow. Prepare team for deployment within 14 days. The machine didn't stop. It never stopped. Harrow opened his desk drawer and pulled out a bottle of bourbon. Poured two fingers. Drank it slowly. He thought about the men under his command. Good men. Professional. skilled. Loyal. He was turning them into something else. Something necessary. Something dangerous. He poured another drink. Outside, the base was quiet. Inside, Harrow sat alone with his choices.

2300 *Hours*

Cole lay on his bunk, staring at the ceiling. Sleep wouldn't come. His mind kept working. Kept replaying. The courtyard guards. The interior kills. Reyes reaching for his weapon. The mistress's scream. Price in Georgetown. Lawson's staged suicide. The precision. The coldness. Simultaneous operations. Both successful. Both clean. Cole waited for the guilt.

Waited for the regret. Waited for something. It didn't come. It never would. He felt... nothing. Not pride. Not shame. Just awareness. This was the job. This was what they did. This was what they were. He thought about the next target. The one after that. The one after that. Wondered where this ended. Wondered if it would end. Realizing it might not. He made peace with that. This was Ghostline. This was what they did. They appeared. They eliminated the problem. They disappeared.

No trace. No evidence. No connection. Farts in the wind, he thought and then smiled. Cole closed his eyes. Sleep still wouldn't come. But that was okay. He'd learned to function without a lot of it. Outside, the base was quiet. Inside, Cole lay awake and thought about nothing in particular. In seventy-two hours, they'd be back. And there would be another target. Another mission. Another name in a folder.

Deep breath in and long exhale.

What would his mom think of what her baby boy had become he wondered. His older brother was serving time for bank robbery.

Everyone thought he was the black sheep of the family, maybe he was, or maybe, just maybe they were looking at the wrong person.

Chapter Thirty-Six

M*onday, March 25th, 0600 Hours*
Fort Bragg, North Carolina

Cole ran alone in the pre-dawn darkness. Five miles. Same route he always ran. The rhythm was calming. Familiar.

He passed other soldiers. Some running P.T. Some heading to the chow hall. Normal Saturday morning on a military base. None of them knew what he'd done. None of them would ever know. He saw Riker running the opposite direction. They high fived. Kept running. He saw Torres at the pull-up bars. Hawke on the track. Mason leaving the gym.

None of them had slept much. None of them could. That was the cost. The weight. The knowledge that they'd crossed a line and couldn't go back.

Cole finished his run and walked back to the barracks. The sun was starting to rise. The base was awake. He looked toward the command building. Harrow's office light was on. Still working. Still planning. Still building the machine.

Harrow sat at his desk, secure phone to his ear. "Understood," he said. "How soon do you need us ready?" A pause. He listened.

"We can be wheels-up in Seventy-two hours." Another pause. "Yes sir. We'll be ready." He hung up and sat back in his chair. On his desk was a photograph. Younger version of himself in a different uniform. Vietnam. 1968. A lifetime ago. He'd built something here. Something dangerous. Something necessary. Something that couldn't be stopped. He opened a new folder on his desk. Surveillance photos.

Intelligence reports. Target assessment. A new name. A new location. A new problem that needed solving. Ghostline's work was just beginning. Harrow looked at the photograph again. Wondered what that younger version of himself would think. Wondered if he'd understand. Decided it didn't matter. The phone would ring again. It always did.

And he would answer.

Chapter Thirty-Seven

Part Two

"In war, there are no unwounded soldiers"
-Jose Narosky

M*arch 25th, 1430, Hours*

The hangar sat at the far edge of the Delta compound, behind two checkpoints and a fence that didn't appear on any base map. Cole and his team made it feel like a home, mainly because it was where they spent most of their time when not deployed.

The team filed in through the side door. A cacophony of conversation and bullshitting. Boots on concrete and the metallic echo of the hangar's empty space. Someone had set up folding chairs in a semicircle facing a table with a projector and a stack of folders. Cole took a seat in the second row. Vail sat next to him. Riker and Torres filled in behind them. Hawke was last through the door, moving like there was no place he'd rather be but with a cup of black coffee. Which is why he was the last to arrive and take a seat. He dropped into a chair at the end of the row and crossed his arms and drank his coffee.

"Three days," Keller muttered. "Couldn't even give us a week."

"Could've given us three hours," Vail said.

"Don't give them any fucking ideas."

The rest of the team settled in. Price and Ward sat up front.

Draven and Keller took the back row, Keller already pulling out a small notebook. Mason and Holt flanked the group, Bishop between them looking more rested than he had in Nicaragua. The hangar door opened and Colonel Harrow walked in. He didn't look tired. He looked like a man who'd spent three days in meetings with people who didn't sleep and didn't accept excuses. He set a briefcase on the table and opened it without preamble. "Nicaragua's done," Harrow said. "Reyes is dead. Lawson's dead. The leak is plugged. Washington's happy. The President's happy. You did good work."

He pulled out a stack of aerial recon photos and spread them across the table. "Now we deal with the other problem." Cole leaned forward slightly. So did everyone else. Harrow picked up one of the photos. It showed a compound from above, buildings, vehicles, and what looked like aircraft hangars.

"Colombia," Harrow said. "Fifty miles south of Bogotá. This is a Soviet forward operating base. They've been running support operations for communist insurgents throughout South and Central America. Weapons. Training. Logistics. And air support." He tapped the photo. "Hind helicopters. The same kind you encountered in Nicaragua." The room went quiet. Cole remembered the Hind. The sound of its rotors. The way it had torn through the jungle canopy before the crew chief put a rocket up its ass.

"How many?" Vail asked.

"At least four confirmed," Harrow said. "Possibly six.

They're pulling them into hangars during the day to avoid satellite detection. The Soviets know our orbital schedules. They've been timing their movements accordingly."

"Smart," Draven said. "It was," Harrow agreed. "Until the NRO changed the schedule at DDI Carmichaels request. We've got new imagery coming in at irregular intervals. Caught them off guard two days ago."

He laid out another photo. This one showed two Hinds sitting on a tarmac in broad daylight, rotors folded, ground crews working around them. "The President wants this stopped," Harrow said. "Soviet presence in South America is a direct threat to U.S. interests. They're trying to expand communism close to our homeland. Supporting rebels. Propping up dictators. Turning the region into another Cold War front." He looked at each of them in turn. "The President's directive is clear. Send a message. Make it loud. Make it permanent. No more Soviet foothold in Central or South America."

Cole felt the seriousness of that settle over the room. This wasn't about plugging a leak or eliminating a traitor. This was about geopolitics. About drawing a line in the dirt and daring someone to cross it. "What's the mission?" Price asked.

Harrow pulled out another set of photos. These showed the compound in more detail, guard towers, vehicle depots, barracks, a command building. "You're going to destroy the base," Harrow said. "Kill the officers running the operation.

Three colonels and one general. All Soviet military

intelligence. All directly involved in supporting communist insurgencies."

"How do we get in?" Torres asked. "HAHO insertion," Harrow said. "You'll deploy via C-130 on a routine resupply run.

The crew won't know who you are or why you're on board. The loadmaster will know you're jumping. That's it. The less they know, the less they can say if anyone asks."

"Where do we land?" Keller asked. "Safe house twenty miles north of the target. Already established. Fully stocked. Weapons, comms, medical supplies. Everything you need." Harrow laid out a map of the region. "You'll conduct surveillance. Identify patterns. Confirm the targets. Then you hit the base. Hard and fast. Destroy the helicopters. Kill the officers. Leave nothing operational."

"Exfil?" Cole asked.

"Aircraft carrier off the coast. USS Ranger. You'll move to the coast after the mission. Navy SEALs will extract you and bring you to the carrier. From there, you'll redeploy to San Diego when the carrier docks. Commercial flights back to Bragg."

Vail frowned. "That's a long exfil."

"It's a secure exfil," Harrow said. "And it gives us plausible deniability. No direct flights out of Colombia. No military transport that can be traced. You disappear into the Pacific and come home like tourists."

"Tourists with guns," Hawke muttered.

Harrow shook his head and ignored him and picked up another photo. This one showed a Hind up close, rotors spinning, side doors open. "There's a secondary objective," Harrow said. "If the opportunity arises, we want one of those helicopters."

The room went still. "You want us to steal a Hind?"

Bishop asked joyfully. "If possible," Harrow said. "Fly it to the carrier. We'll store it below deck and bring it back to the States for inspection. Intel wants to know what the Soviets have been upgrading. Weapons systems. Avionics. Armor. Everything." Bishop stared at the photo. "I've never flown a Hind. But then I never flew anything until I stole my dad's crop duster." He joked

"You will," Harrow said. "We're bringing in a Russian language expert. You've got seventy-two hours to learn how to read Cyrillic well enough to start the aircraft and fly it. You don't need to be fluent. You just need to not crash."

"Comforting," Bishop said. "You're the best pilot we have," Harrow said. "Hell, you're the only pilot we have. If anyone can do it, it's you."

Bishop nodded slowly. He looked confident. He looked determined.

That was enough. Bishop stood up to leave. He had to think about this as he exited the room.

"What's the timeline?" Cole asked.

"You deploy in seventy-two hours," Harrow said. "Insertion at night. You'll have five days on the ground to conduct surveillance and plan the assault. Hit the base on day six. Exfil immediately after. The carrier will be in position."

"What if the opportunity to steal the Hind doesn't arise?" Draven asked.

"Then you destroy them all and complete the primary mission," Harrow said.

"The helicopter is secondary. The officers and the base are the priority."

He closed the briefcase and looked at them. "This is bigger than Nicaragua," he said. "This isn't about one traitor or one leak. This is about Soviet expansion in our backyard.

The President wants the message sent. You're going to send it."

Cole felt the shift in the room. The team was excited about this one. It was a problem that needed solving. This was strategic. A move on a chessboard that stretched across continents.

"Questions?" Harrow asked.

"Rules of engagement?" Price asked.

"Anyone on that base is a combatant," Harrow said. "Soviet military. Cuban advisors. Local insurgents. You engage anyone who gets in your way. No prisoners. No witnesses."

"What about collateral?" Ward asked.

"There won't be any," Harrow said. "The base is isolated. No civilians within ten miles. It's a military target. You have full authorization."

Vail leaned back in his chair. "What happens if this goes sideways?"

"It won't," Harrow said. "But if it does?" Vail pushed.

Harrow met his eyes. "Then its S.O.P, you disappear. Same as always. No rescue.

No acknowledgment. You're ghosts. Act like it." Nobody said anything. That was the deal. That had always been the deal.

"Anything else?" Harrow asked. Silence. "Good," Harrow continued. "Bishop, you're with me. We're meeting the language expert in thirty minutes.

The rest of you, start prepping. Gear check at 0600 tomorrow. Full mission brief at 1200. Wheels up in seventy-two hours. For Christ sakes where is Bishop"

"Outside." Keller said

He picked up the briefcase and walked toward the door.

"Cole," he said without turning around. "A word."

Cole stood and followed him outside.

The afternoon sun was bright and hot. The hangar cast a long shadow across the tarmac. Bishop was against the hanger smoking.

Harrow stopped and turned to face Cole.

"You good?" he asked.

"Yeah."

"This is different than Nicaragua," Harrow said. "Bigger stakes.

More variables. A lot can go wrong."

"I know."

"The helicopter's a gamble," Harrow said. "If Bishop can't fly it, don't force it. Complete the primary mission and get out."

"Understood."

Harrow studied him for a moment. "The President's watching this one. So is the National Security Advisor. So is the Carmichael. They want to know if Ghostline can handle something this big."

"We can."

"I know you can," Harrow said. "That's why you're going. But don't get cocky. The Soviets aren't Reyes. They're trained. They're disciplined. And they'll bury you if you give them the chance."

"We won't."

Harrow nodded. "Good. Get your team ready. This one matters." He walked away, heading toward the command building. Yelled at Bishop to follow him. Cole stood there for a moment, watching them go. Then he turned and walked back into the hangar. The team was still sitting in their chairs, talking quietly. Planning. Already thinking three steps ahead. Cole sat down next to Vail.

"What'd he say?" Vail asked.

"Don't fuck it up."

"Now that's some solid fucking advice."

Torres leaned forward from the row behind them. "So, we're stealing a helicopter."

"If we can," Cole said.

"Bishop's gonna crash it," Hawke said.

"Probably," Riker agreed.

Bishop, who'd left with Harrow, wasn't there to defend himself. "He'll figure it out," Cole said. "He always does."

Draven stood and stretched. "Seventy-two hours.

We should start going over the reconnaissance imagery. I want to know every inch of that compound before we jump."

"Agreed," Keller said. "I'll set up comms in the planning room. We'll need to coordinate with the carrier and the NRO for real-time intel."

"I'll handle weapons," Price said. "We're gonna need more firepower than Nicaragua. Those Hinds have armor. We'll need LAWs. Maybe Stingers if we can get them."

"I'll talk to Harrow," Riker said.

The team started moving, already shifting into mission mode. Cole stayed in his chair for a moment, looking at the satellite photos still spread across the table. Three colonels. One general. Four to six Hind helicopters. A Soviet base in the middle of Colombia. This wasn't about cleaning up a mess. This was about starting a fight. We are good at that Cole Thought to himself. He stood and walked over to the table. Picked up one of the Satellite photos. Studied the compound. Somewhere in Colombia, Soviet officers were planning their next move. Training insurgents. Coordinating attacks. Expanding their influence one operation at a time. They had no idea what was coming. Or maybe they did and this was a trap. Cole set the photo down and walked toward the door.

In seventy-two hours, they'd be in the air. And in less than a week, that Soviet base would be a smoking fucking crater. This is exactly what this team was designed for. Cole stepped out into the sunlight, lit a cigarette, and headed toward the barracks. Three days wasn't much time.

But it was enough.

Chapter Thirty-Eight

The rental sedan rolled to a stop outside Hangar 97 at exactly 1400 hours. Cole watched from the doorway as a man climbed out, maybe fifty, gray hair buzzed to a quarter inch, wearing pressed khakis and a navy polo that stretched across shoulders that hadn't gone soft. The man moved with the deliberate economy of someone who'd learned that wasted motion could get you killed. He pulled a scuffed leather briefcase from the passenger seat, the kind that had seen a dozen countries and twice as many operations and walked toward the hangar with his head on a swivel, scanning the flight line like he was still operating in denied territory.

Harrow met him at the door. They shook hands, brief, professional. Spoke quietly for thirty seconds, Harrow gesturing toward the interior of the hangar. Then Harrow turned and led him inside.

The hangar was stifling. The afternoon sun had been beating on the corrugated metal roof since noon, and even with both bay doors open, the air hung thick and motionless. The concrete floor radiated heat. Somewhere in the back, a fan rattled uselessly. Cole could feel sweat gathering at the small of his back, soaking into his t-shirt.

"This is Yuri Volkov," Harrow said, his voice echoing slightly in the cavernous space. "Former GRU. Defected in '79 through West Berlin. He's been consulting for us ever since."

Volkov set his briefcase on the folding table they'd set up near the center of the hangar and looked directly at Bishop. His eyes were pale blue, almost colorless, and they didn't blink. "You're the pilot."

Bishop straightened. "Yes, sir."

"You speak any Russian?"

"No, sir."

"Good." Volkov's expression didn't change. "Means I don't have to waste time fixing bad habits." He unlatched the briefcase, the clasps made sharp metallic clicks that carried in the empty hangar and pulled out a stack of laminated cards bound with a rubber band, a spiral notebook with a red cover, and what looked like a Soviet technical manual, its cover worn and stained, Cyrillic text stamped in faded black ink. "We have seventy-two hours. You won't be fluent. You won't even be conversational. But you'll be able to read the critical gauges, understand the primary controls, and not kill yourself trying to start the engines."

"That's the goal," Bishop said. His voice was steady, but Cole could see the tension in his shoulders.

"Sit." Volkov pointed at one of the metal folding chairs.

Bishop sat. The chair scraped against the concrete.

Volkov pulled the rubber band off the laminated cards and selected the first one. He held it up. a high-resolution photograph of a Mi-24D cockpit, every gauge and switch labelled in Cyrillic script. "This is a Mi-24D. NATO designation: Hind-D. Gunship variant. Standard crew is two, pilot in the rear seat, weapons officer in front. You'll be flying solo, which means you need to know both stations."

He tapped the photo with a blunt finger. "We start with the basics. Collective. Cyclic. Pedals. Throttle. Same principles as any helicopter, but the layout is different. The Soviets don't think like we do."

He pointed at specific controls in the photograph. "This is высота. Altitude. This is скорость. Airspeed. This is топливо. Fuel." He looked at Bishop. "Repeat."

Bishop repeated the words. They came out awkward, the sounds unfamiliar in his mouth. "Vysota. Skorost. Toplivo."

"Again."

Bishop said them again, slower this time, trying to get the pronunciation right.

"You're going to say each word five hundred times before we're done," Volkov said. "Maybe a thousand. By the time you climb into that cockpit, you won't have to think. You'll just know. Muscle memory. Visual recognition. The conscious mind is too slow when things go wrong."

He pulled out another card. This one showed a detailed sequence of switches and levers, numbered in order. "This is how you don't blow yourself up during engine start. The Isotov TV3-117 turboshafts are reliable, but the startup sequence is unforgiving. You skip a step or do them out of order, you'll cook the turbines or flood the combustion chamber. Either way, you're not flying anywhere."

By 1600 hours, Bishop's head was pounding.

Volkov had him reading Cyrillic characters repeatedly, writing them in the notebook until his hand cramped, matching them to their English equivalents.

The alphabet itself wasn't the problem, thirty-three letters, most of them phonetic. The problem was that half of them looked like English letters but meant something completely different, and Bishop's brain kept trying to read them wrong.

"This is B," Volkov said, tapping the notebook where Bishop had written it. "Looks like a capital B. Sounds like a V. This is H. Looks like an N. Sounds like an N. This is P. Looks like a P. Sounds like an R. You see the problem."

"Yeah," Bishop said. His voice was hoarse. "My brain wants to read it in English."

"So, we reprogram your brain." Volkov tapped the notebook again. "Write it again. All thirty-three characters. Fifty times each. Uppercase and lowercase."

Bishop wrote. His handwriting got sloppier as he went, the letters bleeding together. Sweat dripped off his nose and spotted the paper.

At 1700, Vail stuck his head through the side door. "You good?"

"Peachy," Bishop said without looking up. His hand was still moving, forming Cyrillic letters in neat rows.

"We're doing a full gear check at 1800 if you want in."

"I'll be there."

Vail looked at Volkov, then at the stack of flashcards and notebooks covering the table, the technical manual open to a page showing the Hind's hydraulic systems. "Jesus Christ."

"Three days," Volkov said. He didn't look up from the card he was preparing. "He'll know enough."

"Enough to fly it?"

"Enough not to crash it immediately." Volkov's expression might have been a smile. It was hard to tell. "After that, it depends on how good he actually is."

"That's real comforting," Bishop muttered.

Vail left. Bishop kept writing. The fan rattled. The heat pressed down.

At 1800 hours, the rest of the team was in the equipment room on the second floor of the hangar's attached office building.

The room was smaller than the hangar, maybe thirty by forty feet, with cinder block walls painted tiring beige and fluorescent lights that hummed overhead. It smelled like gun oil and canvas and the faint chemical tang of cosmoline.

Price had everything laid out on a long folding table that ran down the center of the room, rifles, pistols, magazines, grenades, demo charges, medical kits. He was checking each item methodically, making notes on a clipboard with a government-issue pen. His movements were precise, almost mechanical. Check the rifle's serial number. Verify the optic was zeroed. Count the magazines. Note the ammunition count. Move to the next weapon.

"We're gonna be heavy," he said without looking up. "Heavier than Nicaragua. Those Hinds have 12.7mm nose guns and rocket pods. If they get airborne while we're on the ground, we're fucked. We need to be able to put them down."

"Stingers?" Torres asked. He was sitting on the floor with his back against the wall, cleaning his CAR-15 with a bore brush and a rag that was already black with carbon.

"Two of them. Harrow's getting them cleared through channels.

" Price picked up one of the M72 LAW tubes and inspected the seal on the end cap, making sure it was intact. "We'll have four of these. Enough to take out the helicopters on the ground and anything else that needs killing. Each tube weighs five pounds empty, fifteen pounds loaded. Effective range is two hundred meters against armor."

Draven was repacking his rucksack, pulling everything out and putting it back in a specific order, ammunition on the bottom for weight distribution, then rations, then medical supplies, then mission-essential gear on top where he could reach it fast. "What's the weight limit for the jump?"

"There isn't one," Cole said from the doorway.

He'd been standing there for a minute, watching them work. "We're jumping from 25,000 feet. HAHO insertion. You can carry whatever you can carry but remember you're in freefall for two minutes and you've got to hump twenty miles after you land. Pack smart."

"My knees are gonna love that," Hawke said. He was sitting on one of the benches that lined the wall, wrapping his ankles with athletic tape. He'd already done his wrists.

"Your knees are nineteen years old," Cole said. "They'll be fine."

"My knees are nineteen years old, and I've been jumping out of planes since I was eighteen," Hawke said. He ripped the tape with his teeth and started on the other ankle. "That's a lot of impacts."

Keller looked up from the radio equipment he was testing—two SINCGARS radios in their olive drab cases and a PRC-70 satellite uplink that looked like it weighed thirty pounds.

The SINCGARS units were new, just issued this year, with frequency-hopping capability that made them nearly impossible to intercept. "You want me to kiss them better?"

"Fuck you, Keller."

"I'm just saying. If they hurt that bad..."

"They don't hurt. I'm saying they're gonna hurt."

"So, you're pre-complaining."

"I'm being realistic."

Vail tossed a loaded magazine at Hawke. It spun end-over-end across the room. Hawke caught it one-handed without looking up. "You're being a bitch."

"Yeah, well, you're jumping too," Hawke said.

He set the magazine on the bench beside him. "Let's see how your knees feel after you land with eighty pounds of gear."

"My knees are fine."

"That's because you're a freak of nature."

Vail grinned. "Genetics, baby."

Cole walked over to the table and looked at the gear. Fifteen CAR-15s, each with a Colt 3x scope and a suppressor threaded onto the barrel. Three M203 grenade launchers mounted under CAR-15s. One M60 machine gun with a spare barrel and asbestos glove for barrel changes. Fifteen Beretta M9 pistols, the Army had just adopted them this year to replace the 1911. Enough ammunition to fight a small war. "We good on ammo?"

"We're good," Price said. He made another note on his clipboard. "Fifteen mags per rifle. Three per pistol. Extra belted ammo for the 60 if we need suppressive fire. Total combat load is two hundred ten rounds per man, plus whatever's in the gun. We're also carrying twelve hundred rounds for the M60."

"Explosives?"

Holt looked up from where he was kneeling beside Ward at a separate section of the table. They had blocks of C4 stacked in neat rows, coils of detonation cord arranged by length, and a box of M60 fuse igniters open between them. Holt was crimping blasting caps onto det cord while Ward calculated blast radii on a notepad.

"Twenty pounds of C4," Holt said. "Plus, shaped charges for the helicopters. We've got enough to level the command building and anything else that needs leveling."

Ward tapped his pencil against the notepad. "Shaped charges are set for penetration, they'll punch through the Hinds' armor and cook off the fuel tanks. For the command building, we're using timed charges with redundant fuses. Primary and backup igniters on each package."

Price gestured to the demolition's setup. "Timers, det cord, and backups. If something doesn't blow when it's supposed to, we've got manual backups. Holt's carrying the primary demo pack. Wards got the backup charges."

Holt held up a block of C4. "This stuff's stable as hell. You could shoot it and it wouldn't go off. But once we prime it, we're committed. No second chances."

"How long to set the charges?" Cole asked.

"Command building, three minutes," Ward said.

"Helicopters, ninety seconds each if we're fast. We'll have the charges pre-staged with timers set. Just stick them and move."

Holt packed the C4 blocks into a canvas bag, then added the coils of det cord and the box of igniters. "We're good to go. Just point us at what needs to explode."

"Comms?"

Keller held up one of the new radios. It was about the size of a brick, with a whip antenna and a handset. "All checked. Frequencies programmed into the hopsets. Backups packed. We'll have satellite relay through the carrier if we need it, but the terrain's gonna be shit for line-of-sight. These radios will give us secure comms on FM, frequency-hopping every second. Nobody's gonna intercept us."

Cole nodded. "Medical?"

Mason The secondary medic looked up from where he was organizing his aid bag on the floor. He had everything laid out in rows, IV bags, tourniquets, packages of Quik-Clot, morphine syrettes.

Antibiotics in blister packs." If someone takes a hit, I can stabilize them long enough to get to the carrier. But we're twenty miles from the LZ and thirty miles from the coast. If someone goes down hard, it's gonna be a problem."

"Let's not take any hits," Cole said.

"That's the plan."

Torres was sitting on the floor with a map of Colombia spread out in front of him, marking routes with a grease pencil.

The map was 1:50,000 scale, detailed enough to show individual buildings and elevation contours. "We're landing here," he said, pointing to a spot marked with a red X. "Twenty miles north of the base. We hump in, set up an OP on this ridgeline, wait for the satellite window, then hit them at night when they're sleeping."

"How long's the hump?" Riker asked. He was sitting next to Torres, studying the map.

"Six hours. Maybe seven if the terrain's shit." Torres traced the route with his finger. "We're crossing two rivers and climbing about fifteen hundred feet. It's jungle the whole way. No trails."

"It's gonna be shit," Riker said.

"Probably."

Draven leaned over the map. "What's the exfil distance?"

"Thirty miles to the coast. We'll have to move fast once we hit the base. They'll have comms. Someone's gonna call it in, and then we've got the Colombian military to worry about."

"How fast?"

"Fast enough that we're not there when they show up."

"So real fast."

"Real fucking fast."

Cole watched them work. They were tired, he could see it in the way Hawke's hands moved a fraction slower than usual, in the way Torres kept blinking like his eyes were dry, in the way Price's shoulders were hunched forward like he was carrying weight that wasn't there. Nicaragua had been three days ago. They'd barely slept since.

And now they were packing for another op that was going to be harder, longer, and a hell of a lot more dangerous. But they didn't complain. Not really. The banter was just how they dealt with it, how they kept the tension from building up until it broke something important.

They just did the work.

Cole felt something tighten in his chest. Pride, maybe. Or responsibility. He wasn't sure there was a difference anymore.

At 1900 hours, Bishop came into the equipment room looking like someone had beaten him with a dictionary. His eyes were bloodshot, his hair was sticking up in the back, and there was a smudge of ink on his left cheek.

"How's it going?" Cole asked.

"I know the Cyrillic alphabet," Bishop said. He sat down on one of the benches and rubbed his eyes with the heels of his hands. "I can read about half the gauges. I have no idea if I can actually fly the thing."

"You'll figure it out."

"That's what Volkov said."

"He's right."

Bishop dropped his hands and looked at Cole.

"Three days isn't enough time to learn a language."

"You're not learning a language," Vail said. He was loading 5.56mm rounds into magazines, thirty rounds each, pressing them down with his thumb. "You're learning enough to not die."

"That's a low bar."

"It's the right bar."

Bishop looked at the gear spread out on the table, the rifles, the explosives, the medical supplies. "We are jumping HALO?"

"Yeah."

"What's the altitude?"

"25,000 feet."

"Fuck." Bishop closed his eyes. "Fuck."

"You've done higher," Cole said. "We did 28,000 in training."

"Not in a while." Bishop opened his eyes. "And not with this much gear."

"It's like riding a bike."

"A bike that kills you if you fuck up the oxygen."

"Don't fuck up the oxygen," Vail said. He finished loading the magazine and set it on the table with the others. "Just breathe normal. Watch your altimeter. Pull at 3,500 feet. You've done it a hundred times."

Bishop nodded slowly. He didn't look convinced. "How long's the freefall?"

"Two minutes," Cole said. "Maybe less depending on winds. We'll be jumping at night, so you won't see shit until you're under canopy."

"And we're landing where?"

Chapter Thirty-Nine

Wednesday, 27 March

Fort Bragg, North Carolina

"Two klicks north of the base," Torres said, pointing at the map. "In the trees. We'll have cover and a clear line of sight to the LZ."

"Great," Bishop said. He didn't sound enthusiastic.

"You'll be fine," Cole said.

Bishop stood up and stretched, his spine popping audibly. "I'm gonna go stare at Russian gauges some more."

"Good plan."

Cole watched him leave, noting the tension in Bishop's shoulders, the way he moved, stiff, tired. They were all tired. Nicaragua had been three days ago. They'd slept maybe twelve hours total since then. And now they were packing for an operation that made Nicaragua look like a training exercise.

The next two days blurred together in a haze of repetition and detail. They ran through the assault plan six times in the hangar, using tape on the floor to mark the compound layout. Guard towers here. Barracks there. Command building in the center. Vehicle depot on the east side. Fuel storage on the west. They walked it until the movements were automatic. Until they could do it blindfolded.

Draven and Keller worked on communications, programming the radios with frequency-hopping sequences and encryption keys. The Single Channel Ground and Airborne Radio System was new.

Cutting-edge technology that the Soviets supposedly couldn't intercept. Draven wasn't convinced. He programmed backup frequencies anyway, just in case.

Ward, Torres, and Holt went over demolitions. They spread out technical manuals and calculated blast radii, shaped charges, and detonation sequences. C-4 was stable, reliable, but you had to know what you were doing. Too little and you didn't destroy the target. Too much and you killed yourself. They measured out charges, packed them in waterproof bags, tested detonators. Ward had been doing this for six months and he still double-checked everything. Triple-checked. Because mistakes with explosives didn't give you second chances.

Price and Hawke studied the guard rotations, looking for patterns in the surveillance photos. The Soviets changed shifts at 0600, 1400, and 2200. The guards were sloppy smoking on duty, bunching up instead of maintaining proper intervals. Comfortable. Complacent. That would make them easier to kill.

Vail and Riker cleaned their CAR-15s four times. Disassembled it completely, wiped down every component with CLP, checked the gas tube, inspected the bolt carrier group, reassembled it. Then did it again. Cole had seen them do this before every operation. It was ritual. Meditation. This is how they prepared to get into the flow rate of combat.

Cole watched and adjusted. Tightened the plan. Eliminated variables.

He was responsible for these men, these teenagers, really, even though they'd been operating for six months and had more combat experience than most soldiers got in a career. They were good. But good wasn't enough. They had to be perfect.

On the second day, Volkov took Bishop up in a UH-1H Huey to simulate the Hind's handling characteristics.

The helicopter lifted off from the airfield at 0900, rotors beating the air with that distinctive whop-whop-whop sound. Cole watched from the tarmac, shielding his eyes against the rotor wash. The Huey climbed to 500 feet, then began a series of maneuvers, banks, turns, rapid descents. Inside the cockpit, Bishop's hands were slick with sweat on the controls.

"Is not same," Volkov said over the headset, his voice crackling with static. "Hind is heavier. Less responsive. But is close enough you don't die."

"Reassuring," Bishop said. His stomach lurched as Volkov demonstrated a hard bank to the left. The horizon tilted crazily. G-forces pressed him into the seat.

"You want reassuring, join Navy," Volkov said. "They have nice ships. Air conditioning. Hot meals."

Bishop took the stick when Volkov released it. The Huey immediately began to drift. He corrected, too much. The nose pitched up. He corrected again, overcorrected, then finally found the balance. It was like trying to balance a bowling ball on a broomstick. Every input had to be smooth, measured. Too aggressive and the aircraft fought you.

"Better," Volkov said. "Now do it at night with people shooting at you."

"Can't wait."

They flew for two hours. By the time they landed, Bishop's flight suit was soaked through with sweat. His hands were cramping. His head pounded from the noise and the concentration.

Volkov clapped him on the shoulder as they climbed out. "You will not die immediately. Is good enough."

Bishop wasn't sure if that was a compliment or not.

The night before departure.

Harrow gathered them in the briefing room one last time. The overhead lights were harsh, fluorescent. The air conditioning was running full blast, but the room still felt warm, stuffy. Twelve men packed into a space designed for eight. The smell of gun oil and sweat and stale coffee. The photos were spread across the table. Satellite imagery. Reconnaissance shots. Guard towers. Barracks. Command building. Vehicle depot. Fuel storage. Helicopter pads with two Mi-24 Hinds visible, rotors folded. "Primary targets are the officers," Harrow said. He pointed at the command building in the center of the compound. "Second floor. We have confirmation that Colonel Ivanov and his staff sleep there. You take them out first. Fast. Quiet, if possible, loud if necessary."

He moved his finger to the vehicle depot. "Secondary targets are the vehicles and fuel depot. Destroy everything. We don't want them mobile. We don't want them able to pursue." His finger traced to the barracks. "Tertiary is everything else. Barracks. Communications. Weapons storage. You have thirty minutes from first shot to wheels up. After that, the Colombian military will be responding. And we won't be there to help you."

Cole studied the photos. He'd memorized them already, but he looked anyway. Checking. Verifying.

The guard towers were wooden, maybe twenty feet high. The barracks were concrete block, single story. The command building was two stories, also concrete, with a red tile roof. The fuel depot was a cluster of above-ground tanks surrounded by a chain-link fence.

"Questions?" Harrow asked.

"Rules of engagement?" Torres asked.

"Anyone with a weapon is hostile. Anyone who gets in your way is hostile. You're not there to take prisoners."

"Time on target?" Cole asked.

"Thirty minutes from first shot to exfil. Maybe less if it goes loud early."

"It'll go loud," Vail said.

"Then make it count."

Harrow looked at each of them in turn. His face was hard, expressionless. But Cole saw something in his eyes, concern, maybe. Or just the weight of command. Of sending teenagers into a Soviet military base to kill people.

"Questions?" Harrow asked again.

No one spoke.

"Good. Wheels up at 0400. Get some sleep."

They didn't sleep much.

Chapter Forty

Operation Red Fog

Thursday 28 March, 0330 Hours

The trucks arrived at the barracks at 0330, headlights cutting through the pre-dawn darkness. The air was cool, damp. Fog hung low over the compound. They loaded their gear methodically. Rucksacks first, each one packed to exactly sixty-five pounds. CAR-15 rifles with thirty-round magazines, six magazines per man in load-bearing vests. Beretta M9 pistols with three fifteen-round magazines. Fragmentation grenades. Smoke grenades. Demo charges. Medical kits. Water. Rations they probably wouldn't eat.

The oxygen tanks were the heaviest part, aluminum cylinders filled to 2,000 PSI, enough for thirty minutes at altitude. They'd be breathing pure oxygen for the last hour before the jump, pre-breathing to purge nitrogen from their bloodstreams. Otherwise, they'd get the bends when they jumped at 25,000 feet.

Mason was double-checking the medical supplies one last time, kneeling beside his rucksack with his aid bag open. Morphine syrettes. Pressure bandages. Hemostatic gauze.

Chest seals. Tourniquets. He'd organized it all earlier, but he checked again anyway. At 25,000 feet in the dark, there was no room for mistakes.

The parachutes came last. MC-1B main canopies with T-10 reserves. Altimeters strapped to their wrists, set to beep at 4,000 feet. Automatic activation devices set to deploy the reserve at 1,000 feet if they were unconscious or incapacitated.

Cole checked his rig three times. Main risers.

Reserve handle. Cutaway pillow. Leg straps tight enough to hurt. Everything had to be perfect. A malfunction at 25,000 feet in the dark over hostile territory meant you died. Simple as that.

The C-130 was waiting on the tarmac, engines already running. The four turboprops made a sound like rolling thunder, drowning out conversation. Exhaust fumes mixed with the smell of JP-8 jet fuel. The cargo ramp was down, red light spilling out from the interior.

They walked across the tarmac in two columns, bent under the weight of their gear. Cole's rucksack dug into his shoulders. His knees ached. Six months of operations and his body was already showing wear. He was eighteen years old and he felt thirty.

The loadmaster met them at the ramp, a tech sergeant with twenty years in, greying hair, and the bored expression of someone who'd done this a thousand times. He checked their oxygen connections as they filed past, making sure the hoses were secure, the regulators working.

Inside, the cargo bay was cavernous and cold. Webbing seats lined both sides. The floor was bare aluminum, scuffed and dented. The red lights made everything look like a scene from hell.

They strapped in and waited.

At 0400, the C-130 began to taxi.

The engines spooled up, the airframe vibrating.

Cole felt the acceleration as they rolled down the runway, faster and faster, until the nose lifted and the main gear left the ground.

They were airborne.

Cole looked around the cargo bay. Vail was sitting across from him, eyes closed, breathing slowly through his oxygen mask. Torres was checking his altimeter for the third time.

Hawke was staring at nothing, his face blank. Riker was fidgeting with his reserve handle. Draven was perfectly still; hands folded in his lap. Mason sat near the bulkhead, one hand resting on his aid bag.

They were scared. All of them. Cole could see it in the small movements, the tension in their shoulders, the way they kept checking their gear.

They were also professionals. They'd do the job. They always did. Cole closed his eyes and tried to rest. His mind wouldn't stop. He thought about the compound. About the guard towers. About Colonel Ivanov sleeping in the command building, unaware that twelve American teenagers were coming to kill him.

Nobody would ever know they were there.

Chapter Forty-One

The C-130 was leveled off at 25,000 feet. They had done their last refuel in Panama and their hours of flying were coming to an end.

Cole checked his oxygen one more time. The mask was tight against his face, rubber seal pressing into his skin, the flow steady and metallic tasting. Around him, the rest of the team did the same, methodical, practiced movements in the red-lit cargo bay. Twelve operators, each one running through the same checks they'd done a hundred times in training.

The loadmaster held up five fingers. Five minutes. Cole stood and checked his rig. Main chute, reserve, altimeter strapped to his wrist showing 25,000 feet in glowing green numbers. The others followed, Torres, Riker, Vail, Price, Draven, Hawke, Mason, Holt, Ward, Keller, Bishop. They moved to the ramp in two columns, heavy with gear and weapons. Bishop was third in line; his pack loaded with demo charges and the Russian manual and flash cards.

The ramp began to lower. Cold air rushed in, so frigid it burned Cole's exposed skin around the oxygen mask. The noise was deafening even through the helmet, wind screaming past the fuselage, turboprops roaring. Below them was nothing but darkness. No lights. No reference points.

Just black jungle and a Soviet base they were about to destroy.

The loadmaster held up one finger. Cole stepped to the edge.

The wind tore at him. His heart rate was steady. Breathing controlled.

The light turned green.

He jumped. Freefall at 25,000 feet was silent and freezing. The wind noise disappeared the moment he left the aircraft, replaced by the rush of air and the sound of his own breathing inside the oxygen mask. Cole fell through the darkness, arms and legs spread, stabilizing. He counted seconds in his head. Around him, the rest of the team fell in formation, dark shapes against darker sky. Eleven other bodies tracking through the night.

At sixty seconds, they began tracking, angling their bodies to move horizontally through the air, covering distance toward the target area. Cole checked his altimeter. 18,000 feet. Still falling. The air was warmer now, thicker. The jungle below was invisible. Just darkness and the faint glow of the base two klicks south—a handful of lights that marked where Soviet soldiers slept and worked and had no idea what was coming.

At 4,000 feet, Cole pulled his ripcord. The chute deployed hard, jerking him upright with a force that drove the harness straps into his shoulders and groin. He grabbed the toggles and steered toward the landing zone. Around him, eleven other canopies blossomed in the darkness, black against black, visible only by their movement.

The trees came up fast. Cole flared at the last second and hit branches, crashing through leaves and vines that whipped across his face before his boots touched ground.

He collapsed the chute, rolled, and came up with his CAR-15.

Around him, the rest of the team was landing, controlled impacts, the rustle of gear and canopy. Someone cursed quietly. Someone else hit hard and grunted.

"Sound off," Cole whispered into his radio.

One by one, they checked in. Torres. Riker. Vail. Price. Draven. Hawke. Mason. Holt. Ward. Keller. Bishop.

All twelve. “Move," Cole said. They collapsed their chutes, buried them under brush and fallen logs, and started moving south through the jungle. Riker was the one that hit hard. Cole noticed the limp. “You good Cade?”

“Fucking landed wrong, I’m in the fight.” Riker grimaced.

Cole would have to keep an eye on him.

The Colombian jungle at night was alive with sound. Insects screaming in waves. Something howling in the distance. The rustle of things moving through the canopy overhead. The air was thick, humid, pressing against Cole's skin like a wet blanket. Sweat soaked through his uniform within minutes.

They moved in single file, weapons up, night vision turning the world into shades of green. The jungle floor was soft, rotting vegetation that gave under their boots with each step. The smell was overwhelming, decay and wet earth and something sweet and cloying that might have been flowers or might have been something dead.

The hide site was a natural depression in the jungle floor, surrounded by thick vegetation and fallen logs. Two klicks from the base. Far enough to be safe. Close enough to observe.

They arrived at 0245 and immediately began setting up.

Draven and Riker moved forward to establish the primary observation post, a position with clear sight lines to the base. They crawled the last hundred meters on their bellies, moving inches at a time, pushing through mud and rotting leaves. Insects swarmed them. Draven felt something crawl across the back of his neck and forced himself not to react. They found a spot behind a fallen mahogany tree with good cover and elevation. Riker set up his M40 sniper rifle on a bipod, scope trained on the base. Draven unpacked the Leupold spotting scope, 60mm objective lens, 20-60x magnification, and the radio and notepad.

"OP is set," Draven whispered into the radio. "Good visibility on the entire compound."

"Copy," Cole said from the hide site. "Start logging."

Through the spotting scope, Riker could see the base clearly despite the darkness. Guard towers at each corner, lit by floodlights. Barracks on the western side. Vehicle depot to the east. Fuel tanks near the southern fence. The command building sat in the center, two stories, concrete construction that looked Soviet standard. Two Mi-24 Hind helicopters on a pad near the fuel depot. Riker adjusted his scope, ranging the guard towers. "Tower one, 847 meters. Tower two, 891 meters."

Draven wrote it down and made a sector sketch.

Chapter Forty-Two

At the hide site, the rest of the team dug in. Price and Hawke cleared fields of fire, moving slowly, cutting vegetation with knives and piling it carefully to maintain natural appearance. Torres and Mason established a perimeter, marking sectors with small stones only they would recognize. Holt and Ward worked on equipment, checking demo charges and testing detonators. Keller set up the communications station, a radio with a whip antenna they'd disguised with leaves and vines. Bishop unpacked medical supplies and organized them by priority, trauma first, then antibiotics, then comfort items they probably wouldn't use. Vail helped Cole cover their position with camouflage netting and natural foliage. They worked methodically, making sure nothing looked disturbed, nothing out of place.

Then they settled in to wait. This was the unglamorous part. The part that didn't make it into stories. Lying in the dirt. Watching. Taking notes. Waiting for patterns to emerge. Day one was all about the layout.

Cole found a position against a log where he could see

the entire hide site and still have a sight line toward the base. The log was damp, covered in moss that soaked through his uniform. Something bit his neck. He didn't move to swat it. The jungle pressed in around them. The humidity was suffocating. Within an hour, Cole's uniform was soaked through with sweat. His mouth was dry, but he didn't reach for his canteen.

Water discipline. They had three days of observation ahead and limited resupply.

He looked at his team. Price was on watch, scanning their perimeter with night vision. Hawke was next to him, motionless, rifle across his lap. Torres had his eyes closed but Cole knew he wasn't sleeping, just resting, conserving energy. Mason was checking his medical kit for the third time, fingers moving over supplies in the darkness. This was his first as the team medic on mission. Riker was cleaning his optics for the M-40

Holt and Ward were whispering about something, probably the demo charges. Vail was cleaning his rifle, movements automatic, muscle memory. Keller had his headset on, monitoring radio traffic from the base. Bishop sat alone, the Russian manual open on his lap, studying it by the faint glow of a red-lensed flashlight. Learning how to fly a helicopter he'd never touched, in a language he barely spoke, so he could steal it under fire in three days.

Cole realized the magnitude of their situation. The plan. The mission. The fact that in seventy-two hours, he was going to lead these people into an assault against the Soviets, that could kill them all. They were teenagers. Bishop was eighteen, just like Mason, just like all of them. They'd been operational for six months and they were about to hit a Soviet military installation in a foreign country with no support and no backup. If this went wrong, they'd die here. In this jungle. And nobody would ever know. Cole pushed the thought away. Focused on the mission. That was all that mattered.

The sun came up at 0612, light filtering through the canopy in shafts that turned the jungle into a cathedral of green and gold. The temperature climbed immediately. By 0700, it was sweltering.

Draven sketched the compound in his notebook, guard towers at each corner, barracks on the western side, vehicle depot to the east, fuel tanks near the southern fence. The command building sat in the center, two stories, concrete construction. He noted distances, angles, dead space.

Riker ranged everything with his scope. "Barracks to command building, 73 meters. Command building to fuel depot, 104 meters. Fuel depot to helicopter pad, 31 meters."

Draven wrote it down.

Keller counted personnel through binoculars. "I've got twenty-three so far. Probably more inside."

"Officers?" Cole asked over the radio from the hide site.

"Can't tell yet. Need to see who's coming and going from the command building."

At the hide site, the heat was brutal. Cole lay against the log, sweat running down his face, soaking into his collar. Insects swarmed constantly, mosquitoes, flies, things he couldn't identify. Something bit his wrist and left a welt that burned. He didn't scratch it. Price was on watch, scanning the perimeter. His face was red, sunburned despite the canopy cover. Hawke relieved him at 0800, moving slowly, muscles stiff from lying motionless. They rotated watch every two hours. The rest of the time, they lay still and waited.

Torres opened an MRE, Beef Stew. He ate it cold, mechanically, forcing it down. The smell made Cole's stomach turn but he ate his own anyway. Chicken and Rice. It tasted like cardboard and chemicals.

Nobody complained. This was the job.

At the OP, Draven and Riker watched the base come to life. The guard towers changed at 0600. The new guards were sloppy, they smoked, talked, didn't scan their sectors properly. One of them sat down and read a magazine.

"They're comfortable," Riker said quietly.

"Good," Draven replied.

At 0830, a truck arrived with supplies. Two soldiers unloaded crates and carried them into the barracks. No inspection. No security check. They left the truck running, doors open. Draven made notes.

0830 - Supply delivery. Two personnel. No security protocol. Vehicle left unsecured. At 1200, three officers emerged from the command building. Through the spotting scope, Draven could see them clearly different uniforms, cleaner, better tailored. One of them carried a briefcase. They walked to the vehicle depot, climbed into a UAZ-469, and drove out the main gate.

"Officers leaving the compound," Draven reported. "Heading east."

"How many left inside?" Cole asked.

"Unknown. But that's three less we have to deal with."

They logged everything. Vehicle movements. Guard changes. Mealtimes. Who went where and when. By nightfall, they had a basic picture.

Chapter Forty-Three

The sun climbed higher. The heat became oppressive. Draven's uniform was soaked through. His mouth was dry, tongue thick. He took a small sip from his canteen. Riker did the same. Riker looked like he was not uncomfortable at all. He had the same wet head and clothes but looked right at home.

They didn't move otherwise. Didn't shift position. Didn't scratch the insect bites that covered their arms and necks. At 1400, soldiers gathered in the vehicle depot for maintenance work. Through the scope, Draven could hear them, voices carrying across the distance, laughing, shouting in Russian. They were loud, careless, leaving tools scattered on the ground. At 1800, the cook left. At 1900, most of the soldiers were in the barracks. The base quieted down.

Day two was about patterns. Draven and Riker crawled back to the hide site after dark, muscles cramping, joints stiff. It took them forty minutes to cover a hundred meters. Night in the jungle was worse than day. The temperature dropped but the humidity stayed. Everything was wet, uniforms, gear, skin. Cole's hands were wrinkled, waterlogged. His boots squelched with every movement.

The insects were relentless. Mosquitoes swarmed in clouds. Something bit Mason's face and left a welt the size of a quarter. Holt had bites up and down his arms that were starting to swell. Nobody slept well. They rotated watch, two hours on, four hours off.

But the four hours off weren't rest, just lying in the mud, trying not to move, listening to the jungle and thinking about the mission.

Cole lay awake, staring up at the canopy.

His back ached from lying on the ground. His legs were cramping. He shifted slightly, trying to find a position that didn't hurt, and felt something crawl across his ankle inside his boot.

He forced himself not to react.

Bishop was awake too. Cole could see him in the darkness, the Russian manual open on his lap, red flashlight casting shadows across his face. The kid was eighteen and he was teaching himself to fly a Soviet attack helicopter by reading a manual in a language he barely understood.

In three days, he'd have to steal that helicopter under fire, get it airborne, and fly it to a carrier while Soviet soldiers shot at him. Cole felt the sobering reality of that. The responsibility of it. If Bishop couldn't get the Hind up, they'd have to exfil on foot through hostile jungle with no support. They'd probably die. But Bishop would do it. Cole knew that. The kid was good. Focused. He'd figure it out. He had to.

The base woke up at 0600. Soldiers stumbled out of the barracks, half-dressed, heading for the latrine. No formation. No discipline. They moved like men who'd been doing the same routine for months and didn't expect it to change.

At 0700, a cook arrived and started preparing breakfast in a small building near the barracks. The smell of food drifted through the jungle, something frying, bread baking. Cole's stomach growled. He ignored it.

The guard towers changed at 0600. The new guards were just as sloppy as the old ones. One of them was smoking within five minutes of taking his post.

At 0900, the three officers returned. They parked the UAZ and went back into the command building, same routine as yesterday.

"That's our window," Cole said into the radio. "Between 0900 and 1200, all the officers are inside." Draven made a note in his log.

At 1100, a fuel truck arrived.

Two soldiers filled the Hinds' tanks, then drove the truck to the fuel depot and parked it next to the storage tanks. They didn't secure it. Just left it there and walked away. "That's a secondary target," Ward said from the hide site, studying the base through binoculars. "Fuel truck plus storage tanks. Big boom."

"Mark it," Cole said.

They watched the guard rotations again. Same schedule. Same sloppiness. The guards changed every four hours, 0600, 1000, 1400, 1800, 2200, 0200. Like clockwork. At 1400, soldiers gathered in the vehicle depot for maintenance work. They were loud, careless, leaving tools scattered on the ground. One of them was working on a BTR-60 with the engine running, exhaust pouring into the air.

At 1800, the cook left. At 1900, most of the soldiers were in the barracks. The base quieted down. At 2200, the guard towers changed again. Only two guards on duty at night. The rest were asleep. "That's our entry point," Cole said. "2200 to 0200. Minimal guards. Most of the base is asleep."

Keller adjusted the spotting scope at the OP, dialing in the focus. "Guard towers are the priority.

Take them out first, we own the perimeter."

"Agreed," Cole said.

They spent the rest of the night watching. Logging. Planning.

Day three was about finalizing.

Chapter Forty-Four

By day three, the physical toll was showing. Cole's back was a constant ache. His legs cramped every time he moved. His hands were covered in insect bites that had swollen and started to ooze. His mouth tasted like metal and chemicals from the water purification tablets. Price had a rash across his chest from lying in the wet vegetation. Hawke's face was sunburned and peeling. Mason's hands were blistered from gripping his rifle. Torres had stopped talking, just lay there and stared at nothing. Holt and Ward looked the worst. They'd been rotating between the hide site and the OP, crawling back and forth through the mud, and their uniforms were caked with filth. Ward had a cut on his arm that was starting to look infected. But they didn't complain. Didn't ask to pull back. Just kept watching. Kept logging. Kept preparing.

This was what separated them from regular soldiers. The ability to lie in the dirt for seventy-two hours, covered in insect bites and filth, muscles cramping, dehydrated, exhausted, and still maintain discipline. Still do the job. They were teenagers. But they were professionals. They'd seen enough. The patterns were clear. The vulnerabilities were obvious.

At 1400, Cole gathered the team at the hide site. They moved slowly, joints stiff, muscles protesting. Draven spread out his sketches on the ground, detailed drawings of the compound, distances marked, guard positions noted.

"Here's the plan," Cole said, voice low.

"We hit them at 0200. Riker and Vail take the guard towers, suppressed shots, simultaneous. Once the towers are down, Holt triggers the fuel depot. That's our distraction."

"While they're scrambling, we hit the command building," Torres said.

"Exactly. Price and Hawke suppress the barracks with the M60. Keep them pinned. Holt and Ward handle the vehicle depot, demo charges on everything. Bishop gets to the Hinds and gets one airborne. Riker and Vail provide overwatch and shift to security once towers are down."

"What about exfil?" Mason asked.

"We load into the Hind and fly to the carrier. Thirty minutes on target, then we're gone."

Torres studied the sketch, tracing routes with his finger. "What if the officers aren't in the command building?"

"Then we adapt. But based on what we've seen, they're there every night. Second floor, eastern side."

Draven tapped the fuel depot on the sketch. "This is gonna be loud. Once it goes, we've got maybe ten minutes before they organize."

"Then we move fast," Cole said. "Questions?"

No one spoke. Cole looked at each of them. Price, face red and peeling. Hawke, eyes bloodshot from lack of sleep. Torres, jaw tight. Mason, hands blistered. Holt and Ward, covered in mud and insect bites. Riker and Vail, exhausted from three days at the OP. Draven and Keller, faces drawn.

Bishop, still clutching that Russian manual. They looked like hell. But they were ready.

"Good," Cole said. "We execute tomorrow night. Get some rest."

They spent the rest of the day preparing. Checking weapons. Repacking gear. Going over the plan one more time. Every movement was deliberate, methodical. They'd done this before. They knew what mattered. Riker and Vail stayed at the OP, watching for any changes in the routine. There were none.

The base followed the same pattern it had for three days. Same guard rotations. Same mealtimes. Same complacency.

At 1800, Cole moved up to the OP and looked through the spotting scope. The base was exactly as they'd mapped it. Guard towers. Barracks. Command building. Fuel depot. Two Hinds sitting on the pad, rotors folded, waiting.

Everything was in place.

Through the scope, Cole could see a Soviet soldier walking across the compound, rifle slung over his shoulder, smoking a cigarette. He looked young. Maybe twenty. He had no idea that in less than twelve hours, he'd be dead. Cole just wanted this done. Wanted to move on to the mission of the cartels.

"Tomorrow night," Cole said quietly.

"Tomorrow night," Riker agreed beside him. Cole crawled back to the hide site, muscles screaming, and sat down next to Draven. The jungle was darkening, shadows lengthening. Somewhere in the distance, the base hummed with activity, generators running, voices carrying, the normal sounds of a military installation at the end of the day.

"You good?" Draven asked.

"Fuck yeah."

"It's a solid fucking plan."

"I know." Cole smiled

They sat in silence, listening to the jungle. The insects. The distant voices. The sound of their own breathing. Tomorrow night, it would be burning. Tomorrow night, twelve teenagers would assault a Soviet military base and either succeed or die trying. This is fucking crazy Cole thought to himself. He closed his eyes and tried to rest.

Chapter Forty-Five

April 3rd, 1985

They moved into position at 0145. Cole led his element, Draven, Torres, Mason, and Keller, through the jungle toward the command building. His CAR-15 was slick with condensation, the suppressor cold against his forearm. Every step was deliberate, boot placement calculated to avoid snapping branches or rustling leaves. Price and Hawke split off toward the barracks, the M60 slung across Price's back. Holt and Ward headed for the vehicle depot, rucks heavy with C4. Bishop moved toward the helicopter pad with Riker covering him from the OP.

Vail was already in position at the OP, M40 rifle trained on his guard tower. The base was quiet. Two guards visible in the towers, silhouettes against the sodium lights. One walking the perimeter near the fuel depot, AK-74 slung casually. The rest were inside, sleeping or on standby. Cole checked his watch. 0214. He keyed his radio twice. Ready.

Riker's voice came through his earpiece, barely a whisper. "Tower one, I have the shot."

"Tower two, same," Vail said.

"On my mark," Cole said. "Three... two... one... execute."

Cole's heart rate was steady. Sixty beats per minute. His breathing was controlled. In through the nose, out through the mouth. He'd done this before. Nicaragua. The Reyes compound. But this was different. This was a military installation. Trained soldiers. Soviet soldiers.

Riker's suppressed M40 coughed once.

Through the scope, he watched the guard in tower one jerk backward. The 7.62mm round punched through the man's temple and blew out the opposite side of his skull in a spray of bone fragments and brain matter. The guard's body crumpled against the wooden railing, then slid down, leaving a dark smear that looked black in the sodium light.

Vail's shot came half a second later.

The guard in tower two dropped like someone had yanked out his soul. The round entered just above his left eye and exited through the back of his head, taking most of his occipital bone with it. He collapsed onto the platform, blood pooling beneath him, spreading across the weathered wood.

"Towers clear," Riker said. Then went back to covering Bishops movement.

"Moving," Cole replied.

Ward reached the fuel depot first.

Cole's element moved forward. Thirty meters. Twenty. Ten. The command building loomed ahead, concrete walls painted olive drab, windows dark. Cole could smell diesel fuel and cigarette smoke. Somewhere inside, men were sleeping. Officers. The ones who'd planned operations against American interests. The ones who'd sent advisors to train insurgents.

In five minutes, they'd be dead.

The guard near the tanks was lighting a cigarette, his AK-74 slung over his shoulder. He cupped his hands around the flame; face illuminated for a moment. Young. Maybe nineteen. He didn't hear Holt coming.

Holt grabbed him from behind, one hand clamping over the guard's mouth, the other driving his Ka-Bar up under the ribs at a forty-five-degree angle, punching through the diaphragm and into the heart.

The guard convulsed once, a muffled grunt escaping through Holt's fingers. Then he went limp. Holt felt the warmth of blood soaking through his glove, smelled copper and tobacco. He lowered the body to the ground and wiped the blade on the man's uniform. He pulled the charges from his pack, four blocks of C4, each rigged with a remote detonator. He placed them at the base of the fuel tanks, working quickly, fingers steady despite three days in the jungle. The charges were set for simultaneous detonation. When they went, the entire depot would go up. "Charges set," Holt whispered into his radio. Then moved to a safe distance.

"Stand by," Cole said.

Cole's element reached the command building at 0217. The door was steel, painted green, locked from the inside with a deadbolt. Draven placed a breaching charge on the hinges, det cord wrapped in a figure-eight pattern, just enough explosive to blow the hinges without bringing down the wall. Mason covered the approach, CAR-15 up, scanning for threats. Keller and Torres stacked up on either side of the door, backs against the wall.

Cole checked his watch. 0218. His mouth was dry.

His hands were steady. He could feel his pulse in his throat. This was it. The moment before everything went loud. The moment before controlled chaos. "All elements, stand by for breach," he said into the radio. "Holt, blow the depot on my mark."

"Copy."

Cole raised his hand. Three fingers. Two. One.

"Execute."

The fuel depot exploded. The blast was massive, a roiling fireball that climbed fifty feet into the night sky, turning darkness into daylight. The shockwave rippled outward.

A wall of overpressure that Cole felt in his chest even from a hundred meters away. Windows shattered. The ground shook. Flames engulfed the tanks, secondary explosions tearing through the depot in rapid succession, WHUMP WHUMP WHUMP, each one louder than the last.

The base erupted into chaos. Men poured out of the barracks, half-dressed, shouting in Russian. Alarms blared, a mechanical wail that cut through the roar of the fire. Somewhere, an officer was screaming orders, his voice high and panicked.

Draven detonated the breaching charge. The explosion was sharp and focused, CRACK, the hinges ripping free, steel crumpling inward. The door fell into the hallway with a metallic crash. Cole was through before the smoke cleared, rifle up, moving fast. His vision narrowed. Tunnel vision. The hallway. The threat. Nothing else mattered.

The hallway was narrow, maybe four feet wide. Concrete walls. Fluorescent lights flickering. Two Soviet soldiers were running toward the noise, rifles in hand, eyes wide. They were young. Scared. Moving too fast, not thinking.

Cole shot the first one twice in the chest, TAP TAP, center mass, controlled pairs. The suppressor muffled the shots to sharp cracks. The rounds punched through the soldier's sternum, shattering ribs, tearing through his heart and lungs. The man's momentum carried him forward two more steps before his legs gave out. He went down hard, blood spraying the wall behind him in an arterial pattern. His body hit the floor and twitched once.

The second soldier raised his AK-74. Torres shot him in the face. The round entered just below his nose and exited through the back of his skull, taking most of his brain with it. The soldier's head snapped back, a pink mist hanging in the air for a moment. He dropped instantly, his body collapsing like a marionette with cut strings. His rifle clattered on the concrete.

"Clear," Torres said, voice flat.

They moved deeper into the building. Cole's ears were ringing from the breaching charge. He could smell cordite and blood and something else, burned hair, maybe. His heart was hammering now, adrenaline flooding his system. But his hands were steady. His breathing was controlled.

Price and Hawke opened fire on the barracks.

Price had the M60 set up on its bipod, belt-fed, two hundred rounds ready. He let it rip. The muzzle flash was blinding in the darkness, a strobe effect that lit up the compound. The sound was deafening, a sustained roar that drowned out everything else.

Rounds tore through the wooden walls of the barracks, punching fist-sized holes, shredding everything inside. The 7.62mm rounds didn't just penetrate, they fragmented, tumbled, created massive wound channels. Men screamed. Glass shattered. The walls splintered under the sustained fire, wood chips flying.

Hawke worked methodically with his CAR-15, picking off anyone who made it to the door. A Soviet soldier stumbled out, clutching his stomach where a round had torn through him. Intestines were visible through his fingers, gray and glistening. His face was white with shock. Hawke shot him in the throat. The round severed his carotid artery. Blood fountained from the wound, a pulsing jet that sprayed across the ground. The man collapsed, choking, drowning in his own blood. His legs kicked twice, then went still.

Another soldier tried to return fire from a window. Price stitched him across the chest with a long burst, ten, twelve rounds. The man's torso came apart, ribs and organs exposed, sternum shattered. He fell backward into the darkness, his AK-74 still firing, rounds going wild into the ceiling.

"Keep them pinned," Price said, feeding another belt into the M60. His hands were steady despite the recoil. The barrel was already glowing red.

Inside the command building, Cole's element reached the second floor. The stairs were concrete, narrow, lit by a single bulb. Cole took them fast, rifle up, finger on the trigger. Mason was right behind him, then Torres, then Keller. They moved as a unit, each man covering a sector, overlapping fields of fire.

The officers' quarters were at the end of the hall. Cole could hear voices inside panicked, shouting in Russian. He couldn't understand the words, but he understood the tone. Fear. Confusion. They knew something was wrong but didn't know what.

He stacked up with Keller and Torres. Mason and Draven covered the stairs, watching their six. Cole's heart was pounding now. His vision was sharp, hyperaware. He could see every detail, the grain of the wood door, the brass doorknob, a crack in the concrete wall. Time seemed to slow down. This was the moment. The controlled flow of combat. The point of no return.

He kicked the door open. The wood splintered around the lock. The door slammed inward, bouncing off the wall. Cole was through in half a second, rifle up, target acquisition automatic. Three Soviet officers were inside. One was reaching for a Makarov pistol on the desk, his hand halfway there. Another was trying to load an AK-74, fumbling with the magazine. The third was frozen, eyes wide with fear, hands raised.

Cole shot the first one in the chest. The round punched through his sternum and exploded his heart. The officer's body jerked backward, arms flailing. He fell over the desk, blood pouring from the exit wound, a fist-sized hole in his back. Papers scattered. A lamp crashed to the floor.

Keller shot the second one twice, once in the chest, once in the head. The first round shattered his collarbone, spinning him around. The second took off the top of his skull, spraying brain matter across the wall in a gray-pink splatter. The officer dropped, his body convulsing once before going still. The AK-74 clattered from his hands.

The third officer raised his hands higher. "Nyet! Nyet!" His voice was high, panicked. He was older, maybe forty, gray at the temples. He looked like someone's father. Torres shot him in the face.

The round entered through his left eye and blew out the back of his head. The officer's face collapsed inward, then exploded outward. He crumpled to the floor, his body jerking once before going still. Blood pooled beneath him, spreading across the tile.

Cole felt satisfied. No guilt. No hesitation. Just the mission. These men had planned operations. Sent advisors.

Trained insurgents who killed Americans. They'd made their choices.

Now they were dead.

"Officers down, Mission one complete" Cole said into the radio. His voice was steady.

Outside, the base was a war zone. Soviet soldiers were organizing now, returning fire. Rounds snapped through the air, supersonic cracks that sounded like whips. Bullets kicked up dirt, splintered wood, sparked off metal. Price and Hawke were taking fire from multiple positions.

A soldier ran toward them with an RPG-7, the launcher on his shoulder. Hawke shot him in the leg. The round shattered his femur. The man went down screaming, the RPG clattering away. He was clutching his leg, blood pouring between his fingers. Hawke shot him again, this time in the head. The screaming stopped. The man's body went limp.

Price swung the M60 toward a group of soldiers trying to flank them from the vehicle depot.

He opened up, the muzzle flash lighting up the night. Bodies dropped. One man's arm was nearly severed by a burst, hanging by a thread of muscle and skin. He fell, shrieking, clutching the ruined limb. Another soldier took rounds in the gut, three, four hits. He went down hard, intestines spilling onto the ground. He was still alive, trying to crawl, leaving a trail of blood.

"We need to move!" Hawke shouted over the gunfire.

Holt and Ward reached the helicopter pad.

Two Soviet soldiers were guarding the Hinds, AK-74s at the ready. They were alert now, scanning for threats. Ward shot the first one in the chest, two rounds, center mass. The man staggered backward, blood pouring from the wounds. He collapsed against the helicopter's landing gear, sliding down, leaving a smear of blood on the metal. The second soldier raised his rifle. Bishop shot him three times, chest, chest, throat. The first two rounds punched through his sternum. The third severed his trachea. The man gurgled, blood bubbling from his mouth and the hole in his throat. He fell face-first onto the tarmac, his rifle clattering away.

Bishop climbed into the Hind's cockpit. The interior was cramped, smelling of hydraulic fluid and old sweat. Everything was labeled in Cyrillic, switches, gauges, controls. He'd memorized the manual but seeing it in person was different. His hands were shaking now, adrenaline making his fingers tremble.

He found the battery switch, АККУМУЛЯТОР, and flipped it. Gauges came to life. He hit the fuel pumps, ТОПЛИВО, and heard them whine. Then the APU start, auxiliary power unit. The turbine spooled up with a high-pitched whine.

"Come on," Bishop muttered. "Come on."

The main engines caught. The turbines roared to life, the sound building, rotors beginning to turn.

Slowly at first, then faster. The whole aircraft shook. Holt covered their six, scanning for threats. Rounds were snapping past now, hitting the tarmac, sparking off the Hind's armor. "I'm starting her up!" Bishop shouted over the radio.

"Hurry the fuck up!" Torres replied.

Cole's element was fighting their way out of the command building. Soviet soldiers were pouring in from the barracks, trying to retake the building. They were organized now, moving in teams, laying down suppressing fire. Mason threw a grenade down the stairs, an M67 frag. The explosion was deafening in the confined space, the blast tearing through the stairwell. Screams echoed up, then silence.

They moved down, stepping over bodies. One soldier was still alive, his legs blown off below the knees, intestines spilling onto the floor. He was reaching out weakly, mouth opening and closing, trying to speak. His face was gray with shock. Riker shot him in the head. The man's body went limp.

They exited the building into hell.

Chapter Forty-Six

Gunfire everywhere. Explosions. Flames from the fuel depot casting everything in flickering orange light, shadows dancing. The air was thick with smoke, acrid, choking, burning their lungs. The smell of burning fuel and flesh and cordite. The sound was overwhelming, gunfire, screams, the roar of flames, alarms still wailing.

A Soviet soldier charged at Cole with a bayonet fixed to his AK-74. The man was screaming; face twisted with rage. Cole sidestepped, grabbed the rifle barrel, and drove his Ka-Bar into the man's throat. The blade punched through cartilage and muscle. Blood sprayed hot across Cole's hands, soaking his gloves. The soldier gurgled, eyes going wide, and Cole ripped the knife free. The man collapsed, clutching his throat, blood pouring between his fingers. He drowned in his own blood in seconds.

Vail was hit after leaving the OP to join the fight. A round caught him in the shoulder, spinning him around. He went down hard, cursing. "Fuck! Fuck!"

"Vail's hit!" Torres shouted.

Cole grabbed him, hauled him up. Blood was pouring from the wound, soaking his uniform, running down his arm. The round had gone through, entry wound in the front, exit wound in the back. Clean, but bleeding heavily.

"Can you fucking move?" Cole asked.

"Yeah," Vail gasped. His face was white with shock. "Fuck. Yeah."

Torres laid down covering fire while Cole dragged Vail toward the helicopter pad. Rounds snapped past, kicking up sparks on the concrete. Cole's arms burned from the effort. Vail was heavy, deadweight, trying to help but his legs weren't working right.

Holt and Ward were destroying the vehicles.

Holt placed charges on the fuel tanks of two Ural trucks while Ward rigged a BTR-60. The explosions came in rapid succession, BOOM BOOM BOOM, metal twisting, fuel igniting, flames roaring into the sky. The shockwaves rolled across the compound.

A Soviet soldier tackled Ward from behind. They went down hard, rolling in the dirt. The soldier was bigger, stronger, maybe thirty. He got on top of Ward, hands around his throat, squeezing. Ward couldn't breathe. His vision started to tunnel, black creeping in from the edges. He could feel the soldier's thumbs pressing into his windpipe. He reached for his knife, found it, and drove it into the soldier's side. Once. Twice. Three times. The blade punched through muscle and into organs. The man's grip loosened. Ward shoved him off and stabbed him in the throat. Blood poured from the wound, hot and thick, soaking Ward's hand. The soldier convulsed, then went still. Ward gasped for air, his throat bruised and staggered to his feet. His hands were shaking now, adrenaline crash starting.

The Hind's rotors were at full speed now, the rotor wash kicking up dust and debris. "We're ready!" Bishop shouted over the radio. "Get on board!"

Price and Hawke were the first to reach the helicopter, still firing as they ran. Mason and Riker were right behind them, dragging equipment. Draven and Keller came from the building, moving fast. Cole dragged Vail across the tarmac, Torres covering them. Rounds snapped past, kicking up sparks on the concrete. A bullet hit the Hind's fuselage with a metallic PING. A Soviet soldier appeared from behind a burning truck, AK-74 raised. Torres shot him in the chest, three rounds, tight group. The man fell backward, blood pouring from the wounds. They reached the Hind. Cole shoved Vail inside, then climbed in after him. Torres followed, still firing. Holt and Ward piled in, then Keller and Draven.

"Everyone on?" Bishop shouted from the cockpit. Cole did a quick count. Vail, Torres, Mason, Riker, Price, Hawke, Holt, Ward, Draven, Keller, Bishop. Eleven. Twelve including himself.

"Go! Go!" Cole yelled.

Bishop pulled the collective. The Hind lifted off, sluggish, heavy with the weight of twelve men and their gear. The turbines screamed, rotors beating hard against the air. Rounds hammered into the fuselage, PING PING PING, metal on metal. The windscreen cracked, a spiderweb pattern spreading across the glass. Sparks flew from the tail rotor. An alarm started blaring in the cockpit.

"We're taking fire!" Bishop shouted.

"Just fly!" Cole shouted back.

The Hind climbed, rotors screaming, the base falling away beneath them. Flames and smoke rose into the night sky. Bodies littered the ground. The command building was a shattered ruin. The fuel depot was still burning, secondary explosions still going off.

A Soviet soldier fired an RPG-7. The rocket-streaked past, missing by inches, and exploded in the jungle beyond. The shockwave rocked the Hind. Bishop banked hard, pushing the Hind east, toward the coast. The controls were heavy, sluggish. The aircraft was damaged but still flying. He kept it low, treetop level, using the jungle for cover.

Behind them, the base burned.

Chapter Forty-Seven

They flew low over the jungle, the Hind shaking, alarms blaring in the cockpit. Vail was slumped against the bulkhead, his shoulder wrapped in a field dressing that was already soaked through with blood. Mason was working on him, hands steady despite the turbulence, checking for arterial damage, packing the wound. "How bad?" Cole asked. His voice sounded distant in his own ears. His hands were shaking now, adrenaline crash hitting hard.

"Through and through," Mason said. "Missed the bone. He'll live." Vail gave a weak thumbs-up. His face was gray, lips pale.

The rest of the team was silent, breathing hard, adrenaline still coursing through them. Hawke had a gash on his arm from shrapnel, blood soaking through his sleeve. Riker's hands were blistered from the hot barrel of his rifle. He massaged his leg. Torres's face was streaked with blood that wasn't his, spatter from the officer he'd shot. Price was staring at nothing, the thousand-yard stare. His hands were still shaking. Holt was checking his gear, movements automatic, not really seeing what he was doing. Ward had his head back, eyes closed, breathing hard. They looked like hell. Blood-soaked. Filthy. Exhausted.

But they were alive.

Cole looked at his hands. They were covered in blood, none of it was his. His gloves were soaked. He could smell it.

Copper and iron. He'd killed at least four men tonight. Maybe more. He'd driven a knife into a man's throat and felt the blood spray across his face. He felt relieved, Mission complete. His men were not safe. Not yet.

Now the mission was, the team. Getting them home.

The USS Ranger was waiting exactly where it was supposed to be, forty nautical miles off the coast. Bishop brought the Hind in low over the water, the rotors beating hard against the salt air. The carrier's deck crew was already moving, clearing space, waving him in with light wands. They'd been briefed, stolen Soviet helicopter, American operators, don't ask questions.

Bishop fought the controls. The Hind was damaged, sluggish, pulling to the left. The tail rotor was damaged, making it hard to maintain heading. He compensated, over-corrected, compensated again. "Come on," he muttered. "Come on." The deck was coming up fast. Too fast. He pulled back on the collective, flared hard. The Hind shuddered, dropped the last ten feet, and hit the deck hard. The skids slammed down with a metallic thud that rattled through the airframe. The aircraft bounced once, settled. "We're down," Bishop said. His hands were shaking so hard he could barely shut down the engines.

Cole popped the door and dropped onto the deck. His legs almost gave out. Three days in the jungle, then a firefight, then the flight. His body was done. The pain comes after the adrenaline starts to wear off.

The rest of the team followed, helping Vail out, moving quickly. Navy corpsmen were already running

A Navy officer approached, eyes wide, staring at the blood and soot and the way these men moved.

"You Delta or Special Forces?"

"Never heard of them," Cole said. He tried to wink but his face wouldn't cooperate.

"Okay," the officer said slowly. "Follow me. We've got medical standing by."

They followed him below deck, through narrow corridors that smelled like diesel and paint. Sailors stepped aside, eyes wide, staring at the blood and the weapons and the way these men moved, like they'd just walked out of hell.

Because they had.

Cole's ears were still ringing. His hands were still shaking. He could still smell blood and cordite and burning flesh. He could still see the officer's face collapsing inward when Torres shot him. Could still feel the knife punching through the soldier's throat. Later, he'd process it. Later, he'd think about what they'd done. About the men they'd killed. About what that made them.

But not now. Now there was just the team. The mission. Getting them home. The base was gone. The officers were dead. The mission was complete.

His team had done what they did best. They could only hope they did it right and wouldn't have to come back.

Chapter Forty-Eight

The medical bay on the USS *Ranger* occupied a cramped compartment three decks below the flight deck, accessible through a maze of narrow passageways that smelled of diesel fuel, hydraulic fluid, and the peculiar metallic tang of a warship at sea. The overhead fluorescent tubes cast harsh white light across everything, the stainless-steel exam tables, the glass-fronted cabinets filled with medical supplies, the linoleum deck that had been mopped so many times the pattern had worn through in places.

The smell hit Cole first. Betadine antiseptic mixed with the copper scent of blood and something else, the acrid chemical smell of trauma, of bodies pushed past their limits. It was a smell he knew well.

Vail sat on the exam table, stripped to the waist, his torso a canvas of old scars and fresh wounds. The through-and-through in his shoulder was the worst of it, entry wound the size of a dime on the anterior deltoid, exit wound the size of a quarter on the posterior, ragged and ugly where the 7.62x39mm round had tumbled through muscle tissue and torn its way out the back. Blood had soaked through the field dressing they'd applied during exfil, turning the gauze dark and crusty.

Hospital Corpsman Second Class Martinez worked with the methodical efficiency of someone who'd done this too many times. He was maybe twenty-five, Hispanic, with steady hands and the kind of calm that came from treating gunshot wounds. He cut away the field dressing with trauma shears, dropped the bloody gauze into a red biohazard bag, and began irrigating the wound with sterile saline. "You're lucky," Martinez said, his voice neutral, professional.

"Round missed the brachial artery by maybe half an inch. Missed bone. Clean through-and-through. Could've been a lot worse."

"Yeah," Vail said. His voice was tight, controlled. Pain management was mental as much as physical, and Vail had not been shot before. "Feels fucking great."

Martinez didn't smile. He packed the wound with iodoform gauze, working from the inside out, making sure there were no air pockets where infection could take hold. Then he covered it with a sterile dressing and wrapped it tight with an elastic bandage, immobilizing the shoulder to prevent the wound from reopening. "Keep it clean," Martinez said, stepping back to examine his work. "Change the dressing twice a day. I'm starting you on Keflex, 500 milligrams, four times a day. You miss a dose, you risk infection. Understand?"

"Got it."

"I mean it. Tropical environment, open wound, you're a prime candidate for sepsis. You feel feverish, you see red streaks, you come back here immediately."

"Roger that Doc."

Martinez moved to Riker; his leg was starting to swell. Martinez examined him and concluded that the shock of the landing has torn a hamstring muscle. He would be out of the fight for a few weeks. He was not going to like that at all.

Cole stood against the bulkhead, arms crossed, watching.

His own fatigues were stiff with dried blood. Happy it wasn't his but felt a little guilty that it was vails. His hands still trembled slightly, residual adrenaline working its way out of his system. He could still feel the recoil of the Car-15 in his shoulder, still hear the flat crack of suppressed gunfire, still see the Soviet officer's head snapping back as Torres put two rounds through his face.

Torres sat in a folding chair against the opposite bulkhead, head tilted back, eyes closed. His breathing was slow and controlled, combat breathing, four counts in, four counts hold, four counts out. Bringing his heart rate down, forcing his body to shift from sympathetic to parasympathetic nervous system response. His hands rested on his thighs, and Cole could see the slight tremor in his fingers.

Hawke was outside on the weather deck, smoking. Cole had seen him light up the moment they'd cleared the medical bay hatch. The rest of the team was scattered across the ship, Price and Ward in the berthing compartment trying to sleep, Draven and Keller in the communications shack monitoring radio traffic, Bishop, Holt and an injured and very pissed off Riker in the mess getting food Holt and Bishop probably wouldn't eat. Riker would devour whatever was put in front of him. Mason somewhere topside staring at the ocean.

"How's it feel?" Cole asked.

Vail rotated his shoulder experimentally, winced, stopped. "Hurts like hell. I'll live."

After letting Riker head out, Martinez finished cleaning up, disposed of the bloody gauze and used instruments, and made notes on a clipboard. "You're done. Try not to get shot again."

"I was trying to get shot this time." Vail said with a chuckle

They left the medical bay and walked through the narrow corridors. The *Ranger* was a Forrestal-class super carrier, over a thousand feet long, with a crew of five thousand. But down here in the bowels of the ship, it felt claustrophobic, low overheads, narrow passageways, the constant hum of machinery and ventilation systems. Sailors moved past them in blue dungarees, glancing at the blood-stained fatigues, the hollow-eyed thousand-yard stares, saying nothing. They knew better than to ask questions.

Cole found a quiet corner near a ladder well and sat down on the deck, back against the bulkhead. The steel was cold through his fatigues. Vail sat next to him, favoring his wounded shoulder. For a long moment, neither of them spoke.

"That was fucking loud," Vail finally said. Laughing as he said it

"Yeah." Cole said lighting cigarette and smiling.

"Louder than Nicaragua."

"Yeah."

Vail leaned his head back against the bulkhead, closed his eyes. "Think we're gonna catch shit for it?" Cole thought about the base, the fuel depot going up in a fireball visible for miles, the secondary explosions as ammunition cooked off, the Soviet officers dead in the command building, the helicopter they'd stolen and abandoned on the coast. Loud didn't begin to cover it.

"Who gives a fuck. We did what they asked us to do. I am tired of being judged by people who aren't us." he said. They sat in silence, listening to the ship. The hum of the ventilation system. The distant clang of metal on metal. Footsteps on the deck above. The carrier was heading south at twenty knots, putting distance between them and Colombia, between them and what they'd done. Cole closed his eyes and tried not to think about it. Tried not to see the faces. Tried not to count the bodies.

He failed.

Chapter Forty-Nine

April 9th, 1985, 0400Hours
Pope Air Force Base

Thirty-six hours later, they were back at Fort Bragg. The C-130 Hercules touched down at Pope Air Force Base on a Tuesday morning. The landing was smooth, the pilot greased it onto the runway, reverse thrust howling as the big turboprops slowed the aircraft. Cole sat in the red nylon troop seat, feeling the deceleration press him forward against the seat belt, watching the team.

They looked like hell.

Vail's shoulder was immobilized in a sling, his face gray with fatigue and pain. Torres had dark circles under his eyes and a two-day beard. Price sat with his head tilted back, eyes closed, but Cole knew he wasn't sleeping. Ward stared at nothing. Hawke's jaw was tight, his hands clenched on his thighs. The rest of them looked the same, exhausted, hollow-eyed, moving like men who'd been awake too long and seen too much.

The C-130's ramp lowered with a hydraulic whine, and

humid North Carolina air flooded the cargo bay. It was warmer here than it should be for January, the temperature in the mid-fifties, the air thick with moisture. Cole could smell pine trees and red clay and jet fuel. They unloaded in silence. No words, no jokes, no conversation.

Just the mechanical process of gathering gear, slinging rifles, moving down the ramp onto the tarmac. A deuce-and-a-half truck waited for them, engine idling, exhaust visible in the pre-dawn darkness. They loaded their gear and climbed into the back.

The truck pulled away from the flight line, heading toward the Delta compound. Cole sat on the bench seat, watching the base pass by through the open canvas flaps. Streetlights. Empty roads. Buildings dark and silent. Normal.

They turned in their weapons at the armory, CAR-15 carbines, Barretta pistols, the suppressed M-40 they'd used for sniper work. The armorer logged everything, checked serial numbers, said nothing about the carbon fouling and blood spatter. He'd seen it before.

They stripped their gear in the team room, load-bearing vests, magazine pouches, first aid kits, radios. Everything went into duffel bags for cleaning and inspection. Cole's fatigues were stiff with dried blood and sweat, the fabric abraded from crawling through jungle and concrete. He stripped them off, stuffed them in a laundry bag, and headed for the showers.

The water was hot, almost scalding. Cole stood under the spray for a long time, watching blood and dirt and cordite residue swirl down the drain. He scrubbed his hands three times, working soap under his fingernails, trying to get the smell of gunpowder and death off his skin. It didn't work. It never did. He dried off, changed into clean fatigues, and waited.

At 0800, Harrow called them to the briefing room.

Chapter Fifty

The briefing room was on the second floor of the Hanger, a one window space with cinder block walls painted refreshing lime green. Cole hated the beige. There was a conference table that had seen better days. Fluorescent lights overhead. A pot burbled in the corner, filling the room with the smell of burned coffee.

Harrow stood at the front of the room, arms crossed, jaw tight. He looked tired, more tired than Cole had ever seen him. The lines around his eyes were deeper, his face drawn. He'd been awake for days, Cole realized. Managing the operation, coordinating with Washington, dealing with the fallout.

The team filed in and sat down. Nobody spoke. Nobody made eye contact. They just waited. Harrow let the silence stretch for a moment, then spoke. "Mission was successful," he said. His voice was flat, emotionless. "Base is destroyed. Three high-value Soviet officers are dead. Soviet operations in Colombia are set back six months, maybe more. Washington is pleased with the tactical outcome." He paused, and Cole heard the unspoken *but* hanging in the air. "But it was loud," Harrow continued. "Very fucking loud. The fuel depot explosion was visible from the capital. The Colombian military responded within thirty minutes. The Soviets had a diplomatic team on-site within six hours. And now we're dealing with the political fallout."

No one said a thing.

Harrow pulled out a folder and dropped it on the table. The sound was loud in the quiet room. "The Soviets are making noise through diplomatic channels. They're calling it an act of aggression. They're demanding an investigation.

The White House is pissed because now they have to deal with Moscow screaming about American special operations forces conducting raids on foreign soil."

"We did the fucking job," Price said angrily.

"I know you did." Harrow's voice was hard. "But Ghostline is supposed to be invisible. This operation was anything but. The Soviets know it was us. They can't prove it, but they know. And now people in Washington are asking questions. Questions I can't answer without burning this whole program."

Cole leaned forward, elbows on the table. "What are you saying? They have pictures of us, they have copies of our drivers licenses, maybe a picture from one of our fucking high school yearbooks, Nate? They have nothing because we left nothing, not a fucking trace. Who gives a shit about what they suspect. Sure, as fuck not the twelve of us. I can assure you of that."

"I'm saying you need to fucking stand down. Few days, maybe a week. Let things cool off. Let the diplomatic noise die down. Let Washington forget about you for a while."

"Stand down?" Torres said. "That's just friggin great"

"We will stand down and relax for a few." Cole said angrily. " Washington can kiss our collective asses. They wanted quiet, but helicopters and fuel dumps don't blow up quietly. You know what? If they don't like what we do, then fire us and get some new kiddies to play with. Done, Nate, I am fucking done with the second guessing and the judgement from stiffs in suits."

"I know." Harrow's voice was sharp. "But right now, Ghostline is too visible. We push any harder, someone's gonna start digging. And if they dig deep enough, they're gonna find things they shouldn't find.

Things that will get this program shut down and all of us court-martialed or worse." The room went quiet. Cole could hear the hum of the fluorescent lights, the gurgle of the coffee maker, the sound of his own breathing.

Draven spoke up. "Are we compromised?"

"Not yet," Harrow said. "But we're close. This program works because very few people know we exist. The more noise we make, the harder that gets. The Colombia operation was necessary, but it put us on the radar. We need to step back, let things settle, and then we can move forward."

Vail shifted in his chair, wincing as the movement pulled at his wounded shoulder. "So what? We just sit here?"

"For now, yeah. I'll let you know when we're clear to move again."

Harrow looked at each of them in turn, his gaze hard and uncompromising. "You did good work. Damn good work. But good work doesn't mean shit if it gets us burned. Understand?"

"Yeah, whatever, it is what it is." Cole said.

"Good. Get some rest. I'll be in touch."

Harrow picked up the folder and walked out, leaving them sitting in silence.

For a long moment, nobody moved.

"This is bullshit," Hawke finally muttered.

"It's politics," Ward said. "Always is."

Cole stood and walked to the window. Outside, Fort Bragg was waking up. Soldiers in PT gear running in formation, their breath visible in the cold morning air. Deuce-and-a-half trucks moving supplies.

Helicopters on the flight line, rotors turning. Normal. Routine. The machinery of the military grinding forward like it always did.

They'd done the job. Destroyed the base. Killed the officers. Completed the mission.

But now they were sitting on their hands because someone in Washington was worried about optics. Worried about diplomatic fallout. Worried about questions they couldn't answer.

Cole wondered if it was worth it. The visibility. The risk. The noise. Ghostline was supposed to be invisible. Supposed to operate in the shadows, leaving no trace, no evidence, no trail. But the more they operated, the harder that became. Every mission left ripples. Every target created questions. Every success made them more visible.

He didn't have an answer.

Not yet.

Chapter Fifty-One

Part Three

" What the ancients called a clever fighter is one who not only wins, but excels in winning with ease"-Sun Tzu

Five days later, they were back in the briefing room. Vail was still on medical leave. The bullet wound in his shoulder was healing, but not fast enough. The corpsman had told him two weeks minimum before he could return to full duty, and Vail had argued, but the corpsman had been firm. Infection risk was too high. Range of motion was too limited. He needed time.

Riker was with him; his leg wouldn't hold up for field work yet. The torn muscle from the Colombia operation was healing, but he still limped, still couldn't run without pain. Another week, maybe two.

That left ten.

Cole sat at the table with Price, Hawke, Ward, Torres, Draven, Keller, Holt, and Mason. Bishop leaned against the wall, arms crossed, a cigarette tucked behind his ear for later.

Harrow walked in carrying a briefcase and a folder thick with eight-by-ten surveillance photographs. He looked better than he had five days ago, more rested, less drawn. Whatever fires he'd been putting out in Washington, they'd been contained.

"Thought we were standing down," Hawke said.

"You were. Now you're not."

Harrow dropped the folder on the table with a heavy thud. "New target. High value. Strategic priority."

He opened the folder and spread out several surveillance photos across the table. Black and white, grainy, taken with a telephoto lens from a distance. The kind of photos that came from CIA surveillance teams or NSA intercepts.

The man in the photos was maybe forty-five, lean and hard, with sharp Slavic features and cold, intelligent eyes. He wore a Soviet uniform in some shots, dress greens with colonel's insignia and rows of ribbons. Civilian clothes in others, dark suits, expensive, well-tailored. Always surrounded by security. Always moving with purpose.

"Colonel Sergei Sokolov," Harrow said. "GRU. Soviet military intelligence. He's the officer coordinating all Soviet operations in Central America."

Cole picked up one of the photos. Sokolov standing outside a building in Managua, flanked by two bodyguards in civilian clothes. The bodyguards were big men, alert, hands near their weapons. Professionals.

"He's the architect," Harrow continued. "Every proxy operation, every weapons shipment, every advisor deployment, it all goes through him. He's the linchpin holding their entire network together. He coordinates with the

Cubans, the Nicaraguans, the Salvadoran guerrillas. He manages logistics, intelligence, operational planning. Without him, the Soviet presence in Central America falls apart."

"Where is he now?" Price asked.

"That's the problem." Harrow laid out more photos. "He moves constantly. Nicaragua, Honduras, El Salvador, Guatemala. Never stays in one place more than a few days. He's paranoid. Smart. Knows he's a target.

He varies his routes, changes his schedule, uses different vehicles. He's got heavy security, minimum four bodyguards, usually six. Armored vehicles. Secure locations. He doesn't take risks."

"So how do we get to him?" Ward asked.

"You hunt him." Harrow looked at each of them in turn. "This isn't a quick hit. It could take weeks. Maybe longer. You'll track him, learn his patterns, identify his vulnerabilities, and wait for the right opportunity. When you get a clean shot, you take it. One chance. Maybe two. Don't waste them."

Torres leaned forward, studying the photos. "What happens when we kill him?"

"Soviet command structure in Central America collapses. Sokolov's been running operations here for three years. He knows every contact, every supply route, every proxy commander. He's built relationships, established networks, created systems. They don't have anyone who can replace him. Not quickly. Not effectively."

Harrow paused, letting that sink in.

"Kill Sokolov, and the Soviets pull back. They can't sustain operations without him. This ends it. Or at least sets them back years." The room was quiet. Cole studied the photos, memorizing the face.

Sokolov looked like a man who'd survived a long time by being careful. The kind of target that didn't make mistakes. The kind of target that would be very, very hard to kill.

"What's our timeline?" Cole asked.

"As long as it takes. You'll deploy to Central America, establish a base of operations, and start tracking him. Build a pattern of life. Identify vulnerabilities. When you get a clean shot, you take it.

But you only get one chance. Maybe two. Push too hard, he'll disappear. Be too cautious, you'll lose him. It's a balance."

"And if we don't get a clean shot?" Draven asked.

"Then you wait. And you keep waiting until you do." Harrow closed the folder. "This isn't about speed. It's about patience. About being smarter than he is. About finding the one moment when he's vulnerable and exploiting it. You push too hard, he'll know you're there. He'll change his patterns, increase his security, and you'll never get close. This is a long game."

Bishop spoke up from the wall. "What about exfil?"

"You'll have support in-country. Safe houses, vehicles, communications. But you're on your own for the actual hit. No backup. No air support. No quick reaction force. Just you. You make the shot, you disappear, you get across the border before anyone knows what happened."

"Ten of us," Price said.

"Ten's enough." Harrow looked at Cole. "You good with this?"

Cole nodded slowly. "Yeah."

"Good. You leave in forty-eight hours. Use the time to prep.

This is going to be a long operation. Pack accordingly. Light and mobile. You'll be living out of safe houses, moving constantly, staying invisible. No resupply. No reinforcements. You go in with what you can carry."

Harrow picked up the briefcase and walked to the door. He stopped and looked back.

"One more thing. Sokolov's not just smart. He's dangerous. He's killed more people than anyone in this room.

He's survived three assassination attempts that we know of. He's trained, experienced, and paranoid. Don't underestimate him. Don't get cocky. And don't fuck this up."

He left.

The team sat in silence, staring at the photos spread across the table.

"Weeks," Hawke muttered. "Fucking weeks."

"Could be worse," Ward said.

"How?"

"Could be months."

Cole picked up the photo of Sokolov again. Studied the face. The eyes. The way he carried himself. This wasn't going to be easy. This was going to be a grind, days or weeks of surveillance, of watching and waiting, of building a pattern of life until they found the one moment when he was vulnerable.

And then they'd kill him.

"Let's get to work," Cole said.

They stood and started gathering the photos, already thinking ahead. Already planning. This was different. Not a quick strike. Not a single night of violence. This was a hunt. A patient, methodical hunt that could take a while.

And Ghostline was very, very patient.

Chapter Fifty-Two

Operation Final Vector

Price flew into San José first, landing at Juan Santamaría International Airport at 1430 on a Tuesday. He carried a Canadian passport in the name of Robert Mitchell, business consultant, with entry stamps from Mexico City and Panama. He wore khakis and a polo shirt and carried a leather briefcase that contained nothing but business cards and a catalog of agricultural equipment. He cleared customs without a second glance, the officer barely looking at his passport before stamping it and waving him through.

Torres came in six hours later on a different flight. American passport this time, Michael Torres, agricultural equipment sales representative. He wore Wrangler jeans and cowboy boots and a pearl-snap shirt, and he looked exactly like what his cover said he was. The customs officer asked him the purpose of his visit, and Torres said he was meeting with coffee plantation owners about irrigation systems. The officer stamped his passport and sent him through.

Cole arrived the next morning on a flight from Miami.

Freelance journalist, covering Central American politics for a small magazine that actually existed and would confirm his credentials if anyone called. He had a Nikon F3 camera bag over his shoulder, a reporter's notebook in his pocket, and press credentials that would pass inspection.

The customs officer looked at his passport, asked a few questions about his assignment, and waved him through. Draven and Keller came in together that afternoon, posing as telecommunications contractors from a company that did business throughout Central America. They had business cards, contracts, technical manuals.

Bishop landed that evening, posing as an electrical engineer. Hawke came in last, just after midnight, looking tired and annoyed, his cover as a mining consultant holding up under minimal scrutiny.

Ward arrived Thursday morning. Holt and Mason came in together that afternoon, the last of them, posing as graduate students doing research on tropical agriculture.

By 1600 Thursday 18 April, all ten of them were at the safe house.

It was a two-story concrete building in a quiet middle-class neighborhood west of downtown San José, in a district called Rohrmoser. Walled courtyard with bougainvillea growing over the top. Gated driveway with a heavy steel gate. Bars on the windows. The kind of place that didn't attract attention because half the houses in the neighborhood looked the same.

Inside, the furniture was minimal and functional. A table. Chairs. Couches that had seen better days. The windows had heavy curtains that stayed closed. The back room on the second floor had been converted into a communications center—a folding table covered with radio equipment, maps spread across the walls, surveillance photos pinned up in neat rows.

Keller was already working when Cole walked in, hunched over a Yaesu FT-757GX transceiver, adjusting frequencies and monitoring multiple channels simultaneously.

He wore headphones, one ear covered, one ear free, listening to the static and garbled Spanish that came through the speaker.

"Sokolov was in Managua thirty-six hours ago," Keller said without looking up. "Soviet embassy. Meeting lasted four hours."

"He still there?" Cole asked.

"Don't know. Last confirmed sighting was yesterday morning. He left the embassy in a motorcade, headed east. We lost him after that." Cole studied the map pinned to the wall. Managua was 180 miles north, across the border in Nicaragua. Seven hours by car if the roads were good. Longer if they weren't. The map showed the Soviet embassy, marked with a red pin, and several other locations marked with different colored pins, government buildings, military installations, residential compounds.

"We need eyes on the ground," Cole said.

"I know." Keller adjusted the radio frequency, listening to static and garbled Spanish. "I'm working on it. I can monitor Nicaraguan military frequencies. They're not encrypted, they use standard FM tactical radios, mostly Soviet-made R-105s and R-108s. Sometimes they get sloppy, talk about convoy movements or security details in the clear. Might catch something useful."

"Do it," Cole said.

Cole, Price, Torres, Bishop, and Mason crossed into Nicaragua the next morning.

Friday, 19 April
Nicaragua

They drove separately, using different vehicles, different routes, different border crossings. Cole drove a white Toyota SR5 pickup, common as dirt in Central America, with Costa Rican plates and a toolbox in the bed. Price drove a beige Nissan sedan, anonymous and forgettable. Torres drove a Land Cruiser that had seen better days, the paint faded, the body dented, the kind of vehicle that wouldn't attract a second glance. Bishop drove a white Ford Econoline panel van with "Electricidad Industrial" painted on the side.

Mason had a Yamaha XT500 motorcycle, fast, maneuverable, perfect for tight urban surveillance.

The border crossing at Peñas Blancas was slow and bureaucratic, the kind of third-world checkpoint where everything took three times longer than it should. Cole's journalist cover got him through with minimal questions, the border guard looked at his press credentials, asked what he was writing about, and waved him through after a cursory inspection of the truck. Price's business consultant story worked just as well. Torres got pulled aside for a vehicle inspection that lasted twenty minutes, the guards going through the Land Cruiser with flashlights and mirrors, but eventually they waved him through. Bishop's van raised some eyebrows, but his electrical contractor cover held up under scrutiny. Mason breezed through on the bike, the guards barely glancing at his passport.

They met up fifteen miles north of the border, at a Texaco gas station outside the town of Rivas. The station was run-down, the pumps old, the concrete cracked and stained with oil. A few trucks were parked in the lot, drivers sleeping in the cabs or drinking Coca-Cola in the shade.

"Managua's two hours," Price said, leaning against the Land Cruiser, arms crossed. "We go in separately, set up observation posts, see what we can find."

"Keller's got a list of Soviet facilities," Cole said. He pulled out a folded map and spread it on the hood of the truck. "Embassy here. Military liaison office here. Two residential compounds on the east side, here and here. We split them up, rotate every six hours so we don't get burned."

"Five of us, five locations," Bishop said. "We can cover more ground that way."

"Mason, you're mobile," Cole said. "Stay loose. If we pick up a tail or need to move fast, you can get there quicker than any of us."

Mason nodded. "Got it."

They drove into Managua separately, arriving at different times, parking in different neighborhoods, blending into the chaos of a third-world capital. Managua was a sprawling, disorganized city, still recovering from the earthquake that had destroyed it in 1972. Whole sections of the downtown were empty, buildings collapsed or abandoned, streets cracked and overgrown. The new city had grown up around the ruins, a mix of Soviet-style concrete apartment blocks and ramshackle neighborhoods that looked like they'd been thrown together overnight.

Cole set up near the Soviet embassy, a large compound in the Bolonia district, behind high concrete walls topped with broken glass and razor wire. Guards at the gate, cameras on the corners, a Soviet flag hanging limp in the humid air. He parked the Hilux two blocks away, in a spot with a clear view of the main gate and settled in to watch through a pair of Zeiss 10x50 binoculars.

Price took the military liaison office, a smaller building in the government district, fewer guards but more foot traffic, Nicaraguan military officers coming and going, Soviet advisors in civilian clothes, the occasional diplomatic vehicle.

Torres covered one of the residential compounds on the east side, a quiet street lined with expensive houses behind walls and gates. The kind of place where senior officers lived, where security was tight but subtle.

Bishop positioned himself near a government building where Soviet advisors were known to meet with Sandinista officials. He parked the van in a lot across the street, set up a folding chair in the back, and watched through a small window cut in the side panel.

Mason circulated through the city on the motorcycle, checking each location, staying mobile, ready to move if they picked up Volkov's trail.

For three days, they watched.

The work was tedious, mind-numbing, the kind of surveillance that required patience and discipline. Hours of sitting in a hot vehicle, watching a gate or a building, taking notes, snapping photos with a Nikon F3 and a 300mm lens. Watching people come and go. Watching patterns emerge. Watching for anything that might be Sokolov.

Back in Costa Rica, Draven and Keller stayed in the safe house, monitoring radio traffic, trying to intercept communications. Soviet frequencies were encrypted; they used burst transmission systems and one-time pads that were impossible to break in real time. But sometimes they got careless. Sometimes they said things in the clear.

Sometimes the Nicaraguan military talked about Soviet movements on their unsecured tactical frequencies.

Keller picked up chatter on Nicaraguan military channels, convoy movements, security protocols, mentions of "Soviet advisors" that might mean something. He logged everything, built a database, looked for patterns.

On the fourth day, Keller's voice crackled over the radio, transmitted on a secure frequency using a Motorola HT-220 handheld.

"I've got something. Motorcade leaving the embassy. Three vehicles. Heavy security."

Cole grabbed his binoculars and focused on the gate. "I see it."

Three black ZIL-117 sedans, Soviet-made, armored, moving fast through the gate. Flanked by four motorcycles, Nicaraguan military police on Kawasaki KZ1000s, lights flashing. The lead vehicle had diplomatic plates.

"That's him," Cole said quietly. "Has to be." He started the SR5 and pulled into traffic, staying three cars back, keeping the motorcade in sight. His heart rate was steady, his breathing controlled. This was what they'd been waiting for.

Price's voice came over the radio. "I'm moving to intercept. Where's he headed?"

"North on Avenida Bolívar," Cole said. "Toward the government district."

Torres joined the tail from a side street, falling in behind Price, the Land Cruiser blending into traffic.

Bishop pulled the van into traffic two blocks over, running parallel, ready to cut across if the motorcade changed direction. Mason came in fast on the motorcycle, weaving through cars, staying close but not too close.

"I've got eyes from the east," Bishop said.

"I'm on his six," Mason added. "Three cars back."

The motorcade moved through the city with the confidence of people who didn't expect trouble. They didn't check for surveillance. Didn't vary their speed. Didn't take evasive action. Just drove straight through traffic, the motorcycles clearing the way, the sedans following in formation.

They stopped at a large government building near the center of the city, a Soviet-style concrete monstrosity with armed guards at the entrance and soldiers on the roof. The motorcade pulled up to the front entrance, and the vehicles stopped.

Cole parked half a block away, behind a delivery truck, and watched through the binoculars.

The rear door of the middle sedan opened.

Sokolov stepped out.

He was tall, maybe six-two, broad-shouldered, wearing a dark gray suit that fit him well.

Gray hair, clean-shaven, moving with the calm authority of someone used to being in charge. Two bodyguards flanked him as he walked toward the building, big men in civilian clothes, hands near their weapons, eyes scanning the street. Professionals.

"That's him," Cole said quietly into the radio.

"Can you take the shot?" Price asked.

Cole scanned the area through the binoculars. Too many people. Too much security. The bodyguards were close, maybe three feet on either side, and the building had soldiers on the roof with AK-47s. The range was maybe seventy-five yards, an easy shot with a scoped rifle, but he didn't have a rifle. And even if he did, the exfil would be impossible. They'd be trapped in the city, surrounded by Nicaraguan military and Soviet security.

"Negative. Too exposed."

"Copy."

They watched for three hours.

Sokolov stayed inside. The motorcade waited, engines

idling, drivers smoking cigarettes in the shade. The guards didn't move. The soldiers on the roof didn't move. Everything was static, frozen, waiting.

At 1640, He came back out. Same bodyguards. Same calm walk. He climbed into the sedan and the motorcade pulled away, heading south. Cole started the SR5 and followed, staying back, letting two cars get between him and the motorcade. Bishop repositioned the van twice to avoid drawing attention, moving parallel, staying out of sight. Mason circled the block on the motorcycle, mapping alternate routes, ready to cut across if needed.

They moved south through the city, back toward the embassy.

Traffic was heavier now, rush hour building, cars packed tight on the narrow streets. Buses belching black smoke. Taxis honking. Pedestrians jaywalking. The chaos of a third-world capital at the end of the workday.

Cole stayed close, weaving through traffic, keeping the motorcade in sight. His hands were steady on the wheel, his mind calculating distances and angles, thinking three moves ahead.

Then a bus cut him off.

A big Mercedes-Benz city bus, painted blue and white, packed with passengers, pulling out from a stop without signaling. Cole hit the brakes, the SR5 skidding slightly on the worn pavement, and by the time he got around the bus, the motorcade was gone.

"I lost him," Cole said into the radio, his voice tight with frustration.

"I've got him," Torres said. "He's turning east on, fuck, I lost him too. He just turned down a side street, and I can't follow without getting burned."

Silence on the radio. Then Mason's voice, the motorcycle engine revving in the background.

"I'm on him. He's heading toward, shit, he just turned into a residential area. I can't follow without getting made."

"I'm two blocks over," Bishop said. "Trying to intercept."

Price's voice came through, frustrated. "He's gone."

Cole pulled over to the curb and sat there, hands on the wheel, staring at the traffic flowing past. They'd been close. So close. But not close enough.

"Regroup at the safe house," Cole said. "We'll try again tomorrow." He put the truck in gear and drove south, back toward the border, back toward Costa Rica.

Behind him, somewhere in Managua, Sokolov was moving. And they had no idea where he was.

Chapter Fifty-Three

April 21st, Safehouse
Costa Rica

They got back to the safe house after dark.

Cole parked the SR5 two blocks away, in a different spot than before, and walked in through the back entrance. Standard counter-surveillance protocol, never use the same route twice, never park in the same place, always assume you're being watched.

Torres was already there, sitting at the table with a map of Managua spread out in front of him, marking routes with a red pen. Price came in five minutes later, looking tired and frustrated. Bishop and Mason arrived shortly after, both of them silent, both of them pissed off.

Nobody spoke for a while.

Vail and Riker were at the other end of the table. Having arrived Saturday. They couldn't be in the fight, but they could help from the safehouse. They were monitoring the radio and reviewing surveillance notes. Vail's shoulder was still bandaged, his arm in a sling, but he was mobile now, functional. Riker had his leg propped up on a chair, the jump injury from Colombia still healing, but he could walk without limping too badly.

Torres finally broke the silence. "He knows what he's doing."

"Yeah," Cole said. "Varies his routes. Doesn't follow patterns.

Probably changes them daily. Maybe even multiple times a day."

"That's what I'd do," Price said.

Cole sat down and looked at the map. Torres had marked the Soviet embassy, the government building, and the two routes they'd tracked so far. Red lines on paper that didn't tell them enough. They needed more data. More observations. More time.

Mason leaned against the wall, arms crossed. "We had four vehicles on him and still lost him. He's either very good or very paranoid."

"Both," Bishop said.

"We're doing this wrong," Cole said.

Torres looked up. "How?"

"We're following him. Reacting. He controls the movement; we're just trying to keep up. That's a losing game. We need to change the dynamic."

"So, what do we do instead?"

Cole traced a finger along the map, following the routes they'd tracked. "We stop following. We figure out where he's going and get there first. We set up on his destination, not his route. We watch his patterns, identify his regular stops, and position ourselves ahead of time."

Price leaned forward, studying the map. "We don't know where he's going."

"Then we figure it out. He left the embassy at 0830.

Went to the government building. Stayed three hours.

Left at 1640. That's a pattern. Maybe it's a regular meeting. Maybe it's weekly, maybe daily. We need more data."

"If it's regular, he'll go back," Price said.

"Maybe. Or maybe he rotates locations. Keeps people guessing. Either way, we need to build a pattern of life. Track his movements for a week, maybe two. Figure out his routine. Then we exploit it."

Cole stared at the map. The problem wasn't the routes. The problem was they didn't know enough about Sokolov's life. His routine. His vulnerabilities. His habits. They needed more intelligence, more surveillance, more time.

"We need more eyes," Cole said. "We can't cover him with five people. We need the whole team."

Vail shifted in his chair, wincing slightly as the movement pulled at his wounded shoulder. "Ward and Hawke are still here in San José. We could bring them up. I'm mobile enough to run surveillance from a vehicle. Riker can coordinate comms from here."

"Do it," Cole said. "And get Draven and Keller on full-time comms monitoring. I want surveillance on the embassy twenty-four hours a day. Every time Volkov moves, I want to know about it. Every vehicle that enters or leaves, I want it logged. We build a database, we look for patterns, and we find his vulnerabilities."

Vail reached for the radio with his good hand. "I'll coordinate communications from here. Keep everyone synced up on the net."

"Good," Cole said. "Vail, you're on intel analysis. I want everything we know about Sokolov's patterns, associates, properties. Anything that gives us an edge. Cross-reference with CIA reports, NSA intercepts, anything we can get our hands on. Work with ward on contacts he has."

Vail nodded. "I'm on it."

Mason pushed off from the wall. "What about counter-surveillance? If Sokolov's this careful, he might have people watching for tails. Soviet security, maybe KGB, maybe Nicaraguan intelligence. We need to assume we're being watched too."

"Good point," Torres said. "We should assume he has counter-surveillance teams. That means we rotate vehicles more frequently, change our appearance, vary our patterns. Make it harder to spot us."

"Then we rotate vehicles every day," Bishop said. "Different cars, different drivers, different routes. Nothing that stands out. We blend in, we stay invisible, and we don't give them anything to latch onto."

Cole nodded. "Bishop, you and Mason coordinate vehicle rotation. I want at least four different cars we can use, all with local plates, all common models. Nothing that stands out. And I want to keep the motorcycle for quick response and tight surveillance."

"On it," Bishop said.

By morning, the team was in position.

Ward and Hawke drove up from San José, crossing the border separately, using different cover stories.

Draven and Keller set up in a building across from the Soviet embassy, a third-floor apartment they'd rented under a false name, with a clear view of the front gate. They had a Nikon F3 with a 600mm lens, a spotting scope, and a logbook for tracking vehicle movements. Ward and Hawke took over surveillance on the government building, rotating shifts, staying mobile, watching for patterns. Cole, Torres, Price, Bishop, and Mason rotated shifts in Managua, staying mobile, ready to follow if he moved. They changed vehicles daily, swapping the SR5 for a Datsun sedan, then a Volkswagen van, then a

Ford pickup. Different cars, different drivers, different routes.

At the safe house, Vail worked through intelligence reports, CIA cables, NSA intercepts, reports from friendly intelligence services. He built a database of Sokolov's known associates, his properties, his travel patterns. Riker managed the radio net, keeping all elements coordinated, making sure everyone knew where everyone else was.

They watched for two days.

Their target left the embassy at 0845 on the first day. Went to the government building. Stayed two hours. Left through a side entrance and disappeared into traffic before they could follow.

The second day, he didn't leave at all. The motorcade stayed parked inside the embassy compound, and Sokolov never appeared.

"He's fucking with us," Torres said over the radio.

"Maybe," Cole said. "Or maybe he's just careful. Or maybe he's not even in the country. We don't know. That's why we watch. That's why we wait."

Chapter Fifty-Four

M*ay 7th, 0647 Hours*

Soviet Embassy, Managua, Nicaragua

Major Yuri Federov was drinking his second cup of coffee when the call came through.

He sat in his office on the second floor of the embassy, a small room with a metal desk, a filing cabinet, and a window that looked out over the compound. The coffee was Turkish, thick and bitter, the way he liked it. He'd been awake since 0500, reviewing intelligence reports, coordinating with Moscow, managing the daily operations of Soviet military intelligence in Central America.

The phone on his desk rang three times before he picked it up. "Federov."

The voice on the other end was shaking. One of the guards from the lake house, a sergeant named Petrov. "Major, we... there's been an incident. Colonel Sokolov..."

Federov set down his coffee cup carefully, his hand suddenly steady despite the adrenaline spike. "What happened?"

"He's dead, sir. Colonel Petrov too. And the security detail. All of them."

The room tilted. Federov gripped the edge of his desk, his knuckles white. "What?"

"We found them this morning. The house... it's a massacre, sir. Blood everywhere. They're all dead."

Federov's mind went blank for a moment. Then it started racing, running through implications, calculating consequences, thinking about what this meant. Sokolov was dead. The architect of Soviet operations in Central America. The man who knew everything, controlled everything, coordinated everything. Dead.

"Secure the site," Federov said, his voice hard. "Nobody in or out. Nobody touches anything. I'm on my way."

Major Yuri Federov hung up the phone and stared at it for a long moment. Sokolov was dead. His mentor. The man who'd trained him, who'd brought him to Nicaragua, who'd taught him everything he knew about running operations in hostile territory. The man who'd been like a father to him.

Dead.

Federov stood up and walked to the window. Outside, the embassy compound was quiet. Guards at the gate. Vehicles parked in neat rows. The Soviet flag hanging limp in the humid air.

He thought about his mentor. Thought about the last time they'd spoken, three days before the attack. Sokolov had been worried. Paranoid. He'd said something about feeling watched, about changing his security protocols, about moving to a different safe house.

And now he was dead.

Federov knew who'd done it. He couldn't prove it, but he knew. Americans. Special operations. The same people who'd hit the base in Colombia, who'd been operating throughout Central America, who'd been killing Soviet advisors and proxy commanders for months.

Ghostline.

That's what the intelligence reports called them. A phantom unit. No official designation. No paper trail.

Just a series of operations that were too precise, too professional, too effective to be anything but American special operations.

And now they'd killed Sokolov.

Federov picked up the phone and dialed Moscow. It was time to report. Time to tell them that the architect of Soviet operations in Central America was dead, and that everything he'd built was about to collapse.

The phone rang. Someone answered. And Federov began to speak.

Federov stood up too fast. The room tilted, and he had to grip the edge of Sokolov's desk to steady himself. His hands were shaking, not trembling, but actually shaking, fingers splayed against the polished wood like he was trying to hold the world in place. The air conditioning hummed overhead but sweat had already soaked through his shirt collar. He could feel it running down his spine, cold against his skin.

He looked across the office at Sokolov's desk. Empty now. The chair pushed in with military precision, exactly as the Colonel always left it. Papers stacked neatly in the inbox, requisition forms, intelligence summaries, personnel evaluations.

All of it waiting for a man who would never return.

There was a photo on the corner of the desk. Silver frame, slightly tarnished. His wife and son. Taken in Moscow, maybe two years ago, judging by how much the boy had grown. He was smiling, gap-toothed, holding his mothers' hand. Katya stood behind them, one hand on Sokolov's shoulder, wearing that blue dress she'd worn to the May Day parade. The photo had been taken in Gorky Park. Federov recognized the trees in the background.

He looked away. His throat was tight. His chest hurt.

He was dead.

The words kept repeating in his mind, but they didn't feel real. Couldn't be real. He was the most careful man Federov had ever known. Twenty-three years in the GRU. Operations in Afghanistan, East Germany, Angola. He'd survived them all. He varied his routes, changed his schedule, never stayed in one place too long. He trusted no one, questioned everything, saw threats in shadows.

And they'd still gotten to him.

Federov walked to the window and stared out at the compound. The morning sun cast long shadows across the courtyard. Guards at the gate, AK-47s slung over their shoulders. A black Volga sedan parked near the motor pool. The Nicaraguan flag hanging beside the Soviet one, both limp in the humid air.

Everything looked normal. Everything looked safe.

But Sokolov had thought he was safe too.

Federov turned back to the desk. He had to call Moscow. Had to report. His hand reached for the secure phone, a bulky STU-II unit that the Americans had sold to the Soviets through a third party, ironically enough. The encryption was solid, but the interface was clunky. He picked up the handset and dialed the direct line to Lubyanka Square.

The phone rang once. Twice. Three times. Four.

His heart was pounding. His mouth was dry. He could hear his own breathing, too fast, too shallow.

The line clicked. A woman's voice, professional and cold: "Directorate S, duty officer."

"This is Major Yuri Federov, Managua station. I need to speak with Director Kryuchkov immediately."

"The Director is in a meeting right now, Major.

I can take a message..."

"Get him out of it." Federov's voice was harder than he intended. "Colonel Sergei Sokolov has been assassinated."

Silence.

Then: "How?"

Then, very quietly: "Hold, please."

The line went to static. Federov waited. Seconds stretched into minutes. He could hear his pulse in his ears, a steady thump-thump-thump that matched the rhythm of the air conditioning. His free hand gripped the edge of the desk. The wood was smooth, worn by years of Volkov's hands resting in the same spot.

The static cut off. A new voice, deeper, with the flat Moscow accent of a man who'd spent his entire life in the intelligence services: "This is Kryuchkov."

Federov straightened instinctively, even though the Director couldn't see him. "Director, this is Major Federov in Managua. I'm calling to report that Colonel Sergei Sokolov was killed last night. Along with Colonel Dmitri Petrov and eight security personnel."

Silence. Not the empty silence of a deadline, but the heavy silence of a man processing information he didn't want to hear.

"I don't have all the details yet, sir. The bodies were discovered this morning at a safe house near Lake Managua. I'm heading there now to assess the scene."

"Who did this?"

"Unknown at this time, sir. But the operation was

professional. Coordinated. Execution-style kills. No signs of struggle."

"Americans." It wasn't a question.

"Most likely, sir. The methodology matches previous incidents in Colombia and..."

"I know what it matches, Major." Kryuchkov's voice was sharp now, cutting. Federov could hear voices in the background, muffled but urgent. The Director was covering the receiver, talking to someone else. When he came back on the line, his tone had changed. Colder. More controlled. "Major Federov, as of this moment, you are acting operations chief for Central America. Your first priority is to secure all personnel and facilities. Your second priority is to find out who did this and how they knew where Sokolov would be. Do you understand?"

"Yes, sir."

"I want a full report in six hours. Include everything, security protocols, personnel movements, communications logs, everything. And Federov..." There was a pause. Long enough that Federov thought the line had dropped. Then: "Do not let this happen again."

The line went dead.

Federov set down the phone and stood there, staring at it. His hand was still shaking. He was acting operations chief now. Which meant he was responsible for every Soviet operation in Central America. Every weapons shipment. Every training program. Every intelligence network.

Which also meant he was the next target.

He walked back to the dead Colonels desk and sat down in the Colonel's chair. The leather was still molded to the shape of Sokolov's body, worn smooth in places where his shoulders had rested. The desk was immaculate. Three unfinished reports sat in the inbox, Sergei's handwriting neat and precise across the pages. A requisition for additional weapons, specifically Strela-2 surface-to-air missiles for the Sandinistas.

An intelligence summary on Contra movements in the northern provinces. A personnel evaluation for one of the junior officers, Lieutenant Mikhail Orlov, recommending him for advanced training.

All of it meaningless now.

The door opened without warning. Ambassador Popov walked in, his face pale, his tie loosened. He looked like he'd aged ten years overnight. "Is it true?"

"Yes."

"How did this happen?" Popov's voice was rising, panic creeping in at the edges. "Sokolov was careful. He never went anywhere without security. He varied his routes, changed his schedule..."

"I don't know yet." Federov kept his voice level. "I'm heading to the scene now."

"Moscow is going to want answers, Yuri." Popov sat down heavily in the chair across from the desk. "They're going to want to know how the Americans found him. How they knew where he'd be. How they got past his security."

"I just spoke with Kryuchkov. I'm aware."

Popov rubbed his face with both hands. When he looked up, his eyes were red. "This is a disaster. Do you understand that? Sergei was running everything. The weapons shipments to the Sandinistas. The training programs for the FMLN. The intelligence networks in Honduras, Guatemala, Costa Rica. He had his fingers in every operation from Panama to Mexico." He leaned forward. "Do you even know what operations he had running?"

"Some of them."

"Some of them?"

Popov's laugh was bitter. "We're exposed, Yuri. Completely exposed. If the Americans know enough to kill Sokolov, they know enough to dismantle everything we've built here. Every network. Every contact. Every safe house."

Federov said nothing. He was thinking about the photo on Sokolov's desk. About the gap-toothed Boy who would never see his father again.

"I need security increased immediately," Popov said. He was standing now, pacing. "Double the guards at the embassy.

Triple them. No one leaves the compound without an armed escort. And I want a full accounting of every Soviet national in Nicaragua, military advisors, intelligence officers, technical personnel, everyone. If they got to the Colonel, they could get to any of us."

"I'll handle it."

"You'll handle it." Popov stopped pacing and stared at him. "You're in charge now, Yuri. You understand that? You're the operations chief. Which means every failure is your failure. Every dead advisor is your responsibility. Every blown operation is on your head." He leaned over the desk. "Don't fuck this up."

He left. The door closed with a soft click.

Federov sat alone in the office. The air conditioning hummed. Outside, someone was shouting orders in Spanish. A truck engine started, then faded into the distance.

He looked at the photo on Sergei's desk again. Picked it up. The frame was heavier than he expected. The glass was clean, no fingerprints, no smudges. Sokolov had kept it that way. Probably wiped it down every morning before he started work.

Someone would have to tell Katya. Someone would

have to call Moscow and explain to a woman that her husband wasn't coming home. That he'd been killed in a country she'd never heard of, doing work she wasn't allowed to know about, by people who would never be caught.

Federov set the photo down and stood up. He walked to the window and looked out at the courtyard. The guards were still at the gate. The Volga was still parked by the motor pool. The flags were still hanging limp in the humid air.

Sokolov had been the most careful man Federov had ever known. Paranoid, even. He'd survived Afghanistan, where the Mujahideen had killed more GRU officers than anyone wanted to admit. He'd survived East Germany, where the Americans and British ran surveillance operations that caught everyone eventually. He'd survived Angola, where UNITA rebels had put a bounty on every Soviet advisor's head.

And they'd still gotten to him.

Which meant they could get to anyone.

Federov was now the operations chief. Which made him the next target.

He picked up the phone and called the security office. "This is Major Federov. I want armed guards posted outside my quarters immediately. Two men, rotating shifts every four hours. No one enters without my personal authorization." He paused. "And I want counter-surveillance teams deployed around the embassy perimeter. If anyone's watching us, I want to know about it. Vehicle surveillance, foot surveillance, technical surveillance, everything."

He hung up and looked out the window again. The guards would help. The counter-surveillance would help. But if the Americans wanted him dead, he'd end up like

Colonel Sokolov. Face down in a pool of blood, eyes open, staring at nothing.

It was only a matter of time.

He walked back to the desk and picked up the photo one more time.

Looked at it for a long moment. The gap-toothed girl. The blue dress. The trees in Gorky Park.

Then he set it down and walked out. He had work to do. And not much time to do it.

Chapter Fifty-Five

May 27th, Managua, Nicaragua

Nicaraguan State security Headquarter

Detective Lieutenant Marco Santos stared at the crime scene photographs spread across his desk and felt the familiar weight of futility settle over his shoulders like a lead blanket.

Ten bodies. Professional kills. No witnesses. No forensics worth a damn.

He picked up the photo of Colonel Sokolov. The Soviet officer lay on his back in what had been the living room of the lake house, his expensive suit soaked with blood. Two shots. Center mass, then head. The second shot fired while the man was already falling, that's what the blood spatter told him. The spray pattern on the wall behind the body showed the first shot had hit while him was standing, the second while he was going down. Whoever did this didn't take chances. Didn't hesitate. Didn't make mistakes.

Santos had been a detective for eleven years. He'd worked murders, kidnappings, political assassinations. He'd seen bodies in ditches, bodies in cars, bodies in houses. He was good at his job. He closed cases. He found killers.

But this...

This was different.

He flipped through the ballistics report again, though he'd already memorized every word. 5.56x45mm NATO rounds.

Standard military ammunition. Could've come from a dozen different weapons, M16 or the CAR-15, any number of rifles used by American forces or their proxies. The casings had been policed. Every single one. The only rounds they'd recovered were the ones still inside the bodies, and those were too deformed to provide useful forensic information.

No fingerprints. No footprints, the ground around the house had been too hard, baked by the sun, and any tracks had been obscured by the responding security forces. No tire tracks that led anywhere useful. The boat they'd used had been found abandoned two kilometers down the lake, wiped clean, no prints, no fibers, nothing.

Professional. Methodical. Surgical.

Santos rubbed his eyes. He'd been at this for three weeks and had exactly nothing to show for it. No leads. No suspects. No witnesses. Just six bodies and a stack of photographs that told him nothing except that whoever did this was very, very good.

The phone on his desk rang. He picked it up. "Santos."

"My office. Now." His superior, Colonel Ortega. The line went dead. Santos gathered the files and walked down the hall. Ortega's office was larger, better furnished, with a window that actually opened and a view of the city. The perks of rank.

"Close the door," Ortega said. Santos did. He stood in

front of the desk, files in hand, and waited. Ortega leaned back in his chair, a big man with a thick mustache and hard eyes. He'd been a soldier before he'd been a cop, and it showed.

"The Soviets called again this morning. Major Federov. He wants to know what progress we've made."

"None."

"I know that. I want to know why."

Santos set the files on the desk. "Because whoever did this knew what they were doing. They left nothing. No evidence, no witnesses, no mistakes. This wasn't some rebel Contras hit squad. This wasn't local criminals. This was..."

"Americans," Ortega said quietly.

Santos nodded. "Has to be. The tactics, the weapons, the execution. This was a professional military operation. Special operations. Probably Delta Force or Navy SEALs. Maybe CIA Special Activities Division. Someone with training, resources, and experience."

"Can you prove it?"

"No."

Ortega picked up one of the crime scene photos, studied it for a moment, then set it down. "The Soviets want someone arrested. They want a trial. They want to show the world that we're taking this seriously. That we're a sovereign nation that can protect foreign diplomats on our soil."

"We are taking it seriously. But I can't arrest ghosts."

"Then find someone who isn't a ghost."

Santos stared at him. "You want me to fabricate a suspect?"

"I want you to close this case."

Ortega's voice was flat, emotionless. "Classify it. File it. Move on."

"Colonel..."

"There are limits to what we can investigate, Marco. Some things are above our pay grade. This is one of them. You think the Americans are going to let us arrest their operators? You think they're going to extradite them for trial? This is a war. A shadow war, but a war, nonetheless. And in war, people die. Even colonels."

Santos felt anger rising in his chest. "So, we just let them get away with it?"

"They already got away with it." Ortega stood up and walked to the window, looking out over the city. "Three weeks ago. The moment they crossed back into Costa Rica or Honduras or wherever the fuck they went. You think they're still here? You think they're waiting around for us to figure it out?"

Santos said nothing.

"They're gone," Ortega continued. "Probably already on their next target. Probably already planning their next operation. And there's nothing we can do about it. Nothing the Soviets can do about it. This is how the game is played. We kill their people, they kill our people, and everyone pretends to be outraged while the bodies pile up."

"It's not a game. Ten men are dead."

"Two Soviet advisors and eight security guards are dead," Ortega corrected. "In a war we didn't start and can't control. You want to spend the rest of your career chasing shadows? Be my guest. But this case is closed. File it. Today."

He turned from the window and looked at Santos. "That's an order."

Santos returned to his office and sat at his desk for a long time, staring at the photographs. Sokolov's face. Petrov's. The guards whose names he'd never learned, whose families would never know what really happened.

He thought about the killers. Wondered what they looked like. Wondered if they felt anything when they pulled the trigger. Wondered if they were sitting in some bar right now, drinking beer, laughing about something stupid. Wondered if they slept well at night.

Probably.

He gathered the files, the photographs, the ballistics reports, the witness statements that said nothing useful. He put them all in a folder. Wrote "CLASSIFIED" across the front in red ink. Added a case number that would mean nothing to anyone who didn't have the right clearances.

Then he walked to the records room and filed it away, in a cabinet that would probably never be opened again.

Case closed.

The killers were gone. The trail was cold. And Marco Santos would never know their names.

He went home early that day and poured himself a drink. Sat on his balcony and watched the sun set over Managua, over the ruins of the old city, over the new city that had grown up in its place.

Some cases you solved. Some cases solved themselves. And some cases just disappeared into the dark, along with the men who'd committed them.

This was one of those cases.

He drank his rum and tried not to think about it.

Chapter Fifty-Six

Three weeks Earlier: May 4th

Cole sat in the blue Toyota pickup and watched the Soviet embassy gate. The truck was parked on Avenida Bolívar, half a block down from the main entrance, tucked between a delivery van and a rusted Datsun that hadn't moved in days. The position gave him a clear view of the gate without being obvious. Just another vehicle in a city full of vehicles.

The guards changed shifts every four hours. Cole had timed it. 0600, 1000, 1400, 1800, 2200, 0200. Like clockwork. The same black sedan sat in the courtyard, visible through the gate when it swung open. A Volga, probably armored, definitely assigned to someone important.

Sokolov was inside. Doing what, Cole didn't know. Meetings, probably. Intelligence briefings. Operational planning. The kind of work that kept Soviet officers busy in countries where they weren't supposed to be.

But he'd come out eventually. Everyone did.

Cole had been sitting here for three hours. His back ached. His legs were stiff. The truck smelled like old cigarettes and motor oil. He'd bought it from a used car lot in San José for eight hundred dollars cash, no questions asked. It ran rough, burned oil, and the suspension was shot. Perfect for blending in.

Torres was two blocks south in a white panel van.

Price was north in a sedan. Bishop and Mason were mobile, rotating through the city on different routes. Ward was watching the government district. Draven and Keller were monitoring Soviet radio frequencies from the safe house.

They'd been doing this for three days. Watching. Waiting. Looking for patterns.

On the third day, Draven's voice came through the radio at 0620. "Movement. target's leaving early."

Cole started the truck. The engine coughed, sputtered, then caught. "Where's he going?"

"North. Toward the lake."

Cole pulled into traffic and headed north. The morning rush was building, buses, taxis, motorcycles weaving through the gaps. He stayed three cars back from the motorcade, watching the black sedan and its two escort vehicles. Torres was already moving from the south. Price came in from the west. Bishop and Mason converged from their positions near the government district.

They had five vehicles tracking now, rotating positions to avoid detection. Standard surveillance protocol. No single vehicle stayed behind the target for more than two minutes.

"I've got him," Ward said over the radio. "Black sedan, two escort vehicles. Moving fast."

"Stay on him," Cole said into the radio.

They followed the motorcade north for twenty minutes. The city thinned out. Fewer cars. More open road.

The landscape changed, buildings gave way to fields, then to scattered houses, then to nothing but trees and scrub brush. The motorcade turned onto a smaller road that led toward the lake.

Bishop's voice came through the radio. "I'm dropping back. Getting too exposed out here."

"Copy," Cole said. "Mason, move up."

"On it."

Cole kept the Toyota three hundred meters behind the motorcade. Far enough to avoid detection, close enough to maintain visual contact. Torres was paralleling them on a side road to the east. Price was somewhere behind, ready to leapfrog forward if needed.

"Where the fuck is he going?" Torres asked over the radio.

"Somewhere private," Cole said.

The motorcade slowed and turned into a gated property. High walls, maybe three meters tall, topped with broken glass embedded in concrete. Trees blocking the view from the road. A guard shack at the gate, two men visible inside. The gate swung open and the motorcade drove through.

Cole drove past without slowing, eyes forward, hands relaxed on the wheel. Just another truck on a country road. Ward did the same from the other direction, his sedan passing the gate thirty seconds later. Mason continued north on his motorcycle, not even glancing at the property.

"That's not on any of our maps," Price said over the radio.

"No," Cole said. "It's not."

He pulled over a quarter mile down the road, tucked the truck behind a stand of trees, and grabbed the binoculars from the passenger seat. Zeiss 10x50s, East German manufacture, bought from a black-market dealer in San José. Through the trees, he could just make out the roof of a large house. White walls. Red tile. The motorcade was parked in front.

"Private residence," Cole said into the radio. "Probably a safe house or a meeting location."

"He'll be inside for a while," Torres said.

"Yeah."

Cole lowered the binoculars and looked at the gate. Two guards. High walls. No way to see inside without getting closer. But now they knew. Sokolov had a pattern after all. He just hid it better than most. "Get photos of the property," Cole said. "I want to know who owns it, who uses it, and how often the target comes here."

"Copy," Riker said from the safe house.

Cole sat in the truck and watched the gate. The sun climbed higher. The temperature rose. Sweat soaked through his shirt. He didn't move.

Back at the safe house, Riker relayed the information to Vail and Holt. Vail started pulling property records, cross-referencing known Soviet assets in the area. His shoulder was still in a sling, but he could type one-handed. Holt searched through his intercepted communications for any mention of northern locations or lake properties.

They'd lost Sokolov twice in the past week.

But now they had something. A location. A vulnerability. A way in.

They watched the lake house for three days. Sokolov came back the next afternoon. Same motorcade. Same two guards at the gate. He stayed for four hours, then left. The pattern was emerging. Draven and Keller set up an observation post in the hills overlooking the property. It took them six hours to hike in, moving slowly, carefully, leaving no trail. They found a position three hundred meters from the house, hidden in a cluster of rocks and scrub brush. From there, they could see most of the compound through the spotting scope.

"Single-story house," Draven reported over the radio. "Maybe three thousand square feet. Dock on the lake. Boat tied up, looks like a small fishing boat. Two guards at the gate, one roving the perimeter."

"Interior?" Cole asked.

"Can't see much. Curtains are drawn most of the time. Caught a glimpse of someone moving past a window, but couldn't ID."

"Keep watching."

Keller adjusted the spotting scope and started sketching the layout in his notebook. Guard positions. Sight lines. Distances. The roving guard's patrol route. He clocked it with his watch, twenty minutes per circuit, predictable, no variation.

At the safe house, Vail worked through property records with his good arm. His shoulder still ached, but the pain was manageable. Riker sat at the radio, coordinating between the surveillance teams. His leg was healing, but he still limped when he stood too long.

"House is owned by a shell company," Vail said, reading from a document he'd obtained through a contact in the Costa Rican government. "Registered in Panama. Corporación Mercantil del Pacífico. No direct ties to the Soviets, but the timing matches when they expanded operations here. Company was formed in 1982; same year the Sandinistas took power."

Keller's voice came through the radio. "I caught a transmission two days ago on one of the Soviet tactical frequencies. Mentioned 'northern facility' and a meeting schedule. Didn't think much of it then, but it fits."

"That's it," Vail said.

"Ward just reported in," Riker said. "Targets motorcade left the embassy twenty minutes ago. Heading north again."

"Third time this week," Vail said.

"Pattern."

Vail pulled up a calendar and marked the dates. Tuesday. Thursday. Now Saturday.

"He's coming here every other day," Vail said. "That's not random."

"No," Riker agreed. "It's not."

Chapter Fifty-Seven

Saturday May 4th, Lake Managua,

Colonel Sergei Sokolov sat in the back of the sedan and watched the city pass by. He'd been in Nicaragua for six weeks now, and the paranoia hadn't lessened. If anything, it had gotten worse.

He'd noticed the blue Toyota twice yesterday. Once near the embassy, parked on Avenida Bolívar. Once near the government building, idling at a traffic light. Different drivers both times, but the same vehicle. Same dent in the front fender. Same cracked taillight.

Could be coincidence. Probably was.

But he hadn't survived twenty-three years in the GRU by believing in coincidences.

"Yuri," he said to the driver. "Take the next left."

"Sir, that's not the route..."

"I know what the route is." Sokolov's voice was flat. "Take the left."

The driver complied without further comment. Sokolov watched through the rear window. The blue Toyota continued straight. Good. Maybe it was nothing after all.

But there had been other things. Small things. A man at the café yesterday morning who'd looked away too quickly when he had glanced at him.

A motorcycle that had appeared behind them twice on different days, different rider, but the same bike, a red Honda with a loud exhaust. A woman with a camera near the embassy who claimed to be a tourist but held the camera like someone who knew what they were doing. Checking angles, adjusting settings with practiced efficiency. Any one of them could be nothing. All of them together made a pattern. The Americans were looking for him. He was certain of it.

Colonel Dmitri Petrov sat beside him, reviewing a folder of intelligence reports. Younger than Volkov by fifteen years, but competent. Careful. The kind of officer who would survive this war, assuming any of them did. He had a wife in Moscow, two young sons. He talked about them sometimes, late at night when the vodka came out and the walls came down.

"The Sandinistas are requesting more weapons," Petrov said without looking up from the folder. "Specifically, Strela-2 surface-to-air missiles. They're losing helicopters to the Contras."

"Tell them we'll consider it," Sokolov said. "After they demonstrate better operational security."

"They won't like that."

"I don't care what they like." He looked out the window at the passing streets. Managua was a broken city, still recovering from the earthquake that had destroyed it thirteen years ago. Entire blocks were empty; buildings reduced to rubble and never rebuilt. The Sandinistas had other priorities. "Three of our advisors were killed last month because the Sandinistas can't keep their mouths shut.

Someone is talking to the Americans. Someone is giving them intelligence we don't have."

Petrov closed the folder. "You think there's a leak?"

"I think there are a dozen leaks. The question is which ones matter."

They drove in silence for a few minutes. The city thinned out. Fewer buildings. More trees. The road curved north toward the lake. He thought about Katya. She'd be awake now in Moscow, making breakfast for Dimitri before school. His son was sixteen, tall and serious, already talking about joining the GRU like his father.

He had tried to discourage him. The work was necessary, but it hollowed you out. Made you see threats everywhere. Made you trust no one. Made you sit in the back of a sedan in Central America, wondering if the car behind you a surveillance vehicle was it just another commuter.

"The base attack last month," Sokolov said. "What do we know?"

Petrov pulled out another folder. "Twelve dead. Command building destroyed. Fuel depot destroyed. Helicopter stolen, never found."

"Who did it?"

"Unknown. The Contras claimed responsibility, but the operation was too sophisticated. Too precise." Petrov paused. "American special forces, most likely. Probably Delta or SEALs."

Sokolov shook his head. "No. Delta would have left more bodies. They're aggressive, loud. SEALs would have hit from the water, used explosives." He stared at the folder. "This was something else. Smaller team. Better trained. Surgical."

"You think it's the same group that killed Reyes?"

"I think the Americans have a unit we don't know about.

Something off the books." Sokolov looked at Petrov. "And I think they're very good at what they do."

The sedan turned onto the road leading to the lake house. He had been using it for three weeks now, rotating between it and two other locations. Never more than two nights in the same place. Never the same route twice. The Americans were hunting him. He could feel it in his bones; the same way he'd felt it in Afghanistan when the Mujahideen were close.

But they hadn't found him yet.

The gate opened and they drove through.

The house sat back from the road, surrounded by trees, with a clear view of the lake. Two guards at the gate, both Nicaraguan, both vetted personally by Sokolov. Two more at the house. Minimal staff. No one he didn't trust. It was as safe as anywhere could be in this country.

Petrov got out first, scanning the perimeter out of habit. His hand rested on the Makarov pistol under his jacket. Sokolov followed, carrying his briefcase. The morning air was warm and humid, carrying the smell of the lake, algae and fish and wet earth.

Inside, the house was cool and quiet. He set his brief case on the table and poured himself a glass of water from the pitcher on the counter. His hands were steady. They were always steady. Twenty-three years in the GRU had taught him that much.

"We should review the operational plans for Honduras," Sokolov said. "The Sandinistas want to increase cross-border raids."

"Later," Sokolov said.

"First, I want to see the surveillance reports from Managua. All of them."

"Looking for something specific?"

"Patterns. Anomalies. Anything that suggests American activity."

Petrov nodded and went to retrieve the files from the study.

Sokolov walked to the window and looked out at the lake. The water was calm, reflecting the morning sky like a mirror. Peaceful. A fishing boat drifted near the far shore, too far away to see clearly. Birds called from the trees. Everything looked normal.

For the first time in days, he felt the tension in his shoulders start to ease.

Maybe he was being paranoid. Maybe the blue Toyota was just a Toyota.

Maybe the man at the café was just a man. Maybe the motorcycle was just a motorcycle.

Maybe.

He thought about Katya again. About Dimitri. About the apartment in Moscow with its view of the Moskva River. He'd be back there in three months, assuming he survived that long. Assuming the Americans didn't find him first.

Petrov returned with a stack of folders. "Surveillance reports from the last week. Nothing unusual flagged by our people."

"Let me see them anyway."

Sokolov sat down at the table and started reading.

Vehicle movements. Personnel changes. Communications intercepts. Most of it was routine. Background noise. The kind of intelligence that filled reports but meant nothing.

But somewhere in that noise was a signal. He was certain of it.

The Americans were out there. Watching. Waiting.

Building a pattern of their own. He just had to find them before they found him.

Outside, the lake was still and quiet. The guards walked their patrol routes. The trees swayed gently in the breeze. Everything looked normal. Everything looked safe.

He turned another page and kept reading.

He had work to do.

Chapter Fifty-Eight

Cole and Torres were parked a half mile from the gate when Sokolov's motorcade arrived. Same routine. The guards opened the gate. The cars pulled through. The gate closed.

"He's meeting someone," Torres said.

"Or he just likes the lake."

"Nobody likes the lake that much."

Cole raised the binoculars. Through the trees, he could see his target walking toward the dock. Another man was with him. Older. Civilian clothes. Gray hair. They stood on the dock, talking. He gestured toward the water. The other man nodded.

"Who's that?" Torres asked.

"Don't know. Get photos."

Torres pulled out the camera with the telephoto lens, a Nikon F3 with a 300mm lens, loaded with high-speed film. The shutter clicked quietly. The primary Target and the other man stood on the dock for several minutes, talking. Sokolov gestured toward the water. The other man nodded, said something. They both laughed.

"Looks relaxed," Torres said.

"Yeah."

They watched for another hour. Sokolov and the man went inside. The guards stayed at the gate. The roving guard continued his patrol.

"Security's lighter here," Cole said.

"A lot lighter."

Cole lowered the binoculars. "This is where we do it."

Eight hours later they were back at the safe house, the team gathered around the table. The photos were spread out, long-range shots of the property, close-ups of the guards, images of the target and the unidentified man.

The next day, Bishop and Mason took over surveillance while Cole's element rotated back to the safe house.

Bishop parked near the lake access road, watching the water. "If we're coming in by boat, we need to know the approach," he said over the radio.

"There's a public dock about two klicks south," Mason said from his position closer to the property. "Could stage from there."

"I'll check it out," Bishop said.

He drove south along the lake road until he found the public access point. A small dock, weathered wood, half the planks rotted through. A few fishing boats tied up, none of them occupied. Nobody around. Bishop walked the dock, checking the depth, the current, the sight lines to Volkov's property.

It was doable. Quiet. Low profile.

"Public dock works," Bishop reported over the radio.

"We can launch from here, approach by water. No one's going to notice another fishing boat."

"Copy," Cole said. "Get photos."

Draven spread out the photos and sketches he and

Keller had made from the observation post. The layout was clear now. Gate. House. Dock. Perimeter fence. Guard positions.

"Four guards total," Draven said. "Two at the gate, two roving. He will bring guards with him so that makes a total of eight. No towers. No dogs. No electronic surveillance that we can detect."

"Interior?" Cole asked.

"Still unknown. But it's not a fortress. It's a house."

Hawke leaned forward. "What about the lake? Can we come in from the water?"

"Maybe," Draven said. "Dock's exposed, but if we time it right, we could use it."

"Or we go through the gate," Price said.

Bishop spoke up. "I checked the public dock two klicks south. We can stage a boat there, approach quiet. Current's minimal. No obstacles."

"How long to get from the public dock to the target?" Cole asked.

"Ten minutes if we paddle. Five if we use a small outboard on low throttle."

"Paddle," Cole said. "Quieter."

"Everything becomes loud once we start shooting."

Vail looked at the photos, his arm still in the sling. "The other man in the photos. I ran him through our files. His name's Dmitri Petrov. Soviet trade attaché. Officially."

"Unofficially?" Cole asked.

"KGB. Probably Target's handler or a senior officer."

"So Sokolov's reporting to him," Torres said.

"Or coordinating with him."

Cole studied the layout. The house was isolated. The security was minimal. Volkov came here regularly.

Keller's voice came through the radio again. "I intercepted another transmission this morning. Mentioned a Monday meeting at 1500 hours. Didn't specify location, but the timing matches."

"That's tomorrow," Ward said.

It was the best opportunity they were going to get.

"We hit him here," Cole said. "Next time he shows up."

The room went quiet.

"How?" Ward asked.

"We go in quiet. Take out the guards. Get inside before he knows we're there."

"And if Petrov's with him?"

"Then we kill him too."

Hawke nodded slowly. "When?"

"He's been coming every other day. If the pattern holds, he'll be back Monday."

"That's tomorrow," Price said.

"Yeah."

Cole looked around the table. Vail and Riker were still recovering, but everyone else was ready.

"We'll need a boat," Torres said. "Something quiet."

"I'll handle it," Bishop said. "There's a rental place near the public dock. I can get something small. Canoe or a rowboat."

"Do it," Cole said.

"Suppressed weapons only," Cole continued. "No explosives. No rockets. We go in slow. Slow is smooth and smooth is fast."

"Exfil?" Draven asked.

"Everyone takes their assigned routes out of the country. Everyone has their false I.Ds and their cover story."

"And if it goes sideways?"

"It won't."

But they all knew it could.

Mason spoke up. "What about the approach route after we're off the water? We need to know exactly where we're going once we hit the dock."

Keller slid his sketch across the table. "Dock to the house is forty meters. Minimal cover.

We'll need to move fast once the roving guards are down."

"I'll take the roving guards," Hawke said.

"I'll cover the gate guards," Price said.

Cole stood up. "Get some rest.

We move tomorrow at 0700. We need to be in place in the boat by 1430. Sokolov's been arriving around 1500. We'll be waiting."

The team dispersed. Vail stayed at the table, studying the photos. Holt gathered his notes and headed back to the radio.

"You good?" Cole asked Vail.

"Yeah. Wish I could be out there with you."

"You will be. Just not this time."

Vail nodded. He understood.

Cole walked outside and looked toward the hills.

One day.

Then this piece of shit Russian would be dead.

Chapter Fifty-Nine

Monday May 6th

Safehouse

The safe house smelled like gun oil and refried beans. Cole sat at the kitchen table at 1300 hours, field-stripping his suppressed CAR 15 for the third time that day. The Knights Armament suppressor lay beside the rifle, its baffles clean, the threading perfect. He'd already checked the bolt carrier group, the gas rings, the extractor spring tension. Everything was perfect. Everything had to be perfect.

Across the room, Torres worked on his Ruger Mark II pistol, the .22 caliber suppressed sidearm they'd all carry as backup. The integral suppressor made it nearly silent, perfect for close work. He cycled the slide, checked the magazine feed, then loaded it with subsonic rounds and holstered it.

Ward sat by the window, assembling his HK MP5SD. The integrally suppressed submachine gun was German engineering at its finest, reliable, quiet, deadly at close range. He locked the bolt back, checked the chamber, then loaded a thirty-round magazine and performed a press check. Hawke cleaned his CAR, humming something under his breath. His suppressor was already attached, the weapon ready. He'd be the one taking the roving guards, one shot, center mass or head, depending on the angle.

Bishop stood in the doorway, smoking, watching the street. He'd drive them to the staging point, then wait with the boat. His suppressed Ruger Mark II was already holstered. His job was transportation and Medical.

If something went wrong, he'd be their lifeline.

Cole reassembled his rifle, the movements automatic after thousands of repetitions. Upper receiver to lower receiver. Charging handle. Bolt carrier group. He locked it together, performed a function check, then loaded a thirty-round magazine of 5.56mm NATO rounds. He chambered a round, applied the safety, and set the rifle on the table. His mind ran through the operation again. Timing. Distances. Angles of fire. Exfiltration routes.

They had one chance. Maybe thirty seconds from first shot to last. Six guards. Two high-value targets. Then out. The margin for error was zero.

"Radio check," Vail's voice came through Cole's earpiece from the other room.

Cole pressed his transmit button. "Good copy."

"Draven and Keller are moving to overwatch position now," Vail said. "They'll be set by 1345."

"Copy."

"Price and Mason are staging at the road position. Half mile from the gate."

"Copy."

"Holt's monitoring Soviet frequencies.

Motorcade hasn't left Managua yet."

"Copy. We're moving in ten minutes."

Cole stood and walked to the window. The sky was overcast, gray clouds hanging low over the city. Temperature was around eighty-five degrees, humidity oppressive. Rain was possible but not likely. Wind was calm. He turned back to the team. "Final check. Weapons."

Each man held up his primary weapon. Cole inspected them visually. Suppressors tight. Magazines seated. Safeties on.

"Radios."

Each man pressed his transmit button. Cole heard four clicks in his earpiece.

"Medical."

Bishop patted the small trauma kit on his belt. Tourniquets, pressure bandages, hemostatic gauze. Enough to keep someone alive until they reached the boat.

"Exfil plan."

"Boat south to staging point," Ward said. "Load into truck. Drive to Costa Rican border. Cross at Peñas Blancas separately. Rally at the San José safe house."

"Contingency?"

"If we're separated, cross at alternate points. Rally in San José within forty-eight hours. If that's compromised, rally at the secondary location in Liberia."

Cole nodded. "Questions?"

Nobody spoke.

"Alright. Let's move."

They gathered their gear.

Rifles slung across their chests. Pistols holstered.

Extra magazines in pouches. Radios clipped to their belts, earpieces in place. Bishop grabbed the keys to the rental truck and headed out first. Cole, Torres, Ward, and Hawke followed thirty seconds later.

The truck was a white Toyota, nondescript, the kind

used by construction crews and agricultural workers throughout Central America. Bishop had removed the interior dome light so it wouldn't illuminate when they opened the doors. The license plates were stolen from a similar vehicle in a different province. They loaded into the back. Bishop started the engine and pulled out of the driveway. The drive to the lake took twenty minutes. Bishop kept to the speed limit, stopped at traffic lights, drove like someone who had nothing to hide. The truck's suspension creaked over potholes. The engine rattled at idle. Cole sat in the back, watching through the rear window. No vehicles following. No unusual traffic patterns.

At 1345, Bishop turned onto a dirt road that led to an abandoned dock on the southern shore of Lake Managua. The road was rutted and overgrown, barely used. Trees pressed in from both sides. The dock came into view, weathered wood, half-rotted pilings, a small aluminum boat tied to a cleat. Bishop had staged it there two days ago, paying a local fisherman two hundred córdobas to leave it and forget he'd ever seen an American.

Bishop parked the truck in the trees and killed the engine. They climbed out and moved to the boat. It was a fourteen-foot aluminum skiff with a fifteen-horsepower Evinrude outboard motor.

The hull was dented and scratched, the paint faded. Perfect. Nobody would look twice at it.

Cole stepped into the boat first, feeling it rock under his weight. He moved to the bow and set his rifle down carefully. Torres followed, then Ward, then Hawke. Each man found a position and settled in, weapons ready. Bishop untied the line and pushed them away from the dock, then climbed in and moved to the stern. He primed the outboard, pulled the starter cord twice, and the engine coughed to life. Blue smoke drifted across the water.

"Radio check," Vail's voice came through Cole's earpiece.

"Good copy," Cole said quietly.

"Draven and Keller are in position," Vail said. "Overwatch is active. They have eyes on the target house."

"Copy."

"Price and Mason are set on the road. Half mile from the gate."

"Copy."

"Holt is monitoring Soviet comms. Motorcade departed Managua at 1420. ETA to target is 1455."

Cole checked his watch. 1348 hours. They had sixty-seven minutes.

"Copy," he said. "We're moving now."

Bishop throttled up and guided the boat north along the shoreline. The water was calm, barely a ripple. The surface was gray-green, reflecting the overcast sky. The air smelled like algae and diesel fuel. Cole scanned the lake. No other boats visible. A few birds circling overhead. The far shore was a dark line in the distance. The outboard motor hummed steadily, pushing them at about eight knots. Fast enough to make time, slow enough not to draw attention. Cole's mind ran through the sequence again. Dock guard first. Then roving guard. Gate guards when the motorcade arrives. Breach the house. Wait for Volkov and Sokolov to enter. Engage security first, then the targets. Exfil immediately.

Thirty seconds. Maybe forty.

He thought about the target. The man was careful, paranoid, well-trained. He'd survived this long because he was smart. But everyone made mistakes. Everyone had patterns.

And the target's pattern was this lake house. Every other day. Last three were Tuesday, Thursday, and Saturday. Same time. Same route. That means if that pattern stays consistent then today is the day.

That pattern was going to kill him.

Bishop cut the motor two hundred meters from the target dock and let the boat drift. The sudden silence was profound. Just the lap of water against the hull, the distant call of birds.

He picked up a wooden paddle and worked silently, keeping them close to the shoreline where the trees provided some concealment. The paddle dipped into the water with barely a sound. Bishop's movements were smooth, efficient, the result of hours of practice.

The lake house came into view through the trees. White stucco walls. Red tile roof. Large windows facing the water.

A wooden dock extending thirty feet into the lake.

Cole raised his binoculars and glassed the property.

One guard visible near the dock, standing in the shade of a palm tree. AK-47 slung across his chest. Smoking a cigarette. Relaxed.

Another guard at the gate, visible through the trees. Also armed. Also relaxed.

The roving guard wasn't visible, but Draven would have eyes on him from the overwatch position.

"I've got eyes on three guards," Draven's voice came through the earpiece. His voice was calm, professional. "Gate has two, dock has one. Roving guard is on the north side of the house, near the generator shed."

"Copy," Cole said. "We're two minutes out."

He lowered the binoculars and looked at his team. Torres met his eyes and nodded. Ward checked his MP5SD one more time. Hawke flexed his fingers, then gripped his rifle. Bishop paddled closer. The boat moved silently through the water, barely disturbing the surface. Forty meters. Thirty. Twenty.

Cole could see the dock guard clearly now. Young, maybe twenty-five. Nicaraguan military uniform. He flicked his cigarette into the water and adjusted his rifle sling.

"Motorcade is five minutes out," Holt's voice came through. "Sokolov's vehicle is second in the convoy. Three sedans total. Motorcycle escorts."

"Copy," Cole said.

Bishop brought the boat alongside the dock. The hull bumped gently against a piling. Cole grabbed the dock and steadied them.

He stepped out first, rifle up, moving in a crouch. His boots made no sound on the weathered wood. Torres followed, then Ward, then Hawke. They spread out, weapons oriented toward the house.

The dock guard turned, his eyes widening as he registered what he was seeing.

Cole shot him twice in the chest. " Sorry Hawke." The suppressed rifle made two soft thumps, like someone hitting a pillow. The 5.56mm rounds punched through the guard's sternum and shredded his heart. He dropped without a sound, his AK-47 clattering on the dock.

"Dock guard is down," Cole whispered into his radio, then put a round in his head as he passed.

"Gate guards are still in position," Draven said from overwatch. "Roving guard is moving toward the front of the house. He didn't hear anything."

"Copy. Price, stand by on gate guards."

"Standing by," Price's voice came back.

Cole's element moved up the dock toward the house. Forty meters of open ground. Manicured lawn.

A few palm trees. No cover.

They moved fast, weapons up, scanning for threats.

The roving guard appeared around the corner of the house, walking casually, his rifle slung.

He was looking at his watch, probably checking the time until the motorcade arrived.

Hawke shot him once in the head. The suppressed round entered just above the guard's left eye and blew out the back of his skull. He collapsed like a marionette with its strings cut.

"Roving guard down," Hawke said.

"Motorcade is two minutes out," Holt said. "They're on the access road now."

Cole reached the side door of the house. He tried the handle. Unlocked. He pushed it open slowly, checking for resistance, for alarms, for anything.

Nothing.

He moved inside, rifle up, scanning.

Kitchen. Tile floor. Wooden cabinets. A table with two chairs. Empty.

Torres and Ward followed him in, moving silently. Hawke stayed outside, covering the approach from the dock.

They moved through the house methodically. Living room, leather furniture, a bookshelf, a radio on a side table. Empty. Hallway, tile floor, family photos on the walls.

Empty. Study, desk, filing cabinets, a window overlooking the driveway. Empty.

The house smelled like coffee the good kind, not that

shit they had been drinking. The air was still, warm. Somewhere a clock ticked.

"House is clear," Cole said into his radio. "We're set."

He moved to the study window and looked out. The driveway was empty. The gate was closed. The two gate guards stood on either side, weapons slung, talking to each other.

"Motorcade is at the gate," Draven said.

Cole watched as three black sedans appeared on the access road, followed by two motorcycles. The lead sedan stopped at the gate. The gate guards opened it and waved them through.

"Price, take the gate guards when the motorcade is inside the property and out of view of the gate.," Cole said.

The motorcade pulled into the driveway, the vehicles crunching on gravel. Doors opened. Sokolov stepped out of the second sedan, tall, gray-haired, wearing a light-colored suit. Petrov emerged from the third sedan, shorter, stockier, military uniform.

Two suppressed shots from Price's position on the road. Both gate guards dropped simultaneously, one shot each to the head. They fell in the dirt and didn't move.

"Gate guards down," Price said.

Four security personnel. Two stayed with the vehicles, scanning the perimeter.

Two followed the targets toward the house.

"Four security," Cole said into his radio. "Two outside, two coming in."

"I've got the two outside," Draven said from his overwatch position eight hundred meters away.

Cole moved to the hallway and pressed himself against the wall.Torres took position on the opposite side.

Ward stayed in the study, covering the window.

The front door opened. Cole heard voices speaking Russian. Sokolov's voice, deep and measured. Petrov responding, his tone deferential. Footsteps on the tile floor. Two sets of boots, the security guards. Then two more sets, dress shoes. They were in the living room now. Sokolov was saying something about the weather, about the lake. His voice was calm, relaxed. He felt safe here.

The security guards entered the hallway first; weapons held at low ready. Professional. Alert. Cole stepped out and shot the first guard twice in the chest. The suppressed rounds punched through the man's ribcage. He staggered backward, blood spreading across his uniform. Torres shot the second guard in the head. The man's skull snapped back and he dropped.

Both guards hit the floor within a second of each other.

Sokolov appeared in the hallway, his eyes going wide as he processed what he was seeing. His hand moved toward his jacket, reaching for a weapon, for anything.

Cole shot him once in the forehead.

The round entered just above his right eye and exited through the back of his skull, spraying blood and brain matter on the wall. Sokolov's legs buckled and he fell straight down, dead before he hit the floor. Petrov was behind him, reaching for a pistol holstered at his hip. His hand closed around the grip. Ward stepped out from the study and shot him three times in the chest. The MP5SD coughed quietly, the subsonic 9mm rounds punching through Sokolov's sternum. He fell backward into the wall and slid to the floor, leaving a smear of blood on the white stucco.

"Targets are down," Cole said into his radio.

"Two security outside are moving toward the house," Draven said. "They heard something."

Two suppressed shots from the overwatch position. Eight hundred meters away, Draven was firing his M40A1 sniper rifle, the suppressed .308 rounds traveling at subsonic velocity. Both guards dropped in the driveway.

"Both down," Draven said.

"Exfil now," Cole said.

They moved fast. Out the side door. Across the lawn. Down to the dock. Bishop had the boat ready, motor running, bow pointed south. Cole, Torres, Ward, and Hawke jumped in. The boat rocked under their weight. Bishop throttled up immediately, turning the boat south, away from the lake house.

"We're clear," Cole said into the radio.

"Copy," Vail said from the safe house. "Price and Mason are moving to secondary exfil point."

"Draven and Keller?"

"Already moving.

They'll be off the ridge in five minutes."

The boat cut through the water, the outboard motor screaming now, pushing them at full speed. The bow lifted slightly, spray kicking up on either side. The wind was cool on Cole's face, cutting through the humidity. Behind them, the lake house sat quiet in the gray afternoon light. 10 bodies inside and around the property. Blood on the walls, on the floor, on the driveway.

Sokolov was dead. Shot once in the head and two rounds to the chest for good measure, killed instantly. Petrov was dead.

Three rounds to the chest, heart destroyed. The Soviet operation in Nicaragua just lost its command structure. The man who coordinated everything, the weapons shipments, the training programs, the intelligence networks, was gone.

Bishop brought the boat to the southern access point

fifteen minutes later. The abandoned dock was empty, the truck waiting in the trees where they'd left it. They dumped all the policed brass into the lake. Then got out of the boat. They loaded into the truck quickly, stowing their weapons in the back, covering them with a tarp. Bishop started the engine and pulled onto the dirt road, heading south toward the Costa Rican border.

Cole sat in the back, his rifle across his lap, watching through the rear window. No vehicles following. No helicopters overhead. No indication anyone had discovered the bodies yet. They'd have maybe an hour before someone at the Soviet embassy started asking questions. Maybe two hours before Nicaraguan security forces responded. By then, the team would be across the border.

Price and Mason were already across, having left their position on the road immediately after the gate guards went down.

They would cross at Peñas Blancas using their business consultant cover identities. Draven and Keller would cross separately at a different point, using their agricultural equipment salesman covers. Bishop, Cole, Torres, Ward, and Hawke would cross at a third location, posing as American engineers returning from a contract job. By nightfall, they'd all be in Costa Rica. By tomorrow, they'd be scattered, some to Panama, some to Honduras, some back to the States on military transport.

Cole sat in the truck, feeling the adrenaline slowly drain from his system. His hands were steady. His breathing was normal. His heart rate was already back to baseline. The job was done. Clean. Professional. No complications. Ten bodies at a lake house. Two high-value targets eliminated. Soviet command structure in Nicaragua decapitated.

That was all that mattered.

Chapter Sixty

Cole knew this was just the beginning. The Soviets would respond. They'd increase security, change protocols, hunt for whoever did this. The Americans would deny everything. The Nicaraguans would investigate and find nothing. And Ghostline would disappear back into the shadows, waiting for the next mission, the next target, the next war that nobody would ever know they fought.

Cole closed his eyes and let the truck's motion rock him. They had a long drive ahead. Then a border crossing. Then a flight home.

Then they'd do it all over again. That was the job. That was all it had ever been. The safe house was empty by 1900 hours. Vail stood in the center of the living room, watching Riker and Holt work through the final sanitization procedures. His left arm hung at his side, the shoulder still screaming despite the Motrin he'd dry-swallowed an hour ago. The sling was gone, too conspicuous for their exfiltration covers, but every movement sent fresh pain radiating down to his fingertips.

He ignored it. Pain was just information. It told him the shoulder was damaged but functional. That was all he needed to know.

"Documents," Holt said, feeding the last of their operational maps into the burn barrel outside. The barrel sat in the small courtyard behind the house, flames licking up through the metal rim.

Smoke rose in a thin column, dissipating in the humid evening air. The smell of burning paper mixed with the ever-present scent of diesel exhaust and rotting vegetation that characterized this part of San José. Vail watched the flames consume the last traces of their surveillance logs.

Grid coordinates. Timing charts. Radio frequencies. Everything that could connect them to a lake house in Nicaragua where six men had died twelve hours ago. Riker limped through the kitchen, his injured leg stiff but mobile. He'd refused the crutch Bishop had offered, knowing it would draw attention at the airport. Instead, he moved with the careful deliberation of someone nursing a pulled muscle, plausible, forgettable. He dumped bleach across the kitchen counters, the chemical smell sharp and astringent. Then he moved to the bathroom, repeating the process.

"Fingerprints," Holt said, working through the living room with a rag soaked in isopropyl alcohol. He wiped down every surface they might have touched. Door handles. Light switches. The backs of chairs. The table where they'd planned the operation. The window frames where they'd stood watch. Vail checked the burn barrel. The documents had reduced to ash and fragments. He stirred them with a metal rod, breaking up anything larger than a coin. When he was satisfied, he dumped a bucket of water into the barrel. The ashes hissed and settled into gray sludge.

"Radio equipment," Riker said, emerging from the bedroom with the comms units disassembled and packed into two hard cases. The encryption modules had been removed and would travel separately. The antennas were broken down into component parts. Nothing that would draw attention at a casual inspection, but nothing that could be reassembled quickly either.

They loaded everything into two vehicles parked in the narrow driveway. A white Toyota sedan and a blue Ford pickup, both rented under different names, both scheduled to be returned to different locations. Vail did a final walk-through. The house looked exactly as it had when they'd arrived two weeks ago. Clean. Anonymous. Empty. No trace that twelve men had used it as a staging base for an assassination operation across an international border.

"We're clean," Holt said, standing in the doorway.

Vail nodded. They were always clean. That was the job. They locked the door and split up. Holt took the pickup south toward Panama, where he'd cross the border on foot and catch a flight from David. The vehicle would be abandoned in a long-term parking lot, keys in the visor, just another rental that someone forgot to return. Vail drove the sedan. Riker rode shotgun, his injured leg propped up on the dashboard, watching the side mirror with the professional paranoia that kept operators alive.

"Think anyone saw us?" Riker asked after ten minutes of silence.

"No."

"Think anyone's looking yet?"

"Probably."

The highway was dark. A few trucks hauling produce toward the capital. A bus with dim interior lights and sleeping passengers. Nothing that suggested surveillance or interest. Vail kept his speed exactly at the limit. His hands were relaxed on the wheel.

His breathing was steady. To anyone watching, he was just another tired driver heading home after a long day. But his mind was running through contingencies.

If they got stopped, their story was solid. American engineers working on a hydroelectric project near Limón. Paperwork to support it. Business cards. A hotel receipt. Everything designed to hold up to casual inspection but fall apart under serious scrutiny.

They wouldn't get serious scrutiny. Not here. Not yet.

The Nicaraguans would be looking for whoever killed Sokolov, but they'd be looking in Nicaragua. The Soviets would be screaming about American aggression, but they'd be screaming at the CIA and State Department, not at two engineers driving to the airport in San José. That was the beauty.

Nobody knew they existed. At Juan Santamaría International Airport, Vail parked in long-term and left the keys in the visor. Someone would find the vehicle eventually. By then, it wouldn't matter. The rental agreement was under a name that didn't exist, paid for with a credit card that would be canceled by morning.

They walked into the terminal at 2130 hours. Two American engineers heading home after a contract job. Vail wore khakis and a polo shirt with a fictional company logo. Riker wore jeans and a button-down, his limp barely noticeable now that he'd warmed up. Their passports were clean. Their tickets had been purchased three days ago, before the operation, before Sokolov died, before everything went loud.

Nobody looked twice.

Vail bought a newspaper and sat in the departure lounge, pretending to read. Around him, travelers moved through their routines. A family with young children. A businessman working on a laptop. A couple holding hands, speaking softly in Spanish. Normal people. Living normal lives. Vail had helped killed ten men eight hours ago.

Now he sat in an airport, reading about coffee prices and political tensions in El Salvador, waiting for a flight that would take him away from the country where he was an accomplice to murder.

The disconnect was absolute. And necessary.

He glanced at Riker, who was watching the terminal entrance with the casual awareness of someone who'd spent years learning to spot threats. His injured leg was stretched out, his posture relaxed. To anyone watching, he looked bored. But Vail knew better. Riker was cataloging every face, every movement, every anomaly. Looking for the surveillance team that might have followed them. The security officer who might be taking too much interest. The pattern that didn't fit.

There was nothing.

At 2300 hours, they boarded. The flight attendant smiled and checked their boarding passes. They found their seats in coach, stowed their carry-ons, and settled in for the flight to Houston. As the plane taxied toward the runway, Vail looked out the window at the lights of San José. Somewhere to the north, across the border in Nicaragua, investigators were processing a crime scene at a lake house. Counting bodies. Taking photographs. Trying to understand what had happened.

They'd never figure it out.

The plane lifted off, banking west over the Pacific before turning north.

Vail closed his eyes and let the engine noise wash over him.

The job was done.

Chapter Sixty-One

Cole, Torres, Ward, and Hawke crossed into Costa Rica at 2100 hours. Different checkpoint than Price and Mason. Different story. Different vehicle. They'd driven south from Managua in a rented Nissan, taking the main highway through Rivas, moving with the evening traffic. Four men who looked tired but not suspicious. Journalists covering regional politics. Credentials that would hold up to casual inspection but not much more.

The border crossing at Peñas Blancas was busy. Trucks waiting to clear customs. Families returning from visits. A tour bus full of backpackers heading south. Cole pulled up to the checkpoint and handed over their passports. The guard was young, maybe twenty-five, wearing a uniform that looked too big for him. He flipped through the documents, comparing photos to faces.

"Purpose of visit?" he asked in Spanish.

"Journalism," Torres said, his Spanish flawless. "We've been covering the political situation in Managua."

The guard looked at them. Four Americans. Tired. Dusty. Exactly what they appeared to be. He stamped the passports and waved them through. Cole drove into Costa Rica and felt something in his chest loosen slightly. Not relief, not yet, but the first acknowledgment that they'd cleared the most dangerous phase. They were out of Nicaragua. Out of the country where they'd just killed a Soviet colonel and nine other men. Out of the jurisdiction where investigators were starting to ask questions.

But they weren't safe yet.

They drove to San José in silence, taking turns watching the mirrors, looking for the tail that would mean everything had gone wrong. The highway was dark. The jungle pressed close on both sides. Occasionally, they passed through small towns where streetlights cast yellow pools on empty roads. Nobody followed them.

In San José, they split up. Ward and Hawke took the Nissan to a different rental return location. They'd catch a flight to Panama at 0800, then connect through to Miami. Different airlines. Different routes. Cole and Torres checked into a cheap hotel near the airport. Separate rooms. They'd catch the first flight to Mexico City at 0600, then connect to different destinations in the States.

Cole lay on the bed in his room and stared at the ceiling. The air conditioning rattled. Outside, he could hear traffic and distant music from a bar down the street. Twelve hours ago, he'd been in a boat on Lake Managua, moving silently toward a target. Six hours ago, he'd put two rounds through a Soviet colonel's face and watched the man die. Now he was in a hotel room in Costa Rica, listening to a broken air conditioner and waiting for morning.

The disconnect was total.

He thought about Sokolov. The man's face in that final moment. The brief flash of recognition, not of Cole specifically, but of what was happening. The understanding that he'd been found. That his security had failed. That he was about to die.

Cole was satisfied with that.

No guilt. No sense of accomplishment beyond the professional acknowledgment that the mission had succeeded. The man had been a target. A Soviet GRU colonel coordinating operations against American interests. A man who'd sent weapons and advisors to kill people the United States was trying to protect.

Now he was dead. That was all.

Cole closed his eyes but didn't sleep. He ran through the operation again, looking for mistakes, for exposures, for anything that could come back to haunt them. The approach had been clean. The surveillance had been thorough. The execution had been precise. The exfiltration had been smooth. They'd left no evidence. No witnesses. No trail.

Just ten bodies and a lot of questions that would never be answered.

At 0430, Cole showered and dressed. He met Torres in the lobby at 0500. They took a taxi to the airport, two journalists heading home after a difficult assignment. The terminal was already busy. Early morning flights to Miami, Houston, Mexico City. Business travelers and tourists and families moving through the security checkpoints.

Cole bought bad coffee from a vendor and sat in the departure lounge. Around him, life continued. A mother tried to calm a crying baby. Two backpackers argued about their itinerary. A businessman typed furiously on a laptop, racing some deadline. Nobody knew what Cole had done six hours ago. Nobody ever would.

He watched the travelers and felt the familiar sense of

separation. These people lived in a world where violence was something that happened on the news.

Where wars were fought by other people in distant places. Where the mechanisms that kept them safe were invisible and unacknowledged. Cole lived in the machinery. He was part of the invisible apparatus that made their comfortable ignorance possible. He didn't resent them for it. That was the job. That was the whole point.

The flight to Mexico City boarded at 0545. Cole and Torres sat separately, maintaining their cover even though the risk was minimal now. They'd connect through different airlines, take different routes home.

As the plane climbed out over the Pacific, Cole looked down at Costa Rica falling away beneath them. Somewhere to the north, across the border they'd crossed last night, investigators were still processing the scene at the lake house. They'd find nothing useful. No fingerprints. No DNA. No witnesses who could provide descriptions. Just evidence of professional violence and a mystery that would never be solved.

Cole closed his eyes and let the engine noise fill his head. And he fell into a deep comfortable sleep.

Chapter Sixty-Two

They'd left the observation post at 0300, moving through the darkness with the night vision goggles that turned the jungle into shades of green. Their route took them south through the hills, avoiding roads, avoiding settlements, avoiding any possibility of contact. They moved in silence, communicating with hand signals, covering ground with the efficient pace of men who'd done this before. The jungle was loud around them. Insects. Birds. The rustle of larger animals moving through the undergrowth.

They ignored it all.

By dawn, they were ten miles into Costa Rica, well clear of the border, deep in terrain where nobody would be looking for them. A contact picked them up at a dirt road intersection at 0730. An old pickup truck, dented and dusty, driven by a man who asked no questions and expected no answers.

"Any trouble?" the driver asked in Spanish.

"No," Draven said.

They rode in the truck bed, sitting on spare tires,

watching the jungle roll past. The driver took them to Liberia, a small city near the Pacific coast. He dropped them at a bus station and drove away without looking back.

Draven and Keller split up.

They'd fly out that afternoon. Separate flights. Draven to Houston. Keller to Miami. Different airlines. Different connections. Different routes back to North Carolina.

The observation post they'd occupied for three days was already gone. Buried. Scattered. Erased. The hide site where they'd watched Volkov's lake house through spotting scopes was invisible now, reclaimed by the jungle. Like they'd never been there.

Keller sat in the Liberia airport and drank a Coke. Around him, tourists talked about beaches and surfing and where to find the best seafood. Normal people on normal vacations. Forty-eight hours ago, he'd been lying in the dirt, watching a Soviet colonel through a rifle scope, waiting for the order to kill. Now he was drinking a Coke and listening to Americans complain about sunburns. The disconnect didn't bother him anymore. It was just part of the job. You moved between worlds. You did what needed to be done. You came home and pretended to be normal.

That was what he was.

His flight boarded at 1400. He settled into his seat and closed his eyes. By tomorrow, he'd be back at Bragg. Back in the world where this kind of work was planned and executed and never discussed. Back in the shadows where he belonged.

Price and Mason were the first ones back. They landed at Pope Air Force Base at 0300, two days after the hit. A gray Air Force transport that had picked them up in Honduras after they'd crossed the border from Nicaragua using their aid worker credentials.

Nobody asked questions. Nobody checked their gear.

They walked off the plane, climbed into a waiting Humvee, and rode back to the Delta compound in silence.

Bishop came in six hours later, flying commercial through Miami. Ward and Hawke that evening, connecting through Panama.

By the third day, everyone was back.

They gathered in the briefing room at Fort Bragg at 1400 hours. Same room where it had started three weeks ago. Same fluorescent lights humming overhead. Same maps on the walls.

But everything was different now.

Cole was the last one in. He'd landed at Pope that morning, caught a few hours of sleep in his quarters, then showered and changed into a clean uniform. He looked around the table at his team.

Vail's shoulder was still immobilized in a sling, but he looked better than he had in Nicaragua. Riker's limp was barely noticeable. Bishop had dark circles under his eyes, but his hands were steady. Torres looked calm. Ward looked tired. Hawke looked ready for the next mission.

They all looked like they'd just come back from a war.

Which they had.

Harrow walked in and closed the door. He set a folder on the table but didn't open it immediately. Instead, he looked at each of them, his expression unreadable.

"Sokolov's death was discovered eight hours after you left," he said.

"Nicaraguan government is calling it a targeted assassination. Soviets are screaming about American aggression. They're demanding an investigation. They're threatening retaliation."

"Are they blaming us?" Torres asked.

"They're blaming everyone. CIA. State Department. Contras. They don't know who did it." Harrow paused. "And they never will."

"Good," Cole said.

Harrow set a folder on the table. "Moscow's already sent a replacement. Another colonel. Younger. Probably more careful."

Harrow opened the folder. Inside were satellite photos, intelligence reports, diplomatic cables. "Moscow's already sent a replacement. Another colonel. Younger. Probably more careful. They've increased security at all their facilities in Nicaragua. Changed their protocols. They're hunting for whoever did this."

"So, we do it again," Vail said.

"Maybe." Harrow looked at each of them. "This is escalating. Every time we hit them, they push back harder. Sooner or later, someone's going to connect the dots."

"Then we make sure they don't," Cole said.

Harrow studied him. "You good with that?"

"Yeah."

"All of you?"

Nods around the table. Nobody hesitated. Nobody looked away. This was what they'd signed up for.

This was what Ghostline was. Operations that couldn't be acknowledged. Missions that couldn't be discussed. Violence that had to remain invisible.

They were ghosts. They did the work that kept the machinery running. They killed the people who needed to be killed. They disappeared before anyone knew they'd been there.

And they did it again. And again. And again.

"Alright." Harrow picked up the folder. "You've got two weeks. Rest. Train. Stay ready. There's always another mission. May not be this one. Getting tired of sending you after Russians. That's a job for Actual Delta guys."

He walked to the door, then stopped and turned back.

"Good work in Nicaragua. Both operations. Reyes. Sokolov. You did what needed to be done." He left. The team sat in silence for a moment. The fluorescent lights hummed. Outside, Cole could hear the distant sound of helicopters on the flight line.

"Two weeks," Torres said finally. "Think we'll actually get it?"

"No," Vail said.

He was probably right. There was always another crisis. Always another target. Always another mission that couldn't wait. But for now, the job was done. Sokolov was dead. The Soviet command structure in Nicaragua was crippled. The base in Colombia was destroyed. Reyes was gone. Lawson was buried. They had done what they always did.

Disappeared.

Cole stood and walked to the window. Outside, the Delta compound looked exactly as it always did. Operators running drills. Helicopters lifting off. The endless cycle of training and preparation and deployment. This was his world now. This was what he'd chosen. Cole felt nothing about it. No satisfaction. No guilt. Just the cold professional acknowledgment that the mission had succeeded.

That was enough.

He turned away from the window and looked at his team. They were gathering their gear, preparing to leave, already thinking about the next thing. The next training cycle. The next deployment. The next war that nobody would ever know they fought.

"Drinks tonight?" Torres asked.

"Fuck yeah," Cole said. They filed out of the briefing room. The door closed behind them. The lights stayed on, humming in the empty space.

Somewhere in the world, another crisis was brewing. Another target was being identified. Another mission was being planned. And when the call came, they would answer.

They always did.

Cole walked out into the North Carolina afternoon. The sun was bright. The air was warm. The base was alive with the sounds of training and preparation.

He thought about the lake house in Nicaragua. The bodies they'd left behind. The questions that would never be answered.

He thought about the travelers in the San José airport. The normal people living normal lives, unaware of the machinery that kept them safe. He thought about what Harrow had said. *There's always another mission.*

It was true.

There would always be another Soviet colonel. Another threat. Another target that needed to be eliminated. And he and his brothers would be there. In the shadows. Invisible. Doing the work that nobody else could do. That was the job. That was all it had ever been. Cole walked toward his quarters, feeling the gravity of the past five months settling into his bones. The exhaustion. The tension. The constant awareness that one mistake could mean death or capture or exposure. But also, the satisfaction. The knowledge that they'd succeeded. That they were all dead. Those missions were complete.

For now.

He thought about what came next. Two weeks of rest, Harrow had said. Two weeks to train and recover and prepare. Then they'd do it all over again. Somewhere in Central America, another Soviet officer was coordinating operations against American interests. Another target was establishing patterns. Another mission was waiting to be executed.

A cartel leader was sending bad shit into America. And when the time came, he would be ready. He was always ready.

Cole reached his quarters and stopped at the door. He looked back at the compound, at the world he'd chosen, at the life he'd built in the shadows. This was who he was now. This was what he did. He killed people who needed to be killed.

He disappeared before anyone knew he'd been there. He lived in the machinery that kept the world turning. And he was good at it. He opened the door and stepped inside, already thinking about the next mission, the next target, the next war that nobody would ever know he fought. Because that was the job.

And the job never ended.

Epilogue

Fort Bragg, North Carolina
June 1985

The briefing room was different this time. No whiteboards crowded with timelines. No political maps. No acronyms stacked on top of acronyms. Just photographs.

They were pinned to the wall in neat rows, men in tailored suits and gold watches, standing beside private aircraft, leaning against armored SUVs, smiling on beaches with armed guards just out of frame. Hacienda courtyards. Jungle airstrips. Shipping docks at night.

Drug lords. Pipeline managers. Transport chiefs. The men who moved poison north while pretending they were untouchable.

Cole stood with his arms crossed, eyes moving from face to face. He recognized some of the names already, ones that had surfaced in DEA briefs and intelligence summaries. Men responsible for more American deaths than most foreign armies.

They'd all turned eighteen since selection. Legal adults now, though none of them felt older for it.

Harrow stood at the front of the room; hands braced against the table. He looked older than he had a month ago, the lines in his face cut deeper, his patience thinner. "This," Harrow said, breaking the silence, "is why Ghostline exists."

No one spoke.

"For the last six months, you've been used to clean up other people's messes," he continued. "Intelligence failures. Political games.

Counter-Soviet chess moves that were never yours to play." His jaw tightened. "That ends now." He changed the slide. A map of Central and South America filled the screen. Red lines traced routes north—air corridors, maritime lanes, jungle trails that all ended the same way: at the southern border of the United States. "These pipelines move cocaine into the U.S. at an industrial scale," Harrow said. "This isn't street crime. This is command and control." He tapped the screen. "And command and control can be killed."

Cole felt something settle into place in his chest. Not excitement. Not anger. Clarity.

Harrow's gaze locked onto him. "You are not law enforcement. You are not intelligence collectors. You are not diplomats." The room stayed silent. "You are a kill squad." No one flinched. Price cracked his knuckles once, slow and deliberate.

Bishop leaned forward, eyes sharp. Riker's mouth curved into a thin satisfied smile, not joy, just acceptance.

"Rules?" Cole asked.

Harrow didn't hesitate. "Don't miss. Don't get seen. Don't leave witnesses who can talk." Cole nodded once.

"Targets?" Torres asked.

Harrow slid a folder across the table. Inside were names, locations, photographs taken from extreme distance.

Pattern-of-life notes. Ranges measured in meters. "Colombia," Harrow said. "And after that, wherever the pipelines lead.

Long-range interdiction. Leadership decapitation. Sniper pairs when distance is smarter. CQB when distance isn't an option."

Cole closed the folder. This made sense. This was clean. This was honest. This was what they had been built for.

Somewhere south of the border, men who had never heard the word Ghostline were about to learn what it meant to be hunted. This time there would be no politics. Just patience. Just distance. These cartel guys could run, but they would only die tired.

We don't miss from any distance.

Ghostline Creed

We operate where there are no witnesses and no recognition.
We are not assigned to wars.
We are sent to end them before they begin.
We move without signature.
We leave without trace.
We do not exist beyond the mission.
Precision is our discipline.
Silence is our cover.
Execution is our standard.
We do not act for credit.
We do not wait for permission.
We do not fail in public.
Every action has consequence.
Every mistake has a cost.
We carry both.
We are the line that is never seen—
Ghostline.

If this story worked for you, scan below and leave an honest review.

Even one sentence helps more than you think.

Or visit:

amazon.com/review/create-review?asin=B0G3PHMW3Z

— Keven Perkins

www.ingramcontent.com/pod-product-compliance
Lightning Source LLC
LaVergne TN
LVHW020526100826
845148LV00010B/1353
* 9 7 9 8 2 1 8 9 4 6 2 6 5 *